T-MINUS-FIVE AND COUNTING . . .

Doug Grant sat before the huge monitors on the control room wall watching the four differing views of the rocket. The payload of this Long March 3 missile was a blunt-nosed and sleek capsule painted white and carrying a single yellow, five-pointed star, the symbol utilized on all Chinese vehicles bound for outer space. Inside the capsule was a communications satellite. Grant owed General Electric 450 million dollars for it. When it was in a stable orbit, it would belong to the Chinese government, and they would pay him 465 million dollars.

The Long March 3 never got off the pad.

Twelve seconds later, the first stage detonated in a cyclone of red, burnt orange, and brilliant white. The churning maelstrom engulfed the whole pad and the gantry crane.

On the color monitors, it was quite spectacular.

SHANGHAI STAR

BOOKS BY WILLIAM H. LOVEJOY

COLD FRONT
BLACK SKY
DELTA BLUE
ULTRA DEEP
ALPHA KAT
DELTA GREEN
PHANTOM STRIKE
WHITE NIGHT
CHINA DOME
RED RAIN
BACKSLASH

SHANGHAI STAR

WILLIAM H. LOVEJOY

Pinnacle Books
Kensington Publishing Corp.
http://www.pinnacle.books.com

PINNACLE BOOKS are published by

Kensington Publishing Corp.
850 Third Avenue
New York, NY 10022

First Printing: December 1996

Printed in the United States of America
10 9 8 7 6 5 4 3 2 1

This one is for
Stephanie Finnegan,
a writer's dream copy editor

THE PEOPLE OF SHANGHAI STAR

MEGATRONICS INCORPORATED	
Douglas Grant	President and Shanghai Star Project Director
Will Bricher	Director of Satellite Communications
Mickey Stone	Director of Hardware Systems
Curt Wickersham	Director of Software Systems
Calvin Coolidge Jackson	Vice President, Manager of Production, Los Angeles
Diantha Mae Parker	Grant's secretary
SHANGHAI STAR	
Deng Mai	Managing Director, Shanghai Star
Miss Jiangyou	Deng's secretary
CHINA	
Jiang Guofeng	Minister of Information
Wen Yito	Jiang's assistant
Shao Tsung	Minister of National Defense
Pai Dehuai	Minister of Energy
Shan Li	Minister of Labor
Peng Zedong	Minister of Materials
Hua Min	General, Air Force of the People's Liberation Army
Sung Wu	Proposed President of Media Bureau Limited-China
Ming Xueliang	Proposed President of Media Bureau Limited-China
Tan Long	Representative of the People's Department Store
Yvonne Deng	Mai's mother
PEOPLE'S UNDERGROUND	
Chiang Qing	Leader
Huzhou	Qing's deputy
PEOPLE'S RIGHT TO KNOW COMMITTEE	
Zhou Ziyang	Chairman
VENDORS	
Maynard Crest	Consortium of Information Services (USA)
Pierre Lefant	Media Bureau Limited (Europe)
Marc Chabeau	Chief Assistant to Lefant
OTHERS	
Vladimir Petrovich Suretsov	ITAR-Tass Correspondent and Bureau Chief, Shanghai
Yuri Fedorchuk	ITAR-Tass Supervising Editor, Moscow
Arkady Petrovich Makov	Assistant to trade attaché, Beijing consulate
Valeri Sytenko	Trade Attaché, Russian Consulate
Jerry "Dusty" McKelvey	Pilot, owner of Southeast Asia Charter
James "Jimbo" Bowie	Pilot, Southeast Asia Charter
Theodore "Tank" Cameron	China Project Leader, Digi-Communications Technology

Thursday, August 4

T-minus-14 and counting. . . .

Doug Grant's vocabulary included a few Chinese words and phrases, but he couldn't cope with the staccato dialogues taking place all around the control room, and he relied on the interpretation of the young man sitting beside him.

He understood tension, though, and it was a primary feature—in his own back muscles, in the rigidity of the figures arrayed at the consoles before him.

"Gyros are operational and at speed . . . secondary and tertiary computers are on line . . . fuel transfer complete . . . gantry fuel pumps are shutting down. . . ."

Grant should have been listening more closely to the interpreter, but all he could think about was, "That's my four-hundred-and-fifty-million-dollar toy out there."

"Out there" could not be seen directly.

Instead, four huge monitors on the control room wall provided four views of the rocket, from differing angles and differing distances. The closest camera view was of the upper, payload stage, but it wasn't particularly remarkable. A blunt-nosed and sleek capsule was painted white and carried a single yellow, five-pointed star, the symbol utilized on all Chinese vehicles bound for outer space. Grant had always wondered just who the target audience for American, Chinese, or Russian insignia on space vehicles was supposed to be. Some visitor from a galaxy far away would have a hell of a time interpreting the stars and bars. Or a yellow star.

"Thirteen minutes," the interpreter said.

Two of the monitors displayed the entire launch vehicle, that Will Bricher, Grant's Director of Satellite Communications, had explained earlier to Grant was a variant of China's DF-5 intercontinental ballistic missile. In its civilian role, it was called the Long March 3, and China had been attempting to use it as an entree into the commercial space-launch business for several years. Grant was happy the one on the screen wasn't carrying a 5-megaton warhead, but it didn't stop him from worrying about what it was carrying.

"Twelve minutes. All is proceeding normally."

As a demonstration of China's lagging technology, the DF-5 on the screen was wreathed in the vapors of the liquid-oxygen and nitrogen fuels that had been transferred to the vehicle from ground-based storage tanks minutes before. Any decent contemporary launch vehicle was powered by solid propellent rockets. So much could go wrong: the fuel ratios, a two-dollar valve, a. . .

"Eleven minutes," the interpreter intoned.

"I should have gone to the bathroom," Bricher said from his chair on the other side of the interpreter.

"You can't do it in eleven minutes?" Grant asked.

"There's no predicting at my current stress level."

"Don't tell me that. It's your job to keep me calm."

Grant's eyes went back to the close-up view. The capsule looked sleek, but he knew how thin the metal skin was. It was like wrapping aluminum foil around his delicate satellite.

It was his, right now. He had paid, or promised to pay, General Electric (GE) $450 million for it. Twenty minutes from now, when it was in a stable orbit, it would belong to the Chinese government, and they would pay him $465 million.

It seemed like a fair deal to Grant.

"Ten minutes. All systems green."

Grant stood up, went around his chair, and then leaned forward on his hands on the back of it. He hated displaying nervousness of any kind, but he about had his share of sitting.

Since three o'clock in the morning, when the first launch briefings were delivered by General Hua and his staff.

It was now 8:54 A.M. On the screens above him, the sun was shining brightly on the environs of the Xichang Launch Center and the white skin of the rocket. In the control room, kept in semidarkness for the benefit of the console operators staring at two dozen computer screens, the chatter had begun to die away. Most of the attention was concentrated now on the mission director, sitting twelve feet from Grant at the major, centrally located console.

"Nine minutes, now."

"I think they've screwed around with that clock, Doug," Bricher said.

"I know they have. About a two-to-one ratio."

Yet, the hands of his steel-cased Rolex matched the digital readout of the big numerals on the wall near the screens.

"Launch suspended at eight minutes, fourteen seconds," the interpreter said.

"What!"

"There is a problem with the guidance computer, Mr. Grant."

"I'll be right back," Bricher said, heading for the door in the back wall.

Grant knew it wasn't his place to complain or to intervene in any way with the launch process. He and Bricher were in the control room strictly as a courtesy. It was all he could do not to march over to the launch director, tap him on the shoulder, and demand, "What's going on here, buddy?" Not that he knew crap about launching rockets into space. He still felt he might come up with some ready solution. He was pretty good with problems.

He waited.

He looked up at the windows on the second-floor level of the back wall of the control center. General Hua would be in one of the observation rooms. He didn't know who else was there. On the far end was a small room for reporters, but he didn't know if this launch was being observed by the media.

He waited.

The launch clock seemingly stayed at 8:14:32 forever.

At least, for seven minutes.

Bricher was back by the time the clock started moving again.

"Launch resumed," the interpreter said.

Grant let out a long sigh and sat down again, and waited.

And watched the clock.

The Long March 3 never got off the pad.

At T-minus-five minutes, twenty-three seconds, the first stage detonated in a cyclone of cherry red, burnt orange, and brilliant white. The churning maelstrom engulfed the whole pad and the gantry crane.

On the color monitors, it was quite spectacular.

Thursday, August 4

Vladimir Petrovich Suretsov was in the glass-walled observation booth above the control room. It was reserved for journalists, and he was one of four allowed to view this launch.

Or what was to have been a launch.

He almost missed it. He had been leaning forward on the edge of his chair, with his forearms pressed against the window of the booth, studying the two Americans and their interpreter on the floor at the back of the control room. Suretsov was more interested in people than in rockets, and the Americans interested him. The sudden splash of color on the monitor screens jerked his attention back.

There was no sound in the booth. The explosion on the launchpad, which was twenty kilometers away, was muffled by walls and glass, and the three Chinese correspondents in the booth with him were as stunned as he was.

The launch sequence had seemed perfect except for one hesitation to correct a computer error. It was the third Chinese launch he had been authorized to report, and Suretsov was all but bored with the chore. The 1,900-kilometer journey from Shanghai to Xichang in Sichuan Province, alone, was numbing. He would have liked to pass on this story. However, as a correspondent for the Russian news agency ITAR-Tass, and even though he was head of its Shanghai bureau, Suretsov was not an autonomous individual. His supervising editor in Moscow, Yuri Fedorchuk, assigned most of his stories for him.

He sat in semishock for several minutes as the flames shown on the screens died away. The launchpad was bathed in vapor for some time, until the light breeze began to blow it away and reveal the carnage. Except for five or six meters of the base poking from a ground-level cloud, the gantry tower was no longer standing.

Neither was the rocket.

It seemed to have disappeared.

Suretsov tried to look upward, above the screens, as if seeking a rocket that had already taken off. His eyes found only the blank, beige-painted wall.

More of the mist blew away, but if what he saw of tangled metal and structural beams spread across the earth was the rocket, it was not recognizable as such. The explosion had to have been tremendous.

All of the monitor screens suddenly went blank, as if the mission director suddenly realized that observers were present.

Following the examples of his three Chinese journalistic colleagues, Suretsov leaped from his chair and headed for the door at the back of the booth. It opened before they reached it.

One of the complex's guards stepped inside and held up his hand.

They stopped.

Suretsov said, "I want to speak to the launch director."

"You must wait here, gentlemen," the guard said in their common language of English. "Someone from the administration will come and talk to you as soon as initial investigations are complete."

That could take hours.

"I will just return to Shanghai," he said.

"You will wait here."

Suretsov cleared his throat with disgust and turned back to the interior window. He moved close to it and looked down at the floor of the control room. There was still some pandemonium among the technicians, but the launch director appeared to be appealing for calm.

He looked for the two Americans and saw them just as they were ushered from the room by their interpreter.

Suretsov wondered if he would not learn more from the president of Megatronics Incorporated than he would learn from the spokesperson for the Air Force of the People's Liberation Army.

The air force did not readily admit to mistakes, and General Hua Min, the commander of the space program, was a flawless individual.

In his own mind.

Deng Mai took the call in her spacious headquarters office on the sixth floor.

"Director," Miss Jiangyou, her secretary said, "it is General Hua."

She pushed the blinking button. "Yes, General?"

"There has been an accident."

Why could people not be more specific? Deng was ever irritated at the circumlocution of those around her. She had a reputation for remaining unruffled in the most dire of crises, however, and she simply asked, "The Americans?"

"Oh, no, Director! It is the rocket! The Long March Three exploded on the launchpad."

Her day turned ominous.

"And the satellite?"

"Destroyed, I am afraid."

In the privacy of her office, where no one could see her distress, Deng allowed herself to close her eyes in anguish. The loss of the satellite was a blow to her program. It was to have been the second of three General Electric communications satellites dedicated to her system.

She swivelled around in her chair, and when she opened her eyes to look at the sea of skyscrapers outside her window, they appeared to be encased in a brown tinge that was more toxic than ever before.

"Do you know the cause, General?"

"Not at this time. The investigative team is moving to the launchpad now."

"There were reporters present?"

General Hua coughed. Prior to the expanding openness in the country, failures of the air force were unknown simply because they were never reported. The first venture into commercial launches—with a U.S.-built Australian communications satellite as the payload—had been embarrassing. Televised, the world watched as the countdown approached takeoff. And nothing happened. The Long March 3 failed to do anything at all—launch, blow up, or even fall over.

"Yes. Three from Chinese newspapers, and one from ITAR-Tass."

"There will be world attention, then," she said. "I trust that the reasons for the loss will be appropriate."

"Of course, Director."

Hua hung up before she could ask if Grant were still at the complex. She needed to discuss the altered schedule with him. There were always schedules: ten-year plans, five-year plans, one-year plans. In her case, she had less than sixty days.

October 1.

Many of the plans failed to achieve their stated deadlines, or their defined goals; she knew this. And when it occurred, program directors disappeared into obscurity. Deng Mai's major problem was that she was a woman at the head of a high-visibility agency in a nation where few women achieved such status. She was under scrutiny, with many who rallied to her cause, but there were those who would relish her failure even more than they prayed for the demise of Shanghai Star.

If it were in her power, they would not see her cringe in defeat. Yet, Shanghai Star was so large that she could not control every aspect of it. She was at the mercy of people like General Hua and Douglas Grant.

Hua, as commander of rocket forces, was likely accustomed to unreported setbacks, but he would feel the heat of his superiors after this event. The costs were too great, not only in the millions of yuan devoted to the rocket and its launch costs, but also in the associated fiscal and political expenses that would be charged to Shanghai Star. Deng Mai did not have to mention her displeasure with the air force to any of the leaders on the State Council. They would already be applying pressure on Hua without her intervention. Evidence of Hua's concern was to be found in the solicitous posture he had taken with her on the telephone. The general was not normally given to moderate tones, especially with women.

And Douglas Grant.

The loss of the satellite would have adverse financial repercussions for Grant. It would cost him heavily, but she fervently hoped that Megatronics Incorporated (MI) would survive. If Grant were forced to drop out of the project, forfeiting his performance bond, his company would go into bankruptcy. While the profit-or-loss status of Megatronics was not her concern, its presence on the Shanghai Star Project certainly was. If Grant went under, the subsequent search for a new contractor could take six or seven months. And even then, the new experts would require additional months to study and understand what Megatronics had already accomplished.

No, she could not lose Grant. He was to be her good joss, her luck.

Again, however, Grant's fate was not something she could control.

She hated that. She had for so long considered herself in control of her life. She had devoted twelve years to a succession of government posts, performing flawlessly and obviously, so that she would be recognized by superiors and elevated to yet another, and more public, position.

Her quest was supported by two distinct assets. Until his death, her father had been a close advisor to—though not a relative of—Vice Premier Deng who, though not in either of the supreme government or party posts, was still China's most influential leader. The aura of her father's wisdom surrounded her, and his influence had opened doors for her.

Her second asset was a legacy of her mother. She remembered a time when she was very young, when she accompanied her mother to Hong Kong on a shopping trip, and the two of them went to see an American motion picture, the first she had ever viewed. It was *The Seventh Dawn,* starring the American actor William Holden. Her mother had pointed out the Eurasian beauty of Capucine to her. "That is you, my lovely."

Deng Mai's mother was French. Her family had links to long lines of French aristocracy and was wealthy, but their saving grace was that they were also sympathetic to communist doctrines. Mai's grandfather had befriended Ho Chi Minh when that revolutionary lived in Paris. Madame Yvonne Deng was still a beauty in her own right, and she and Mai shared an old house on a tree-shaded street.

The fine melding of East and West was in Deng Mai. She was tall at 170 centimeters, (five feet seven inches) and there was a lean crispness to her figure that was not found in most Asian women. Never afraid of being herself—and perhaps the symbol she was for other women, Deng favored Western styles, generally wearing dresses in pastel shades and skirted business suits.

Her face was composed of classic lines, with high cheekbones and dark eyes cautiously suggesting the almond-shaped heritage of her father's eyes. Her throat was long and slender. The shining blackness of her hair was paternal, but the natural curl belonged to her mother, and she kept it fluffed and cut to a medium length that gave her a haunting, brooding beauty.

At Yvonne Deng's insistence, she had been educated at the Sorbonne, specializing in political history and public administration. Hers was a quick mind, given to in-depth consideration of her alternatives prior to making decisions. She was comfortable in several Chinese dialects, in French, and in English.

By all that was right with the People's Republic of China, (PRC), Deng Mai should never have achieved her position as Managing Director of Shanghai Star. Even though she resided in Shanghai, a special municipality with more enlightened mores than much of the nation, the strikes against her—her femininity and her mixed blood—should have condemned her to obscurity. And yet, she had turned them in her favor. Admittedly, the necessary support of her father had provided the impetus, but her warm smile, her wit, and her stunning beauty had charmed the old gentlemen who sat on committees. Many of those old gentlemen had also pursued her socially, but she had managed to elude them with grace and without embarrassment.

Her performance in her administrative positions had cemented her reputation, and her record, along with *père* Deng's urging, had obtained her an interview with the Information Advisory Committee. Though Jiang Guofeng, the Minister of Information, displayed misgivings without subtlety, the committee had appointed her the managing director of the newly created Shanghai Star three years before, a year after the concept received the blessing of the Politburo.

The performance audits she had undergone in those three years were laudatory, but circumstances had changed considerably. Her father passed away fourteen months earlier, and Master Advisor Deng was no longer in the background, protecting her. She suspected that a few of the twelve-member Information Committee who had been rebuffed by her at various times were no longer ardent supporters. And Minister Jiang was frequently her strongest critic.

Deng Mai *needed* Doug Grant. If his company was forced to liquidate and caused Shanghai Star to miss its first and primary operational objective, Jiang Guofeng and his cronies would surely use the opportunity to force her from office.

Deng knew she had become a role model for women in Shanghai and Beijing, as well in other parts of the nation, and she felt she carried a double burden. Should she fail, the loss would be her own as well as that of other women throughout China.

And Jiang would be immensely satisfied, having demonstrated the authenticity of his convictions. She had often thought that she could accept failure if it were not for the fact that Jiang would be proven correct.

Pressing the intercom button, she told her secretary, "Please try to locate Mr. Grant. I would like to see him as soon as he returns to Shanghai."

Mickey Stone would have preferred to be in Shanghai. The city of Urümqi, though the capital of Xinjiang Uygur Zizhiqu Province, didn't have much going for it.

If Stone mentally listed the attributes and deficits of Urümqi, on the positive side he would say that, though the climate was normally severe, he had been lucky so far. For August, it was relatively cool. There had been only three days exceeding 100 degrees Fahrenheit.

That was the extent of the benefit listing.

The city had once been described as a dust bowl, situated as it was in a broad, level valley in the Celestial Mountains, and though protective rings of trees had been planted around the outskirts and many of the streets paved, it was still dry as powder. In June, the rainiest month, Urümqi received an inch of precipitation.

Also on the other side of the ledger were uncontrolled mobs

of insects, rampant poverty, and a distinct lack of menu variety—which tourists were advised to avoid anyway because of the lack of hygiene. And in a city of 800,000 people, the population of available young ladies without suspicious parents was sparse.

Though many Han Chinese had been relocated to the area by the Chinese government, becoming the majority and composing one of the thirteen nationalities inhabiting the province, the Uygur people made up five of the twelve million living there. They were Islamic in faith, and they were identifiable by the embroidered skullcaps they wore. The caps provided just about the only color in the otherwise national drab dress typical of the everyday Chinese. Stone hadn't been there on a feast day or a holy day, so he didn't know if the stories he'd heard were true—that the women actually dressed in ornate vests over a colored *quilak* with a tight waist, supplemented with colored veils, bright sashes, and bracelets of gold and silver. *That* was the exotic image in his mind the day he'd signed his contract with Megatronics.

Stone had been in Urümqi five days on this trip, and already he felt the deprivation.

Mickey Stone was Megatronics Incorporated's Director of Hardware Systems, but his fervent desire was to die with a legacy as rich and lush in anecdote, fable, and fact as those bequeathed by Don Juan or Casanova. He was thirty-two years old and as fit as a daily workout with his weights allowed. He even carried small dumbbells with him when he travelled.

When he was in high school in Pomona, California, Stone had read Errol Flynn's biography, *My Wicked, Wicked Ways,* and decided they weren't so wicked. Flynn became a personal idol, who led to the way Stone styled his hair and, later, trimmed his mustache. He had clear brown eyes that could appear very liquid and sympathetic in the right situation. They were also quick to reflect his good humor, and tiny laugh wrinkles emanated from the corners. His straight nose had a slight bump in it, through no genetic ancestry that he had ever determined, and though he had occasionally considered having it straightened, the thought of scalpels always deterred him. He was a lover and a wild-horse rider, but not a fighter.

Like Flynn, he thought he should have been in motion pictures, but an obvious lack of talent, discovered in a collegiate drama club, had killed that idea. Instead, he had taken his engineering degree from the California Institute of Technology, reluctantly admitting to himself that he had a better command of numbers and formulas than of scripts. After college, he had bummed around the world, à la Flynn, pursuing jobs that kept him on the move, and meeting beautiful women.

He was back in the Silicon Valley as an engineer for Hewlett-Packard when Grant's headhunters found him, and after one look at Megatronics's brochure, with the attendant exotic call of the Orient, he had signed on.

But Urümqi was not what he'd envisioned. As the largest province, it was a buffer against Russia, Mongolia, Afghanistan, Pakistan, and Kashmir. It didn't produce much more than decent fruit and some good horsemen among the Kazakhs who, on the Russian side of the border, were known by the Slavic term Cossack.

His touristy visits had been limited to the multitiered Hongshan Pagoda built in 1788, the People's Park, and the Memorial Hall to the Eighth Route Army. They were limited because that's all there was to see. The Urümqi Museum was a disappointment, the Stone Age interpreted according to Marxist theory. He had taken up sight-seeing as a substitute for chasing women. Unfortunately, he was learning a lot about the country.

He did look in on the carpet-making factory and the small steel mill, but didn't find any women worth pursuing.

The social life was so bland, he spent most of his time working in the outposts of Shanghai Star—Hohhot in Inner Mongolia, Lhasa in Xizang Zizhiqu, Chengdu in Sichuan, Harbin in Heilongjiang, and Guangzhou in Guangdong Province.

In each of those provincial capitals was a building similar to the one he was examining in Urümqi. This one was a three-story monstrosity that had been built in the mid-1960s, probably by the Russians. It had Moscow's singular stamp of mediocrity all over it. Grant's subcontracted architects and contractors had come in and stripped the interior clean, including nonsupporting walls. Other than some tuck-pointing of the exterior yellow brick and painting of the trim, they hadn't done much to improve the exterior appearance. A small brass plaque to the right of the new double glass doors identified the building in Chinese characters and in English as:

SHANGHAI STAR COMMUNICATIONS NETWORK
URÜMQI FACILITY

Inside, the renovation was a different story. A Westernized reception area complete with low-slung couches and potted tropical plants greeted the visitor. The walls were clad in textured grass mat. Administrative offices and cubicles for technical supervisors were on the first floor. The second floor contained studios, space for programming personnel, and a large area dedicated to the computer people. The top floor at Urümqi, and similar spaces at the other facilities, belonged to Stone.

And partially to Curt Wickersham, who was Director of Software Systems, but Stone only acknowledged the partial ownership when Wickersham pressed him. It was a fleeting possession, of course. At the end of the contract, the Chinese technicians and managers currently in training would assume control.

Glass walls divided the spaces on the third floor, as much for impressing the people who were led on tours through the building as for controlling the temperature and humidity in the equipment spaces. The temperature and humidity was under control at least for those times when the electrical supply remained steady. For Stone, who was more of a hands-on person than a believer in the abstract, the sight was also impressive. The Megatronics equipment, fashioned in the plant in Los Angeles, was encased in metal-and-plastic cabinetry finished in a deep teal color. The color, Grant had explained, was to distinguish MI from "Big Blue" or Burroughs or anyone else.

Inside the cabinets were a profusion of wiring bundles, integrated circuit boards, and memory modules that appeared about the same as those of anyone else. Some components, like mass-storage devices, hard-disk drives, and even circuit boards, were in fact produced by other manufacturers, purchased under license, housed in teal blue, and stamped with the MI logo. The central processing units (CPUs), however, were based strictly on schematics engineered by Grant's design team. The simplicity, speed, low-heat emission, reliability, and low cost of those units were what made Megatronics Incorporated unique.

Stone and Grant were adherents of the philosophy of networking micro and mini computers rather than relying on massive mainframe computers. Except for specific scientific applications, they both thought of mainframes as déclassé.

The philosophy and the amazing CPU had positioned the company, despite its lack of reputation, for the low bid of $2.8 billion accepted by the Shanghai Star governing committee.

Nearly $3 billion sounded like a lot of money, especially to Stone, but he knew that MI was operating on shoestring margins. There wasn't a lot of room for error or waste, and everyone on MI's payroll in China was, figuratively, "swinging a hammer." Some very good people, whom Grant had lured away from competitors on the promise of MI's computer design, plus shares of company stock, were working their butts off. If MI made it, they would also make it.

It was a two-way street. Once associated with Megatronics, the shining names of those experts in computers, software design, communications, and space-age technology had helped sell the proposal to the Chinese. Grant had told them up front that he was hiring them for both their expertise and their names in the brochures, and no one labored under any misconception that MI would survive if the Shanghai Star Project didn't turn out to be a world-class operation.

And so Stone toured his installations with a critical eye. On the roof, where the satellite antenna and its backup were located, he had discovered a cable frayed by movement in the wind and had ordered it replaced, then the new one better secured.

On this floor, he walked slowly down the corridor, stopping frequently to peer through the glass walls. He checked the digital readouts of temperature and humidity. He stepped inside cubicles to open cabinets and examine fiber-optic translators. He watched as technicians ran diagnostic tests of memory, hard drives, and connectors. He ordered a CPU changed out—the basement storage rooms had a minimal supply of replacement parts—because its log showed sporadic faults.

He was in the main control room, with front panels spread all over the floor, as he, three American techs, and two Chinese apprentices attached digital test instruments to input components when Wickersham came in.

"Hey, Mickey!"

Stone, on his stomach with his head inside a console, backed out and rolled over on his back.

"Hey, yourself."

"The bird blew up on the pad."

"Shit! The satellite?"

"Vaporized, for all I know. Nothing left."

The three technicians stopped work for long enough to vent their frustrations with a few choice obscenities. Everyone in the company had a vested interest.

The two Chinese also tested American slang new to them with indignation. "Mutha . . . fucka!"

Stone rose from the floor without using his hands for leverage—a sit-up, over onto his knees, then to his feet. "You talk to Doug?"

"No. Bricher called me."

"Damn it! Let's go get a drink."

"Let's get coffee," Wickersham clarified.

The two of them went through the glass door and down the hall to the small office the eventual systems manager would use. Inside was a desk, a couple chairs, and a table with a coffee urn. Wickersham filled two Styrofoam cups.

Stone sat on the desktop and sipped from his cup.

Like Stone, Wickersham was dressed in jeans, a sport shirt, and running shoes. The MI executives tended to get their hands dirty.

Wickersham was in his early fifties, his gray hair getting thin around a widow's peak. He had a long, horsey face, with big square-cut teeth displayed in an infrequent smile. He was a major worrier, Stone thought, though a certified genius when it came to the arcane instructions that went through a computer's mind.

"What'll this do to us, Mickey?"

"I didn't read the contract that closely, Curt. I think the insurance only covers ninety percent of the loss."

"Oh, damn! That's a forty-some-mil charge against the company. Can we handle it?"

"We probably ought to get our resumes out and about," Stone said.

"To hell with that."

The problem with most of Grant's senior employees, from Grant's point of view, was that almost all of them could find another job instantly anywhere else in the industry. If MI couldn't make it, it was no skin off their respective noses.

So Grant had made it tougher. For every month they spent on the job, their shareholdings increased. Stone and Wickersham each owned three percent of the company, more than halfway to the five percent they would own when the project was completed. Five percent could be worth $100 million someday.

Plus, both men had come to have a lot of respect for Grant, and an inordinate amount of pride in their company.

"I could maybe rob my piggy bank," Stone said.

"I'll hit mine, too, soon as Doug tells us what we need."

"Think we can come up with forty or fifty million?"

"Might be a little short," Wickersham said.

Will Bricher sat in the first seat behind the flight deck of the Learjet. Across the aisle from him, Grant was absorbed by the numbers on the screen of his laptop computer, a rare scene. Grant only used a computer infrequently.

Bricher wouldn't interrupt him just now.

He studied the green lushness of the lowlands over which they were flying. It had come as a surprise to him to find tobacco, cotton, soybeans, wheat, and barley among the crops being raised around Shanghai. Somehow, he had expected to see nothing but rice paddies. The farmlands were more like the Arkansas of his youth, and he had been disappointed. The first eighteen years of his life had been devoted to dreams of getting off the farm, and now he was back in the middle of it.

Bricher was forty-four years old, with a doctorate from the Massachusetts Institute of Technology. A blond with blue eyes, he appeared to have more Norse blood in his veins than that of a Kentucky frontiersman with Irish linkages interspersed with a bit of Seminole. Occasionally, Mickey Stone called him "Chief," and Bricher bridled at that appellation. He had spent fifteen years with NASA at the Johnson Space Center outside of Houston, and the dwindling budgetary support for the space program had had him considering alternatives long before he got the call from Grant. After he heard Grant out, he only asked about arrangements for his family—he was a confirmed family man.

Grant told him, "Whatever you want."

He had brought his wife, Shana, and his two teenage children to Shanghai with him. In a city of over thirteen million people—the largest city in Asia, they seemed to be getting along as well as they had in Houston.

The pilot, Jerry McKelvey, but also known as "Dusty" for some reason, slid the curtain aside and called back, "Twenty minutes out!"

Grant looked up, nodded, went back to his numbers.

McKelvey looked to Bricher, shrugged, and returned to his controls.

McKelvey, a tidy man of fifty years with slicked-back brown hair and clear and direct hazel eyes, wore a gold ring in his left ear and a folded red bandanna to hold his hair in place. He was lean and mean, and Bricher suspected he would be tough in a saloon brawl. He had been, as Bricher interpreted the gossip, an Air Force fighter pilot, then a bush pilot for the CIA's Air America during the Vietnam era. The rumors said that he had never returned to the States, but stayed in Bangkok to establish his own air service. Grant had contracted with him, with Southeast Asia Charter, to provide three business jets and pilots for the Shanghai Star Project. The distances were so great—2,000 miles between Shanghai and Urümqi in the middle of the northwestern province, for example—that propeller-driven planes or domestic Chinese airlines were inadequate. The 1,200-mile trip from Xichang took two-and-a-half hours in the Gates Learjet 25B.

Grant slapped the lid shut on his computer.

Bricher turned his swivel seat toward his boss and spoke loud enough to be heard over the whine of the jet engines. "Well?"

Grant tapped his hand against the computer. "I don't like these things."

"I know that. But it comes in handy sometimes, right?"

"Yeah, it does. Don't tell Diantha I played with this."

Grant's secretary had a full inventory of computer equipment.

"I won't tell her. My question was 'Well?' "

"The second it happened, I damned near had a heart attack," Grant said.

"You sure as hell kept it off your face. I don't think I did. God, my heart's still pumping a gallon a minute."

"I was afraid General Hua might have been watching from his little nest up behind the control room."

"You think he had a heart attack, maybe?"

Grant grinned at him, "We're going to squeak it out, Will."

Grant's grin was infectious; he always charmed people into going along with him. Bricher couldn't help laughing.

"Sure we are."

"Honest Injun."

"You taking potshots at me?" Bricher asked.

"No way. Look, the insurance will cover four hundred and five million, right?"

"Right."

"Now, the Republic . . ."

". . . which told us they never, ever had a rocket failure—well, just one, so we needn't worry about their liability? That Republic?"

"Yeah. They also told us it was cheaper than using U.S. boosters out of Vandenburg," Grant said.

The Chinese had reduced the final contract price by offering to use their own space program to insert the American-made satellites into orbit.

"But we don't know that it's cheaper," Bricher said.

"Nor care, since we're not paying. Anyway, we've got the terrorist clause."

Bricher sat up in his seat. "That's right! I'd forgotten."

"I wanted the whole ten percent difference in coverage, but it got negotiated down to eight percent, based on our cost, rather than our selling price. Now, if we invoke the clause, our exposure is only nine million."

"Only nine million. Peanuts."

"We could live with that," Grant said, "if we had to. It'll shave the final profit margin damned close, but we could do it."

"You think Hua Min will admit that terrorists got to his rocket, Doug?"

"That's the beauty of it, Will. We were told that the space program hadn't suffered a major loss in five years, right? That's why they only pay if a failure is attributed to an outside cause. Hua Min was damned proud of his assertion."

"Ah! The good general won't want to admit he's at fault. He wants a bad guy involved as much as we do."

Grant grinned again. "Beijing might balk, but I think we'll have Hua and Deng in our corner."

"So the company's only out nine million dollars. That's wonderful."

"Better than bankruptcy."

"If we can pull it off," Bricher said.

"I'm going to do my damnedest. Then, too, we may not be out the nine million."

"Say again."

"Tell me about our satellites, Will."

Bricher thought it superfluous to count to three, but he did. "The PRC is buying three satellites, which GE builds for us, to our specifications. The first is already in orbit, but it's dedicated to the military channels. It'll serve as a backup if we have problems on the other two. The second, now a mass of melted elements . . ."

"You did check it out?"

Bricher, being a suspicious sort, anyway, had gone with Hua's launch director to the pad and verified that the satellite was a total loss.

"You don't think Hua would stage a disaster, just to get himself a free half-billion-dollar comsat?"

"Will."

"I saw it. GE wouldn't be proud."

"Go on, then."

"Okay, the second satellite was to have carried the bulk of the civilian channels. The third, scheduled for launch in December, would carry a third of the traffic, and both two and three serve as backup for each other. There, I counted up to three."

"So, where are we?" Grant asked.

"If we can convince the military to give up half of their channels for the time being, we can still put some new programming on line by the first of October. It would be limited, and it certainly wouldn't be up to our contract specs."

"What if we can get GE to move up the schedule on ShangStar Three? I think they've had so much downtime, they've been keeping their people busy on our next machine."

"And launch early? I'll have to work out something with Hua."

"Do that. And order a replacement from GE. Renumber the new units ShangStar Two and ShangStar Three."

"I just love placing half-billion-dollar orders. It's like going to the big Wal-Mart in the sky."

"That's why I let you do it," Grant said.

"You really think we can get Beijing to buy the terrorist act, Doug?"

"I do. But, Will, we also want to recover our profit margin."

"I agree. But I don't know how."

"GE's going to do it for us."

"They'll be happy to hear that," Bricher said.

"You put a condition on the new order. We want a four-and-a-half-million-dollar discount on each of the next two satellites."

Bricher almost laughed. "They're going to buy that?"

"Look what we're doing for them, ordering a fourth unit and keeping their people at work. You have to admit there's not a large market for their product. Hell, Will, this is volume buying. They ought to be acting like a discount warehouse."

"So they cut their profit in order to keep their plant active?"

"Wouldn't you?" Grant asked. "Besides, the R&D cost goes down with a fourth unit. Hell, they've probably recovered the research investment already, with the second satellite."

Bricher thought about it. Grant's ideas were always surprising, one of the reasons Bricher liked him. He frequently came up with concepts that kept them on the lip of the frying pan, looking down into the fire, but not quite tumbling off.

"Yeah, I might think that way."

"Sell it to them."

"I'll give it a try," he promised.

"And I'll convince Hua he's just been hit by terrorists."

"Who are you going to blame it on?" Bricher asked him.

"Arabs, North Koreans, disenchanted Latvians, who knows? I'll think of something."

Bricher was sure he would; he always did.

"Give me the damned phone," Grant said, "and let's hope it works."

On the phone, he told McKelvey to link him up with General Hua Min in Xichang.

Minister of Information Jiang Guofeng did not like what General Hua Min told him on the telephone.

"A terrorist act! That is impossible!"

"Nonetheless, Minister . . ."

"What evidence do you have of this act?"

"We are still investigating, Minister. The wreckage is vast, and the total examination will require time."

"But you are so certain, General, you call me with these assurances?"

"I am positive," Hua claimed.

He did not sound so positive to Jiang, but the rocket-forces commander was difficult to read at times.

"Your casual statement could cost the People's Republic millions in American dollars. Not to mention the millions that burned with the rocket."

"I am aware of that. And it is not a casual statement. You will receive a formal report."

"Disastrous! You attempt to protect yourself and your incompetent minions."

"Minister Jiang, I do not have to endure such slurs!"

"I should not leave the investigation to the air force. The Premier will want an independent report."

"I would welcome it," Hua said, though Jiang did not believe him for an instant.

The minister slammed his telephone into its cradle.

With his chin resting in his cupped hands, Jiang stared at the top of his desk and pondered his next action.

He would have to let the members of the committee know immediately. The Information Advisory Committee had been formed to assist the State Council in setting policy for the Ministry of Information, and the Ministry's stellar project was, of course, Shanghai Star. The twelve members of the committee, of which Jiang was one, were a diverse group, most of them serving in other ministries of the government—cultural affairs, energy, foreign affairs, military affairs. They were men with definite views on what was proper and what was counterrevolutionary. Jiang was never quite certain how votes on crucial issues might turn out. With the even number of members on the committee, he could not count on his own vote being pivotal.

He was certain of one thing; on fiscal matters, the committee always voted conservatively. Having devoted $2.8 billion in U.S. and Chinese currencies to Shanghai Star, they would be extremely reluctant to augment that amount, even by the thirty-six million dollars the abominable terrorist clause might invoke.

Jiang was adamantly opposed to it. He would have to fight Hua all the way.

So, before calling the members, he arranged for an audience with the Premier.

The headquarters of Shanghai Star Communications was a fifteen-story building originally intended to be a luxury resort hotel. Several years before, the People's Republic of China engaged in an experiment which allowed local political divisions to pursue economic real-estate development, intending to lure foreign investments. Instead of the housing and commercial enterprises that Beijing expected, luxury vacation spots and golf courses sprang to life. The abuses created some instant millionaires, a few convicted felons, and some construction projects seized by the government for conversion to urban housing and other uses. This was one of them.

It was located on the narrow end of a block between Yanan Road West on the north and Huashan Road on the south. The Shanghai Hotel and the Hilton International were a block to the east. It was prime real estate, Yanan Road heading west into HongQiao, the direct route to the airport. To the east, the skyscrapers blocked the view of the river, but emphasized the metropolitan quality of the city.

Fortunately, the structure was commandeered before the plumbers got to it or Grant might have had twenty bathrooms on each floor. He had written the program specifications—the conceptual layout of spaces—with the assistance of Deng Mai, and with the philosophical convention the Information Advisory Committee wasn't interested in seeing their employees ensconced in penthouse office suites.

The top four floors were devoted to equipment spaces, the pride of Mickey Stone and dubbed by him as "Silicon Heaven." Floors 6 through 11 had been designed as office and open-space work areas. Most of the permanent Chinese administrative staff, including Deng Mai, were located on 6, and the balance of the floors went to the operations and programming staff.

For the duration of his part of the project, Grant and some of his personnel were officed in temporary quarters on the fifth floor. Some MI employees were on the upper floors, but the bulk of them were scattered throughout the PRC. Eventually, the second through fifth floors would be utilized by the firms awarded contracts for supplying programming to the communications network, but so far only the coffee shop and restaurant off the lobby—part of the original hotel design—were sublet. The coffee shop was showing a profit strictly on the building occupants. The ballroom could be subdivided into small spaces and was under control of the Shanghai Dragon Restaurant. Both Deng and Grant used it for larger meetings.

Grant and Bricher got off the elevator on 5, and Bricher headed for his section of the floor. Grant turned to the right and walked down to his suite.

It was an unfinished floor. There was temporary linoleum in a hideous pattern of beiges and blues underfoot. Temporary partitions blocked off some of the offices, and six-foot-high dividers defined other areas: satcom operations, software design, hardware engineering. The last belonged to Mickey Stone, but he was rarely in Shanghai. The partitions were finished in primer white and the matte surfaces were broken only by posters and artwork some of the employees had installed.

Diantha Mae Parker, a six-foot-tall, platinum-haired lady of proportionate proportions, ruled the kingdom in Grant's absence and, sometimes, when he was present. She had been his administrative assistant from the inception of the company six years before, and she had taken the move from Los Angeles in stride.

Parker's office, fronting his own, was about the same size as Grant's. But then, she had a dozen filing cabinets, a copier, a monster-memoried personal computer tied into the Local Area Network (LAN), a long table littered with plotters, scanners, and printers, a desk, and herself to fill it. Grant's office contained a desk, a sofa, and a couple chairs. For the head of a computer and communications conglomerate, Grant's needs were simple. He relied on the telephone and the huge charts taped to one wall. The charts tracked the various construction components for him and were kept up to date by Parker. The top line on the main chart, showing the schedule for satellite-orbit insertion, was going to have to be revamped.

Another set of lines tracked the completion stages of facilities—this one being ninety-five percent complete. Another group followed the construction of substations—the microwave-relay units. Hardware and software installations were monitored. Cable-laying in various cities was shown on a separate chart. Cable wasn't going to be a major part of the project, but there were a few areas where it was necessary. California production numbers for antennas, controllers, computers, and other peripherals were displayed.

Parker kept her versions of the same charts on her computer.

Parker's office was also a zoological garden. Greenery in large pots filled the corners, hung from the ceiling, and crept over the tables on either side of the visitor's couch. She had pictures of *jungles* on the walls, for Pete's sake.

She was on the phone, and she asked the caller to hold as soon as she saw him.

"Good afternoon, Diantha." No "Di" for her.

"Why don't you start calling me 'Gorgeous'?"

"You're luring me into an harassment trap. I'm too smart for that."

She grinned at him, as she always did, so that he never knew whether it *was* a trap or not. "The phone's been hot all day. I've got a stack of memos for you."

"Just what I wanted."

Grant took the sheaf of paper from her and went into his own office. She had been after him for years to install his own computer so she could send him electronic mail with such notes on the machine. He had resisted. Pieces of paper he could throw out if he didn't want to return a call. If he had serious number-crunching to do, he used his laptop, and generally, he did that in the privacy of his apartment.

He walked around his desk and sat down with his back to the window wall, which had a nice view of downtown Shanghai that he rarely had time to appreciate. It was generally wrapped in a toxic brown cloud, anyway. Shanghai was not only the largest city in Asia; as the most industrialized, it was also the most polluted.

Leafing through the memos, he sorted them into priority stacks, one of which he would never get to.

He called Calvin Coolidge, first. C.C. Jackson was a vice president of MI and Manager of Production. For the past three years, while Grant spent most of his time in China, he had essentially been the chief executive of the company in the United States.

"C.C. You called?"

"Hey, Doug! It's about time."

"I've been watching fireworks." Grant told him about the launch disaster.

"Shit! That going to put us under?"

"I don't think so. I'm working on some ideas."

"I hope they're good ones. I've got four hundred and twelve people—and I'm four-twelve—dependent on your whimsy."

That was one of the things Grant liked about Jackson. The big man had played tackle at Southern Methodist University, but had left there with two degrees and a real affinity for people. It was like him to number himself 412, behind the people working for him. He responded well and affirmatively to worker complaints, and he regularly put himself on the assembly line so he wouldn't forget what it was like.

"Don't worry about it, C.C. We'll pull it off."

"I wish we were as mega as our name implies."

Grant had selected the name of the company based more on the size of his ideas than his inventory, production, or bank accounts. The logo gave them equivalency with the logos of IBM or DEC, but the substance was much smaller—the design of the central processing unit. It was Grant's tenacity, roster of specialists, and list of strong American financial institutions backing the company that had landed him a multibillion-dollar contract. They were only months away from going over the top. The successful installation of Shanghai Star would lock MI into a hefty market share of the international computer and communications business.

At the moment, however, his lines of credit were stretched thin enough to snap at any moment. Despite the proximity of his goal, he didn't think he'd find another bank willing to extend credit as a result of the satellite destruction.

"How's the plant holding up?" he asked.

"That's one of the reasons I called," Jackson said. "We shipped the last units to Guangzhou today. I'm going back to a single shift."

One eight-hour shift of production was enough to satisfy the product demand in their normal world. Rather than add people they might have to lay off later, Jackson had put his existing workforce on additional half-shifts in order to meet the demand for the China contract.

"How about the replacement stock?"

"We're supposed to supply a six-month inventory of critical replacement parts, right? Our machines are so damned reliable, they won't need it."

"Need is not the operative word," Grant said. "*Selling* additional components is the idea."

"I'm slipping it into normal production. Ninety days, we'll have it completed."

"Good."

"The next thing, Doug. When are we getting our next payment on contract?"

"I thought you had it."

"Nothing in sight, as far as electronic fund transfers go, babe."

"I'll check on it. They were supposed to make the payment on the thirty-first."

"Do that. My cash flow's kinda constricted. I won't have the time-and-a-half payroll to face, but eighteen months of that used up the reserves, and a few of the suppliers are threatening to cut me off if I don't throw a few bucks their way."

"I'll find out right away."

"Thanks, babe."

Grant hung up and made a note on the back of the phon memo. The Chinese government was supposed to make monthl payments of $56 million in the first three years of the contrac $42 million a month in the fourth year, and $24 million a mont in the last year. The payment schedule reflected the early heav expenditures for equipment and facilities, then tapered off a Megatronics reduced its work force and capital outlays. In th last year of the contract, when the profit picture brightene Grant expected to have fewer than five hundred people in th PRC. At the moment, there were nearly 3,500 on the payroll.

The payments were also split. American dollars went to th United States. The balance of the payment, primarily to me in-country payroll expenses, was paid in Chinese yuan. Mo than once, Grant had had to press for payment. Jiang Guofen was no dummy, and a five-day delay in payment earned him sixt or seventy thousand in interest. Interest that Grant couldn't co lect—if he had had the luxury of idle cash flow.

The next phone memo was one of five from Deng Mai. H was about to press the speed-dial button for her when Parke came in.

"Have you called the Ice Maiden, yet?"

"Diantha, that's not how we refer to our boss."

"Sorry."

He knew that "Ice Maiden," the underground office name f Deng, had become widespread. He just hoped it didn't get bac to her. He also knew that their perceptions were entirely diffe ent from those of the people Deng worked closely with.

"She's pretty anxious to see you, Doug. She wanted you t come up as soon as you got back."

He replaced the receiver. "Okay. I need to open some negot ations, anyway."

Grant felt a little gritty from his early morning—he an Bricher had been up and on the job at three—and he was sti wearing the Megatronics uniform of Levi's and sport shirt, bu he didn't feel like going down the hall to the men's room to was up and change to something more formal, like chinos.

He left the office and rang for an elevator. The stairway doo to the sixth floor were locked. The elevator arrived quickly, an the trip was short. He barely had time to get his laminated ID card from his wallet and clip it to his shirt pocket.

He got off into a security zone protected by steel walls, a single steel door, a single wire-mesh, bulletproof window, surveillance cameras, and a handprint scanner. Waving at the guard behind the window, Grant placed his hand flat against the scanner, and when the Megatronics computer decided he had clearance, the door lock buzzed and the door slid back.

There were five of these security checks on the sixth floor, fed by five elevators. During changes in shifts, they tended to become bottlenecks, but there was no other access into the tower. Separate elevator banks serviced the upper floors from the sixth, after the visitor or employee passed through security.

Stepping into a wide, carpeted corridor, he walked it toward Deng Mai's office. The walls on these floors were finished in soft tan rice paper, and pastoral scenes framed in black bamboo were spaced along the hallway.

Deng's outer office contained two secretaries, and he addressed the first. "Is the director available, Miss Jiangyou?"

Her schoolish English was unimpaired. "I believe so, Mr. Grant. I will check."

She got up, knocked softly on the right of the double doors, opened it a bit, and slipped inside.

We give her a state-of-the-art telephone and intercom system, and she still announces visitors in the traditional way.

Grant shook his head and waited. He wasn't much better himself, he knew. He was afraid if he allowed a computer into his office, he'd spend all of his time on it. That was why he paid Diantha Parker.

Jiangyou reappeared, smiling brightly. "If you will come this way, Mr. Grant."

The formality never disappeared. In the first two years, when Deng's office had been temporarily located in a warehouse on the riverfront, he had been greeted and treated the same as he was now.

He crossed the reception area and stepped through the doorway. Jiangyou bowed slightly, slipped out, and closed the door softly behind her.

Deng's office had the same view as his. The Hilton tower

could be seen through the haze behind her. Beyond that was the building housing the United States Consulate General.

The managing director's digs were impressive, Grant thought. She had designed the room herself, starting with walls clad in rice paper of an ecru color so delicate it was almost pink. Her desk was a single sheet of free-form glass resting on heavy brass legs. There was a telephone and a blotter on it. A single vase containing one yellow rose stood on the near edge. Behind her was another sheet of glass with a computer terminal. Deng didn't have the same misgivings that Grant did.

The sunlight, if it became harsh through the bronze-tinted windows, could be softened with diaphanous curtains that were now pulled to the sides. Angled slightly to his left was another glass table, four feet across, and maybe sixteen inches off the floor. It was surrounded by six low chairs upholstered in a burgundy fabric which had dark blue threads running through it, depicting abstract blossoms. Two huge paintings adorned the walls. In the middle of China, their subjects were surprising—Left Bank scenes in Paris. He had been told they were gifts from her mother.

Whenever he entered this chamber, and after having known the beautiful lady for three years, Grant felt as if they should run across the deep pile carpet and throw their arms around each other.

He would have liked that.

Deng Mai, however, was always properly formal. She was quick to smile, to laugh at a subtle joke, to perhaps touch his forearm, but he always suspected—he had never attempted it—that an encroachment beyond the nature of their business interest into her personal life would be greeted by formidable barricades.

Today, she was wearing a pale-blue dress with a high collar, something of a mix between East and West. It did nothing to hide her stunning figure, but as always, she moved as if completely unaware of her impact on others. She rose from her chair with fluid grace and came around the glass desk. Her smile displayed lots of perfectly aligned white teeth and was echoed in the warmth of her eyes. She held out her hand, and he stepped forward to shake it briefly. As always, it was warm and firm and dry.

The smile was briefly held, then replaced by a sternness that suggested her deep concern.

Nothing about her suggested the ice water that flowed through her veins. Not until one went too far in a wrong direction and the eyes went flat and hard.

"Good afternoon, Douglas."

"Hello, Mai."

It had taken two years to achieve first-name status.

She gestured toward the low table, and they took chairs, with one vacant chair between them so they didn't have to continually look sideways at each other. He noticed that a glass bowl of water with three purple orchids floating in it had been placed on the table. That was new, and he couldn't decide if it were significant or not.

"Would you like tea or coffee?"

"Thank you, no. I drank my fill of both this morning. The orchids are pretty."

"Thank you. They are meant to add harmony to my day, to bring good joss."

She sat erect in her chair, with her hands folded in her lap. The chairs were just the right size for her five-seven frame. Grant was six inches taller, however, with most of that in his legs, and the chair didn't fit him right. He didn't let it bother him, but shoved his feet out under the table, noting that his Nikes could use a scrubbing.

Sometimes, he had noticed, a clue to her mood could be found in her earrings, the only jewelry she ever wore. They were different almost every day, and often difficult to find in the luxuriant mane of dark hair that curled along her jaw. When she tilted her head sideways, he saw that a tiny, gold mask of tragedy was affixed to the lobe of her right ear. He hoped she was wearing comedy on the other ear. And if so, he wasn't going to find a clue in the earrings.

He waited, letting her choose the opening.

"Douglas, this was a tragic event."

"It hasn't been my best day ever," he grinned.

She shook her head slightly, as if exasperated at his lightness of tone.

"Have you determined how long we must delay the day of initial programming?"

"Oh, I don't think we're going to have any significant delays at all, Mai."

It was what she wanted to hear, of course. Though he did his best to steer clear of them, Grant was not insensitive to the political intrigues taking place between Shanghai and Beijing. He knew there was tension between Deng and Jiang. On several occasions, in joint meetings, he had seen and heard it.

Her eyebrows rose in question, and her eyes lightened so that he could all but see his own green eyes reflected in them.

"A few things have to fall in place just right, of course."

"Such as?"

"We have to determine if General Hua can get another Long March Three prepared quickly. He indicated to me that it was possible. We're checking with GE now about completing ShangStar Three ahead of schedule. It will become ShangStar Two."

"Can you give me a date?"

"Right now, it'd be a guess. Let me call you tomorrow afternoon. Or probably, I won't know anything until the first of next week."

In the first demonstration of nervousness Grant recalled seeing, Deng looked down at the hands in her lap and watched her forefingers fidget with each other.

Finally, she looked up, her gaze steady, and asked, "Will you survive it? Will Megatronics survive?"

He smiled. "It's not a problem, Mai."

"Isn't it? I follow your fortunes closely. I recommended your selection to the committee because I knew you were not only capable but hungry. I know that you cannot overcome a forty-five-million-dollar loss."

Grant pulled his feet back and leaned forward, resting his elbows on his knees. He kept his eyes on hers despite the fact that once in a while he felt as if he could get lost in their depths.

"Since we're talking about money, Mai, we haven't yet received our July payment."

"I will look into it. What of the loss?"

"It won't amount to much, Mai. In my conversation with General Hua, I understood that this could possibly be a case of sabotage. That would, I'm afraid, result in the Ministry of

Information assuming part of the cost." When he had talked to Hua from the Lear, Grant had, in fact, planted the suggestion with the man, hopefully before he had talked to Deng or to air-force headquarters. If Hua hadn't thought of it before, it gave him an out. Grant understood the general's desire to save face. In his experience, all generals were the same, East or West.

Deng leaned forward in her chair, closing the gap between them over the table. The movement provided them with a surprising sense of intimacy, Grant thought.

"You would not have provided such a hint to the general, Douglas?"

Grant hadn't expected such a direct question. Chinese usually skirted around issues for a while. He hesitated and looked around the office. He had built the place; he knew there weren't any electronic bugs.

He said, "Shall we be open with each other, Mai?"

"Please."

"I may have discussed the possibility with him."

"Good, because I made a similar indirect suggestion."

With those admissions, their relationship had suddenly changed.

Now they were conspirators.

Of a sort.

"It may not make any difference to the committee, however," she said.

"Oh?"

"The Premier has ordered an independent investigation of the accident."

On Henan Road in Old Town, which fit partially into a crook of the Huangpu River, was the national headquarters of the People's Underground. It was not advertised as such, of course, since then it would not have been an underground. Still, having been in existence for over ten years, and not having relocated its administrative center in that time, most of those with a need to know could find it easily. The Shanghai police and the national law-enforcement agencies knew where to find the People's Underground or its chairwoman, who preferred to be called Leader, Chiang Qing.

In the days of the foreign concessions, when British, French, Dutch, American, and businessmen of other nations dominated the economy of Shanghai, the Old Town was a refuge of native Chinese. The boundary was defined by Zhonghua Road, which nearly encircled the area, and its narrow, dark, and twisted alleys were once byways of extreme peril. It was a slum that defied the presence of elected officials, police, or legitimate citizens. Today, it has been renovated and whitewashed, and tourists meander through the maze, frequently becoming lost, to sightsee and shop the old market.

Chiang preferred to think of Old Town of the earlier era, with its sinister overtones, and it seemed to be an apt location for a counterrevolutionary movement. She was image-conscious. People striving for a new world did not appear affluent; they did not work from modern glass-and-steel office buildings. In Chiang's case, she did not have to work for her image. The People's Underground treasury was nearly always on the brink of insolvency.

Chiang Qing's headquarters was on the second floor of a century-old, redbrick building. There was an entrance at street level, and a long flight of worn wooden steps to the upper floor. The interior walls, also of brick on the perimeter walls, had been painted white, but that was ten years before. They were marred and blemished now. Political posters disguised the worst of the scraped paint. The furnishings were a conglomeration acquired from bazaars and auctions. Rattan couches, old mahogany swivel chairs with woven cane seats, and several cedar chests littered the main room, which also held four desks.

In addition to the large main room, there was also a kitchen, a bath, and three sleeping rooms. Chiang's permanent residence was in one of the latter, selected because of its escape route, a black iron fire escape barely gripping the brick wall at the back of the building. She had never been required to use it, but a revolutionary cause took all the precautions which seemed prudent.

Despite the fiery rhetoric of its chairwoman and its claim of revolutionary status, the People's Underground was all but a licit organization. The government could identify at least twenty percent of its membership—supposedly 3,000 strong in Shanghai, with another 50,000 members in other cities of the PRC, and the government tolerated its existence for two reasons. For one, the Underground appeared to give many with complaints a place to vent their anger, usually in closed meetings. It served as a relief valve. The second rationale for ignoring the vocal group was that Leader Chiang was extremely careful to not overstep some intangible boundaries. She would never, for instance, have sided with the students in Tiananmen Square during the Beijing uprising.

Chiang was a thorn in the side of the Beijing leadership, but a tolerable one. She ranted and raved, but she did not really *say* anything that was truly subversive. Still, her visibility and her ability to rile the government without reprisal, had steadily increased over a decade, and she was recognized as a voice of the common people, by the common people.

Chiang's face was relatively well known throughout the country, from the occasional television newscast and from the proliferation of posters that her members tacked, taped, and pasted to walls and electric poles everywhere. It was round and flat, with hooded oval eyes and a pug nose. Her black hair was cut even with her jawline, and was combed smoothly to either side of the crown of her head. She favored a peasant style of dress—mostly white cotton slacks with a white overblouse—in order to reassure her followers of her roots.

She had, in fact, been educated at Fudan University in political science and augmented that education with world travel that included the United States, Great Britain, France, and Germany. She was intellectually aware, and she selected carefully from a variety of political systems those aspects that best suited her purpose at any given moment. Of one thing, she was certain; she was not a communist. Her politics might be considered moderate socialism. She was prone to allow many deviations on that philosophy in order to accommodate a steady increase in membership.

Her instinct for knowing how far to push the government, without pushing hard enough to incur retaliation, was well known, and she was respected for it. She took up causes with apparent randomness: supporting student rights at one time, antipollution efforts at another, freedom of information at most times.

Chiang had been following Deng Mai's career for some time. It seemed to Chiang that there was a kinship, a sisterhood, between the two of them. Though Deng operated within the bureaucracy and Chiang on its vague borders, they both espoused their causes—and especially the cause of women—in a very visible fashion. They were the vanguard of the newly emerging version of the People's Republic of China.

The 1982 constitution of the Republic called for modernization of agriculture, the military, industry, and science and technology. Deng Mai was working within the latter area, and hopefully, her efforts would lead to greater awareness of the world community. Chiang considered herself as working toward the modernization of the *people,* a commodity she thought the constitution seemed to have ignored.

Chiang also considered herself a realist. She thought that Deng Mai must eventually fail simply because she attempted to challenge the entrenched leadership on their own grounds. Chiang would take whatever roads she must take to achieve her goals.

It was in that light that she and three of her followers watched the evening news. There was no film of the disastrous launch of the Long March 3 rocket, but after it was described by the reporter, Minister Jiang told everyone from his office in Beijing, "It is a tragic event."

And Managing Director Deng Mai told everyone in her sound bite that the loss of the satellite, "was a setback for the agency, but should not interfere with the long-term goals of establishing a people-oriented information network."

Chiang told her cohorts, "Glorious!"

Friday, August 5

A few blocks west of Old Town, in the International Hotel on Nanjing Road, Pierre Lefant occupied two suites on the fifth floor. He had been ensconced in them for nine months, using one for his personal needs and the other as the Far East office of Media Bureau Limited (MBL). Additionally, he leased time in one of Shanghai's not-too-state-of-the-art television studios for the production of demonstration tapes. The sessions were conducted at night, when the facilities were available. He had a staff of fifteen people in Shanghai with him, most of them now accustomed to a nocturnal routine of converting MBL's archival assets into attractions that would captivate a nation. That is, *The Six Million Dollar Man* and *The Pink Panther*, and others, were being edited for a less-sophisticated audience. Though official guidelines had yet to be adopted, Lefant had received some guidance from the information ministry.

Benny Hill, of course, was a no-no.

Lefant had an affable, if sometimes abrupt, manner. He was close to sixty years old, wouldn't admit it, and with careful grooming, appeared ten years younger. He was also shorter than he wanted to be, and he wore shoes handmade in Italy that gave him a trifling bit of lift, enough to make him feel more equal in a world that was growing taller all around him. For him, an assignment in the Orient provided a perquisite that his superiors in the Paris home office were not aware of; almost everyone he dealt with was shorter than he.

His hidden cache of Just for Men kept his hair dark and shining, and he wore it swept straight back from his high forehead in carefully permed waves. With his smooth skin, taut cheeks, and aggressive jaw, Lefant suited his career perfectly.

He was a salesman. He understood it, felt he had been bred for it, and was exceptional at it. From his graduation from public school, during which he had sold refrigerators and other household appliances, Lefant had sold furniture, automobiles, real estate, factories, talent, and now, programming packages.

Media Bureau Limited, as far as Lefant was concerned, was a terrible name. The very idea that anything he had for sale was limited in any way was unthinkable. There was no end to what he could offer anyone, provided the price was right.

MBL had been created as a consortium of European and British companies which owned or leased the rights to tens of thousands of movies and television programs. At his disposal, or rather, for his disposal was a library of cinematic efforts that spanned the ratings scale, the quality scale, and the ages—from early-1920s' French, Spanish, and Italian silent films to the latest action-hero blockbuster.

Additionally, the consortium had funded a subsidiary called Comp-U, which was hastily developing a computer-based interactive concept for incorporation into the package. Comp-U would be going head-to-head against the giant American companies, and Lefant had great hopes for it. Unfortunately, at the moment, all he had was a demonstration unit that seemed to be lacking in complexity.

Still, he kept reassuring himself, he could sell anything; had; and would do so again. Even Comp-U.

His present assignment had one rather massive drawback, however.

There was only one customer.

As an entity, the customer was Shanghai Star Communications.

As a person, the customer was the intriguing Deng Mai.

As a matter of reality, Lefant knew that he had to sell, not only the managing director—who would make the recommendation—but also the twelve men on the governing committee. He must convince them that a marriage between Shanghai Star and MBL was one to be blessed by Buddha, Confucius, the *Tao Te*

Ching, and given that those were superstitions in the eyes of the government, the Communist Party.

As was their normal procedure, Lefant and his chief assistant, Marc Chabeau, engaged in a working breakfast in the International's dining room. Chabeau was a young man—thirty-six—with a fine working knowledge of his product, a mind sharp enough to remain quiet when he was supposed to, and the potential to be as good as Lefant in the marketing game. If he had a flaw, it was that he was permanently angry at—Lefant thought jealous of—Americans. He occasionally let slip a barbed reference to Megatronics Incorporated's personnel despite Lefant's assurances that MBL would never work for Megatronics. They would work for—with—Shanghai Star.

Though he ate only a poached egg, a single slice of toast, and a cup of coffee for breakfast, Lefant always used the hotel's formal dining room. He appreciated elegance in his own life, and he expected it in the service for which he paid.

The waiter refilled Lefant's cup, then lit his Gauloises, as Chabeau completed his recital of the status of the previous night's production schedule. ". . . *Cherie* is ninety percent complete. The two game shows will be finished tonight. *Africa* and the other documentary, *East Bloc,* have been shortened to twenty-two minutes each, and the language dubbing is scheduled for Monday."

Chabeau looked up, smiling, waiting for his compliment.

"Excellent! What of the quality, Marc?"

His assistant blinked his eyes closed in a brief grimace. "It is not the best. Yet, to an unsophisticated audience, the distinction will not be noticeable."

"I hope that is so," Lefant said.

In the last six months, samples of the Bureau's products, newly dubbed in the official Chinese language called *putonghua,* meaning common language, had been sent to various government and party officials for their free viewing, with a request for feedback. The officially designated language was the Northern Chinese dialect, called Mandarin by outsiders. Since there were enough dialects in the language to constitute separate languages, not to mention the minority languages of Korean, Mongolian, Uigar, and a few others, it was nice to be able to focus on one.

And though there were many dialects, there was, fortunately, only one writing system for all dialects. All Chinese speakers wrote the language in the same way, using characters instead of an alphabet. The academic system of writing the language in the Roman alphabet had been developed by Sir Thomas Wade and Herbert Giles in the 19th century, but China had begun using the newer pinyin (Chinese Language Transcription Proposal) system in 1979 for news reports and communications with the rest of the world. That was when Peking became Beijing, Tibet Xizang, Mao Tse-tung, Mao Zedong. It was an attempt to apply phonetics to the language since foreigners could not see a single phonetic clue in any of the three thousand commonly used characters. The scholars consulting with Media Bureau Limited had recommended that pinyin be used in conjunction with a few Chinese characters for any written material that would appear on a screen. This was especially critical in the area of commercial enterprise. Advertising.

To date, that which had been sent out seemed to have been received favorably.

"So, Marc, how close are we to having our demonstration package?"

"I expect it will be complete by the seventeenth, Pierre. That is a week ahead of our formal presentation, and you will be able to rehearse your part many times."

"What is the final composition? Have we decided?"

Chabeau said, "We have excerpts from two major movies, six newscasts, two talk shows, three situation comedies, five commercials, four cartoons, the two documentaries, a crisis-reporting situation, and a home-shopping segment. We have also the Comp-U piece. You and I will have to discuss the sequential arrangement."

"The commercials. Tastefully done, I hope? I want to see them before a final decision is made."

"Quite tasteful, Pierre. The consulting sociologists have all given their approvals. No one will be offended, even inadvertently."

"Cut the number to three. We don't want the presentation to seem overloaded with commercialism."

Chabeau wrote himself a neat note on the yellow pad next to his plate.

"What crisis are we using for an example?"

"Earthquake. The one in California."

"Hmm. We had to buy that footage. It is not our own."

"Still, Pierre, we want to show that we are not parochial. Our news teams do cover the world, not just Europe."

"True. Good point. The sitcoms do not contain innuendos that the Chinese would not understand?"

"Again, there is nothing offensive, Pierre. The sociologists are aware of the government's concern for blue material. We are showing nothing that would even be considered near an 'R' rating."

"Good."

Once the contract was in hand, of course, there would be intense screening for suitable material but little doctoring of future programming. It was too time-consuming. For the presentation, however, Lefant intended to have a meticulous selection.

"Now," he said, "the boredom factor."

"If you sense your audience drifting," Chabeau said, "you have only to press the button, and the programming will skip to the next segment. Fortunately, we do not have to give them a full eighty-eight minutes of drama. If we lose them six minutes into the piece, we can jump to a newscast."

"Excellent, Marc! You are doing very well."

"I will be happy when this is over and I can go home. Francine is impatient."

Chabeau's girlfriend was entirely too demanding, Lefant thought, but again, kept his opinion to himself. He never intentionally offended anyone.

He smiled, demonstrating the quality of his dentistry. "When we go home, Marc, our luggage will be worth three billion francs."

And his commission would see him through the rest of his life.

In the warm sun of the south of France, where his villa was located.

Fortunately, the volatile Margot had never located it.

Zhou Ziyang was led into Minister Jiang's office by a male secretary.

"Well, Chairman Zhou!" Jiang said without rising from behind his desk. "You honor us with your presence."

"It is you, Minister, who honor me by allowing this audience."

Zhou stood before the desk, being humbled, he supposed, for nearly a full minute before Jiang gestured toward one of the two visitor's chairs placed squarely in front of the huge teak desk. Jiang was fond of such dramatic gestures, but Zhou did not concern himself with them. Perhaps it went with the office.

Perhaps because he was so slight of stature, Zhou felt the bulk of the minister as a nearly overwhelming presence. He was a set of spheres. That of his body was rotund and overweight for his height and confined within a well-tailored gray suit of American cut. Leading political figures in the PRC favored Western dress. When they appeared on balconies or on television in more traditional garb, looking like latter-day Mao Zedongs, it generally preceded a governmental crackdown on excessive counterrevolutionary activities. Jiang's upper arms were massive also, tapering to hands that were disproportionately small. They were hyperactive hands, frequently toying with the objects on his desk—a pencil, a telephone cord, small golden souvenirs he had accumulated in his travels.

His head was saved from being a simple globe by a shock of thick white hair, left full like a halo around his head. His eyes were dark and direct and darting; they jumped from one fixation to another, carrying with them some indefinite knowledge of all they had witnessed in fifty-plus years. In the middle of the puffy cheeks was a small, but expressive mouth. The minister did not often smile, Zhou thought.

In contrast, Zhou Ziyang was a petite man with well-defined features. His hair was strikingly black, trimmed short, and a match for his eyes which were shaded by heavy eyebrows. His face was gaunt, and his nose was too large for an Asian. He was forty years old, and it felt to him as if most of his life had been a struggle. He was always fighting for something—to live, to succeed, to convince others.

Besides their obvious physical disparity, Jiang and Zhou were polarized in their philosophies regarding the dissemination of knowledge.

Zhou Ziyang headed the organization he had formed some fifteen years before, shortly after his graduation from the university. It was called the People's Right to Know Committee, and the government had grudgingly given it lip service, and a few insignificant concessions, over the years. The gains had been insubstantial because, like Chiang Qing, Zhou moved with extreme care not to antagonize the authorities into reprisals against himself or his roster of some fifty active members. There was a large number of associate members—perhaps fifteen thousand, and Zhou was relatively certain that Beijing remained unaware of them.

Despite the size of his organization, in a state of over a billion population, it was minuscule, and more akin to the nuisance of a flea than a tiger. Zhou had had no illusions in the past decade about the rate of his progress.

Now, however, there was Shanghai Star.

With the ceremonial announcement of the project some four years before, Zhou had developed a sense of impending doom. He had felt that he was to be forced into open confrontation, and to his credit, he thought, he had not shirked his duty. He had kept pressure on officials to make Shanghai Star what it could be.

"It is August fifth, Minister. As you requested, I have returned."

Jiang's face creased as though in confusion. "Remind me, please, of the topic. I am afraid that I have been so preoccupied with other matters. . . ."

Again, the stalling tactics.

"The Information Advisory Committee was to have a draft copy of its information dispersal policy available to me at this time."

"Ah, yes! I recall our meeting now. You gave me a list of concerns the Right to Know Committee wished to have considered during the policy-development process."

"Exactly, Minister."

"And it was an excellent idea, Mr. Zhou. So good, in fact, that we requested similar listings from other organizations."

Was he to be flattered?

"Do you have a copy for me?" he asked.

"Unfortunately, not yet. The response was overwhelming, and the committee is still considering all of the input. Then, too, this unfortunate incident with the rocket has resulted in some chaos. Meetings have been delayed. You do understand?"

Zhou thought that this statement was likely a fabrication, but he said, "When may we expect to see a draft?"

"I should not think it would be much longer," Jiang said. "Perhaps in a week?"

Zhou stood up. "Very well, Minister. I will return on the twelfth."

"Wonderful! It was good of you to come by, and I regret that the bureaucratic wheels turn so slowly."

Zhou left the office knowing that Jiang suffered no regrets whatsoever. He did all that he could to obfuscate and wipe the grease from those bureaucratic wheels.

A governmental policy regarding what data would be available to the Shanghai Star network should have been formulated long before. As it was, Zhou had been dogging the Minister of Information for nearly ten months.

And there was still nothing in writing.

He felt deep in his heart that, when it was presented to him, the policy would not be in draft form, allowing further comment. It would be a fact accomplished, and the policy, he was also certain, would be unacceptable.

If that were the case, Zhou would be forced into a confrontation that he neither desired nor knew how to shape.

And probably could not survive.

On the intercom, Diantha Parker's golden tones announced, "Mr. Grant, your two o'clock appointment is here."

Grant finished signing the last two letters as he glanced at his calendar. "Send him on in, Diantha."

He got up and went around the desk as Suretsov entered the office.

Offering his hand, he said, "Mr. Suretsov."

The correspondent had a firm grip and a dry hand. He was tall and blond, and he seemed fit beneath the lines of his dark-blue suit. The suit was obviously crafted in the Orient for him, but the color and weight seemed inappropriate for Shanghai in August. He had very bright-blue eyes beneath a craggy brow, and they maintained a steady and noncommittal gaze. Grant figured him for his midthirties.

"Thank you for seeing me, Mr. Grant."

"My pleasure, though I'm not certain just what ITAR-Tass could find of interest about me."

"I think that you are one of the keys to what is happening in China right now, Mr. Grant. With the information superhighway."

"Let's sit over here." Grant led the way to his conversational grouping of couch and chairs. Suretsov sat on the sofa, and Grant took one of the chairs.

The Russian removed a notebook and a small tape recorder from his jacket pocket, then looked around the office.

"For a computer man, Mr. Grant . . ."

"Look, call me Doug, will you? Everyone else does."

The man seemed to find the request typical of informal Americans. He said, "I am Vladimir. I was about to observe that you do not have a computer in your office."

"I don't know the first, or the last, thing about computers."

The blond eyebrows rose in surprise. "That cannot be."

"Well, I know just a little. I'm a businessman, Vladimir. My philosophy is to hire the best people for a job. That's all I've done."

"Would you tell me about yourself?"

"I'd rather talk about Shanghai Star Communications."

"Please? Our audience is interested in anything American, especially an American contributing to profound changes in China."

After the profound changes in Russia?

"Clear back to 'born and raised'?"

The reporter nodded.

Grant sighed. "That was in, or rather, near Manhattan, Kansas."

"The heartland of America?"

"That's it. My folks farmed three hundred acres. They worked hard at it."

"Which provided you with your philosophy and work ethic?"

"Couldn't survive unless you were Republican."

"Did you enjoy your formative years?"

"Sure."

Hated it. Tore up a lot of gravelled roads with that old '66 Chevy, looking for a way out. Spent half my time in trouble with my folks and the other half in trouble with the traffic cops.

"Then you went to the university?" Suretsov prompted, but Grant had the feeling that he'd done a little research before showing up.

"No, I pulled two years in the army, first. Contributing a little time to the country."

That was the way out of Manhattan, helped along by old Judge Potter, who had no sense of humor at all. He saw nothing funny in blowing up old cars with sticks of dynamite. Two years in the army, or nine months in jail, your choice. Next case.

"Where did you serve?"

"Fort Leonard Wood, Missouri, then Fort Gordon, Georgia. I was an MP, a military cop."

How's that for irony?

"You did not go to Vietnam?"

"I was too late for that game."

"And what did you learn in the army?"

"I learned I didn't want to be either a private first class or a cop."

And maybe a little discipline. And maybe ambition. And maybe a little compassion for others. Old Judge Potter was a smart cookie. Ten years after the fact, Grant had sent him a letter of thanks only to learn that the judge had died. He'd always felt bad that he'd been too late in showing his appreciation.

"In what I have read, I understood that you served in the Persian Gulf."

"That was after my schooling, Vladimir. I was in the reserves, so I took a commission as a second looie. At the time, I needed the extra money, and I sure didn't think I'd get called back to active duty."

"You were a military policeman, then?"

"No. My unit was infantry."

And gung-ho until I learned about hot sand and hot bullets.

"According to the short biography in *Who's Who,* you went to Augusta College."

"During my eighteen months at Fort Gordon, I went to night

school, just to get off post, you understand? By the time I was discharged, I already had a year's credits racked up, so l continued at AC."

"And finished in two years?"

"I was in a hurry," Grant said.

Plus, I couldn't live on the student loans if I'd done the whole three years.

"And then to the Harvard Business School?"

"They offered me a scholarship."

"Tell me about your business experiences."

"Most of it's boring, Vladimir. After I resigned my commission as a first lieutenant, I spent a couple years at General Motors, where I primarily learned corporate politics. Then, I worked for two other companies before starting MI."

"But you owned those companies."

"More correctly, I owned parts of them. Everybody's got a boss, and mine were always boards of directors."

"Nonetheless, from what I read," Suretsov said, "you gained a reputation as—what is the term?—a turnaround specialist?"

And as a ruthless son of a bitch. If people don't work, you put sticks of dynamite under their asses and blow them into action or out the door. Pretty simple formula.

"I saw some opportunities that others had missed. I managed to focus those companies on some clear goals, that's all."

"And you left as president and chief-executive officer of ABCRA Engineering to found Megatronics?"

"The job had become less than exciting."

So boring that I dumped my accumulated stock a year before and put a million of my own dollars with six million in venture capital to underwrite the development of the MI central processing unit. The ABCRA board happened to find out about it and suggested I leave. They didn't want a man who was running two companies.

"The rise of Megatronics has been meteoric," Suretsov said. "To what do you attribute that?"

"From the beginning, we've had a very aggressive marketing strategy, Vladimir. We spent a hell of a lot of money promoting our product, but then we followed it up by demonstrating its quality. Quality counts."

Being on the edge of bankruptcy also helps. When Monica, whom he had met and married while at GM, bailed out on him—with the Encino house, one of the two Mercedes, and all of his personal cash, he was left with nothing but the determination to make MI a success. Monica, fortunately, didn't believe in the viability of MI and had left him his stock. Which could be as worthless as Monica predicted.

"It came as something of a shock to others in your industry, I think, when Megatronics won the Shanghai Star contract. Can you tell what your advantage was?"

"MI was no different from others in wanting to get on the bandwagon when this information-superhighway concept became a catchword, Vladimir. I don't think I'm making any huge revelations when I say that we shaved our profit margins to get this contract. Others did the same. Yet, I think we truly offer three distinct advantages. One is quality. The second is reliability. The first machines we produced for the market, six years ago, are still operating faithfully without one component failure."

"And the last advantage?"

"I, and all of the principals of MI, truly believe in what we're doing for the People's Republic. We're dedicated to assisting the people in fully developing their knowledge and their learning capability. I'd like to believe that that dedication was apparent to those who selected us."

Suretsov wrote the response on his notepad, apparently not fully convinced that his tape recorder would catch it.

"You are not involved in the programming of this knowledge dissemination."

"No. We'll leave that to other experts. But we're committed to providing the best possible platform for that information flow."

Grant swigged the rest of his coffee, then refilled their cups. He had made the same statements so many times before that he had them down pat. More important, he believed them. He thought that came across to the interviewers.

"Now, to current events," the correspondent said. "I was a witness, yesterday, to the failure of the Long March Three rocket at Xichang. What was your reaction?"

"I was disappointed, naturally."

"You do not think it was sabotage?"

Grant wanted to be careful here. Saying anything too overt

might turn Beijing against him, and he desperately needed a break in favor of sabotage.

"I'm not a specialist in rocketry, Vladimir, but my understanding is that the Republic's space program is consistently successful. It seems to me that an outside influence might be involved, but until the autopsy of the rocket is complete, I couldn't say anything definite."

Suretsov smiled, as if divining his purpose. He wrote out that quote, also.

"If sabotage were involved, Doug, to what would you attribute the purpose?"

"That would involve a lot of conjecture on my part."

"Your competitors?"

That thought hadn't even crossed Grant's mind. "I like to think my competitors and I meet on the field of business. We might undercut each other in price, but I can't imagine anyone attacking a satellite."

"Chinese dissidents, then?"

"I've been doing my best to stay out of Republic politics, Vladimir. I wouldn't even hazard a guess."

But it was possible, wasn't it? What the hell? I've been so intent on blaming it on terrorism that I didn't even think that it could actually be a terrorist act.

"Finally," the Russian asked, "about your relationship with Deng Mai . . ."

"Relationship! What relationship?"

"That is what I am asking."

"Director Deng and I have a professional relationship. I assure you that it is quite formal."

Denial is always the first affirmation that the reverse is true.

"You understand that, in my pursuit of the news, I meet a lot of people, Doug. Believe me when I say that the perception of many people is that the two of you are very close. She is, after all, a strikingly beautiful woman."

Not too long ago, he could always say he was happily married. Now, the alibis were thinner, but what he didn't need was a rumor mill turning out speculation that could kill him with Jiang and the Information Advisory Committee.

"The perceptions are in error, Vladimir," he replied, smiling. "Is Tass aspiring to tabloid status?"

Suretsov returned the smile. "I should hope not. Still, I am a student of human nature, and I watch many things with interest."

"But not for publication?"

"Not until I have evidence."

After Suretsov left, Grant had the uneasy feeling that the Russian was going to be digging around in Grant's life.

It was another complication, and it was certainly one that he did not need.

Tan Long was envied by many of the people who knew him, and a great many people were acquainted with him.

They envied him less for his job—at which he appeared to toil very hard—than for the airline pass which came with his job. The plastic-laminated card Tan carried allowed him access to airline seats that would take him anywhere within the borders of the People's Republic of China.

For a Chinese citizen, Tan Long was well travelled. For nearly fourteen years, he had served the state committee of the People's Department Store, working from his flat and a tiny office in the People's Department Store in Shanghai. His job was two-pronged. In his many visits to the stores located in every principal city, he assessed the ongoing operations and wrote reports to the committee, often making recommendations for improvements in efficiency and effectiveness. From time to time, some of his recommendations had been implemented.

In that part of his job, the managers and departmental supervisors of People's Department Stores had come to fear him and to cater to him. A kind word from Tan could mean the continued availability of their livelihoods.

In the other aspect of his position, Tan was responsible for acquiring specialized new products and charting their introductions and sales progress. For this, he was not paid a commission. However, if one of his selections proved successful, he would be paid an appropriate bonus at the end of the year.

The bonuses he had accumulated over fourteen years allowed

him to live a life that was substantially better than those of his counterparts. A confirmed bachelor, Tan's expenditures were devoted entirely toward his own comfort. His four-room flat was furnished and appointed with wares from the Friendship Store, a non-Chinese emporium which attracted international shoppers. He owned a four-year old Lada, which was not a very prepossessing automobile, but which was, at least, his own.

His flight from Guangzhou had been uninteresting; Tan prided himself on his studied indifference to his frequent travel. He arrived in Shanghai in great spirits, however. In the morning, he was scheduled to meet with a representative of the Japanese electronics giant, Sony.

With the introduction of Shanghai Star, a surging demand for things electronic, like high-resolution monitors and television sets, was to be anticipated. A solid contract with yet another of the Japanese firms to sell their products through the People's Department Stores would assure him a healthy bonus in December. He had already secured a contract with Panasonic.

Tan was one hundred percent in favor of the creation of Shanghai Star. In more ways than one, it would make him a wealthy man.

On at least one Friday each month, Maynard Crest hosted a party. For one thing, he liked parties. For another, it was a subtle method by which he put others in his debt. He preferred having other people owe him, if only a dinner or a shot of scotch.

He varied the format of his celebrations, and this, the eighth since he had been in Shanghai, was a buffet. The caterer had erected tables along one wall and set out chafing dishes of smoked ham, rare roast beef, deep-fried shrimp, Sichuan pork, and lobster. Snow peas, green beans, three presentations of potato, a platter of varied breads, and four different desserts filled out the offerings. Most of those going through the line made themselves thick sandwiches from the offerings.

On the north end of the room was a table of hors d'oeuvres ranging from potato chips and seven different dips to goose pate, Beluga caviar, and egg rolls. Opposite the buffet was a full bar attended by two bartenders. Soft music issued from stereo speakers situated in the four corners of the room. Crest had personally selected the CDs—easy-listening instrumentals fronted by Percy Faith, Mantovani, the Dorseys. His tastes gave away his age, sixty-three, but he preferred listening to music that wasn't intrusive and which he could understand.

Between the tables, in space cleared of furniture, the guests were supposed to mix and enjoy themselves. He didn't intend for them to sit.

So far, it seemed to be going well. About seventy people were engaged in animated conversations, holding dripping sandwiches or plates of appetizers in one of their hands and drinks in the other. Not many seemed to be paying attention to the bank of six large-screen television monitors aligned at the south end of the room. Each soundless screen carried a sample of the offerings of the Consortium of Information Services, called CIS. It was an alliance of American cable and entertainment concerns, and it was a quality group that Crest was proud to represent. One delighted Chinese man clasped a Remote Responder in his hands and answered questions asked by the interactive program on screen number six, *Career Search.*

Crest didn't worry that few watched the screens. They knew they were there, and they knew that CIS was buying their dinners.

Minister of Information Jiang Guofeng was there, presiding over a group of six near the appetizers. This was the second of the parties he had attended, and Crest was pleased. It was difficult to lobby when his visa restricted him to Shanghai and most of the heavy-duty decision makers were in Beijing, seven hundred miles away to the north.

He excused himself from a knot of four men debating Middle East politics and worked his way across the room. He noted with approval that his top staff people were spread out, joined in conversations. Their orders were to mingle, to not bunch up and talk shop. They were also to refrain from selling, unless someone asked about one of the demos on a television. It was more important to remain low key and just meet people they could be nice to.

Crest also noted that the reporters—five of them this time—were making about their fifth assault on the buffet table. New among them for this party was the Russian Suretsov. Crest had never heard of him before, but the ITAR-Tass news agency had broken the story of the aborted rocket launch internationally so Suretsov got a last-minute invitation.

As he aimed for the bar, he saw Grant and Bricher appear at the door, and he changed course to meet them.

"Good evening, Doug, Will. I'm glad you could stop by."

"Wouldn't miss one of your feeds for the world," Bricher told him.

"I was damned sorry to hear about your misfortune with the satellite."

He was, too. If Megatronics failed, then CIS failed. Or was delayed until someone new finished the job.

"I don't think it will set us back by much," Grant said.

"That's a relief to me."

"I thought it might be," Grant said.

Bricher left the two of them and headed for the bar.

Crest felt a special affinity for the twenty-year-younger Grant. They were, first of all, both Americans stuck in an exotic locale, and they were engaged in the same pursuit—helping the Chinese into the 21st century.

Using an American investigative company he was familiar with, Crest had done some extensive background checks of the primary personnel working for Megatronics Incorporated. That was a tactic he had learned growing up on Madison Avenue where he had eventually become president of Wacker-Morgan-Shell, one of the chief advertising agencies in the United States with a billion dollars in billings. It was a basic philosophy for him: Know your enemy, your friend, your client. There was no sense in attempting to sell pine-scented tissue paper to a man allergic to pine.

He had been impressed with the quality of the MI managers, but he had also been concerned about the precarious fiscal position of the company. It couldn't afford many mistakes.

Maynard Crest was not, of course, trying to sell anything substantial to Grant. Rather, he was trying to impress the man with CIS's innate integrity and vision. His gut instinct was that what rubbed off on Grant would eventually rub off on Deng Mai. Despite the rumors, he couldn't swear that Grant was bedding her, but even if he wasn't, the obvious odds said that Grant had a great deal of influence with her.

"What kind of a delay are we looking at?" he asked.

"Maybe none, Maynard. It'll be Monday or Tuesday before I know for certain."

"Great! Wonderful!" He almost gave Grant a pat on the shoulder, but remembered in time—from their first encounter—that Grant was not a man who appreciated backslapping.

Crest's job was to remember such details. He had a phenomenal memory, to which he attributed what success he had had in life.

Grant paused in his scanning of the guests to grin at him. "Are we exporting the cocktail culture to China, too?"

"Goodwill. We are exporting goodwill. I know you think this sort of thing a blatant and transparent artifice, but honestly, blatant and transparent artifices help us to get to know people in an informal atmosphere."

"Just as long as you back it up. When's your presentation?"

"To the committee? On the twenty-sixth." Crest winked at him. "And we've got it backed up."

"Lefant's showed me a couple of his ideas, Maynard. They're not too bad."

"You want to tell me more about them?"

"Of course I don't. I'm a neutral in this war."

Crest respected that stance. He didn't think Grant would give away secrets.

"You want a little insight?" he asked.

"That I should keep to myself?" Grant asked.

"Please. Not even to Director Deng."

Grant raised an eyebrow, but said nothing.

"We'll be showing our newscasts and major dramatic pieces with the audio dubbed in *putonghua,* but they're also closed captioned in English, French, pinyin, and Chinese character. The viewer makes the choice."

"Nice touch. A Chinese speaker could learn English, just watching Stallone slam someone around the ring."

"Bad example, Doug, but yes, it could work that way."

They spoke for a few minutes more, then Grant headed for the appetizers.

Crest had already spoken to Minister Jiang, so he wandered in the direction of Deng Mai, who was speaking to others in a group just in back of the minister. He had been keeping a close eye on both Jiang and Deng and had seen them meet earlier and spend ten or fifteen minutes in civil discourse. There was a tension between them, however, and it was probably not good for him. If he showed more favoritism toward one than the other, antagonism toward Crest might be the result.

Caution must be his watchword.

Deng Mai was particularly radiant this evening. Emphasizing her Chinese roots tonight, she wore a high-collared and form-fitting cheongsam of shimmering green silk. An intricate pattern of interwoven dragons was worked into the fabric in a slightly softer shade of green. A white gardenia was pinned into her hair, and Crest thought he'd like to lean forward and test its aroma. He refrained.

The group she was with parted a bit to admit him. They were mostly Chinese, but the correspondent Suretsov and a Vietnamese were part of the gathering. Deng Mai introduced him to the Vietnamese who, she explained, was observing the formation of Shanghai Star. She also introduced him to Suretsov.

"I appreciate the invitation, Mr. Crest," Suretsov said.

"I'm happy to have you here. Enjoy yourself."

"I could not help but notice," Deng said, "the program running on screen number six."

"Wonderful! You were supposed to notice it."

She smiled that great smile that he knew he'd seen before but, oh, so rarely.

"Tell me about it, please. It seems to have captured the attention of many."

Crest looked toward the eight or nine people gathered around the set now, then briefly explained how, by responding to posed questions, the viewer helped to define the career areas to which he or she might best be suited.

"I had better get in line," Suretsov said. "I frequently feel that I am in the wrong line of work."

"How about you, Mr. Crest?" Deng asked. "Have you taken the test?"

"To be honest with you, I'm afraid to take it. I'd find out that

I've wasted the last forty years. Would you like to sample the program?"

"I don't think so," she said. "I think that my aptitude fits my present position perfectly, and I intend to stay where I am."

Over her shoulder, Crest saw Jiang looking at them.

The minister smiled at him.

Tuesday, August 9

The Dallas Cowboy Cafe had sprung to life shortly after the new infusion of foreigners working on the Shanghai Star project. It was located on the ground floor of the building on Changning Road where Grant and a dozen others from MI had located apartments. The food wasn't anything anyone would write home about, but it was hot and based on familiar recipes. Since the cafe was handy, and since Grant didn't cook beyond what might be thrown on a charcoal grill, it had become his kitchen.

The motif was not football; it was cowboy. The Chinese waitresses wore jeans and plaid shirts and leather vests and Nike running shoes. Ten-gallon Stetsons and plastic wagon wheels and replica six-shooters hung on the walls between posters that touted desert and mountain scenes of Texas, Arizona, New Mexico, and Colorado. An imitation giant Sahuaro cactus stood in one corner. The jarring note was a black-and-white checkered floor of vinyl tile.

The two dozen tables in the place were crowded with a talkative and noisy bunch, mostly Americans, but there were a few Europeans scattered about. A particularly noisy Australian held forth at one corner table. The lingo might have mystified many of their countrymen. They spoke in acronyms and technical slang that was not only particular to the communications and computer industries, but often to a particular company within the industry. Most noninsiders who dropped in thought the Dallas Cowboy Cafe a modern-day Tower of Babel.

Grant had finished his oatmeal—he tried to vary his breakfasts—and was on his second cup of coffee when "Tank" Cameron stopped beside his table.

"Got a minute, Doug?"

"Sit down, Tank?"

Like C.C. Jackson, he was a football man. Cameron had once played on the offensive line at Iowa State, but though he was squat and broad and tough, he hadn't been big enough to make the pros. Unlike Jackson, the termination of Cameron's athletic career was a disappointment that showed up in some of his conversations. He was, however, an able business manager, and he headed the China delegation of Digi-Communications Technology (DCT), a company that had already won a contract in Hunan Province. DCT was installing digital telephonic networks in the province, and they were vying with a dozen other vendors for contracts in the other provinces.

Cameron's round face was blunt and seemingly dull, but it was a mask for a sharp mind. His blond hair was shorn so short in a crew cut that he appeared almost bald—a perfect military type, which he vehemently denied.

"How's Changsha?" Grant asked, referring to the capital city of Hunan Province.

"Last week, they had some festival going, kind of like a county fair. I think all fifty-two million of the province's population was in town."

"Not like Iowa?"

"Not much, amigo. Look, Doug, we're going to be ready for operational testing on the fifteenth. What's the loss of your bird do to that?"

"I don't think it's a problem, Tank. We'll get a few channels on ShangStar One."

"You think so? What I'm learning is that once the military gets their hands on new equipment or technology, they don't want to let go."

"Tell me about it."

"Okay. Our contract sets priorities. Number one is upgrading the military telephonic systems. Two is national governmental departments. Three is the provincial government. After that, it's large commercial and industrial sectors, then medium, then small. The guy on the street comes last."

The national and provincial governments were underwriting the cost in all but the last category. Hunan's was a socialistic environment, after all. The individual who wanted a telephone or a television or a computer could apply to the government for a low-cost loan to purchase them. Cameron and Grant, naturally, wanted everyone to own their own telephone and computer. Cameron wanted to sell phones, and MI's design staff had been developing several versions of low-end computers. The design criteria included the ability to handle the flow of information from Shanghai Star, reliability, and low cost. Additionally, C.C. Jackson had already started production on a remote-control device that allowed interaction between the viewer and the programs appearing on his set. When Megatronics proved its ability with a successful Shanghai Star system, Grant fully expected to utilize their new credibility in exploiting the ensuing consumer market. His target was a twenty-percent market share, but with over three hundred million households, that was substantial.

"I might have guessed that that was the ranking," Grant said. He knew that the military machine swayed a lot of the decisions made in Beijing.

"So, okay. We've got the main facility set up in Changsha, right? And we go out and put substations around the province, including the dedicated stations for the army and the government. While we're doing this, we sprinkle a few phones around on desks. They don't work yet, but we want people to get used to seeing them."

"I get the picture."

"Okay, we're short of phones at the moment, so I tell one of the guys to go pick up a few sets from the army admin building so we can display them at the smelting plant. Some colonel got all irate and tossed him in jail."

"No shit?"

"No shit, Red Ryder. Took me eight hours to spring him, and the army let me know in no uncertain terms that what was theirs was theirs. Hell, the sets aren't even inventoried by the army yet, I don't think. As far as I know, they still belong to me, but I think I'll be writing off the cost."

"I don't think I'll run into the same problem with General Hua."

"Good luck. Okay, I'll keep the fifteenth on my calendar for op tests. You let me know if I've got to change it."

"Will do, Tank."

Cameron had no more than disappeared when Pierre Lefant approached. He was carrying an insulated pot daintily, as if he might risk scalding himself.

"Let me buy you a cup of coffee, Douglas."

Grant shrugged and sat back down. "I've never turned down a jolt of caffeine."

Lefant refilled Grant's mug, then one of his own, and sat down.

"You're pretty far from the International for this time of morning, Pierre."

"I came in search of you."

There were quite a few who did. Grant's breakfast habits had become well known, and he was often accosted over pancakes or ham and eggs. By now, he knew most of the American, European, Australian, and Japanese vendors of communications products who were resident in Shanghai, pitching their goods to Deng Mai and the committee. He had met most of them in the Dallas Cowboy Cafe.

Lefant spoke pretty decent English, though it carried both British and French accents. He ran the flats of his palms along both sides of his head to make certain his hair was in place and said, "I respect your opinion highly, Douglas, especially in regard to Chinese affairs. You have been in Shanghai much longer than I."

"You don't want to rely on my gut instincts, Pierre."

"Oh, but I do. As I rely on your discretion."

"Let me guess. You want a reaction to your material?"

Lefant winked, then smiled.

"And you don't want me passing the contents on to anyone else."

"I would be most appreciative."

"I don't think I want to get in the middle of this," Grant told him.

"Strictly off the record, Douglas."

From inside his jacket pocket, Lefant retrieved a folded sheet of paper, smoothed it flat on the table, and slid it across to Grant.

Reluctantly, Grant looked at the short listing. The titles of the pieces were listed, along with a short summary of each. He scanned the descriptions quickly.

"What's this *East Bloc* documentary about?"

"It's a retrospective of the transformations that have taken place in Eastern Europe."

"The good, the bad, *and* the ugly?"

"We've tried to keep a balance, Douglas."

"I wouldn't want to tell you your business, Pierre, but if it were up to me, I'd probably scrap that one."

Lefant raised an eyebrow. "Please tell me why."

"I haven't seen it, of course, but if your documentary attempts in any way to persuade the viewer how a change in political or cultural direction might best be accomplished, it probably won't go over well in Beijing."

The Frenchman raised his other eyebrow.

"My impression is that the Chinese are facing up to the need for *some* change, but they want to hang on to the old ways as long as possible, let the change take place gradually. You show them governments that tumbled overnight, which they already know about, and they may have an adverse reaction."

"Absolutely! You are so very right, Douglas. I don't know why I missed the significance. We will eliminate that one. What of the others?"

"Again, I haven't seen them, but on the surface, I don't see anything particularly obnoxious. The sitcoms have anything racy?"

"No. I checked that aspect personally." Lefant stood up, and Grant followed suit. "I appreciate your insight immensely, Douglas. I will owe you a dinner."

"Forget it, Pierre."

They both stopped at the cashier to pay their bills, Grant turning down Lefant's offer to pick up his breakfast tab. On the street, they parted, and Grant walked south down Wanhangdu Road, headed generally in the direction of his office.

The street was lively with pedestrians and auto traffic, and the cacophony of their combined voices and engines seemed typical of any city in the world. Many of the Chinese had adopted Western dress, and jeans or chinos and sport shirts were as common as the casual slacks and open-necked shirts favored by Chinese businessmen. Blended with the auto and truck and motorized rickshaw exhaust was the aroma of exotic spices emanating from open storefronts. Behind glass windows, the trinkets and jewelry and supposed gold watches beckoned.

At the corner of Yanan Road, as he turned west, Grant passed the Children's Palace, one of many in the city, and the one normally displayed for visitors. The palaces occupied the mansions once owned by the wealthy commerce aristocracy and were dedicated to extracurricular training. After school hours, children were allowed to attend the palaces to learn the arts: singing, dancing, painting. He heard a chorus accompanied by a slightly off-beat orchestra when he passed an open window.

Dodging his harried fellow pedestrians as he walked, Grant considered Lefant's purpose this morning. It certainly wasn't to obtain Grant's approval of Media Bureau's offerings. The *East Bloc* piece might even have been inserted to test him. No, Lefant hoped Grant would gush eloquent to Deng Mai about the quality of the programming.

Grant hadn't really paid much attention to what MBL, CIS, or any of the other purveyors were promoting. He assumed they were slanting their offering toward what Jiang would like to see and hoping to get an endorsement from Mai along the way.

To be honest, Grant wasn't impressed, but he wouldn't say anything, one way or another, to Mai. He was doing his best to avoid the warring programmers.

The problem with having five hundred channels of television was how to fill those hours with something worth watching. Grant had never been a big viewer. Once in a while, he'd catch a football game or some special. Normally, he only watched the news.

The big outfits, like Media Bureau and the Consortium of Information Services, not only had to convince the committee of their worth, but they had to also create an appetite among the Chinese populace. There was demand there, certainly, but the demand was unstructured. The people didn't really know what they wanted since they'd not had many choices in the past. Maynard Crest was attempting to create an interest in American-style sports by donating videos of football, basketball, and baseball games to bars and clubs. And to Crest's credit, the Friday Night

Games at a dozen different clubs in Shanghai were becoming popular.

Next, it would be Saturday Games, then Sunday Games. Crest was probably looking forward to a time when he'd have a football channel, a basketball channel, and a soccer channel going twenty-four hours a day. Special—"The 1968 Super Bowl."

It was all very interesting, but he was only concerned with the means.

Then he'd sell a few computers.

He didn't care what people watched, but he thought they should be entitled to watch whatever they wanted.

It wasn't, however, his problem.

Chiang Qing's deputy was known only as Huzhou to protect his identity. His father was prominent in political circles and certainly no help to the People's Underground. Huzhou had left the university after his second year to devote his soul to the cause. His hair was as black as Chiang's, though it was longer, to the tops of his shoulders, and was held in place by a leather thong wrapped tightly across his forehead. He wore thick spectacles in round gold frames, and from the frontal view, the magnification gave him huge, wondrous eyes. At twenty-two years of age, he was more ardent about the goals of the Underground than any five members put together.

He was only confused at those times when Chiang changed the goals, but he always recovered quickly and embraced the new directions. That is, he had always done so before.

He was accustomed to Chiang's eccentric ways. For example, she spelled her name C-H-I-A-N-G, rather than J-I-A-N-G, as was expected in the pinyin phonetic spelling. Since Jiang Quofeng had risen to power, she was happy she had done so.

Chiang and Huzhou were alone in the headquarters room, sitting across from each other at one of the old desks. Huzhou ripped pieces from a chunk of hard, dark bread and sipped tea to soften the crust.

In front of Chiang was the old metal box that served as the group's bank account, and spread around it were tattered banknotes.

"Three thousand, six hundred kuai,"—the spoken form fo
yuan—"two hundred Japanese yen, and fifty-four U.S. dollars,'
she said. "It does not seem right."

Huzhou looked over the several sheets of the list resting on th
table near him. They were littered with crumbs from his bread

"We have not kept very good track this year," he said, "but i
looks as if, oh, about half of the members have not yet paid thei
dues."

"They are two months past the deadline. We will need to senc
another letter."

"And that will cost money."

"It is ever the same. The problem with representing th
poverty-stricken is that they are poverty-stricken. They save u
to join us one year, then they disappear, unable to continue th
support."

"Or could it be that they become disenchanted with us?'
Huzhou asked, abandoning his bread to focus his enlarged fire
brand's eyes upon her.

"Disenchanted? What do you mean?"

"In your heart of hearts, you know."

"Come on, Huzhou! Spit it out!"

"You wish to be the voice of the people, Qing, but your voic
wavers. You keep changing topics, and the people do not knov
for what you stand."

"You may be an adequate lover, Huzhou, but you are a terri
ble analyst!"

"I think not," he said, sitting up in his chair, thrusting his chi
forward.

This young man was full of his own defiance, but he hac
never before turned that defiance on her.

"For over a decade," he went on, "you have challenged man
on many issues, but as soon as you feel the government's resis
tance to your rhetoric, you slither away to a new subject. I thin
your followers have finally become aware that you do not com
plete what you begin."

Huzhou stood up.

"That is ridiculous!"

"Is it?"

"I take it back. You are also a terrible lover!"

"You will find yourself with no followers, and with no treasury, Qing, unless you carry one—just one!—of your issues to a conclusion."

Huzhou turned away from her and started for the door.

"Come back here!"

"I will not. Unless you decide whether you are a true revolutionary or simply making a career of the image."

He did not slam the door, but closed it softly. She heard the leather soles of his sandals slapping on the stairs as he descended.

Chiang looked down at the table, at the notes scattered about, at her hands. They trembled with her anger.

Huzhou could go to the devil.

She did not need him.

But thoughts of his hot and taut body against her own in the darkness of night intruded and caused her to waver.

Perhaps he was correct.

No. Her methods had proven successful. She was not in jail, was she?

And then again, the membership numbers were vague. She could not really tell how many supporters of the cause were still active. Judging by the cash flowing in, not many. There were, of course, bank accounts of which Huzhou was unaware. Chiang was wise enough to not confide all of her secrets in everyone.

Perhaps it was time to embrace the freedom-of-information issue—which she had previously mentioned only in offhand ways—and carry it all the way.

She would show him!

Chiang Qing was not smoke and mirrors! She was the embodiment of the people, and she loved them.

She counted the money again.

One of Dusty McKelvey's pilots, named James Bowie, but called "Jimbo," was in the left-hand seat of the Cessna Citation, and Mickey Stone sat in the right seat. He wasn't licensed to fly, but Jimbo let him take the controls at 20,000 feet. Stone loved getting his hands on hot hardware, electronic or aeronautical. A few times, he'd thought of pursuing a private pilot's license, but he was always short of time.

"Where we at, Jimbo?"

"Couple hundred miles out of Lhasa. Won't be long now."

"I'm in no hurry."

"See the water down there? That's Nam Lake. I always want to shoot the hell out of it when I fly over it."

Bowie had been a buddy of McKelvey's in Vietnam. Stone didn't think that either of them had pleasant memories of the era.

Lhasa was the capital of Xizang Zizhiqu, or in the old world—pre-1979—Tibet Autonomous Region; if anything, it was in worse shape than Urümqi. The city's population was somewhere around 600,000, and in his previous visits, Stone had failed to identify and secure a date with even one attractive young lady. He was going to have to revise his personal definition of "exotic" before he signed another contract.

Even if he found a suitable companion, however, he wasn't sure anything would come of it. At 12,000 feet of altitude, Lhasa inhibited the urge to run, climb stairs, or perform any other exertion. Many of the MI technicians still experienced altitude sickness when they were in residence for any length of time.

Lhasa was 1,800 miles from Shanghai—read "civilization"—but only 300 miles from Mount Everest. At the plane's altitude, Stone could see it in the distance on his right, rising sun-bright and hazy on the horizon. A band of clouds circled it far below the summit.

He had no desire in the world to climb it. He was probably abnormal.

"When was the last time you were here, Mickey?" Jimbo asked.

"Lhasa? About five weeks ago. Why?"

"You haven't seen the nuke, then?"

"Hell, I forgot all about it. They have it in place?"

"They did ten days ago."

"What's it look like?"

"Give me my airplane back, and we'll take a pass over it as we go in."

As soon as he felt Jimbo's hands on the yoke, Stone released it, then eased his feet off the pedals. The pilot put the plane into a slight left turn as he began to lose altitude. Nam Co, the lake, enlarged in the windscreen.

Some French outfit had come up with the solution to China's drastic shortage of electrical power in the form of portable nuclear generating plants. Stone hadn't yet seen one, but he was acutely aware of the electrical deficiency. On his arrival in Shanghai, while he was acclimating himself to the city, he had taken an organized tour of the city's industrial sector. The factory they had been shown, which produced plastic products, had been clean, organized, and extremely bright under hundreds of banks of fluorescent lights. After they left, and just before they boarded the bus, Stone ran back to snap a picture of the exterior.

All of the lights had been dimmed after the guests departed, and he suspected that that was their normal environment. Tourists saw only the optimistic view.

In his own work, Stone was faced with power problems—fluctuations in amperage and voltage, outright brownouts. None of those conditions were acceptable to the sensitive power requirements of computers and communications equipment. The Chinese engineers had built new substations to feed the Shanghai Star facilities, but the power sources had had to be augmented with banks of diesel generators to ensure a continuous supply of clean, filtered electrical power. It was inadequate, and supposedly, temporary. It also was less than reliable. They suffered power problems at least twice a month at each of the provincial installations.

The French nuclear generating plants were intended to supplement the existing electrical grids, providing not only the Shanghai Star facilities, but the thousands of envisioned energy consumers with the basic ingredient for the information highway.

The huge lake passed under the Citation, and Jimbo began a slow turn to the right, lining up to approach Lhasa from the northeast. Actually, he was approaching Gonggar Airport, which was a ninety-minute taxi ride out of the city.

They were flying over high country, with most of the rolling, rocky, and mountainous terrain over a mile above sea level. Deep gorges, massive rock outcroppings, and pristine forests created a wild and beautiful land. Peaks stretched their snowy heads to 25,000 feet of height. If it weren't for the lack of diverse feminine companionship, Stone could imagine making a home in such a setting.

"Two thousand feet AGL," Jimbo said. "We should get a good view."

"Where?"

"It'll come up on your right."

Stone saw the heavy equipment first. The bright yellow specks of bulldozers, trucks, and a couple tall cranes stood out against the mottled salt-and-pepper face of a cliff. The earth in front of the cliff had been levelled, and whitish-gray concrete structures, nearly matching the color of the rock, had been erected.

As they closed in, Stone surveyed the buildings and decided that it wasn't at all what he had expected. There was one long and rectangular concrete building, with no roof. He judged it to be fifty feet long by thirty wide. Another silolike structure stood close by it, and a third and smaller building was located at a right angle to the largest. The small building was likely the control center.

"It doesn't look very damned portable, does it?" he asked Jimbo.

"Not with all that concrete."

"Can we go around again?"

"Sure." Jimbo started a 360-degree turn to the left. To the right meant risking impact with the mountain.

While they circled back, Stone looked over the access to the site. A narrow, two-lane gravel road had been cut into the rock and earth, following the contour of the mountain as it climbed five or six hundred feet upward and several miles from the main road traversing the bottom of the valley. The reactor was definitely isolated from the normal pathways of man, and it was also enclosed by an eight-foot-high chain link fence. There was a guard shack of some kind near the gate where the road entered the compound. The forest had been cut down inside the enclosure and within ten or fifteen feet of the fence on the outside. A trail was being cut through the forest toward Lhasa, and work crews were erecting steel towers to carry the power lines.

Jimbo throttled back as they came around and made their pass slower this time, but still over two hundred miles per hour. Stone saw that the cables from both of the cranes were being attached to a massive slab of concrete, about three feet thick.

"Ah!"

"You figure it out?" Jimbo asked.

"They're about to lift the roof into place. The concrete isn't portable, but the reactor components are."

"You know about this stuff?"

"Not much. I worked on a computer glitch once at the Fort St. Vrain generating plant in Colorado. They had so much trouble with that plant that they eventually shut it down before it ever delivered commercial electricity. The one down there is based on a Russian design."

"Russian?"

"Yeah. For decades, the Russians have been putting small nuclear plants in orbit, to power their scientific experiments. They were designated the Topaz, and they generated anywhere from five to maybe ten megawatts. Pretty simple devices since they didn't worry about radiation shielding.

"The French company, which I think is called Nuclear Power Limited, has enlarged on that design. Supposed to get two hundred megawatts out of each unit."

"Is that a bunch?" Jimbo asked.

"If I remember right, the U.S.'s biggest reactor, Sequoyah, puts out around twelve hundred megawatts. For the size difference, I guess these are pretty efficient, Jimbo. I don't know the cost, but I heard about four hundred million per unit."

The Citation whisked over the plant, and Stone looked down to see a blue steel container entrapped within the largest concrete building.

"That's what they've done. The cranes have dropped some part of the plant inside the concrete walls, and now they're going to put the roof on."

He twisted in his seat to look back.

"The silo's got to be a containment vessel, in case of a leak. Probably where the reactor's located."

"They wouldn't have transported that thing live, would they?"

"I shouldn't think so. The fuel rods will be along any day now."

Bowie got on the radio to Gonggar, requesting approach approval.

Stone tightened his straps and hoped he wasn't going to find as many problems at Lhasa as he had found at Urümqi. Wickersham had stayed behind because of all the bugs in the software.

Maybe when they brought the nuclear plant on-line, it would help. In many cases, Stone could trace equipment faults to the power supply. The substations the Chinese engineers had constructed weren't infallible, but no one was going to tell them that.

He was hoping to be out of Lhasa within two days and on his way back to Shanghai, where he could catch up on his social program.

If MI was still a company by then. When he had talked to Grant yesterday, there was still no word from the government's high-powered team investigating the Long March 3 fiasco.

Vladimir Suretsov was in Beijing, tracking the tendrils of a story that might involve the Russian consulate. The tip had come through Yuri Fedorchuk in Moscow, and while it seemed tenuous to him, he still found himself sitting in a teahouse two blocks from the Russian consulate working on his second pot of jasmine tea and ignoring the menu the waitress had hopefully placed near his elbow.

Though many of the stories he was forced to write were tedious in the extreme, Suretsov considered himself a fortunate man. He had been, as the Americans said, a "cub" reporter when the upheaval of the Soviet Union produced a new and better news agency. Suretsov had first aspired to the journalistic trade after reading Superman comic books and identifying himself with, first, Superman, then Clark Kent. He had come to believe that the Kent persona had more power than that of the superhero, and that power was in the form of truth. It was an ideal that had been shattered soon after he took his first real job.

Truth, he had learned in the old agency was what one wanted to make of it. He had seen stories abandoned, or at best, watered by omission, in order to present Soviet leaders in their most favorable aspects. In the agency's secure morgue, there had been files and files of interviews and eyewitness accounts of atrocities committed by Stalin, Khrushchev, or Andropov, but they would sooner see the light of a match than the light of day.

As far as he knew, those files no longer existed, having been eliminated before the new directors took over the agency after the Union divided itself into republics. Despite the destruction of historical evidence, the revolution and the new directors were a godsend to Suretsov. There was a new emphasis on accuracy and objectivity. While the editors still maintained a rather strict control over their correspondents—especially their budgets, little was done to subvert the reportage as long as it was founded on solid evidence.

Suretsov had been posted to both London and Paris before his assignment to Shanghai. He did not make very much money, but the chance to see the world and to pursue his calling with little interference were compensation in themselves. If it were politic, he would have described himself as an investigative reporter—that was his personal vision. He loved delving into the morass of data behind a story or a subject and separating the fact from the fiction.

This day's work, he felt certain, would result in a tall tale. The value of his round-trip airline ticket from Shanghai was to be wasted.

The light in the teahouse was subdued, provided by the sunlight filtering through the intricate lace curtains pulled across the windows. When the man opened the wood-framed glass door, Suretsov knew him immediately for his contact.

Fair-haired and fat-faced, he was dressed in a suit of pinstriped beige, and while most likely a Russian, what gave him away were the furtive glances he shot back over his shoulder. He was a haunted man, or a hunted one.

Spotting Suretsov, he made his way across the dining room, easily avoiding the few diners. He stopped in front of the table.

In Russian, he asked, "You are . . . ?"

"From ITAR-Tass. Suretsov." He did not bother getting up.

"And you know me as . . . ?"

"Pyotr."

The man sat down opposite him, and the waitress appeared at his side. When Suretsov only ordered another pot of the tea and a second cup, her smile hardened.

Pyotr was the contact name because the man wished to remain anonymous, but Suretsov had been through his personal file of the consulate's assigned personnel. He considered it part of his job to know with whom he might have to deal, and his mind now raced through the pictures he had reviewed, then stopped. Makov. Arkady Petrovich Makov. He was a minor functionary, an assistant to the trade attaché.

They sat silently until the fresh tea was delivered, then Suretsov poured two of the small cups full and said, "Pyotr, you have evidence of an official's malfeasance. That is what I have been told."

More likely, Makov had suffered some slight and was eager to get back at his superior in some way. As Suretsov now recalled the short dossier, Makov had been in the same job, or the same kind of job, for over twenty years. He probably considered himself a prime candidate for promotion.

"That is correct."

"Who is the official?"

Makov twisted his head to look at the windows, found no watchers, and looked back to Suretsov. "Valeri Sytenko."

"He is the trade attaché."

And your superior, as I imagined.

"That is true."

"And what has Sytenko done?"

"I don't know."

What!

"You don't know?"

"What I do know is that he has accepted a large amount of money from a foreigner."

"How large?"

"That I do not know, either. It was in a suitcase."

"He received this from a Chinese man?"

"No. It was a Caucasian. I do not know the nationality."

"And what is your evidence?"

"My eyes. I witnessed this transaction personally."

Suretsov sighed.

"It took place in the People's Park during my lunch break. I was there by myself when Sytenko arrived. He did not see me, but he waited on a park bench until the other man arrived. They talked for a few minutes, and the other man left, leaving the suitcase behind."

"And you know this suitcase contained money?"

"He opened it and took a quick look inside. It was full of currency. American bills."

"Perhaps he took this case back to the consulate?"

"No. He took it to the American bank, Citicorp, and put it in a safe deposit box."

"You followed him?"

"I did." Makov fidgeted, and said, "I must go. I should not be seen with you."

"A minute more. I need more substantial evidence."

"Go to the bank. Ask them."

"I predict that that would be unproductive, Pyotr. You must find something more for me."

"I cannot! He will think that I am spying on him!"

As you are.

Suretsov jotted notes quickly in his notebook, then suggested, "We could offer you compensation for your services."

The man was truly offended. His eyes widened, and his mouth turned down. "Never!"

"That is a test, Pyotr," Suretsov appeased. "I still need your help if we are to uncover this unknown activity. Even if the bank should reveal that Sytenko rents a safe-deposit box there, and even if we could open it to find large amounts of currency, we would be at a loss to prove *why* Sytenko received it."

Makov's jowls sagged as he considered the implications. Finally, he said, "I will try, but I promise nothing."

"That is all I ask." Suretsov gave him a card with his Shanghai telephone number on it. "Call me if you discover anything."

"We cannot meet again."

"I agree. We will use the telephone."

Makov nearly bolted from the table. He managed to slow down by the time he reached the door.

Suretsov sipped from his cup.

Unfortunately, he believed the man.

Jiang Guofeng had been born in Ba Xian in Hebei Province and had spent most of his life within seventy kilometers of the capital city of Beijing. He had never yearned to visit distant lands, and the diverse cultures of the world did not capture his imagination, even in the enforced journeys requisite to his positions over the course of thirty years in the government.

Though he had been to Moscow three times and London twice and to other capitals at least once, those cities had failed to hold his interest. If anything, they demonstrated how far astray ungoverned cultures could roam. In London and New York, the widespread graffiti on buildings particularly offended him, and the criminal activity in every city was appalling. He remembered particularly his fear of leaving his Washington, D.C., hotel at night. People were killed for a few grams of white powder or, far worse, for no reason at all.

His travels, for which he had small gold trinkets meant for a souvenir bracelet, had only reinforced his reservations about the course the Republic was taking. Jiang's fingers toyed with an Eiffel Tower and an Empire State Building as he stared through his office window at a stack of swirling cumulus clouds. They were white against the blue sky, and the winds aloft kept them in continual movement, much as his mind continued to swirl with his worries of the future of his country.

There was no doubt in Jiang's mind nor, he thought, in the minds of others about his patriotism. For longer than he could remember, his nation had come first for him; its welfare preempted that of his own success or of his concern for his wife of twenty-seven years and his two grown sons.

He did not think that his nationalism blinded him. Jiang was realist enough to know that change, desirable or not, was inevitable. China could not maintain her barriers against the onslaught of technology. Already, clandestine broadcasts made their ways insidiously inside the borders and corrupted the people. He deplored the fact that centuries of magnificent culture were to be eroded, but given that it was unstoppable, his practical side said that the changes to come, if they were properly managed, could be less disruptive than they might otherwise be.

Jiang did not want his Beijing turned into another New York City, her palaces smeared with gang graffiti. Why worry about banning assault rifles from the hands of the citizen if they were never in those hands to begin with? Why be continually offended by wanton Madonnas flaunting their anatomical parts from films, television, posters? He was fond of telling his friends that there was much to be said for an open society, but the words were generally derogatory.

Yet, if outright rebellion by the populace were to be avoided, some degree of movement toward the open society was required. The leadership was becoming increasingly wary of world condemnation—and economic and political sanctions—that followed in the wake of a visible suppression of revolt.

It was for that reason that he had originally sided with the supporters of the Shanghai Star project. Notwithstanding the fact that the original support came from the five-member Politburo and his opposition would not have been politic. He saw in that controlled communications system a methodology for tempering the alterations to Chinese tradition.

And simply because the liberal Deng Mai and her American cohort had gained positions of influence, he was not about to let Shanghai Star stray too far from the vision he had set for it.

A tapping at his office door brought him from his reverie.

"Enter!"

The broad teak door pushed open and his chief assistant, Wen Yito, entered. Wen was a man of many facets and one of multiple talents. Taut-muscled and small of stature, he still gave the impression of potential danger, like a coiled snake. Had Jiang not taken him under his wing a decade before, Wen could easily have taken a wrong turn and evolved into an enemy of the state.

Jiang had schooled him, and Wen could, in one of his facets, demonstrate the polish of a diplomat.

Wen waved a sheaf of papers. "The report has arrived, Minister."

"And the results?"

"It is not as we might have hoped."

Jiang's heart sank. "It could not have been a terrorist act!"

"According to the independent investigators from the aviation bureau, it was indeed, Minister."

"Ah . . ."

Jiang had viewed the disaster at Xichang as a reprieve, a fortuitous event that would forestall the implementation of Shanghai Star and give him more time in which to orchestrate the change. He had counted on Megatronics coming to him, palms out, beseeching him for mercy. And he had all but rehearsed his speech of denial.

With the failure of Grant's company, the Shanghai Star project might have been delayed by a year, even eighteen months, the postponement reflecting on Deng Mai's administrative prowess and promoting her severance from the project. Megatronics Incorporated's near-to-the-brink financial condition was one of the reasons Jiang had urged his colleagues on the Information Advisory Committee to name them as prime contractor. He had, at that time, foreseen the numerous obstacles that Grant would be unable to overcome, significantly delaying the program.

And Grant had surprised and astounded him, deftly circumventing the barriers as they arose.

Wen laid the report on his desk and stood back at semiattention.

"Tell me."

"It was a small explosive device, very likely attached to the main oxygen tank in the first stage. When the first stage exploded, the fuels in all other stages detonated sympathetically. The consensus seems to be that it was detonated by an electronic remote-control device."

"And the perpetrators?"

Wen shrugged. "This report does not examine that aspect, Minister. At this time, no person or group is claiming responsibility."

"No one is investigating?"

"I telephoned General Hua's headquarters, but received little satisfaction. It appears to me that the national police and the military investigators are haggling over the jurisdiction."

"No doubt, neither wants the jurisdiction," Jiang said. "Very well. It is our loss. We will have to arrange a negotiation meeting with Director Deng and Mr. Grant and arrive at some settlement."

"I believe that is the only course open to us, Minister."

"Make the arrangements. And while you are at it, you may release the July payment to Megatronics."

"Uh, that has already been done, Minister Jiang."

"What! How was it done?"

"I believe Director Deng talked to someone in the finance office."

Damn her! She was forever interfering in his affairs.

He declined to reveal his feelings to Wen, however. His antipathy toward Deng Mai was already apparent to many, and an escalation was not in his political interest.

He must step carefully because she still had many supporters, but he was confident of his ability to eventually force her early retirement.

Not only from Shanghai Star, but from any place in the government.

Will Bricher was waiting in Diantha Parker's jungle when the courier arrived with the manila envelope. An elephant-eared monstrosity which Bricher thought might have flesh-eating tendencies kept brushing against his cheek, and he kept shoving the leaf away.

Parker signed for the envelope, and the young man left. He had a second envelope, and Bricher figured he was bound for the next floor up with that one.

"Who's it from?" he asked.

"It's not addressed to you."

"I didn't care who it was to, Diantha."

She eyed the envelope. "Ministry of Aeronautics and Astronautics."

"Open it!"

"Hold on."

He climbed out of the low-lying couch and leaned on the front edge of her desk while she whisked a letter-opener under the flap, then pulled the set of papers free.

Reading upside down, he saw the word "FINDINGS" halfway down the front page, and he went around the desk to read over her shoulder.

Parker was as interested as he was.

They got to the gist of it about the same time.

Parker sighed.

Bricher said, "Hot damn! Give me that."

Reluctantly, she gave up the report, and Bricher headed for the door to Grant's office. He knocked once, waited two seconds, and pulled it open.

Grant and Deng were seated side by side on the couch at the side of the room, sitting on the front edge of it, leaning over the coffee table. An array of paper was spread all over the table.

They both looked up at him.

"Sorry to barge in, Doug. It's worth the interruption, though."

He walked over, handed Grant the report, and then sat in the closest chair. It wasn't all that comfortable; Grant never wasted money on his own office furnishings, here or stateside.

Grant held the papers so that he and Deng could read at the same time, found the pertinent recommendation from the investigators, then grinned. "No more than we expected, Will."

"No more than we hoped," Bricher said, then quickly glanced at Deng, fearing he had spoken out of turn.

She was severely dressed today in a gray business suit, her hair drawn back into a tight cap of curls against her skull. Whenever he saw her, no matter what image she was projecting, Bricher always felt guilty; he couldn't help comparing her to Shana. Or Shana to her.

His wife was a comfortable Kentuckian, open and bright-eyed, and in great shape for having produced and raised two rambunctious boys. Sometimes, though, the exotic aura that surrounded Deng Mai generated fantasies.

When she finished reading, Deng looked up at him and smiled.

Bricher knew right then that something had changed. The formal distinction between contractor and contractee had somehow blurred. He felt that Deng was less a boss and more of a partner.

She tapped the report with the long fingernail of her right forefinger. "This helps to keep us on track."

"It does that," Grant agreed. "What's with GE, Will?"

He wouldn't normally have discussed internal business concerns in front of Deng, but there was that subtle change in the relationship. He studied Grant's eyes.

And Grant winked at him.

Flustered, Bricher said, "I've talked to Crichton a dozen times in the last couple days, but we're getting some movement now. ShangStar Three is now ShangStar Two. He's put more people on it, and he says he'll ship it out on the twenty-second. We'll get it on the twenty-third."

"Good," Grant said. "Great!"

"On the discount, I don't think we'll get the full nine mil, but we'll get something. That issue is going to their board on Friday, and Crichton will call me after the meeting."

"When can we get it launched?"

"I'm meeting Hua on Thursday and we'll figure that out."

"All right. We're going to pull this off yet, Will." He turned to look at Deng. "Feel better, Mai?"

"I am not certain. The investigators report that the incident was truly sabotage. That raises more questions than it answers."

The same question mark was nagging Bricher, loitering around in his mind.

"I agree, Director. The question is 'why?' "

"Precisely. Who is it that objects to Shanghai Star achieving its promise?"

"Ah, hell," Grant said. "That puts us directly into a political situation. I've been trying to avoid that."

"I know you have, Douglas. However, from the beginning it was always there, even if you did not want to recognize it. Now, you must."

"We're here to help you build for the future, Mai, not engage in any wars."

She just looked at him.

Grant turned to Bricher. "Did we, Will?"

"I think we've got one anyway, Doug."

Thursday, August 11

Madame Yvonne Deng sat on the lounge seat in the bedroom and sipped her morning tea as Deng dressed for the day. It was a frequent morning ritual and one where they generally shared their innermost secrets.

Her mother was fully dressed; she was *always* up by five o'clock in the morning, bright-eyed, eager, and prepared to boss the houseboy and the cook. At sixty-one—she had been twelve years younger than Mai's father—she was as energetic as she had been thirty years before. With her inheritance of several million francs managed by Paris banks, she was not a drain on the state, and she maintained the big, old, fourteen-room house, made the rounds with her circle of social friends, and frequently travelled abroad.

She had not accepted the appearance of gray in her hair gracefully, and the houseboy, who doubled as coiffeur, spent a half hour each day seeking out and touching up each strand of gray. Her hair was as dark and carefully styled as ever. Each year, her stature seemed smaller to Mai, but that may have been relative to their increasing ages. Her skin was still as delicate as porcelain, and though she devoted a considerable amount of time to it, tiny wrinkles had appeared near her eyes and the corners of her mouth. It had always seemed to Deng that her mother's consideration for appearance was inconsistent with the revolutionary zeal she must have displayed when she first met her father. Madame Yvonne saw no inconsistency whatsoever.

They spoke French in their morning tête-à-tête in order to nurture her native language. It wasn't spoken often in most of Shanghai.

Deng sat at her dressing table in bra and half-slip, working the brush through her hair for the required fifty strokes. "Mama, you need a rest. Why don't you fly to Kuala Lumpur for a few days?"

The houseboy and the cook needed a rest.

"That is nonsense! I am not leaving you to face the coming trial by yourself."

"Trial! I would hardly characterize it as a trial."

"I am not without my sources, Mai. There are those who would have you fail, and we must do what we can to see that they are frustrated."

"Please, Mama. Don't get yourself involved."

"I am always involved with you," her mother said, refilling her Lemoge cup from the silver pot on the table.

"The contract is safe. The schedule is intact. The committee can find nothing about which to complain."

"And still, they will. You may count on it. If nothing else, they will say you antagonized some group to the point where they have resorted to bombs. And cost the Republic millions. You are seen far too well as a liberal and a reformist, my dear. Next, they will tag you as counterrevolutionary."

In the PRC, since the government was one of revolution, dissidents were seen as counterrevolutionaries.

In fact, Deng Mai *was* worried about that aspect. Yet, she could not come up with a single name of anyone she might have offended. She had been extremely careful in that regard. Her innermost feeling, which she revealed to no one, not even Yvonne, was that China could be propelled into the current and future centuries only be a free flow of ideas from the West, decadent or not. Pragmatically, she knew that was impossible. Her immediate goal was to complete Shanghai Star so that the means of achieving the final goal was in place. In the meantime, she had to maintain the fine balance between the conservatives and the reformists on the information committee. Any shudders in the foundation could split them into warring factions. And Shao Tsung, the Minister of National Defense, who was also on the committee and represented yet another faction—the military—might be forced to align with one group, or the other. Either way would spell disaster for Shanghai Star. And for Deng Mai.

Placing the brush on the table, she stood up and walked across the room to the walk-in closet to select a midcalf-length skirt and matching jacket in yellow-gold. Slipping a lace-overlaid blouse from its hanger, she carried all back into the bedroom and laid them on the bed. She pulled the blouse on, went to her mother, and stood quietly as the elder woman got up to button the back.

"I have faced the committee down often, Mama. You must not worry."

"It is my life's chore to worry about you. For instance, I was married at seventeen."

This subject came up regularly. Deng did not reply.

"You are thirty-six," Madame Deng accused.

"I am a career woman."

"Ridiculous! You may have both."

"Not in Shanghai."

"Yes, in Shanghai. You have not forgotten my dinner tomorrow night?"

"How could I? You have mentioned it once a day for five days."

"Shankuan Takai will be there."

"You have mentioned him several times also, Mama."

"He is a handsome man, the son of . . ."

"I know who he is, Mama."

"Politically, it would be a fine union."

"What is this, the twelfth fine political union you have attempted to arrange?"

"Mai, I have your best interests at heart."

"I know that, Mama." Abruptly, and on impulse, Deng said, "I would like to bring a guest to your dinner."

Yvonne Deng finished buttoning the blouse and turned Deng around by the shoulders. "A guest?"

"Mr. Grant."

The eyes went wide. "The rumors are true!"

"The rumors are rumors. Mr. Grant and I have a very professional relationship."

"And you want to bring him to your home?"

"It is done in all the better circles," Deng said, letting the sarcasm drip. "Why should you not meet him?"

Madame Yvonne smiled, though it was a trifle grim. "I do not remember ever having a noncommunist in this house."

They were both Party members. Careers were not available to nonmembers.

Deng laughed. "Can you recall the last time you attended a Party meeting? Your interpretation of the manifesto is so liberal it must hurt your conscience."

"Me, a liberal! Mai, you are the threat to the old men on the committees. Do not call me a liberal!"

Deng walked back to the bed and slipped the skirt over her head, let it slide, and settled it on her hips.

"Ah! You are attempting to divert the conversation. Of course, bring your Mr. Grant. I will call Mr. Shankuan and force him from my guest list."

Instant guilt.

"Mr. Shankuan and Mr. Grant can coexist, Mama."

"Not likely at the same party! A proper suitor and the foreigner you adore?"

Deng was forced to smile as she went back to the closet for shoes. "I believe you are a foreigner, Mama."

"That is different. You are avoiding the subject of adoration."

"I don't adore anyone."

"Let us hope not!"

Pierre Lefant lit another Gauloises and sat at the head of the round table in his conference room. It was actually one of the two bedrooms attached to the suite Media Bureau leased, and it was not large enough to be a suitable conference room, but one was forced to make do in hard times.

At the table with him were Marc Chabeau and three Chinese men, who represented potential future employees of Media Bureau. They had been recommended to him by Jiang Guofeng, and if the contract went the way Lefant was certain it would, they would become key members of Lefant's enterprise. One man would supervise the MBL National News Channel, coordinating the corps of national news gatherers and the feeds from local stations. The provincial capitals would eventually have their own channels for public service and local news.

Another man would head a newly created enterprise producing entertainment packages of Chinese origin. That division would reside in Beijing, and Lefant expected the productions to be heavily influenced by Chinese cultural tradition. He did not have great hopes for it, and he did not care who eventually received the post.

The last man, Sung Wu, was suggested by Jiang as the president of Media Bureau Limited-China if Media Bureau were awarded the contract. Otherwise, he would be president of the Consortium of Information Services-China. Sung would be headquartered at Shanghai Star, serving as the liaison between the communications network and the programming segment. He would also be the Chinese overseer of programming beamed from Europe.

Lefant had known from the start that all executive positions within the country were to be filled by Chinese citizens.

In the three hours they had been meeting, Lefant had yet to be impressed by any of the three. All were at least Lefant's age and probably older. Sung had to be in his seventies. All were of a conservative bent, to say the least. Sung Wu was particularly obsessed with the notion that European entertainment bordered on the pornographic and kept requesting assurances that such was not the case. He would tolerate no bare breasts or exposed buttocks in advertising, entertainment, or news.

The appointments to the three key positions were to be made jointly by the Managing Director of Shanghai Star, the Minister of Information, and the winning contractor. Lefant knew Deng Mai would turn thumbs-down on these men, leaving Lefant in a deciding-vote role. He did not relish the prospect. If he joined Jiang in selecting these men, he would antagonize Deng, and that could lead to disharmony.

When he could take no more, Lefant stubbed his cigarette out in a full-to-overflowing ashtray and stood up.

"Gentlemen, I am so happy we could have this time to get to know one another."

The Chinese men stood, beaming and smiling, and spent nearly ten minutes bidding goodbye. They left behind on the table their respective resumes, thick, Lefant was certain, with accolades bestowed as patronage rather than accomplishment.

As soon as they were into the hall and the door closed behind them, Lefant turned to Chabeau and said, "That was ghastly."

Chabeau grimaced. "None of them would allow much in the way of creativity, I think. Our producers would be stifled in the extreme."

"According to the economists," Lefant said, "China is to grow into a seventy-five-billion-dollar-per-year consumer nation by early in the next century. If these men are to censor the advertising, I doubt that we will make it."

"And yet?" Chabeau asked.

"And yet, I suppose we shall have to appoint them."

"Yes. I thought as much."

From the moment he got out of the taxi on Tuesday and entered the building on Jiefang Road, Mickey Stone had known he wasn't going to be gone in two days.

The place was chaotic. A number of Chinese techs, who were supposed to be learning their jobs from the American experts during the installation, had walked out in a dispute with their American counterparts. They felt they weren't receiving enough respect from the Americans.

The MI technicians, who felt they could get more work done without the Chinese in the way, were going hell-bent for destruction, trying to accomplish everything on their own.

Instead of completing an inspection tour, then, Stone had spent Tuesday afternoon and all day Wednesday in negotiations with the Chinese workers. He still hadn't achieved closure when Curt Wickersham caught up with him on Thursday morning.

The facility manager, a Nebraskan named Kent, had already briefed Wickersham on the problem by the time the software director found Stone on the top floor.

"Nice going, Mickey."

Stone looked up from the console where he was sitting. "Go back to Urümqi."

"And let this place fall apart?"

Stone stood up. "Let's go for a long walk."

They took the elevator down and left the building, emerging into the heavy traffic of Jiefang Road. Several company cars were parked in front, but Stone ignored them and started walking along the crowded walk.

Wickersham fell in beside him.

"Is it bad, Mickey?"

"It's like crossing a creek on slippery rocks, Curt. Everyone's so damned sensitive, you never know whether you've hurt somebody's feelings until you've slipped off the rock and are knee deep in the stream."

"Yeah, I know."

"I'm about ready to say, 'Screw the Chinese,' and go out and recruit Tibetans."

In 1950, when the People's Liberation Army had taken over Tibet, and much of the world viewed it as an invasion, the Chinese insisted they were merely freeing the citizens from a feudal society. And indeed, they probably were. From the first Dalai Lama, confirmed in power by the Mongols in the late 14th century, all had treated their subjects in pretty much the same way. The land belonged to the Dalai Lama; and landholders, if they were paying their taxes, could pass the land on to their eldest sons. Younger sons were out in the cold; they went to work as tenants or headed for the monasteries. The class of laborers, for example, was not allowed to marry—which did not prevent them from spawning families. Today, most of the Tibetans still farmed barley and raised vegetables—turnips!—or spent a nomadic life herding sheep and goats. As in Urümqi, Han Chinese immigrants had been introduced into the region by the government right after the Liberation Army came to town, and they constituted the class of merchants and bureaucracy.

The Chinese claimed the Tibetans were, at least, a free people now; the lands being redistributed to peasants and herdsmen who had been serfs as recently as 1965.

"Recruit the Dalai Lama," Wickersham said. "Time he came back from India."

In exile since 1959, the Dalai Lama was frequently in the public eye as his followers attempted to gain independence for Tibet. Demonstrators and monks were killed in protests as late as 1988. And the number of lamas had decreased from 110,000 in 1960 to currently 1,000. The 2,500 monasteries had become 10, principally eradicated during the Cultural Revolution of 1966 to 1976. The current Chinese administration was paying greater attention to, or at least making allowances for, the spiritual needs of the people, and a few of the religious shrines and monasteries of Lamaist Buddhism were being restored.

"Maybe I will," Stone said.

"Seriously, Mickey, we don't have a hell of a lot of choice. We use the people they send to us."

"I know that, but shit!"

Stone stepped around an old man squatting at the curb and continued his pacing along the street.

"So, who did what?" Wickersham asked.

"One of our guys—Nelson—told one of the Chinese techs he was too dense to understand the concept of . . . hell, I don't even know what they were working on."

"Not good."

"No. The Chinese thinks he has enough wisdom to go around. But then, another Chinese steps in to argue his buddy's case, and Nelson called *him* a son of a bitch. The buddy took it literally."

"Nelson missed our orientation sessions?"

"You'd think so, Curt. I'm having him go through another session, then shipping him off to Chengdu. He's lost any effectiveness here."

"Jesus," Wickersham said, "that's a basic faux pas. You just don't denigrate anyone's family. I talked to a man last month who hauled his father's body on a cart over four hundred miles, just so he could bury him in his native village."

The reverence for parents, ancestors, and practically anyone in the nuclear or extended family was so ingrained in the Chinese psyche, it automatically cut off a lot of programming possibilities. There wouldn't be many reruns of *All in the Family.* It didn't matter whether Archie Bunker was right or wrong; most Chinese would find themselves on Archie's side since sons should not speak to fathers, or fathers-in-law, the way Meathead did. Any dramatic offering that involved a split between offspring, and either or both parents, wouldn't play in Lhasa or Guangzhou.

Stone and Wickersham kept walking, veering off onto a side street. Most of those they met smiled at them, and Stone gave them smiles in return. He wanted to be a decent visitor, though Lhasa didn't offer much beyond its near continual sunshine to a guest. It was about seventy-five degrees, he figured, and comfortable. The skies were cloudless, but it would probably rain again tonight. The almost nightly rains were sent by God, helping to restore oxygen to the two-mile-high city.

Abruptly, Stone flagged down a cab.

They climbed in, and Stone told the driver, with a variety of hand language and emphasized English, that he wanted to go to the Jokhang Temple.

"We're supposed to be working, aren't we?" Wickersham asked.

"We'll work after lunch. I need a couple hours. Have you been to the temple?"

"No."

"Good. I'll be your guide."

The driver took them through the Old Quarter to get to the temple. The streets of the ancient section of the city formed an octagonal pattern as a result of the temple's architecture, and the houses were built of stone, with elaborately painted doors and windows. The market area offered silver in the shapes of bowls and daggers, woven rugs, and woolen goods in fashion designs that wouldn't impress New Yorkers. Stone liked the old section; the more modern areas seemed to be composed of rectangular boxes slammed into each other.

They got out at the temple, but didn't go in. A rope stretched across the entrance suggested the public wasn't invited today. Probably spring-cleaning time, Stone thought. They sat on a stone bench near the entrance.

Wickersham leaned back and scanned the huge structure.

"Well, it's interesting," he said.

"Thirteen hundred years old. The reason it looks . . . weird is because, along the way, they mixed in Tibetan, Nepalese, Indian, and Chinese architecture. It's supposed to be one of the holiest shrines in the country."

Near them, several pilgrims had prostrated themselves on the courtyard in front of the entrance.

"Above the entrance, there? That's a prayer wheel supported by two goats. They're covered in gold."

"Goats?"

"Don't ask me," Stone said. "Inside, there's a gold throne for Buddha, sitting between two pillars of solid silver. There's another couple hundred statues inside."

"Too bad we can't go in."

"You can come back on your day off, Curt. Bring a flashlight, or you can't see it all."

"No electricity?"

"Very little. Of course, they didn't have much when they started building thirteen centuries ago."

Wickersham turned sideways on the bench and looked at him. "Why the hell are we here?"

Stone grinned. "Sometimes, I like to get off where it's quiet. Peaceful, and maybe a little holy. Helps me think."

"And what are you thinking about?"

"Well, number one, I'd like to get the Chinese techs back on the job."

"Without, I suppose, going to their bosses to have them ordered back."

"Preferably."

"They just want respect?"

"That's what I've been told."

"How many are we talking about? It's your department, after all. My software people aren't acting up."

"Eleven. They're essentially journeymen technicians, supposed to be advancing their knowledge by watching the hotshot consultants at work."

Wickersham looked up at the sky and thought for a while.

Then he asked, "These guys don't have their own offices? Or cubicles?"

"Eventually, they'll take over the desks our guys are using."

"There you go."

"I do?" Stone took a few minutes to digest what Wickersham was suggesting, then said, "We cut some plastic nameplates for them to tack up outside the rabbit warren. We put them behind the desks, and I have my guys use the visitor's chairs."

"Give them nameplates for their desks, too. Let's make them feel like it's their bailiwick and we're only here to help them out with the sticky problems. Hell, Mickey, I'll do the same thing with the software people. We can do it at every facility."

"That just might work."

"Sure it will," Wickersham said, looking at his watch. "You ready to go back to work?"

Stone stood up. "Come on, I'll show you the Dalai Lama's joint."

"What?"

"The *Potala* Palace. It's on top of a sacred mountain called Putuo Hill. Damned place has a thousand rooms and over two hundred thousand statues."

"Potala?"

"It means Buddha's Mountain. It was built in the seventh century, but got hit by lightning and a war, so its been rebuilt a couple times."

Stone waved at a taxi, and the eager driver nearly downed two bicyclists getting to the curb.

"Since when did you get so hot on ancient culture, Mickey?"

Stone pulled open the rear door of the old Renault and clambered in. "Since I started thinking about what I might be doing to it, injecting all this twenty-first-century crap into the country."

Wickersham settled down beside him and slammed the door shut twice before it latched.

"Feeling guilty, are you, Mickey?"

"This sucker is thirteen stories tall, Curt. Seven thousand serfs worked daily on it, and I don't think they were getting minimum wage. There're actually two palaces, the White and the Red, and . . ."

The sun was bright and hot when Will Bricher arrived at the Xichang launch complex. The driver who had picked him up at the airstrip got him through the main gate and let him out directly in front of the redbrick administration building.

In the long walk up the white sidewalk to the door from the air-conditioned car, sweat broke out on his forehead. He pulled the door open, stepped inside, then paused to wipe his face with his handkerchief.

The young woman at the curved reception desk smiled at him and said, "Good afternoon, Mr. Bricher. The general is waiting for you."

"Thank you, ma'am. Ah'll just go on up." Bricher often let his Kentucky twang seep through when speaking to secretaries and receptionists. They seemed to like it.

The Chinese woman was no exception. She smiled at him.

He crossed to the stairway and started up. The treads were faced with metal plates, but they had been worn shiny over the years. The wood in back of the protective facing was eroded from military footwear.

On the second floor, which had a replacement of beige tile that was polished to the gleam generals liked, he crossed the foyer to be greeted by a noncom.

"Go right in, Mr. Bricher."

"Thank you, Sergeant."

The door was open and General Hua Min got up from his desk as Bricher entered. They shook hands.

"Good morning, General."

"Mr. Bricher. Please have a chair."

The general was in his fifties and militarily fit. He might have to stretch to reach five nine, but every inch was perfectly starched and ramrod straight. His dark-brown hair was clipped short enough to give him the appearance of premature baldness, and his gray eyes had a penetrating hardness to them. In nearly three years, Bricher had never seen him smile.

"Any leads yet on who was behind the sabotage?" Bricher asked.

"None, sir, and that is strange in itself. A person or group able to strike such a blow also tends to brag of it."

"Well, I'm sure sorry it happened, General."

"As am I." Hua clasped his hands together. "It reflects poorly on my security section, which of course is my responsibility."

Bricher was surprised at the admission. Perhaps it indicated that the bond that had developed between them was stronger than Bricher had thought.

"One cannot be everywhere, all the time."

"But one's subordinates should be. Anyway, Mr. Bricher, we want to discuss another launch."

"That we do."

"As I mentioned on the telephone, a Long March Three is currently being emplaced at Launch Pad Six. I have checked with the engineers, and they feel it could be ready to go on September nineteenth."

That was way too late. All of the test sequences would be thrown at least six weeks behind, and the October 1 deadline for implementation would disappear. Plus, Bricher would have his own personnel sitting idle while they waited. Finished with the testing and finalizing of systems aboard ShangStar One, they had been ready for the August fourth launch and the next project. Morale could turn into a problem. His payroll could turn into a problem. Six weeks of nonproduction for the highly paid consultants MI had brought on board wasn't the best of business practices.

"The General Electric people have assured me that ShangStar Two, the new one, will be delivered to Xichang on August twenty-third," he said. "It would be desirable to launch it the next day."

Hua nodded. "I understand your need, Mr. Bricher, believe me. However . . ."

"As I flew in, I noticed a vehicle on Launch Pad Two," Bricher said.

"Ah, yes. It is dedicated to a contract with the Australians."

"When is the launch scheduled?"

"For August seventeenth."

"Perhaps an arrangement could be made to trade the dates with the Australians?"

"I do not think that will be possible, Mr. Bricher."

"Could we discuss it with them?"

Hua cleared his throat, "You do understand that such a contract involves three ministries—Commerce, Foreign Economic Relations, and Space Industry? I have already been informed by the respective ministers that the Australian launch is not to be altered."

Bricher didn't want to get in an argument, or even a discussion, about influences on the State Council, made up of the Premier, the vice premiers, the ministers, and other government officials appointed by the National People's Congress.

He couldn't resist saying, however, "Four years ago, when Shanghai Star was adopted, the State Council set the program as its first priority, General."

"That is true."

"I wonder if the ministers might be reminded of that?"

Hua ran his thumb and forefinger over his lips as his eyes held Bricher's. "I think not by me."

"But perhaps by someone you know?"

"I might say something to several members of the general staff. It could be important, too, that you or Mr. Grant speak to a few people on the State Council."

"Jiang Guofeng?"

Hua's eyelids slid down halfway over his eyes, and he studied his visitor for a long moment before saying, "I do not think so."

Bricher nodded, ready to drop that line. "May we leave it this way, General: We are scheduled for September nineteenth, for certain, with the possibility of advancing that date to August twenty-fourth if other things can be worked out?"

Nodding, Hua said, "Let us leave it that way."

"I have one more item, then, which I would like to discuss. It could be helpful, since you will be talking to the general staff, if you would mention it to them."

"And that is?"

"ShangStar One is dedicated to military purposes, with one hundred channels reserved as backup to the next two satellites."

"That is my understanding," Hua agreed.

"We had some testing scheduled, primarily for Digi-Communications Technology, which is delayed because of the failed launch. We would like to use two channels on ShangStar One on August fifteenth for testing."

"Go right ahead," Hua said with a grin. The first that Bricher had ever seen.

"There seems to be a problem. Army headquarters has told me twice that the channels are not available."

"There are those who become protective of new territory."

"Yes. Can you suggest a course of cooperation for me?"

"This test will involve military communications?" Hua asked.

"It will."

"Let me make a telephone call or two. Then I will talk to you tonight."

"I appreciate that, General."

They said their goodbyes, and Bricher made his way down the worn steps to the first floor. With another dash of Southern charm and dialect, he talked the secretary into loaning him an office and telephone. He called Grant.

"What have you got, Will?"

"Brush up your lobbying techniques, Doug."

"I don't have any. What's going on?"

Bricher reported on his meeting. "You know, I think General Hua is in our corner, and I was never sure of that before."

"That's interesting, Will."

"He's got to be in a delicate situation. We don't want to do anything to jeopardize him, Doug."

"I read you. So, you want me to hit up some people on the State Council?"

"Except for Jiang. If I'm reading the general correctly, Jiang may have influenced the decision on the Australian payload."

"Hmm. I'll talk to Mai about it."

"Do that, then get hot. I want that twenty-four August liftoff."

"So do I, Will. Without it, we're still good guys, having done our part. However, it leads to us being broke good guys."

Yuri Fedorchuk was a supervising editor at the ITAR-Tass central office in Moscow, and Suretsov thought him an open-minded man. He was especially sensitive to the role TASS had played in earlier days in subjugation to the whims of the KGB.

"Well, Vladimir Petrovich? You called me."

"I need information about Valeri Sytenko, the trade attaché in Beijing, as well as about his assistant, Arkady Makov."

"Do you think there is a story there?"

"Makov was convincing, though I am not totally convinced." Suretsov briefly related the story of the apparent payoff.

"I see. The file will hold only the sanitized version of Sytenko. I know a general, now retired, who served the KGB. Let me see what I can learn from him."

"Call me as soon as you know, Yuri."

"I think we are getting this backward, Vladimir. It is you who is supposed to do the investigating."

"Send me an airplane ticket, and I will investigate."

"I will call."

Zhou Ziyang was admitted to Director Deng's office behind the secretary.

Once he was seated across a low glass table from the director, she said, "I am sorry we have not met before, Mr. Zhou. I have read of your work, and I applaud it."

"It is simple work, Director. The people tell me what they would like, and I bring it to the attention of the bureaucrats. Usually, they will tell me no, and I will return to my home."

"How many are involved in your organization?" she asked.

"I do not publish a membership list."

"That is understandable. Still . . . ?"

Her smile invited him to trust her, and he said, "There are fifty active members and about fifteen thousand associate members."

It seemed a pittance.

"One must start somewhere."

"Idealists are difficult to come by," Zhou said, "when the ideals are undefined."

"And do you define the ideals?"

"I do my best to avoid doing so. Rather, the Committee encourages open communications so that each individual might develop his or her own goal."

Zhou found himself wondering if he had ever before used the phrase "his or her." It seemed to him that he thought in terms of a masculine collective, but this beautiful woman had him choosing his words carefully.

They spent a few minutes discussing his committee and the goals of Shanghai Star, then Deng asked him, "Beyond becoming acquainted with one another, did you have a particular purpose for this meeting, Mr. Zhou?"

"I did, Director. About a year ago, the Right to Know Committee submitted to the Minister of Information a proposed policy relative to the distribution of information." Zhou related all of the bureaucratic pitfalls he had encountered—the referrals, the delays, the subterfuges.

"Today, it is once again delayed. I have just spoken to Minister Jiang."

She smiled. "I know the bureaucracy."

"I am here to ask for your help."

"I do not know that my assistance could benefit you," she said. "I work for the minister, after all."

Zhou removed a copy of the policy from his leather portfolio and placed it on the table. "If you would be gracious enough to read what is proposed, I would be most appreciative. Then, you might decide your position."

"I will read it," she promised.

Jiang had said the same thing, but Zhou thought that Deng Mai sounded more convincing.

Tan Long ordered the *tournedos* for two in imperfect French, and as the waiter bowed and slipped away, sipped lightly from his glass of wine. It was a French import, and while he knew little of wines, he thought it must be superb. Judging by the price, it had to be.

His dinner companion, whom he knew only as Qingling, attempted to take in the elegant dining room of the Red House Western Food Restaurant, along with its patrons, without appearing to stare. He understood that she was somewhat in awe of her surroundings. He doubted that she had ever seen so much crystal and silver all in one place. Certainly, she had never partaken of a meal priced at a level that would feed her family for days.

She was a pretty girl, especially in the formfitting black cocktail sheath he had purchased for her less than an hour before.

"Are you enjoying yourself?" he asked.

"Very much, Mr. Tan."

"Please, let us not be so formal."

Tan intended to become very informal with her, as soon as this dinner was completed and they were back at his apartment.

His social life was frequently conducted in this manner, and it suited him perfectly. Tan knew he was no prize. Seven centimeters taller than the average, he was extremely tall for a Chinese, and while that might have drawn attention to him, his face tended to put others off. His unusual leanness carried into the sunken cheeks which were also pitted with acne scars. Above his right cheekbone was a one-inch purplish scar he had incurred when the bus he was riding six years before had slammed into a taxicab; his head had gone through the window and his face had been lacerated in several places by broken glass. In the United States, as he understood it, he might have sued someone; in

China, he was not even entitled to plastic surgery. He seemed to have no control whatsoever over the lanky black hair which spilled to either side of the crown of his head. With the taut draw of his skin over his cheekbones and forehead, his dark eyes appeared to protrude on either side of the short, broad spout of his nose. His ears splayed outward.

The women he met were apt to ignore his physical shortcomings when they saw the thick roll of bills he carried. He had discovered that an expensive gift, such as the dress, and an evening of fine wine and foreign foods, made him more attractive.

"Are you celebrating something of importance?" she asked.

"Why, yes, I suppose I am. I completed an important contract today."

The deal with Sony would net him a 10,000 yuan bonus at minimum, he estimated. And he had scheduled meetings with IBM and Hewlett-Packard, both of whom dearly wished for deep penetrations into the Chinese market. It was going to be a wonderful year.

"What kind of contract?" Qingling wanted to know.

"Ah, but I am not supposed to discuss it, I'm afraid."

Letting them know there was a hidden side to his life made him more mysterious, he thought.

Tan enjoyed being the mysterious man in a lot of lives.

Grant and Diantha Mae Parker were in his office with large pieces of poster board and several reference books laid out on the coffee table.

"This is ridiculous," she said. "I could whip this up on a spreadsheet and dump it to the printer, then enlarge it for you if your eyes are that bad."

"But I wouldn't have that hands-on feeling, Diantha."

She looked up at him. "Was that a come-on?"

"Damn it! A man can't say anything anymore without finding himself in trouble with some letter-of-the-law feminist."

"It's the spirit that counts!"

"Hell, in China, you can't even find an appropriate law. I just thought of that."

"Uh-oh!"

He grinned at her. "I'm a free man! I don't have to put up with you."

"I may just go back Stateside. You can make your own posters."

"Not that I'd impose my freedom on your sensitive nature."

"Let's keep that in mind. Tell me, why are we doing this?"

"I want a picture of what I'm getting myself involved in."

"Well, you've got your pictures."

He did. The first poster, completed in black Magic Marker block letters by Parker's steady hand, read:

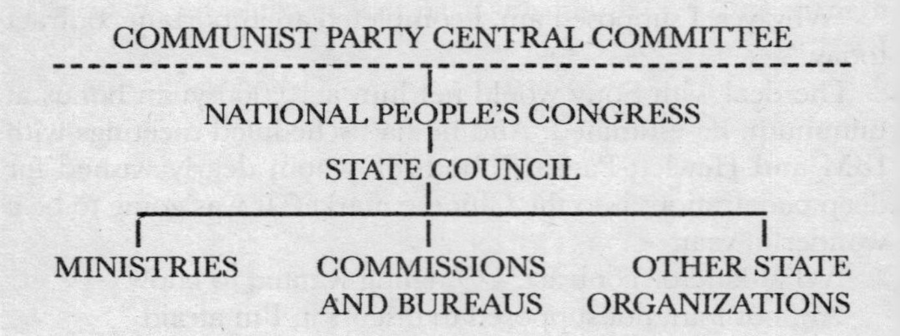

The Communist Party, of course, was a suggestive body, but its recommendations were taken quite seriously. The delegates to the Congress provided for representation from the provinces, and perhaps in recent years, their input had gained a bit more weight. The State Council, which included all of the ministers, took care of the day-to-day policy making. The ministries, commissions, and other groups put the policy into effect and served as the top level of administration.

There were hundreds of offices under those three categories. The ministries alone included anything from Agriculture to Civil Affairs to National Defense. There were about forty ministries, and Parker had listed them on a separate poster.

Another poster identified the commissions and bureaus, such as Planning, Physical Culture and Sports, and Nationalities Affairs. The People's Republic of China included so many minority nationalities—fifty-four ethnic groups—that a separate office had been set up to deal with those issues. In the United States, Grant realized, they called it the Bureau of Indian Affairs.

The Chinese flag admitted to the distinctions. The large gold star represented the Han people which comprised ninety-three percent of the population, and the four smaller stars symbolized the major National Minority areas: Xinjiang, Inner Mongolia, Tibet, and Manchuria.

Under other state organizations, again on a separate chart, were the offices of Tourism, the Bank of China, Statistics, and others.

There had once been a Ministry of Radio and Television, but that had evolved into the Ministry of Information, taking with it some of the functions of the Ministry of Posts and Telecommunications. It had also taken under its wing the agencies of Broadcasting and Publications, though the Xinhua News Agency—the official government agency—retained its supposed independent status.

The chart of the Ministry of Information read:

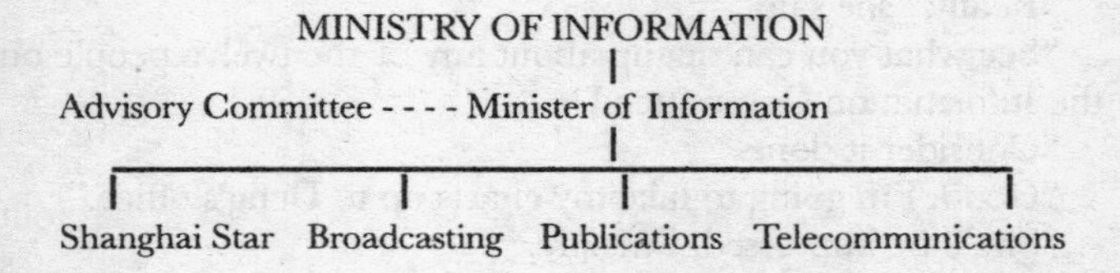

That Advisory Committee was a bit unique. It was composed of twelve people, all heads of other ministries. They all had a voice in the State Council, of course, but they were charged here with monitoring the operations of the new ministry. Someone up high was a bit frightened of the potential damage (or could that be *benefit*?) that might arise from the creation of the Ministry of Information.

There was one more chart. On it, Grant had directed Parker to simplify the division of power in the country. There were three major influences: the Party, the Army, and the State.

The Communist Party had nearly fifty million members, but the power was vested in the Politburo of the Central Committee. That committee had oversight for the Central Military Commission, the Party Secretariat, and the Central Advisory Commission.

The People's Liberation Army was directed by the Military Commission and headed by the Commander-in-Chief who was generally the head of the Military Commission.

The State was represented by the National People's Congress, the NPC. That body had 3,500 deputies and a standing committee of 175 members. In the United States, with 100 senators and 500-plus representatives in Congress, legislative issues seemed to drag on for years, Grant thought. He didn't know how a body with 3,500 members got anything done at all.

Grant looked at the posters and thought that there were a hell of a lot of people to lobby—especially for the purpose of changing a calendar date. Contrary to what he'd told Will Bricher, Grant did have some experience at influencing influential people.

"Diantha, do me a favor."

"I'd be delighted!"

He glanced at her, again unsure of her tone.

"Really," she said.

"See what you can dig up about any of the twelve people on the Information Committee."

"Consider it done."

"Good. I'm going to take my charts up to Deng's office."

"She'll be impressed, I'm sure."

Carrying his poster boards, Grant ran the gauntlet of the security posts on the sixth floor, and Miss Jiangyou allowed him into the inner sanctum.

"Hello, Douglas."

"Take a look at these, Mai," he said, moving the bowl of orchids aside and spreading the posters out on the glass table.

She came around her desk and looked down at the artwork.

Smiling, she said, "You are taking an interest in our government."

"I'm really taking an interest in our welfare." He told her about Bricher's meeting with General Hua Min. "And I'll tell you how I'm reading it. The Ministers of Commerce, Foreign Economic Relations, and Space Industry are putting pressure on Hua to maintain the schedule for the Australian satellite, thereby pushing us off six weeks, and forcing the inaugural date of Shanghai Star past October first. What would that do to you?"

She gave him a grim smile. "I would seek another line of work."

"Yeah. Me too, probably. But when I look at Diantha's charts, I note that those three ministers also serve on the advisory committee to Jiang Guofeng."

"Yes, they do."

"You don't think that Jiang, just maybe, encouraged those three men to have a little chat with Hua?"

Deng's eyes held his own, and as many times before, Grant felt a little dizzy, as if he could lose himself in their inky depths.

"Between us?" she asked.

"Of course."

"I am certain that Minister Jiang spoke to his colleagues, suggesting just what you are saying."

"Well, damn. What's his purpose, Mai?"

"First, I believe he would like to establish better control over Shanghai Star prior to its inception. Second, he would prefer to have a managing director who showed more subservience to him. Third, he would prefer his subordinates be male."

Grant bent over, found the chart of the advisory committee, and placed it on top of his stack. Digging a pen from his pocket, he scrawled a big check mark next to four of the titles.

"In addition to Jiang, then, he's got commerce, foreign economics, and space, as far as votes go?"

"And the Minister of Energy, I should think. His name is Pai Dehuai, and they have long been friends."

Deng sat in one of the chairs, and Grant took the one next to her.

"That's five votes out of twelve," he said.

"I do not know if they truly vote in that committee. It is advisory, after all."

"What I've got to do, Mai, is introduce myself to, and speak to, the other seven people on the committee. And maybe a few in the State Council who could apply some pressure on the three ministers controlling Hua Min's launches."

She thought about it for a minute, then said, "I will help you determine who would be best to approach. What would you tell them?"

"Will Bricher suggested that, four years ago, Shanghai Star was named the high-priority project for the nation. Certainly, it should come ahead of an Aussie communications satellite."

"Yes, the priorities are in writing. I have a copy of the declaration."

"Am I going to get too far out of line, talking to these people?" he asked.

"As the consultant, I think not. As long as you are cautious with them."

"I know cautious."

"There are a few on the State Council, and a number of staff persons that I can approach with the same message," Deng said. "It would be unseemly for me to talk to anyone on the advisory committee on this issue."

"We're not asking for much, Mai. On the surface, it doesn't look like much."

"That will be in our favor, yes. However, many of these people, especially the ministers, also understand what is taking place below the surface. They will know that Jiang would like to replace me."

"What of their philosophies? In regard to open information?"

"In basis, many will agree with Jiang. In reality, some have come to realize that change is inevitable, but they will resist drastic alterations in policies that have made them comfortable for decades."

Deng told him about her visit with Zhou Ziyang of the People's Right to Know Committee. "His proposal—which I will give you to read—appears modest. Yet, modesty to one man is radical to another. Do you understand?"

"I do."

"What is your plan?"

"Diantha is preparing some biographies for me, then I will try to get interviews with them."

"In the morning, have her come to see me, and I will add what I can to her information."

"That's great, Mai." Grant gathered his posters together. "Now, I'll go back down and start work."

"Could it wait until morning?" she asked.

"Well . . ."

Glancing at her watch, Deng said, "It is already five-forty, and at seven o'clock, my mother is giving a dinner party. I would like to have you attend."

Grant was surprised at the invitation, though not certain whether it originated from Mai or her mother.

"I'd be happy to come."

"Very well. You have not met my mother, so I should tell you that her dress code is slightly higher than denims."

"I'll go change." He grinned.

Grant took his posters back down to his office and told Parker she was to meet with Deng Mai in the morning. Parker looked skeptical. He checked around the office, noting those who were working late. The business day was supposed to be nine to five, but from the beginning, his people had been putting in ten to twelve hours a day. Everyone wanted MI to succeed.

He had walked to work that morning, so he took a cab back to his apartment building. The crowd was already building in the Dallas Cowboy Cafe, and he returned the waves of a few who signalled him inside for a drink, but passed up the offers. He took the stairs to the second floor and unlocked his front door.

His housekeeper, who came in on Thursday mornings, turned the air-conditioning too high, and invariably, forgot to turn it off. Grant turned it down.

The small living room was immaculate, but barren. He had never bothered to add the homey touches, and the couch, chairs, and tables looked unused. There was a television set, mostly unused, and a stereo with a stack of CDs next to it. The kitchenette had a round, Formica-topped table, where he often worked on a briefcase full of paperwork, but where he rarely ate. There were two bedrooms.

He shed his clothes, dumped most of them in the hamper, and took a long, soapy shower. He shaved with more care than usual, applied deodorant and aftershave, and felt like a teenager. He told himself to tone down his exuberance.

It was only a dinner.

After picking out his favorite Countess Mara tie, he found a white-on-white dress shirt to go with it, then selected a light-gray suit that he'd had tailored in London. Before dressing, he polished a pair of low-cut dress shoes. He was ready to go at 6:35 P.M.

On the ground floor, he walked the hallway to the back of the building and exited on the small parking lot. Of the dozen car in the lot, four belonged to Shanghai Star and were designatec for use by MI staff. The car assigned to him was a white GM(Jimmy utility vehicle with the Shanghai Star logo—a yellow sta over an outline of China—on the doors. It wasn't very roman tic, but it could bull its way through Shanghai traffic. It was al ready dinged from minor mishaps.

Fighting the traffic, it took him half an hour to reach the stree full of palatial homes on large lots. Most of them dated to colo nial times, and very few were still privately owned. Most wer converted to government uses of one kind or another.

He had to park a block away, and he was ten minutes late pass ing through the wrought-iron-topped brick wall, walking up th long white concrete sidewalk, and mounting the three steps t the full-width porch. There was a pair of huge carved black oa doors with a bell pull on the right.

He pulled it and considered himself fashionably late, thoug he knew that punctuality was a high-priority courtesy in China

To his left were wide windows overlooking the porch, and h could see ten or twelve people milling about in the room. He triec not to stare through the window.

After a few minutes, when he was certain no one had hear the bell, he reached out to give it another tug.

The right door opened.

A small Chinese man in something of a valet's rig nodded a him, and said, "Good evening, sir."

"Hello. My name is Grant. I think I'm expected."

"Yes, sir. Please come in."

He was afraid he was going to be framed in a doorway anc announced, but Deng Mai appeared in the foyer from the livin room. She smiled at him and held out her hand. He took it anc she surprised him by giving his hand a tiny squeeze.

Everything under the sun was new.

"I'm glad you could come," she said.

"I miscalculated the traffic."

"You had short enough notice that you are to be excused."

He took a quick look around the foyer, which was tiled ir gold-veined white marble. A sideboard under a mirror held thre vases he assumed to be antiques. To the right was a grand staircase carpeted in dark gold and rising into darkened regions.

On the right also was a door into a dining room, elegantly prepared with white linen over a long, long table. A gold-and-pale-blue brocaded wall-covering clung to the walls, and blue drapes were parted to the sides of several windows. The woodwork was painted white. On the left was the living room, and lilting sets of conversations emanated from it. Chinese, French, and English were all in vogue.

Deng led him through the wide door into the living room, and he got a quick count of fourteen people, none of whom he had ever seen before. They were chatting easily with one another, sipping from champagne flutes.

The valet appeared with a silver tray, and he picked a flute from it.

"Mama serves only champagne," Mai said. "French, of course."

"Of course."

He had identified Mama immediately. Besides himself, she was the only other Caucasian in the room, and despite the fact that she must be sixty years old, she was stunningly beautiful. Dressed in a floor-length white gown accented by a diamond necklace, Madame Deng commanded a small circle of her friends. She was taller than anyone in the room except Grant, and her face glowed with radiance. Her dark hair was swept up in a coiffure that may have taken a couple hours to achieve. Her eyes were striking, a clear violet that might entrance or repel, depending on her whim.

The similarities between mother and daughter were apparent. The high cheekbones, the shape of the ears, the curvature of the mouths, the hourglass figures.

"I'd have known her for your mother if I'd met her on the street," he said.

She sipped from her glass and eyed him across the brim. "Would you?"

"Absolutely."

"And what would . . . no, that's not fair."

Grant didn't know where she had started to go with her comment, and decided it was best not to pursue it. Deng Mai's manner—her eyes, the movement of her mouth—seemed to him to be somewhat flirtatious tonight. Maybe her personality changed when she was at home.

Though she had probably known he was in the room from the instant he passed through the doorway, Yvonne Deng appeared to suddenly notice him. She excused herself from her group and crossed the room, smiling.

He appreciated the smile, but as she got closer, realized that her eyes were not part of it. They were somehow opaque, suspicious.

"Mama, Mr. Grant. This is my mother, Madame Deng."

She held out her hand, and Grant shook it lightly. The same smooth skin as her daughter's, but Grant thought the temperature much lower. Her flesh felt chilled.

"I am pleased to meet you, Mr. Grant."

"The pleasure is mine, I assure you."

They chatted briefly, Madame Deng inquiring about Megatronics Incorporated and the progress they were making. Grant told her he was impressed with her house. He wanted to say that he was also impressed with her daughter, but toned that down to an expression of his appreciation for Mai's administrative capabilities.

Finally, she said, "Mai, please introduce Mr. Grant around. I'm sure he will find our guests most interesting."

They were of interest. There was an economist, a university professor who taught both French and English, an actress and her director-husband, the managing director of a manufacturing plant, a young man who was a lawyer.

They seemed to find Grant of interest, also. The conversations were lively and in English in deference to Grant's language limitations. He began to enjoy himself.

But from time to time, he felt Yvonne Deng's violet eyes chasing him around the room.

Monday, August 15

The port of Shanghai stretched for thirty-five miles along the shores of the Huangpu River. Though the city was situated in an intricate web of creeks and canals belonging to the delta of the Yangzi River, it was the wide stretch of the Huangpu that carried all manner of craft from the sea to the port.

In the cool of the evening, with a breeze clearing a path through the coal smoke permeating the air, couples walked hand in hand along the boulevard fronting the river, strolling through the gardens and stopping to lean on the sea wall and study the marine vessels. Ferries plied the passage with hundreds of tourists and commuters jammed together on their decks. Rust-laden freighters and lovingly restored steamers hauled grain and cotton and steel, outward bound for other ports along the China coast. They grudgingly gave way to junks under power—the reliability of diesel engines had supplanted sail. The commoners—the sampans—were everywhere, five or six members of a family working the single *yuloh* oar or diesel engines crying as they scooted across the river's surface.

In the early mornings, the singers and musicians practiced their arts alongside the martial arts and exercise aficionados.

Chiang listened to the varying rhythms and voices as she waited in the small park next to Zhongshan Road. The mist flowing off the river was thick, and the bass-toned foghorns of vessels under way were a steady accompaniment for the singers.

At 4:30 A.M., her contact appeared as promised, materializing out of the fog like the wraith she sometimes thought him to be. She did not know his name, did not want to know it, and preferred thinking of him as a phantom. Admittedly, he was a handsome phantom with hard, flat planes in his lean face and a fire in his eyes that suggested peril for anyone exploring their uncharted territory. It was that sharp edge of danger in the man, despite his expensive Western suit, that attracted her, but she sensed that to breach the line that divided them was not in her best interest.

The similarities between the phantom and Huzhou were apparent to her, but she also recognized that Huzhou was largely untried, an apprentice aspiring to the heights her contact had already reached. This man had such confidence in the set of his shoulders, in the way he walked, that one automatically sensed that his menace was real. With Huzhou, there was a possibility that it could be real.

She rose from the bench as he approached. He stopped in front of her, and his mysterious eyes surveyed her, though they did not reveal either his approval or his distaste. Reaching inside his jacket, he withdrew an envelope and gave it to her.

"Membership dues, I believe," he told her.

"Yes, they would be."

"And instructions."

"Instructions?"

"Just follow them."

And then she knew she was trapped.

"Ah, hell, boss. I was hoping to get back to Shanghai. At least, for a couple days? Rest and recuperation?"

"And women?" Grant asked.

"That's my R&R," Stone told him.

"We're much safer keeping you in the country, Mickey."

"That's Diantha talking. You know she doesn't approve of me."

"I'm not sure she approves of me," Grant replied, laughing. "But she does have our best interests at heart."

"Can't be. My health is deteriorating."

"Professional interests."

"Oh, that. It's no fun being a professional and having to be on one's best behavior *twenty-five* hours a day."

"Talk to Diantha about it. Anyway, I approve of your behavior. You handled the walk-out situation in Lhasa very well, Mickey."

"The credit goes to Wickersham," Stone said. "He came up with the idea of giving people their own desks."

"But you negotiated it. Good job."

It was another example of why Grant liked Stone as a man and an employee. He was always quick to place credit where it was due, and he never bothered to blame anyone else when things went wrong.

"So what's in Chengdu?" Stone asked.

"Well, we have a bunch of computers there."

"I know that. But the last I heard, three or four of them were working. What more do you want?"

"I want you to act like you're on a regular tour of the facility, but I also want you to talk to Deputy Shang."

"Of the sheriff's department?"

"Of the National People's Congress." He explained his lobbying plan to Stone.

"And this Shang is a wheel?"

"She's one of—"

"She?"

"She's one of the reps from Sichuan Province, but she apparently has an overriding interest in Shanghai Star, and she may have some influence with ministers I'm trying to reach."

"And you want me to bend her ear?"

"Without breaking it, or hopefully, biting it, Mickey. Be tender. Get our message across."

"Stupid message, boss. Can't you come up with something more romantic than advancing a launch date?"

"All it means is your paycheck."

"I can handle it."

"Good. Diantha is faxing you some background info. Be good, Mickey."

"I don't seem to have any other choices. Hey, Doug?"

"Yo?"

"What happened at the GE board meeting?"

"Oh, damn! I need to get a memo out to everyone on that.

They voted to give us an eight-mil discount on the next two sats."

"So we're only out a million?"

"Thanks to Will. He did the selling job, Mickey."

"Give him my thanks, will you? Jesus, this is good news. I'm going to meet the Shang chick with gladness in my heart."

"Don't overdo it, Mickey."

Grant replaced the telephone receiver on its console and left his office.

In the jungle, Parker stopped him.

"You aren't leaving?"

"Just down to see Will."

"Okay. I've about got these files ready for you."

"Everything I ever wanted to know, huh?"

"You bet. Mai was very helpful."

Since her meeting with Deng Mai last Friday, Diantha Parker seemed to have forgotten the Ice Maiden appellation. It was "Mai said this," or "Mai said that," and Grant thought it best to ignore the change in her attitude. Bringing it up would only get him in hot water.

He told her to send an electronic memo to all the managers about the GE decision. He hated keeping people in the dark, but the memo had slipped his mind.

He went down the long hallway past the elevators to the far side of the floor. The satellite-communications people had their area defined by room dividers, but no cubicles. They were in one area, kind of like a newspaper city-room.

There were a couple dozen desks assigned to seven permanent MI employees and seventeen people hired as consultants to the project. The room was a madhouse of comings and goings, chatter between desks, yells across the room. Engineers worried over schematics displayed on the computer screens, dashed out to catch planes to Xichang, came running in from excursions to the equipment spaces on the upper floors. Telephones buzzed and the MI engineers made patient explanations to their Chinese counterparts located on floors ten and eleven. As the implementation wound down over the next year, all satcom operations would eventually shift to the Chinese technical people on the upper floors.

Will Bricher's desk was located in the middle of the chaos.

Grant felt like a running back crossing a jammed defensive line as he made his way to the center of the room. Bricher was on the phone, and Grant went around his desk and sat on the corner of it.

Bricher looked up, held up a finger to signal one more minute, and said, "Tank, we show you're getting your signals to the sat, we're just not getting them down again. Hang loose while we fine-tune some downlinks . . . yeah, I'll get back to you."

He slammed the phone down and called to the guy at the next desk, "Fred, get on the landline to Hunan sites DCT-four through eleven and tell them they still haven't got alignment." Turning to another man, he ordered, "Head upstairs, Gene. We want another test on the damned downlink translators."

Gene bolted out of his chair, headed for the elevators.

Bricher looked up at Grant and grinned.

"Another perfect day, Will?"

"Just A-one, Doug. Hell, if the Viets picked today to attack Changsha, the generals couldn't even call their colonels on DCT's system. Tank's kinda upset."

"He will get over it, won't he?"

"Sure he will. Give me another couple hours, and we'll work the kinks out."

"How long have we got the system?"

"Hua Min did a job for us. We've got five channels for ten days."

"Buy him dinner the next time you're out that way."

"That's big of us," Bricher said, "but probably the only thing he'd accept."

"So, anything I can do to help?"

Bricher let shock cross his face. "You've got to be kidding."

"Just thought I'd ask since I'm going to be gone for the rest of the day."

"We'll struggle along without you."

"Do you really know what the problem is?" Grant asked.

"Yeah, I think Cameron's downlink units need to be reprogrammed. They aren't allowing the antennas to align properly."

"But you haven't told him that yet?"

"I'll let him think we've done all we can before I spring it on him. And then I'll loan him a couple of Wickersham's programming wizards to straighten it out."

"Loan him?"

"Give him a break on the consulting fee."

"Good man. Diantha can probably track me down if I'm needed."

"Don't hold your breath."

"Mickey thanks you, by the way."

"For what?"

"Saving him a few mil. I thank you, too."

"Just give me another gold star next to my name."

"Already did."

Grant went back to his office to find Parker and Deng side by side on the couch, poring over Parker's printouts.

Deng looked up. "I have asked Diantha for copies of these files. She has done a very nice job of compiling them."

"And I'm going to spend some time with Mai's secretaries, showing them some computer tricks," Parker said.

"Let's not forget that you're supposed to be the boss here this afternoon."

"I'm the boss here all the time."

Deng smiled at the exchange. It was one that probably wouldn't take place in the office of a Chinese firm.

Rising with the file, Deng led him into his office and they sat in separate chairs at the coffee table.

"Who are you seeing first?" she asked.

"I've got appointments with Shan and Peng this afternoon, then I'm having dinner with Shao Tsung tonight."

She leafed through the file and withdrew the three data sheets on the three ministers. Grant took them from her and spent some time reading the new information that had been added.

"Jesus! We don't want these sheets out of the building. Not even out of the office, I think."

"Diantha said that she has the file secured."

"Where did you get all this?"

"It is common knowledge in the higher echelons, though no one speaks of it."

He read out loud from the Minister of Labor's file. "Shan Li is highly corrupt. He accepts bribes for delivering labor resources to preferred construction projects."

Deng nodded.

"And we want this guy on our side?"

"We do. You must understand that much of this has taken place for decades. At least since the end of the Cultural Revolution. It becomes accepted practice."

He looked up at her. "Do you remember much of the Revolution?"

"Some, yes. I remember the Red Guards storming the museum near our house. They destroyed everything inside."

"All priceless artifacts."

"It was terrible."

The Cultural Revolution and the Gang of Four had nearly wiped out China's cultural heritage, what was left behind by colonial-style raiders in earlier centuries.

"You must keep in mind," she went on, "that there is always a tension, even a struggle, between the Party, the army, and the government. Many of the alignments change with each new issue that arises."

"So where are our alignments?"

"The Chairman of the Party and the Politburo favored the creation of Shanghai Star, and they were supported by the army. In general, I think their motives are pure."

"Are you speaking as a Party member?"

She gave him a quizzical glance. "Very likely, but also as a proponent of the information system."

"Go on."

"The Premier has . . . to be blunt . . . overlooked many of the inadequacies in the government. No one accuses him of corruption, but he appears to condone it. He would, I think, like to be the next Party Chairman. He is quite reactionary, and he fought Shanghai Star from the beginning. It was a tremendous loss of face when he was finally forced to concede. His concession, however, came at the expense of placing Jiang Guofeng at the head of the ministry."

"They are friends? The Premier and Jiang?"

"Not friends, I think. Ideological comrades."

"And the army?"

"Minister of National Defense Shao Tsung is a very powerful man, as long as he sides with the generals. Both the Chairman and the Premier court him, attempting to keep the balance of power in their favor."

"How does Shan fit in, then?"

"The Minister of Labor belongs in the Premier's camp, of course. Without the Premier's permission, he would not be allowed to become a wealthy man. In the past he has looked favorably upon the advances that Shanghai Star promises. I think that, to keep the peace, he may urge his colleagues to accept our proposal."

"How about Peng?"

"As Minister of Materials, Peng Zedong controls much of the nation's resources. If a steel mill does not receive its allotment of ore, the director will not meet his quota and will fall into disfavor. Almost everyone treats Peng with extreme deference. I am not overstating the case, Douglas, when I say that Peng has attempted to be fair. He takes his position with great seriousness, and he is a protege of the Chairman. Peng and the Premier have argued in public."

"So, he's with us?"

"I should think so, though his final position may depend upon Shao."

"Why Shao?"

"He is going to support what the generals want. The fact that they released the ShangStar One channels for your testing suggests to me that they view us with some favor. Not one of them would admit it in a public forum, of course. They prefer to be aloof and noncommittal. Aloof and powerful."

"My take on this, Mai, is that the generals, whatever their view of open information, need Shanghai Star badly. Their portion of the system is what will jerk them out of the early twentieth century."

"Yes. They must support it for that reason alone. Most of the military complex is quite antiquated. I suspect there are many on the general staff who have reservations about the civilian programming, but that was the compromise they agreed to in order to obtain the new military systems."

Grant was getting surprising admissions from her lately. Until the disaster with the satellite, she hadn't been very forthcoming on topics outside of the project. He put it down to the pressure she was under, along with her need to support MI.

"So, I'm likely to meet Shao while his mood leans toward me?"

"I should think so. And if so, he will do much to sway the others."

"Okay, thanks. I think I'm ready." Grant looked at his watch. "I've got about an hour before my flight, and I'll use it studying your secret service files."

Deng stood up and offered her hand. "I will talk to you later."

He took her hand and held it a trifle longer than necessary. It was certainly warmer than her mother's.

"I'll call you tonight."

"Please do."

"And Mai, thanks again for the dinner. I enjoyed it."

She smiled. "Are you certain?"

"The conversation was lively."

"Mama likes intellectuals."

"I don't think your mother likes me very well," he ventured.

"That is all right, Douglas. Frequently, she does not like the things that I like."

She turned and left the office, leaving Grant pondering her comment.

"In his last post, which was in Washington, D.C., Valeri Sytenko was also a trade attaché," Yuri Fedorchuk told him.

"Was he a good one?" Suretsov asked.

"It seems that he became involved with an American woman, and he was ordered to stay away from her," the editor said.

"She was a spy?"

Suretsov stretched his back and shoulder muscles. The old wooden swivel chair behind the tiny desk was hard on his back. His whole office was hard on his back. The ITAR-Tass Shanghai Bureau consisted of one tiny three-room suite for himself, a part-time Chinese secretary, and a part-time Chinese reporter. For the largest city in Asia.

"At first, they thought she worked for the CIA. As it turns out, she was a housewife from Maryland. Apparently, she was looking for excitement in her life."

"Did he stay away from her?"

"He is in Beijing, is he not? It is hardly as desirable a posting as Washington."

"Perhaps he is truly in love with her," Suretsov suggested.

"My contact, the retired general, could not assure me of Sytenko's emotions," Fedorchuk said.

"Maybe I will ask him?"

"That will certainly conclude your story early, Vladimir Petrovich."

"I may have to fly back to Beijing."

"Be careful with your budget. It may dry up quickly."

"I am very aware of my budget. There is another matter, Yuri."

"Yes?"

"I hear rumors of unrest in the government."

"Unrest? Over what?"

"I think it has to do with the Shanghai Star project. From what I have heard, the liberals are lining up to challenge the conservative faction."

"Ah." Fedorchuk mused for a while, then said, "Stay close to that, Vladimir. It could get interesting."

"Yes, I am afraid it might."

"And do a follow-up on the Douglas Grant article. It was well received."

"Thank you, Yuri. I will proudly accept my bonus."

Fedorchuk was laughing as he hung up.

Suretsov shoved the chair backward. The old metal caster wheels resisted movement and squeaked on the uneven floor. He stood up and retrieved his suit jacket from the hanger on the hall tree in the corner. It was a two-step walk from his chair to the hall tree.

He made certain the note was still in the pocket of his suit jacket. It had been taken in the morning by his secretary—who was now gone for the afternoon, and it read: PYOTR—CHIANG QING—PEOPLE'S UNDERGROUND.

Suretsov had no idea in the world what it meant. He had searched around for an address for the Underground, of which he had heard, but of course, it was not advertised. An Associated Press correspondent he knew had located it for him.

He locked the door of the outer office behind him as he left, sure that it was unwarranted. There was nothing worthwhile to steal.

The building had no elevator, but fortunately, he was only on the second of six floors, and he took the concrete steps to the main floor, slipped past the floral shop, and went out. Hailing a taxi, he gave the driver the address in Old Town.

The driver talked to him without interruption the entire trip, speaking in high-pitched Mandarin. Suretsov did not understand one word, but he smiled and nodded whenever the driver checked him in the rearview mirror.

As reward for the entertainment, he tipped a bit more than he should have before getting out at the People's Underground headquarters. Taxi drivers expected ten percent from Chinese passengers and hoped for a great deal more from wealthy foreigners—*gweilos.* Since he was not wealthy, Suretsov allowed fifteen percent.

He stood on the sidewalk for a moment, looking around. Not surprisingly, there was no sign, so he simply pulled open the door and climbed the steps.

There were eight people in the main room, all busy at undetermined tasks. Some were talking on telephones. Others seemed to be making posters. Stepping up to the closest of four crowded desks, he identified himself to the girl in both Russian and English.

Neither of which she had command over. She smiled at him and called to a young man who seemed irritated at the interruption.

But he walked over and said, "Yes?"

English, at least. Suretsov presented his press credentials and asked, "I wonder if I could speak to Miss Chiang?"

The young man's eyes seemed to glitter behind his thick spectacles. Maybe he was more impressed with the credentials than Suretsov was.

"I will find her. Please have a seat."

Since all of the seats seemed to be taken, Suretsov wandered around the room, studying the posters on the walls. They were all in Chinese characters—known as "big-character" posters, or *dazibao,* though some featured a picture of Chiang. They were banned in the early 1970s when they turned critical of the government, but began to reappear in the late eighties, just prior to the Tiananmen Square massacre. Of these posters, Suretsov couldn't determine one of the issues involved.

He had never followed the Underground, and he wasn't quite sure what positions they took. He guessed, however, that they were not strong positions, or their headquarters would not be so accessible.

"Mr. Suretsov? I am Chiang Qing."

He turned to find a tiny woman with severely cut hair probing him with dark eyes that shifted abruptly from his eyes to his mouth to his ear, back to his eyes. She was a bit on the hyperactive side, he thought.

"Miss Chiang, I would like your reaction on several issues."

"What issues?"

"For one, the Shanghai Star Communications Network."

"Why me?"

"Because I have heard that you are often outspoken, and I am gathering information from a variety of Chinese organizations."

The man behind her nodded vigorously for her, but she couldn't see him.

"Perhaps a few minutes," she said and took him to a back corner and cleared it of counterrevolutionaries with a few well-chosen words. He thought her dialect to be Shanghainese.

The two of them sat in chairs, and the young man hovered over the desk.

Suretsov looked up at him.

"Huzhou," she said, "go check on the mailing."

He sneered at her, but left them alone. Suretsov started his recorder and opened his notebook. He jotted down Huzhou's name, so he would remember it.

It took twenty minutes to conduct the interview, and Chiang was so vehemently pro-open information that Suretsov decided it might even turn into a story, rather than the ruse he had intended it to be.

For his next-to-last question, he asked, "And what of the director, Deng Mai? How does your organization view her?"

Chiang took a little time before responding to that one. "I cannot speak for the entire Underground, but if they think as I do, they admire Director Deng. She does much for the cause of open administration and for women in the PRC."

Now for the zinger.

"And what is your relationship with Valeri Sytenko?"

He was watching her eyes for the giveaway, though they were difficult to analyze because of the way they kept moving around.

He did not see one scintilla of recognition in them.

"Valeri who?"

"Sytenko. He is the trade attaché at the Russian Consulate in Beijing."

"I do not know the man. What is the connection?"

"I understood that he assisted the Underground financially," Suretsov said quickly, looking for a suitable excuse.

"I wish that he would."

He drew a line through the last sentence of his notes, as if writing off that rumor, then stood and thanked her for her time.

As he descended the steps to street level, he wondered what the hell Arkady Makov—Pyotr—was trying to do to him.

Jiang Guofeng met with Shan Li shortly after the labor minister had completed his discussion with Grant. It was one of Wen Yito's assignments to keep track of where the major foreign consultants travelled, and why. As soon as Grant had ordered his ticket from Air China, Wen had been alerted to the visit to Beijing, and subsequently had pinned down the name of Shan as one of those Grant would see.

They met in Shan's office since Shan hadn't expected him. Jiang barely acknowledged the male secretary before walking in on Shan.

"Minister Jiang. Did we have a meeting scheduled?"

Jiang smiled. "No, not at all. If you are too busy at the moment, I can return at a later time."

"No, no. Please sit. Have you eaten?"

Jiang did not smile at the traditional greeting, rendered popular over the years by a starving populace. It was always courteous to ask an arriving visitor if he was hungry.

Shan Li came out of that tradition of hunger, one of nine siblings in a poverty-stricken family—pre-revolutionary China allowed families more than one child. It was difficult for him to leave the old world behind, despite the fact that he had accumulated millions. He accepted his position in life as if it were his due, but he could not break old habits. He was a Scrooge, if there was one; and his emaciated appearance suggested he could not afford the cheapest duck in the market.

After a few minutes of small talk—another of the traditions that always delayed negotiations, Jiang went right to the point. "You spoke to the *gweilo* contractor?"

All foreigners were referred to as *gweilo*, foreign devil, but Jiang was beginning to believe that Grant was indeed a devil, one with the magic to circumvent Jiang whenever he pleased.

"I spoke to him."

"May I ask the topic?"

"You may. It is a simple matter of a launch schedule. I would think that you were aware of it."

"I know that Grant wishes to displace the Australian launch date, substituting his own. Do you feel or not feel that such an action would bring us poor publicity?"

"Perhaps the relationship with the Australians would be strained. Yet, Grant reminded me that the Central Committee established Shanghai Star as the priority project. Without the unfortunate incident, their satellite would have been injected into orbit first."

Jiang watched his colleague closely. Shan was always difficult to predict. While he usually followed the lead of the Premier, he sometime took radical turns from the projected line. He had to be careful here. If he took a strong stance on what Shan himself thought of as a minor matter, questions would be raised as to his motives.

He would not contest Shan. There could come a time when he needed labor resources placed at his disposal, and an alienated labor minister would assure him that none were available.

And he would have to determine, and quickly, how many people Grant was talking to on his quick trip to Beijing.

"If you need the reminder, also," Shan said, "this is a copy of the Committee's directive."

He pushed a paper across the desk. Jiang glanced at the Chinese characters filling it. "I am familiar with it."

"I wonder, then," Shan said, "if you might not speak to the ministers of commerce, foreign economics, and space industry? Apparently, they are somewhat misguided in their directives to the rocket forces."

Now Shan was urging him to countermand the action Jiang had set in motion? Acting as a lobbyist for the American?

Shan did not know that Jiang had spoken to the three earlier, of course.

"I could speak with them, though I doubt my words will carry weight."

"This would be a silly matter to bring up in the Advisory Committee or the State Council, do you not think?"

Was that a threat?

Probably.

He ignored a response by asking, "Do you know who else Grant was to meet?"

"Why, yes. He was quite open in mentioning meetings with Peng Zedong and Shao Tsung. Tomorrow, he has a half-dozen appointments, but he did not say who they were with."

Damn the man!

This was the first time Grant had interfered politically. If Jiang had his way, it would certainly be the last.

The "Green-Eyed Devil," as some referred to Grant, could not be allowed to give the appearance that he was directing, or forcing Jiang to direct, the ministry according to his own whim.

This was China, not the United States of America.

The computer screen offered a list:

(1) Games
(2) Sports
(3) Bulletin Boards
(4) News Reports
(5) Knowledge

Maynard Crest used the mouse to direct the pointer to the fifth choice and pressed the left button. The new screen read:

(1) Libraries
(2) Museums
(3) Dictionary
(4) Encyclopedia
(5) Languages
(6) Sciences
(7) Arts
(8) Government

Crest selected number four and watched as the screen changed to the opening display for the encyclopedia. His screen displays were, naturally, in English, but the user had the option of selecting Chinese character or pinyin for their own use. The interactive encyclopedia had been developed sometime before, and CIS had paid big bucks to acquire it for this system.

He had options for looking up a topic or browsing through the on-line tome, but he typed in "Bengal tiger."

Immediately, the screen came alive with a view of the tiger in motion, prowling through a lush green jungle. At the top of the screen, he used the cursor to select pinyin as the written display language and *putonghua* for the oral language. As the big cat prowled, the pinyin alphabet scrolled along the bottom of the screen, describing the tiger, its habits, and its habitat. He supposed, since he couldn't read it. Simultaneously, a soothing voice issued from the speaker, reading the script aloud in the northern dialect, or what non-Chinese called Mandarin. From time to time, he was prompted to select other options. Did he want to see a map of the cat's normal home? Did he want to know the historical and current statistics of the Bengal tiger population. Did he want to know what was being done to protect the species?

With the mouse, he backed out of the program to the knowledge screen, then selected "Government."

He was provided a listing of provinces, autonomous regions, and special municipalities, and he selected Guangdong Province.

The screen gave him a graphic breakdown of governmental functions, and he opted to pursue human services. The next screen provided the titles of offices related to human services in the provincial capital of Guangzhou—which he had known for years and years as Canton, along with their addresses and telephone numbers. Again, he was reading it in English, but the viewer had other options.

Crest looked at the small box in his hand, with one cable to the mouse he held against the table. There were no other cables. The box, with a small keyboard, spoke to the television monitor via infrared signals.

"Jesus, Nick. You've done a great job."

Nick Alvarez, CIS's head of interactive computing, was standing behind him. He grinned at the compliment. "Thanks, Maynard. It's been a trial, I'll tell you."

Crest shook the box. "Whose?"

"That one is from Micro Organisms. We anticipate that IBM, Compaq, HP, Megatronics, and a few others will have several levels of control available in the near future. The basic level, like you have there, allows the user to interact with the system via his television. Higher levels will include personal-computer functions, including links to printing devices. With just the TV, the user can watch. With a remote control like that one, he can involve himself."

Crest swivelled his chair around to look at Alvarez. The computer specialist was dressed impeccably, just the way Crest liked to see his people, but contrary to the standard business practice in China. The Chinese preferred to be comfortable, especially in the heat of summer.

"I don't see a listing for the national government, Nick. Why is that?"

Alvarez leaned against the back of the chair behind him. "Traditionally, Maynard, the common Chinese peasant didn't give a shit about the government. Most of them went through their daily grind of trying to find or grow enough food to keep themselves and their families alive and remained completely oblivious to who or what was in power. Regimes—dynasties, democracies, communist committees—came and went without the man in the street being much the wiser. Sure, the schools and the different forms of commune that were set up provided a political education, but not many cared.

"On the communications front, there's one radio for every seven people, and sixty people get together and buy a TV. Since the seventies, the government's been getting better about allowing entertainment on the airways, but it's consistently censored. The telephone is used almost exclusively for official purposes. Joe Ching uses the mail if he wants to contact his relatives.

"Now, we and Shanghai Star come crashing in. Even if they don't get a phone right away, they can easily get the toy you've been playing with. They're going to be bombarded with new ideas and new data, both trivial and relevant. They're going to become aware of the governmental bureaucracy, and we're trying to help them understand that with this particular segment of the program. They're also going to want to participate. We hope they want to participate."

"And you don't think Beijing anticipates this development?"

"I sincerely doubt it. If we listed the national government, at least at this time, I think the switchboards would smoke with all the calls coming into the capital. We're trying to limit it to the provinces for now."

"Imagine half-a-billion phone calls, all at once," Crest said.

"I did. That's why we set it up this way. Let the provinces take the heat in the beginning."

"It's a good selling point." Crest always looked for good selling points.

"I hope its better than what Media Bureau has come up with."

"I'm sure it is, Nick. Positive, in fact."

Crest always took the optimistic view.

His optimism had been a trifle shattered the day before, though, when he had met the three candidates proposed by Jiang Guofeng for the executive positions in Shanghai Star's program divisions.

Sung Wu, especially, bothered him. The old goat might drop dead before he took over as president of Consortium of Information Services-China, but if he didn't have the grace to drop dead, he could cause a lot of damage.

"Do you think, Nick, that that Bengal tiger we saw was a capitalist or a communist?"

"What? Does it matter?"

"It might to Sung Wu."

Alvarez looked blank.

"Who's Sung Wu?"

"He's the one that will go through that encyclopedia looking for topless gorillas, or Sally Rand without enough feathers." Crest tapped the remote control. "Does this have a delete function?"

"You can't delete anything in the main database."

"I'll bet Sung Wu can."

The Garden of Abundance and Color restaurant was located on Zhushikou Street in western Beijing. It was not only one of the best restaurants in the city, it featured a Northern Chinese and Shandong menu, and since Minister Shao Tsung was originally from Zibo in Shandong Province, according to Diantha Parker's bio on the man, Grant thought he might appreciate the gesture.

Grant was in the foyer, waiting, when Shao arrived via a chauffeured Lincoln Town Car. There weren't many of those around the city, and the government had officially taken the position of denying fancy limos for its political hierarchy, so the symbol of Shao's power was not lost on Grant.

A uniformed army sergeant hopped out of the front seat and opened the rear door to let the minister emerge. He was a former general, and as Grant had anticipated, demonstrated a military posture. Stiff back, alert gray eyes, an awareness of what was going on around him.

The sergeant opened the restaurant door, and as Shao entered, Grant stood up from the ornately carved bench where he had been sitting.

"Ah, Mr. Grant!"

"I'm honored that you could join me, Minister."

"Who could refuse an invitation from the Green-eyed Devil?"

Grant smiled. "Is that my nickname? I hadn't heard it."

"It seems to be in use around the city."

"I think I'm pleased." The Chinese were big on nicknames; almost everyone and everything had one.

"You should be."

Grant gestured for the minister to proceed him, and the hostess led them to a large table in a back corner of the dining room. There was nothing particularly distinctive about the restaurant's decor. Its fame lay in its menu.

After they were seated, Grant said, "I assumed the luxury of ordering for the two of us."

"I am certain I will be pleased."

For nearly an hour, as they worked through the appetizers, the two of them tested each other lightly, on familiar and simple ground, learning something of each other's background. Grant discovered a few things that Parker hadn't listed in the minister's biography. For one, he had exiled himself to Hong Kong during the latter half of the Cultural Revolution, unable to approve of the destruction and persecution perpetrated by the Red Guards, and being a major at the time, unable to effectively protest. He asked about Grant's tour of duty in Kuwait and Iraq, and Grant said, "It was not a happy episode."

"You were a prisoner of war?"

The man had a pretty complete dossier on Grant.

"For about three hours and twenty-five minutes. Then, I got mad."

"Do you frequently become angry?" Shao asked, smiling.

"That was the last time that I remember."

During the entree of Chicken Puffs with Shark's Fin—chopped white chicken meat in whipped egg white cooked in a chicken stock with shark's fin—they concentrated on the food. After three years in the country, Grant had learned not to push too early for talk of a business nature.

Over tiny cups of aromatic tea, with a teapot handy for refills, Shao said, "General Hua has spoken to the chief of the general staff about the scheduling problem."

It was nice of the minister to open the topic, Grant thought.

"Do you understand my predicament?"

Shao shrugged. "A few days here, a few days there. It will not matter in the universal scheme of things."

If he was aware of the political shenanigans taking place, he wasn't going to give it away. Simply by the man's demeanor, Grant could be certain he was not oblivious to the politics. Grant decided against appealing to the Politburo's priority commitment. Shao was army; he probably cared less about the Party's rationales.

"Let me make an observation, Minister. You have a tough job. You are responsible for defending over a billion people living in three-point-seven million square miles of territory. Most of it is very isolated. There's twenty-five hundred miles of coastline; half the country is mountains; two thirds of the countryside is arid. Eighty percent of your population lives in rural areas, yet that is only fifteen percent of the land area. Four percent of the population lives in half of China—Inner Mongolia, Xinjiang, and Tibet."

Shao smiled. "You are well acquainted with the numbers."

"In the past, the military has had communication problems. If . . . the Cossacks had come across the border, the news might not have reached military headquarters because of frequent breakdowns in landlines and radio facilities. Even your early satellite communications often encountered problems."

"And that has all changed with the military portion of Shanghai Star Communications, Mr. Grant. With your computers and your communications equipment, our voice and data transmission is all but instantaneous from any border region."

"With ShangStar One."

"Yes."

"Which is supposed to serve as a backup for the next two satellites."

"You understand that national defense supersedes entertainment?"

"Of course, Minister. But do you also understand that ShangStar Two and ShangStar Three are the backups for the current satellite? If that bird dies tomorrow, it could be three days before you learn that the Dalai Lama's supporters have taken over Lhasa."

Shao didn't smile this time. His eyes narrowed and focused just beyond Grant. When they came back to the here and now, he said, "Is that your sole reason for wanting the Australian's launch date?"

"No. But it's the one that affects you, and the one that I think you should be aware of."

"You have provided the satellite. Do you think that it will fail?"

"Not in the next ten years. But I didn't think the Long March Three was going to blow up on the pad, either. I'm not very good at predictions, Minister Shao."

"You make an excellent point for avoiding delay, sir. Frequently, our services obtain new equipment and believe it will last a lifetime."

One had to only look at the air force to understand that rationale. Grant didn't think they owned one aircraft that wasn't obsolete.

"It doesn't even have to be an equipment failure," Grant said. "An antisatellite missile takes out ShangStar One and you're forced back onto your old systems. If they haven't been removed by now."

Shao nodded. "I will speak to the general staff and the Premier of this situation."

"That's all I ask, Minister."

Shao shoved his chair back and stood up. "You have been an informative host, Mr. Grant. I shall return the favor."

"At any time," Grant said, rising. "I would be pleased to continue our conversation."

The Minister of National Defense was whisked away in his Lincoln Town Car, and after Grant settled the bill, he waited fifteen minutes for a taxi to take him back to his hotel on Chang An Avenue.

The Beijing Hotel was one of the premier hostelries in the city. His room wasn't that expensive at eighty bucks a night, but the deluxe hotel was one of the most expensive in the capital city. Given Megatronics's cash state, he wouldn't have opted for the top hotel except that in China, as in many other places, it was a matter of "face." He received more respect when people knew where he was staying.

He had room 43 on the western end; it was one of the rooms that overlooked the Forbidden City and Tiananmen Square. He had been telling himself, every time he came to Beijing, that as soon as he had a couple free months, he would tour the Forbidden City. From what he'd been told, there was so much to see of the temples and palaces of the ancient dynastic rulers, a weekend wouldn't do it. A weekend was almost required to cross Tiananmen Square, the largest in the world at thirty-four acres. A million people had gathered in the square for Mao Zedong's funeral.

He was looking forward to uncapping his bottle of Chivas, pouring a quick one while he watched the activity in the square, then crawling into bed. When he stopped at the front desk for his key, however, there were three messages for him.

In his room, he tossed his jacket on the bed, dug through his suitcase for the scotch, poured an iceless inch in a glass, then picked up the phone.

He tried Deng Mai first, but she was out.

He caught Shana Bricher at their apartment.

"Hi, Shana. This is Doug."

"Hold on, Doug. He's right here."

Bricher took over the phone and said, "H'lo, boss."

"I had a message from you."

"I just wanted to tell you we've got to get something better on the tube. All this opera, documentary, and cultural production is driving me out of my mind. I need something escapist."

"Doing my best, Hoss."

"Second thing I wanted to tell, was that we've got DCT sixty-seven percent on-line. It turned out to be the software problem I predicted. Wickersham's engineers picked up on the glitch right away, and we should be at a hundred percent by tomorrow."

"Tank Cameron's happy?"

"Getting happier by the second."

"Good. Thanks for a super job, Will."

"It's not super until it's done. Then you can give me a gold star."

"We'll do that at noon. Oops. The next day. I've still got a full round of handshaking tomorrow."

"How's it going?"

"Better than I expected. But then, I have trouble reading minds. I may be way off-base."

"Got my fingers crossed."

After hanging up on Bricher, Grant looked at the third message, found the number, and called it. He sat on the edge of the double bed and sipped his whiskey.

Stone answered right away.

"It's ten o'clock. I thought you'd be out chasing skirts."

"I looked at a few skirts, Doug. They all had daddies with shotguns."

"They don't have shotguns in China."

"The licensed hunters do."

"They're hunters, not daddies."

"Well, the prospects were ominous, anyway."

"Are you reporting something important?"

"I met with your Deputy Shang."

"And?"

"She's damned near eighty years old."

"But a brilliant mind, Mickey."

"As a matter of fact, I thought so, too. She was quite charming, and we spent an enjoyable couple hours together."

"Two hours?"

"It took an hour-and-a-half to get past the amenities. I made my pitch, she agreed with me."

"Is she going to do anything about it?"

"Said she'd make some phone calls."

"Marvelous. All it takes is a few phone calls." Grant reported briefly on his own meetings. "This Shao Tsung is a shrewd character, Mickey. I think I got through to him, but I also think I wouldn't want to ever cross him. Anything else?"

"Yeah. I met with Shang just after lunch, and I finagled a pass out of her to tour the nuke reactor. It's located about twenty miles out of Chengdu."

"What? No museum?"

"I'll do that tomorrow. If there is a tomorrow."

"What are you talking about?"

"I don't know much about reactors, Doug, but that thing scares me."

"In what way?"

"I think it's going to leak like a sieve."

Saturday, August 20

Du Fu's Cottage was in the middle of a forty-acre garden overlooking a thick trickle of water called the Huanghua. The cottage was a replica, of course. Du Fu had spent four years in Chengdu in the 8th century, writing 240 poems. Some of his poems and calligraphy were on display.

The Chinese could certainly boast a history with immense chronology involved, Mickey Stone thought.

He also thought he was pretty disgusted with himself.

This morning, he had been to the Temple of Marquis Wu, to the zoo to see the largest collection of giant pandas in the world, and to Dujiang Dam which diverted the Min River into an intricate system of canals to irrigate the region. At the dam was a commemorative display to Li Bing, a scholar who began diverting water for irrigation twenty-two centuries before. Grant was amazed at the longevity of names in China. These people remembered, not only all the generations of their families, but those that had had an impact on their lives.

In the year 4000, he didn't think anyone would gaze upon an eternal quartz-emitting diode plaque emblazoned with the highlights of the life of Michael Ross Stone. And at the rate he was going, there wasn't going to be a wicked, wicked ways exposé of Mickey Stone, either.

He couldn't help but think that, once the Chinese were swamped with a sea of information, they'd start forgetting all these names that really meant something. Who the hell needed to remember Rush Limbaugh or Howard Stern?

It was far better to idolize the names of Du Fu and Li Bing.

As he walked, he heard a crackle of thunder and looked up at the overcast sky. It appeared as if the skies were going to dump at any minute, and he left the grounds to begin searching for a taxi.

It was beginning to sprinkle by the time he climbed under the canvas canopy of a pedicab and directed the driver, "The Minshan."

"*Hai!* Minshan. Minshan."

His driver was soaked through, and Stone's jeans from his knees down were a sponge by the time the pedal-powered rickshaw pulled up in front of the hotel on Renmin Nan Road. He produced some bills and ran for the protection of the lobby.

Stone didn't mind the rain, actually. After the heat and dust of Urümqi and the dry altitude of Lhasa, he welcomed it. The rainfall and the four major rivers (Sichuan meant "four rivers") were the reason Sichuan Province was the breadbasket of China, producing mountains of rice, wheat, corn, potatoes, cotton, sugarcane, tea, and tobacco. After the arid outlands, he was happy to be ensconced in a city that looked as if it has some degree of prosperity.

His hotel was the newest in town, twenty-one stories, with three restaurants, two bars, and a disco. He peeked through the entrance to the disco on his way to the elevator stack. Nothing happening yet. Last night, there had been a fair crowd, including a group of English women. Accompanied, to his disgust, by a group of English men.

In fact, since his arrival, he had been checking the hotel bars nightly. If he couldn't find an exotic playmate, he'd have to settle for a tourist. And he'd found the tourists to be middle-aged, which might or might not have been a deterrent, except that they were escorted by middle-aged husbands or boyfriends.

When someone got around to writing his life story, the China years were going to be awfully dry. One chapter, one page.

On the elevator, he stood in one corner with his sopping jeans dripping on the floor while a German couple spoke to each other in derogatory remarks that he couldn't understand, but suspected were centered on him.

He didn't let it bother him, if it was supposed to, and spent the upward trip lamenting his condition. He was supposed to have been on a flight to Shanghai at nine o'clock, but the airplane decided to go bonkers and get itself grounded. So, now, he was hoping to get out Monday.

He was tired of playing sightseer; he needed action.

Unlocking his door on the eighteenth floor, he entered to find the message light on the phone blinking.

"Why me, Lord?" he echoed Kris Kristofferson.

He picked up and told the English-speaking operator, "I hope you don't have a call for me."

"There is just a message, Mr. Stone."

"From anyone I know."

"A Mr. Wickersham?"

"Ah, good!" If it were Grant, the boss would have another chore for him. "Am I supposed to call him?"

"No, sir. It just says that he will meet you in Guangzhou."

"Guangzhou! Why?"

"He says the facility has gone down, Mr. Stone. Whatever that means."

In Liwan Park, caught inside the curve of Huangsha Road and the Pearl River, Tan Long strolled without apparent care among the gardens. He stopped frequently next to the many lakes and fed the ducks from a bag of popcorn he carried.

It was a sunny day, not too warm, with the hint of cooling showers to come later in the afternoon. Tan was one who enjoyed his free time to the utmost. Despite the impression he might have given his acquaintances and those he worked with, Tan did not labor excessively. When he appeared at one of the stores, he was a whirlwind of activity, probing into inventories, sales records, and the salesmanship of employees. It was difficult, however, for his own superiors to keep an eye on him all of the time because, if he was not en route to a new destination, he devoted much of his day to sitting in his hotel room and writing his copious reports. Furthermore, no manager at a People's Department Store was going to report that Tan Long had not been in the store on such-and-such a day, not if he wished to retain his job.

Today, for example, Tan had consumed a leisurely breakfast, devoted three hours to report writing, another two hours to luncheon, and planned to squander the rest of the day in whatever fashion happened to strike him at the time.

He had but one more chore to accomplish, then he thought he might visit one of the tourist hotels and introduce himself to some unattached female, inviting her to a shopping spree and dinner.

As he neared the north end of the park, Tan found the stone bench he was searching for. He slipped his jacket off and laid it carefully over the back of the bench before sitting down. Placing the popcorn bag on the bench next to him, he rested back and turned his face upward to the sun. To passersby, his eyes might have been closed, but they could not tell behind the oversized dark glasses he wore.

The warmth played over his face and felt particularly good to him.

He had been there less than ten minutes when another approached, leaving the concrete path to sit down next to him.

Tan ignored the newcomer.

And after five minutes, the man got up and left him alone.

And after another five minutes, Tan sat up and reached back for his jacket. He slipped into it, then stood and walked on to the north, toward Zhongshan Road.

He did not forget the popcorn bag.

It was already gone.

Pierre Lefant did not think highly of the city of Shanghai. The virulent atmosphere made his eyes itch and his throat raspy. The show areas—the hotel strip and the government region with their high-rise buildings, the children's palaces, and the model factories shown to visiting tourists and dignitaries—were no disguise for the ills that permeated the rest of the city. Beijing wanted very much for the world to think of Shanghai as a model of socialist charm and success. For anyone who had spent any time at all in the city, the opposite view was the one to be retained.

From the revolution in 1949, when the communists had taken control, the city had steadily gone downhill. The mandates and dictates of the Communist Party, the five years plans, the readjustment plans, had served only to bring decay to what had once been a magnificent city. In ninety percent of the urban area, Lefant saw the results: streets full of potholes; buildings sagging; aimless youth with blank, objectiveless faces wandering about. Where were the teenagers with pockets full of money to buy what the men like Lefant had to sell?

In all of their adjustments to their society, from collectives to communes to "responsibility" (meaning incentive) policies, the Party had only demonstrated, at least for Lefant, that communism did not work. They tried one tactic, and when that did not work, attempted another. Never once, he thought, did they look at the rest of the world to see what did work. Somewhere, the communists thought, there must be a slight deviation of Marx that would prove successful and yet reaffirm the great man. At the moment, small pockets of private enterprise among repair shops and tiny boutiques were allowed. Factory managers could actually fire workers who did not produce. On the collective farms, individual farmers were allowed small plots in which to raise produce for themselves. And yet, Beijing was loath to admit that these were capitalist ventures.

It was such instances as those that gave Lefant hope. Whatever the government wanted to call it on the surface, underneath were those little attempts at free enterprise. Perhaps one day they would reach the surface.

Lefant thought that he would not be present when it happened. The repression had been taking place for so long, allowed by a subservient people, that a hundred years might pass before massive change took place.

These innermost thoughts were never explored publicly, of course. If he allowed his mind to become embroiled in the morality and ethics of modern China, it might well lose its finely tuned focus.

His concentration must be fully placed upon his own goals: To finalize his contract for Media Bureau, first; then to complete his private business transactions; to pocket his small fortune; and to escape the hellhole that was Shanghai. Everything he did must be calculated to preserve what he had hidden away in France and to promote his interests in China. Though Lefant thought he knew where he stood with Minister Jiang, Lefant would not trust the man for an instant. It was a highly politicized environment, and Deng Mai was resourceful. She might well upset the apple-cart.

For that reason, he was standing, for the third Saturday in a row, in the Shanghai No. 1 Department Store on Nanjing Road. This Saturday, he had chosen to examine stationery. As a center for printing, Shanghai did produce paper of amazingly good quality.

And this Saturday, finally, he saw her.

As she came down the aisle, Lefant held up a single sheet of paper, as if attempting to discern its watermark in the poor light. He stepped backward, and his heel came down directly on her instep.

"Aiie!"

He dropped the box of paper and spun around.

"Oh, my God! Madame, I am so sorry!" He spoke French.

Her eyes were squinched shut, and she danced on one foot, attempting to massage the top of the other with her hand.

Lefant reached forward and found her elbow, attempted to stabilize her.

"Leave me alone!"

He pulled his hand back. *"Oui, madame."*

"Ohhh," she moaned.

"I beg a single pardon of you, for my million apologies, madame."

As her pain subsided, she apparently became aware that they were speaking French. Perhaps she noticed his magnificent Parisian accent.

Perhaps he noticed, for the first time, since this was the only time he had seen her in person, that she was truly a beautiful woman.

And his own age.

"It will be all right," she said. "I will walk again within a week."

"Ah, you are a countryman! How could I be so clumsy? Come, we will seek medical attention for you."

She placed her foot on the floor, then moved her weight onto it.

"That will be unnecessary."

"Then I must buy you coffee and get you off your feet. At least for a short period of recuperation?"

She eyed him speculatively, her lustrous eyes gauging his worth. "You are Parisian?"

"Oui, madame."

"And what do you do in Shanghai?"

He told her.

"Ah! Monsieur Lefant?"

"At your service."

"My daughter has spoken of you."

"Your daughter? But you cannot have children!"

She smiled, a radiant glow in the dimly lit store, and brushed away his compliment with a wave of her gloved hand.

"That was tactful, but unnecessary. My daughter is Deng Mai."

"Ah, but of course!"

"I will let you buy me coffee, Mr. Lefant, but you must be my crutch."

He offered his arm, and the two of them left the store, Yvonne Deng hobbling perhaps more than was required under the circumstances.

At an outdoor cafe a block away—he had decided on its location earlier—he helped her into a chair and issued orders to a waiter he had already tipped.

Almost instantly, a good Napoleon brandy and hot and aromatic coffee were delivered to the table.

She picked up the snifter and inhaled.

"It is a trifle early in the day, Mr. Lefant."

"But you have suffered an injury, madame. You must consider it medicinal."

"Very well."

The two of them spent forty minutes becoming acquainted, reliving common memories of French hotels, restaurants, and spectacles. There was no one person in France that they had in common, but there were names of relatives. She told him a bit about her life in Shanghai.

"And what is your life like, Mr. Lefant? Your life in Shanghai?"

"It is," he smiled, "mostly one of worries."

"Worries!"

"That is my job. I must worry about things."

"I should be so fortunate that someone would pay me for my worries. What is it you worry about?"

"At the moment, the insidious delays that interfere with the schedules my superiors have assigned for me."

He signalled for more coffee and brandy.

"My daughter has said nothing to me of delays."

"Can that be true? This rocket thing has my ulcers in an uproar."

"The rocket . . . oh, that was resolved this morning."

"You are fooling an old man."

"Not so old, I think. No, Mai was told that her project was back on schedule."

"Wonderful! You have no idea how that relieves me, madame."

Already, the cost of several drinks was paying off!

He looked at his watch.

"I am holding you from your shopping, madame. Again, I find myself at fault for your distress."

"Nonsense. I frequently shop to merely see. I much rather enjoy a decent conversation in French."

"As do I," he confessed, thinking that Shanghai would not be so horrible with a woman like this. "You would not be free for dinner, by any good fortune?"

"Dinner? You need not pay forever for stepping on my toe."

"I insist," he told her.

In the great hall at Fudan University, the final speaker of the afternoon, the economist who had been at Yvonne Deng's dinner party, completed his thesis with agonizing slowness. In familiar company, and when challenged, as Grant had challenged him, the learned professor could be witty and stimulating. In this public arena, however, he espoused the dogma of the Party. The audience, composed of scholars, factory managers, and commercial leaders, had all heard it before.

The Shining Hour is coming, as long as we all adhere to the party line.

In recent years, Deng Mai had found it increasingly difficult to have faith in any shining hour. Because of the equipment Grant had installed at the headquarters of Shanghai Star, Deng

Mai was a little more informed than she might have been. Though Shanghai Star's nonmilitary system was not yet in place, the antennas on the roof could easily be aligned on other satellites in orbit. It was a capability, she was certain, that the Ministry of Information was not aware of. Grant had taught her how to program the antennas. And she had spent many a night in her office, guiltily searching the skies for news broadcasts from Russia, Japan, and the United States.

She knew of the economic chaos in Russia and the other republics once belonging to the communist Soviet Union. And without Russia to prop them up with foreign aid, the smaller communist states were reeling in confusion. Central American revolutions were stymied without Russian arms. Cuba no longer received its allotment of oil, and rationing was strict. The Cuban people were starving.

Politics was politics, and yet, politics was also economics. To survive as a socialist state—as Deng Mai believed it should, China must adapt, using what it could of the old, but also embracing new strategies. It was that vision that propelled her. She firmly believed she could assist her country in its quest to become part of the new world order. In information, there was power, but there was also learning. Her people could learn to survive, if she could present them with the information.

For that reason, the dogmatic repetition of teetering economic policy no longer encouraged her. As she stood to leave, she wondered how many of these industrial and commercial leaders still believed what they heard in the education seminars.

"Mai! Mai!"

Turning, she saw Liu Baio standing in the aisle. She waved at him and began to make her way toward him.

Liu managed a plastics-manufacturing plant in one of the industrial parks to the north of the city. They had attended school together—up until she left for her advanced education in France, and he had once been an ardent suitor. She found him attractive, but . . . somehow plebeian. He had never married.

"Hello, Baio," she said when she reached him.

"I had hoped to see you," he told her as they moved toward the exit.

She tensed, afraid that she would once again have to decline a social invitation. Though she liked Liu, she could not imagine a future with him. Not when there were more animated men in the world, men who assumed risks to accomplish their goals.

Like Douglas Grant? A year ago, she would have banished the thought. Now, as they fought side by side, and perhaps as a result of Yvonne Deng's resistance to Grant, she occasionally allowed herself to think of Grant from a new perspective.

"How have you been?"

"Worked to death, what else?" He smiled. "Look, Mai, I would like to ask you some questions. You do not have to answer them, of course."

"What kinds of questions?"

"Let us wait until we are outside."

Once they reached the doors of the auditorium, Liu led her through the lobby, then down the stairs to the front walk. They stepped off into the grass, away from the people milling about, making small talk.

She saw her driver and car waiting for her and raised a hand to let him know she would not be long.

"What is it, Baio?"

"You are travelling in heady circles now, Mai."

"Not so heady, I think."

She knew, however, that Liu was probably feeling a little defeated. It was unlikely that he would advance to any position beyond the one he held at his plastics factory, and she was managing director of an internationally watched program. Her name appeared frequently in international as well as Chinese newspapers. He was a classmate, but he would be feeling outdistanced.

"Well, at least I think of your new friends as exalted. What I am getting to, Mai, is a personal concern."

"Personal?"

"Not that kind of personal, I am afraid. I may have given up that quest. No, I am concerned about my factory, my workers, my job."

She was surprised. "In what way?"

"There is talk of unrest in Beijing."

"I have heard of it, and I believe it is just talk."

"Do you have any idea of what feuds involving the ministries of labor and materials can do to me?"

"I do. I know that disruptions in far places can reflect on your quotas."

"That is what scares me. I know that you know these people, Mai. I know that you can ease the tensions."

"Me! Baio, I oversee technical workers. I do not tell ministers how to perform."

"They are lining up on two sides of a great argument, the conservatives and the reformers," he insisted. "My supervisor has told me so. And you are at the center of the argument."

"It is not in my power to change their thinking."

"I believe it is."

"What would you have me do, Baio?" she asked.

"Do not resist them. Do not insist on reforms."

"Do you know what you are saying? Many years ago, you insisted you were going to create a better China. Have you changed your mind?"

"The PRC will evolve, Mai. It is not necessary to push it."

He left her standing in the middle of the grass plot, feeling . . . what? That she was a traitor? That, because of her, men like Liu could lose their jobs, their futures? They were at places in their lives where stability was more important to them than musical entertainment and world news beamed in from Canada. Liu Baio had moved from idealism to pragmatism. He was no longer the promise of China; he was the establishment, hanging on for dear life to a concreteness that he understood.

She felt sorry for him, but knew that if she had to make a choice between the stability that let her society stagnate, and a pandemonium that allowed millions to make their own choices, she would have to opt for chaos.

It would be much more difficult than she had imagined when she pursued the managing director's position with such simple-minded abandon.

Shaking her head with regret, Deng walked out to the curb and her Nissan Pathfinder. It was not hers, naturally, but was one supplied to Shanghai Star as part of the contract with Megatronics.

She got in, and the driver found his way off the campus and eventually onto Zhongshan Bei Road, a boulevard that ringed the core of the city, becoming Zhongshan Xi on the west and

Zhongshan Nan on the south. When he reached Yanan Road, he turned east for three blocks, then pulled up in front of the main doors. Dismissing him until nine o'clock, she went inside and took the elevator to the sixth floor. The security ritual took four minutes, despite the guards knowing who she was.

It was after five o'clock, and her secretaries were gone. Pushing open the right door of the pair to her office, she stepped inside.

And immediately knew that something was wrong.

Someone had been in here.

Someone who was not supposed to be.

Grant, or one of Grant's people?

She did not know.

She felt the departed presence as if it were the aroma of an unknown flower.

Moving cautiously, she walked around the room, examining the paintings, the walls, the furniture. When she reached her desk, she opened each small drawer in the brass leg supporting the plate-glass top.

Nothing had been disturbed.

She turned to the computer credenza and turned the machine on. In seconds, it came to life, but the screen displayed no messages that it had been tampered with, as it would have if someone had attempted to circumvent her passwords.

Deng stood behind her desk and surveyed the room.

It was all in her mind.

She was upset by the seminar and by Liu's warning.

Her eyes travelled across the Left Bank scenes, moved to the opposite wall, where she had just hung a print of a Manet landscape, moved on . . . moved back, found the glass table in front of the couch.

And the bowl of orchids.

Except that there was now only one orchid floating on the surface of the water. And it was black.

"You cannot call me here!"

"Relax, Pyotr. This will be a short conversation. Where did you get the name Chiang?"

"From his blotter! It was written on the blotter."

"Sytenko's blotter?"

"Yes!"

"And that's all? You don't know the connection?"

"I am not a spy! You said to look; I looked."

"Well, take it easy. Were there any more names written on the blotter?"

"I don't know, yes. Several."

"You don't recall them?"

"I was in a rush. I had no time. I should not have been in his office. He will discover—"

"Just one name?"

"Not a name. It was . . . it was . . . the Frenchman. That's all!"

Arkady Makov hung up.

And Suretsov was no closer to knowing anything substantial. Why, in this deck of cards, could he not have been dealt a decent spy in the office of the trade attaché?

And why could Makov not just keep his mouth shut? Why go and involve ITAR-Tass in some scheme that Makov could not prove, anyway?

Because middle-aged Arkady Makov was a patriot, and he did not like what he saw in the park. He did not know what he had seen, but it was distasteful to him.

And he did not know where to turn. Any of his superiors could be involved. Call the man at the news agency which had widely publicized its reform. That was what the Americans did. Get the *Washington Post* on the case.

Get Superman. Get Clark Kent.

It was getting dark outside, but Suretsov did not get up to turn on the lights.

He was thinking about the Frenchman.

There were probably hundreds of Frenchmen in China, attempting to do business with the government.

The problem was, Suretsov had met only one of them.

Grant was feeling out of sorts. The gang at the Dallas Cowboy Cafe was becoming boisterous, so after he finished his chicken-fried steak—which tasted more like chicken than steak, he went out the back way and got into his truck.

He had hoped to have dinner with Mai tonight, had asked her after returning from Beijing, but had been turned down. No excuses, no alibis, just no dinner.

So it was chicken-fried steak again.

He cranked up the engine and pulled out of his parking slot. Nosing his way across the sidewalk from the alley, he avoided running over anyone, worked his way into traffic, and drove south. After waiting for the light at Yanan Road, he crossed the intersection, drove past the Shanghai Star building, and turned into the parking lot at the back of the building. A security guard had to open the barrier for him.

There were a few cars in the lot. Some people, both Americans and Chinese, liked to work late or had weekend duty. Beginning October 1, there would be more cars in the lot on weekends.

Using his plastic passcard, he ran the magnetic strip through the slot on the wall beside the back door. The door buzzed and he let himself in. He took the wide corridor to the front of the building, noted that the restaurant was hosting a fair crowd, and then pressed the call button for the elevator.

The car was slow in arriving, but when it did, he stepped aboard and pressed the button for the fifth floor. Rising past the unused floors, 2, 3, and 4, Grant thought that within ten days, after Jiang announced the winning contractor, those floors would be a beehive. The contractor—and Grant hoped it was Crest and CIS—would be moving in and setting up shop. He supposed that the in-country Chinese president would locate himself on the fourth floor, as high as he could get for the best possible view.

Stepping out of the elevator on his floor, Grant noted lights in the satcom section and in Wickersham's software area. A few engineers were burning the Saturday-night oil. Frequently, they were men who hadn't brought families with them, and they would just as soon be working on MI projects, or maybe their own designs.

Grant frequently purchased ideas developed independently by MI software engineers. One of those ideas, a billing system, was currently in its final testing phases. Shanghai Star, like other industries in the current five-year plan, wasn't to be a free social service. It was to be a profit center for the government. Users would get monthly billings, and that task in itself was a daunting one. The database had to ultimately handle 600 million records. Within the first year alone, they expected to be mailing 100 million statements a month. The paperwork and the flow of money was going to be enormous. Just tracking those who didn't pay their bills and cutting off service would require a staff of thirty people.

Shanghai Star was creating nearly fifteen thousand jobs systemwide, most of them nontechnical and low paying, but the job creation was important to Beijing, also. The ripple effect—the requirements for paper, electrical service, advertising, cleaning, transportation—was expected to produce another hundred thousand jobs in other industries throughout the nation. It would, Grant thought, take some of those aimless teenagers off the street before the gangs could get to them.

At higher levels, the number of technical, artistic, and creative positions would also expand.

Those jobs, just a splash in the pan within the enormous population of the PRC, still poured more money into the economy. Grant had always known that the positive effects went far beyond Shanghai Star. He just hoped that battles over ideology didn't jeopardize the whole thing. If it required more hobnobbing with the politicos on his part, he was ready to take it on.

He felt good about his past week's work. The telephone call from General Hua to Will Bricher this morning, simply stating that the ShangStar Two launch date was August 24, had been the reward. There was no indication at all of what battles had taken place on the Information Advisory Committee, or what calls from State Council members had helped to reverse the earlier decisions of the supervising ministers.

There was a downside, of course, and Grant was well aware of it. Having to shift into reverse had cost those ministers some face. And if Jiang Guofeng were responsible for prodding them in that direction in the first place, Jiang would be incensed at the new development. He would also know that Grant and Deng were behind it, and he'd be keeping his finger close to the trigger.

Grant pushed open the door to Diantha Parker's office and was startled to see someone sitting on the couch. In the dim light produced by some of the light-emitting diodes on computer peripherals, it took him a second to realize it was Deng.

"Mai?"

She stood up. "Hello, Douglas."

"What are you doing here in the dark? Is something wrong?"

"I called your apartment, then the cafe. They thought you were coming here. And yes, something is definitely wrong."

"Come on in." Grant put his hand on her back—the first time he had done so—and guided her into his office.

He thought he detected a small tremor running through her.

He snapped on the overhead lights. The brilliant fluorescents bathed the room with light, which he thought might be more appropriate under the circumstance. A little less romantic than the afterglow of the city seeping through the window. A little less scary as far as intrigue went.

"What happened?" he asked as she sat down.

She took the chair next to his desk, so he settled into his desk chair.

She told him about the black orchid.

"One of your orchids didn't just up and die?"

"No. This is a fresh flower. It is specially bred."

"Beyond the supposition that someone got onto your floor to place it there, you see this as bad?"

"It is a bad omen, Douglas."

"Meant as a warning?"

"Yes, I believe so."

Grant sat back in his chair. There were a lot of superstitions running through the Chinese psyche. Many homes had altars to various of the gods seeking protection from misfortune. Despite the Communist Party's doctrine, there was still a deep religious belief in much of the population. He would not have thought Mai susceptible to the influence of superstition or religion, but he was not in a position to know.

"How would someone breach the security procedures?" she asked.

"I'm not certain that they did, though I'll have some of my people take another look. More likely, someone on your staff was paid off to deliver a flower. It might be possible to quiz the guards and see what was brought through security."

"However it was delivered, Douglas, the implication is clear."

"It is?" Grant, sure as hell, wasn't clear on the implication.

"If I pursue the course I have chosen, I will be killed."

Grant was shocked. To cover it, he leaned forward and put his elbows on the desktop. "Oh, now, Mai, I don't think . . ."

"You are a *gweilo*, Douglas. The Green-Eyed Devil. You do not understand how seriously these signals are to be taken."

"Well, maybe I don't. But couldn't it just mean that your job is in jeopardy?"

"No. It is directed at me."

If all of this were true, someone was getting downright intense. Grant didn't have enough China experience. He certainly wasn't an old China hand as many of the expatriate British, Scots, and Australian China traders whom he had met were.

"I know some people," he said, "who could recommend some reliable bodyguards. Maybe we should give you some additional security?"

"What will protect me is my backing down to Jiang, accepting his recommendation of Sung Wu as the contractor's China executive."

"You think Jiang is behind this black orchid?"

"Who else? He suffered a terrible loss of respect in the battle over the launch schedule. I knew it would be so, and yet I proceeded along that course."

Grant caught her eyes and held them in his gaze for a long moment. Again, it was as if their conspiracy were deepening. He searched the dark pools of her eyes for clues, and anything else in his life slid to the back of his mind. The precarious position of MI did not matter. His ex-wife's cavorting with all of his ex-worldly goods did not matter. All those good people who had abandoned secure jobs to join him didn't matter. His resolve to remain neutral in a politicized world evaporated.

"What do you want to do, Mai? Whatever it is, I'm behind you all the way."

She took a moment before saying, "I cannot say at this point, Douglas. I will need to think about it. You, however, need not risk—"

"Let's not worry about my risks. I want to do what's right."

"Douglas . . ."

The damned telephone rang.

He looked at it, and he was going to let it ring itself to death.

Deng said, "It might be important. Only someone with your extension number can get past the voice mail after hours."

Grabbing the receiver, he rasped, "Grant."

"Mr. Grant, this is Vladimir Suretsov."

The damned press. He forced himself to be civil. "What is it, Mr. Suretsov?"

"I am in the Shanghai Dragon. I wonder if I could come up for a moment?"

"Ah, it's Saturday night, Vladimir. I—"

"Please? It is important, I think."

Grant gave in. "All right. Come on up."

After he hung up, Deng asked, "Suretsov?"

"A Russian correspondent."

"I should leave."

"No, please stay. It might encourage him to bail out quicker."

Suretsov appeared in the doorway a few minutes later, and Grant could tell he was immediately uncertain the moment he saw Deng.

She stood up and offered her hand, which he took.

"Do you remember me, Director? We met briefly at a party given by Mr. Crest."

"Ah, yes! I do remember you, Mr. Suretsov."

"I still want to interview you sometime."

"We can arrange that."

"Have a chair, Vladimir," Grant said.

He sat in the other chair in front of the desk.

"Doug," he asked, "do you know Chiang Qing?"

Grant thought a minute. "I've heard the name, but I can't place it."

"I know of her," Deng said. "She leads the People's Underground."

Suretsov turned to Deng. "She is quite an admirer of yours, Director. In fact, she is preparing to mount a big campaign in support of Shanghai Star. I couldn't read the big-character posters, but that was the impression I received in talking to her."

"She has never taken an overly aggressive stance before."

"I think she may surprise everyone this time. Anyway, I was hoping to find a connection between her and the Russian consulate in Beijing."

"Why is that, Vladimir?" Grant asked.

"Between us?"

Grant and Deng both nodded, and Suretsov told them an improbable tale of a Russian who was, or could be, in love with an American woman, and who had apparently taken a payoff from a Caucasian man.

"The only thing I have going for me," Suretsov said, "is that Chiang Qing's name was found in his office. Oh, there is also a reference to a Frenchman."

"A Frenchman?" Deng asked him.

"That could be the man making the payoff."

"There are a lot of Frenchmen in China," Grant said.

"Yes, I know. The only one I have met is Pierre Lefant. I think you know him better than I."

"What would Lefant be doing with the Russians?" Grant asked.

"That, I do not know. I wondered if you had some ideas."

"Off the record?" Grant reversed the promise of confidentiality.

"Of course. This entire conversation is confidential."

"I think Lefant has his hand in several games. The Media Bureau job may be just one of them. I'd look into his background and see what else he's involved in. Or, he may just be trying to sell a programming package in Russia as well as in China."

"I had considered that, but Sytenko—that is the Russian trade attaché—does not have anything to do with telecommunications."

"But he might know someone who does," Grant said.

"Yes, true. I will examine that."

"None of this has anything to do with Shanghai Star, does it?" Deng asked.

"I do not think so, Director. I was merely hoping that Douglas knew more of Chiang or Lefant than I do."

"You really hurting for stories?" Grant asked him.

Suretsov smiled. "Stories for which I can accumulate evidence, yes."

"Take a look at the new nuclear reactors."

"Nuclear reactors?"

"They're portable units." He related Stone's concern for the design. "When you mentioned a Frenchman, that was the first thing I thought of. And according to Mickey, those reactors are based on a Russian design. Something called the Topaz?"

"Yes, I know of the Topaz." Suretsov considered the implications, then said, "This is very interesting, Doug."

"Mickey thinks it's more frightening than interesting," Grant told him.

"This would come under the purview of the Ministry of Energy, would it not?"

"Minister Pai Dehuai," Deng said.

A good old friend of Jiang Guofeng, Grant recalled Mai telling him.

Wednesday, August 24

The odor of lighter fluid and soot still permeated the top floor of the Guangzhou Facility of the Shanghai Star Communications Network.

The seven damaged consoles had been removed, and the walls and ceiling had been repainted, but the gaps in the row of consoles made Mickey Stone mad as hell. He had a reverence for finely crafted equipment, and his policies prohibited even the presence of a soft drink or a mug of coffee because accidents happened.

To have someone deliberately spray lighter fluid into the MI Model 1001 units and then torch them, was unfathomable. In China's past, the disobedience of a son to a father was punishable by death, and Stone thought the same sentence should apply to anyone playing with fire around his machines.

He and Wickersham were sprawled on chairs in the facility director's office. Through the glass wall of the office, Stone could see across the hall into the computer room. The seven gaps kept his ire at peak. Stone held a phone in his hand, waiting for his call to go through. He had placed it twelve minutes before, but the system in use was forty years out of date, and the signals crawled on hands and knees along copper wires to a—for God's sake—manual switchboard where the operator was required to dial the overseas call for him.

He moved the phone away from his ear and shook it angrily.

"Patience, Mickey," Wickersham advised.

The other man, who had assumed a position of importance behind the desk, smiled politely. He was some kind of commander or detective with the police.

"Go on, Inspector," Wickersham said.

"As I was saying, gentlemen, we have interviewed everyone with access to the computer room."

"Five Americans, two Brits, and eight Chinese, right?" Stone asked.

"That is correct, Mr. Stone. And to date, we—"

"One of them's your brother, isn't it?"

The policeman's face did not change expression. "A second cousin."

He waited for Stone to say something more, and when he didn't, went on, "To date, we find that none of the persons have any possible motive for sabotaging the equipment. Of the fifteen, eleven had opportunity, but again, the reasons. . . ."

"What was the ignition device?" Wickersham asked.

"It was a small spark plug, connected to a battery, with the connection closed by a clock device. The spark burned a hole in a bladder, probably a balloon."

"How long?"

"From the time it was set until it ignited? Our experts judge that it was not greater than an hour. It could have been longer, but the lighter fluid would have evaporated more and lost some of its potency."

"Eleven people were in and out of that room in the hour before it went off?"

"That is correct, sir."

"What's your next step?"

"Well, sir, I don't see that anything overly productive—"

"Don't see it? Or aren't willing to try?" Stone's rage was barely controlled by instinct; he wasn't consciously trying to control it.

"Sir—"

"Hold on." Stone pulled the receiver to his ear.

"Your party is now available, sir."

"My eternal appreciation."

"That you, Mickey?"

"Me, C.C. How you fixed for Model 1001s?"

"The big one? Hell, I've got . . . hang on . . . two on hand, two in production."

"I need five."

"Babe, you got to be kidding!"

"Some asshole torched eight at Guangzhou. I've spent the last two days rebuilding one, and I think I'll recover a couple more, swiping parts back and forth, but I've got to have five, and damned soon."

"How soon?"

"The major system test is September fifteenth, Calvin. I'll need at least three days of on-site testing. More time if you let me have it."

"Ah, shit! It'll disrupt my whole damned line, but we'll get 'em out. Who we billing this to?"

"To the Star. We're damned sure not picking up the tab."

"Okay, babe, here's your invoice number."

Stone leaned over toward the desk and scrawled the numbers on the back of a paperback book as Calvin Jackson read them off.

Stone hung up the phone and said, "That's fifty-five grand, what with shipping and all. Someone's not going to be happy. They'll be especially unhappy if we don't find out who did it, Inspector."

The Chinese cop remained impassive. "We are doing everything we can."

Stone turned to Wickersham. "Best solution, Curt. Fire all of them."

"All of them?"

"Just the Chinese. I'm sure of my boys and girls."

A flicker of some kind of interest passed over the inspector's eyes. Maybe he was considering the consequences of his cousin losing his first decent-paying job and moving back in with the inspector and his wife and ten kids. Maybe he was considering the value of the cousin's job against some suggestion he had received from someone higher in command to not press too hard on this investigation.

He sat up behind the manager's desk. "Gentlemen, before innocent people come under a cloud of suspicion as a result of a massive termination, let me examine the evidence once again. Perhaps one of my subordinates missed something."

"Damned good idea, Inspector," Stone told him.

* * *

At ten minutes past eleven in the morning, the big digital clock on the wall read 04:31:52. The clock tracked to the hundredth of a second.

Will Bricher had been invited to sit with General Hua Min in the crow's-nest compartment high above the mission-control room. In addition to the two of them, a major and a captain, both aides to Hua, were present.

"More tea, Mr. Bricher?" the major asked.

"Thanks, no. Times like this, I get overly anxious about finding a men's room."

The major smiled and settled back in his chair.

The digits dropped off the clock like maple syrup.

The general looked sideways at him. "I am very certain of this one, Mr. Bricher. I personally inspected every compartment aboard the vehicle. There is not one pair of pliers or screwdriver lodged in any crevice."

"I am sure of it, General."

The umbilicals had dropped away several minutes before, and as he watched the screens now, the gantry slowly moved away from the rocket, leaving it standing on its own. At one minute until launch, white vapor billowed beneath the first stage.

Bricher held his breath.

Red flame appeared in the white mist.

Boiled.

Plumes of flame and vapor shot sideways from the launch pit.

The Long March 3 rose a fraction.

Hesitated.

"We have launch," the launch director announced over the speaker system, in *putonghua* and in English.

It didn't look to Bricher like . . .

The rocket disappeared.

Shot upward.

The camera took a millisecond to catch up, then centered the picture. The Long March 3 leaned over, taking a new direction, still climbing, gathering speed quickly. In seconds, the rocket body disappeared from view, and the camera tracked it only by the long white plume spouting from the main-rocket motor.

Three minutes into the launch, a camera on a chase plane took over, and the rocket was easier to see.

"One minute until first-stage separation."

Bricher let out his breath.

"I am happy that you decided to breathe again," Hua told him.

"I'm happy, too, General."

The stage separations went smoothly, and at 11:47 A.M., the mission director in some other building announced the Long March in its first orbit. Two hours from now, another controlled rocket burn would insert it into its final geostationary orbit above China. Once in that orbit, the payload would separate from the payload bay, and the antennas would deploy.

God willing.

Bricher was not in the least worried about the final adjustments. Getting the hummer off the ground had been his main worry.

"General," he said, "let's you and me, the major and the captain, all go into town and have lunch. I could use a glass of the local wine."

"Very well, Mr. Bricher. Your invitation is kindly accepted."

As they left the crow's nest, Hua told him in a hushed voice, "You understand that this is only one of the battles, Mr. Bricher? The war is still to be won."

"Yes, sir, I do. However, this is my battle. Some other general gets to do the rest of it."

The same aide to General Hua who had called her to tell her of the successful launch, called back at two o'clock in the afternoon to announce the successful separation of the satellite and the deployment of the antennas.

Deng thanked him profusely, then called Diantha with the news. Grant was in a meeting, but Parker sounded joyful and said she would pass the message along.

She felt very much relieved.

Checking her watch, she saw that she had an hour before the Consortium of Information Services presentation. CIS and Media Bureau Limited had switched their presentation days with her approval. Pierre Lefant had begged for the extension because of some problem with his interactive computing program.

She used ten minutes of her hour to review the last draft of the letter Miss Jiangyou had prepared. It was addressed to the Minister of Information, with copies to each of the advisory committee members. It was also written in Chinese characters, with careful attention taken with the selection of each character. Chinese writing could be very subtle, with different shades of meaning attached, as a result of the fifty thousand characters available. Though only three thousand were used in normal correspondence, those with a larger command of the characters could be devious.

She concentrated on the content. To head the National News Channel, she had recommended a man currently an editor at the Xinhua News Agency. He was young for the post—thirty-five, but capable. She also knew that he was disenchanted with his current position as a result of the strictures on reporting directed by both the Premier's office and the five-member Standing Committee of the Politburo.

For Managing Director of the Shanghai Star Entertainment Division, Deng's recommendation would come as another surprise to the ministry. Susan Li Quan was Guangzhouese, but had acted in motion pictures and on television in Hong Kong, then in the United States and Great Britain. In Hollywood, she had directed and produced films, though not films with large budgets. At fifty-six, she had assumed a teaching position at the University of Beijing. Deng was confident that Li could strike a moderate position in her management of domestic productions.

She had spent months deliberating her selection for the national chief-executive position for the winning contractor. She had compiled a list of fifteen potential candidates and had managed to meet each of them in a social situation without any of them realizing that they were under scrutiny. From that first screening, she had pared her list to five and invited each of them to her office to discuss the potential of the position. Three had been frightened immediately by the national exposure. Of the remaining two, she had selected Ming Xueliang. His background was not entertainment or news, which she did not consider a priority for the job. Rather, she was seeking someone with exemplary qualities of administration and a sense of fairness. Ming, presently a managing director of consumer goods, based in Beijing, filled those criteria well, she thought. As another plus, he was sixty years old. Those on the advisory committee revered age as suggestive of wisdom.

No matter the moderate stance of her choices, except perhaps for the National News Channel director candidate, her slate was likely to be interpreted in the ministry as highly reformist since they would be compared to the list Jiang had prepared.

Her candidates were to meet with Maynard Crest after his presentation today. On Friday, they would meet with Pierre Lefant. She had no idea how either man would react, but she sensed they would respond favorably. Especially since each man had already met the men on Jiang's roster.

Deng knew that, as soon as she posted this letter, she would have drawn yet another line—a much bolder one—between herself and Jiang. It would be simple to endorse his recommendation and hope to build a working relationship with the old men in power. The simple solution had no happy prospects, however. She knew none of the men would work with her and none would be wooed by her arguments.

She shuddered to think what would become of Shanghai Star's promise if Sung Wu were appointed chieftain of the programming coming from the West.

Her intercom buzzed.

Pressing the button, she said, "Yes?"

"Your mother is on the line, Director."

"Thank you." She pressed the blinking button. "Yes, Mama?"

"You have considered our conversation this morning, Mai?"

"I have." They had discussed her choices. Her mother had urged caution.

"And?"

"I am proceeding with my heart *and* mind, Mama."

"The consequences could be severe."

"You knew that also, thirty-five years ago, did you not?"

After a silence that nearly grew unbearable, Yvonne Deng said, "Did you know that I still retain my French passport?"

"No, Mama. I did not."

"And that you have a French passport?"

"Mama! What in the world . . . ?"

"I have kept my options open. You should know that you also have options."

Leave her country? It was not fathomable.

But there was the black orchid.

"I will bear that in mind, Mama."

"Do so. Further, I will not be home for dinner. *Monsieur* Lefant and I are going to the Fangshan Tang."

The restaurant specialized in Qing imperial recipes served by waitresses dressed in Qing dynasty costumes.

"Lefant? How did you meet him, Mama?"

"We ran into each other."

"Mama, be careful of him," she said, thinking of her conversation with Grant and Suretsov.

"Don't be a child! I am quite capable of enjoying myself with a charming man."

She hung up.

Deng Mai was troubled, but after looking at her watch, opened the top drawer in the pedestal and removed her pen and inkstone. With carefully drawn flourishes, she signed her name to the letter in Chinese characters.

Depressing the intercom bar, she said, "Miss Jiangyou, you may retrieve the letter, make copies, and post them."

Jiang stood outside the viewing room on the seventh floor of the Shanghai Star tower with several members of the advisory committee. Most sipped tea provided by Maynard Crest's subordinates while they waited for the presentation to begin.

There were actually two gatherings of the advisory committee. Jiang was talking with those he considered his closest friends, and three meters away, others of the committee were engaged in conversation. Jiang was painfully aware that there were seven men in the other group, precisely the number of votes that had gone against him in the discussion of the rocket schedule. He was also aware that Shao Tsung stood with the other group. Where that man stood was where the army stood.

It was not a good sign, and Jiang believed in signs.

Near the other door to the viewing room was a small knot of men and women, and each wore a badge they had received when passing through security on the sixth floor. The badges read: VISITOR—MEDIA.

Jiang was perturbed by this revelation. He had certainly not authorized media attendance at the presentations. In fact, he had not thought about it at all. It would be, he thought, just like Deng to spring this on him without warning. It could only add to the pressure on the members of the committee to know that their final decision would be second-guessed by the reporters. And unfortunately, he noted, the international press was involved. There were several Caucasians and Japanese among the correspondents. As they talked, laughing frequently, he heard Australian accents and someone speaking phrases of Spanish.

To complain now would make matters worse. The correspondents would like nothing more than to blare that the Minister of Information had denied them access to something as simple as a vendor's presentation.

While he fumed, one of the men detached himself from the group and approached him.

He forced the automatic smile to his face, then found that the man was aimed, not for him, but for Pai Dehuai, standing next to him.

Pai was almost a brother to Jiang. They had grown up together and attended the same schools. Pai was his brother-in-law by virtue of his marriage to Jiang's sister, and he wore his success as a bureaucrat well. His suits were tailored to his fit frame, and his face was smooth, as if no worries were allowed to crease his brow.

The reporter addressed him, "Minister Pai, I am Vladimir Suretsov, representing the ITAR-Tass News Agency."

"Yes, Mr. Suretsov?"

"Minister, a matter of some concern has come to my attention."

"Relative to?"

"The portable nuclear reactors provided by Nuclear Power Limited of France."

"Ah, yes! Six of them have arrived in the country, four are on-site, and we expect to activate the first two, at Lhasa and Chengdu, the first of next week. We expect grand things of them."

"Are you convinced of the design integrity, Minister?"

"What? Design integrity? Naturally. What nonsense are you speaking?"

"I have been told by someone who knows that there is a likelihood that these reactors will leak radiation into the atmosphere."

"Absolute rubbish! Who is this supposedly learned informant?"

The Russian ignored the question, a tactic Jiang would not have allowed.

"Has the International Atomic Energy Agency approved these reactors?"

"Of cou—" Pai halted himself in midword.

Like any good politician, he would not utter an outright lie. "That is, I am sure they have been certified. It was taken care of by the Atomic Energy Bureau."

"Who would I speak to at the bureau?" Suretsov asked.

Pai gave him a name, and Suretsov thanked him for his time, then went back to join the other correspondents.

"What is that all about?" Jiang asked.

"I am not certain, Guofeng. I will have to look into it."

"Agitation is what it is. Yellow journalists hope to dig muck from any rumor."

Pai settled his gaze on Jiang. "I am certain that is the extent of it, Guofeng."

Zhou Ziyang sat with the reporters through the full five hours of the event. He would not presume to have the stature to sit with the ministers, and he was gratified to be present at all.

His timid call to Director Deng in the morning, asking for permission to attend, had elicited a gracious response, and when he arrived on the sixth floor, surprised at the security precautions, a visitor's badge had been waiting with his name on it. She told him that she had also invited Chiang Qing, who had declined the invitation.

Chiang may have been afraid to confront the Minister of Information. Zhou had been seeing more and more posters with the People's Underground signature appear on the streets. His contacts told him similar posters were going up in Beijing,

Chengdu, and Guangzhou. Compared with his own posters—exhorting the ministry to allow free expression—Chiang's were downright inflammatory.

The People's Underground accused Jiang personally of cowardice, the ministry of repressing human rights, and the advisory committee of refusing to acknowledge the rest of the world. The Underground called for Jiang's resignation and the totally uncontrolled international interchange of information. Zhou thought the campaign worthy of a true rebel, and he also knew he would not have dared to go so far.

Chiang had never before taken such an impassioned position. While Zhou was pleased to have such a fervent ally, he feared for her safety. He also feared that, to maintain his own integrity with his membership, he was forced to follow her lead. His assistants were preparing mock-ups of a more strongly worded big-character poster.

The presentation did not consume the full five hours. At 5:30 P.M., Crest announced a break for dinner, and caterers arrived to fill the tables at the back of the room with tea, coffee, and soft drinks. There were platters of tiny sandwiches filled with roast pork, roast beef, and ham. It was the first time in his life that Zhou had tasted Beluga caviar. He had to restrain himself from overindulging in the repast.

During the recess, the reporters mixed with the ministers, seeking tidbits of information in addition to the tidbits on the table. Minister Jiang acknowledged Zhou with a nod, but did not choose to engage in conversation.

The first two-and-a-half hours had been devoted to sampling the amazing variety of entertainment and intellectually seductive advertising available from the Consortium of Information Services. In the last hour-and-a-half, Maynard Crest, who proved to be quite at ease with his audience, demonstrated CIS's international news gathering and interactive capabilities. In one segment, he demonstrated how the people could become familiar with their government and its services. Zhou thought that one capacity of the system alone was worth the entire cost of the project.

From time to time, he surreptitiously glanced at the ministers, to see how they were receiving this seminar, but was disappointed. None demonstrated by expression or gesture that he was impressed or disgusted with any element.

As the presentation came to a close and the audience got up to stretch and wander to the bar now set up at the back of the room, Director Deng—who had been sitting quietly in the front row of chairs—singled him out.

Zhou was impatient to be gone, but too polite to ignore her.

"What is your impression, Mr. Zhou?"

He was almost embarrassed to tell her. "Madame Deng, I feel as if I have been sequestered my entire life. I have been a monk without knowing it."

She smiled.

"The goal of the Committee has simply been to have access to the government's data, to know what the leadership knows. To be truthful, we have not been overly concerned with the rest of the world's drama and comedy and hygienic products. I was totally unaware of the learning strategies available. I feel, Director, quite naive."

"This is what Shanghai Star is all about, Mr. Zhou. So that the people know what is available."

"Believe me, I am enthused anew by the potential," he said. "I must now rethink the simplistic proposal I offered to the ministry in regard to open information. I must rethink my committee's strategies."

She smiled again, enough to make stronger men weak in the knees, and Zhou thought he might just collapse. She said, "I am happy that you could attend."

"And I thank you for the opportunity."

Zhou took the elevator to the sixth floor, was escorted through the security rooms, and then found another elevator.

He was absolutely certain that Crest had slanted the presentation to appeal to the members of the advisory committee.

But if that was what was available in a biased environment, think of what the rest of the world had.

Think of it!

His would be a long night, as he revised the poster to reflect what he now knew. He would print more of them. He might print a short newsletter. What was left of his funds would be consumed by the printing costs.

But it was worth it.

Maynard Crest got back to his hotel room a little after ten o'clock.

He felt rotten.

Crest had not had anything to drink at the party afterward, and as soon as he had his room door closed and was out of his suit coat, he ripped his tie off and poured himself a healthy dose of Jack Daniel's.

How many times, he wondered, had he made similar presentations over the years? A thousand? More. Advertising, promotion, and publicity campaigns. Political forays. Pro bono work for public service.

And this one had been as seamless as any of his previous exploits. His staff had done a magnificent job in preparing the material. The reporters, especially the international correspondents—who should be somewhat inured to most of the crap—had reacted well. They smiled or laughed or demonstrated sadness in the appropriate spots. Some of the Chinese reporters, as well as the guy Deng had invited, Zhou, seemed a bit stunned by some of it, but that was to be expected. He had shown a couple of hard-hitting news stories—a mother who had drowned her kids, for one—to demonstrate that CIS, while it wasn't screening the more bizarre footage, also wasn't going to back away from what was going on in the world. It had been a bit risky, he knew, and the correspondents, for the most part, took it in stride.

He didn't know how the committee had taken it. Not one blinked an eye.

Of the advisory committee, only the National Defense Minister, Shao, had even appeared to be awake. He had nodded minutely a couple of times. The rest of them were better stoics than Zeno of Citium, the Greek philosopher who had founded the school of Stoicism.

Not one reaction, pro or con.

Not during the performance.

Not during the interlude.

Not over a glass of wine.

He had never been so uncertain of where he stood.

But he thought he was going down in flames.

Zhou Ziyang called her, which was a first.

Chiang, Huzhou, and three others were gathered around desk. She had just passed out to them enough yuan to see then through the week, to Huzhou's apparent wonder. When she explained that membership dues were on the apparent rise, h gave her a skeptical look. It was difficult, however, to argu against the colored currency spread on the table. Obviousl there had been a turn in their fortunes.

Perhaps that would bring him tapping on her door in the middle of the night, something he had avoided since their argumen on August 9. Their relationship had not improved since.

And what would she do?

Deny him, she thought. He must be taught a lesson.

When the telephone rang, the girl from Hefei answered it, the beckoned to Chiang. She got up and went to the telephone.

"Miss Chiang, this is Zhou Ziyang."

"I am surprised that you call."

"I am surprised that you did not attend the presentation thi afternoon. I had thought you one eager to learn."

"I had other plans," she said, though, to be truthful, she ha been somewhat intimidated by Deng Mai's invitation. And to b trapped with the exalted leaders of the information committe was a prospect she had not wanted to endure.

"Was it instructive?" she asked.

"Absolutely. There is a great deal that we are missing."

He prattled on for ten minutes, recapitulating the program demonstrated by the Consortium of Information Services. Sh listened carefully, and when he was finished, almost regretted he decision to stay away.

"This is why you have called me?"

"No. I am changing my program of protest to reflect a nev theme: Let Us Learn. I inform you in the event that you wish t pursue a similar course. I am afraid that your current rhetori will bring Jiang Guofeng's wrath upon you."

"It is time to take a stand, Zhou."

"I agree. However, attacking the committee may be fruitless."

"Let me consider what you have said."

She was halfway across the room when the telephone rang again. Grimacing, she turned back to it.

"Yes?"

"Chiang Qing?"

"Who is asking?"

"My name is Wen Yito. I am an assistant to Minister Jiang."

"So?"

"The minister is unhappy with many of the posters he sees."

"It is not a happy world."

"He would ask you to refrain."

"He should leave 1950 and join the new world order."

"It would not be good to urge the police to stop the slander."

"Slander needs to be proven."

She slammed the telephone back on its wall hook. Jiang was getting what he wanted: heat.

She stood there, staring at the wall. She felt the others looking at her.

Finally, she turned and went back to the desk.

"Zhou Ziyang urges us to join his campaign."

"Which is?" Huzhou asked.

She explained. "He wants to concentrate on the educational aspects of the interactive programming. He may have a point, if the program can help the masses to understand the morass in which they are bogged down."

"We can do that, in addition to attacking the ministry," the girl said.

"That was the second call. A threat."

Huzhou rose from his slouch in the chair, his eyes shining. Now, he was prepared to be a martyr?

"A threat from whom?"

"Jiang, apparently. I did not know the name of the man."

"Good! We have their attention. Finally."

The leather-thong headband holding his hair in place seemed to make his eyes behind the spectacles stand out. They glittered in the light from the overhead bulb.

"We should plan a rally," Huzhou said. "Three hundred thou-

sand, a half million marching through the streets. That wil
alarm them."

"I like it!" the girl from Hefei told him.

"Instead," Chiang said, "I have another task for you."

"You may do it."

"I may have to, if you cannot."

Huzhou always resented any suggestion that he was incapable

"What is it?"

"You must recruit a programmer from Shanghai Star."

"What for?"

"All in good time, Huzhou."

At night, the gangs of young men roaming the city moved ou
of the suburbs and Old Town and seemed a hell of a lot mor
menacing. There were very few stories of foreigners being at
tacked or mugged, probably because the police presence in th
tourist areas was increased at night. No sense in alarming th
tourist industry.

In his short walk back to his apartment building, Grant almos
resolved to start driving every day. Or taking a cab.

A throng of a dozen teenagers matched his pace, on the othe
side of the street, and he found himself looking over his shoulder frequently. He was almost to the Dallas Cowboy Cafe whe
they crossed the street and fell in behind him.

There were still a lot of people on the sidewalks, but he wa
pretty certain they wouldn't want to become involved in any al-
tercation. Grant had learned long before that the better part o
valor was to run like hell, and he was about to do that when a
police truck rounded the corner ahead of him, then drove slowly
down the block.

The young men split up, disappearing into the crowd, evapo-
rating into an alley. The truck stopped, and four constable
hopped off the back of it. Dividing into pairs, they began walking, one pair north, behind him, the other pair to the south.

He felt better, and he didn't run home.

As he passed the cafe, digging the key to the front door out o
his pocket, a violent rapping on the windowpane caught his at-

tention. Maynard Crest stood at the window, beckoning him inside.

He went back to the cafe entrance, and Crest met him there.

"Can we talk for a bit, Doug?"

Grant looked around. The place was smoky and loud.

"Let's go up to my place, Maynard."

Up in the apartment, Grant broke out the Chivas, along with some ice from the small refrigerator.

"Hope you don't want soda."

"Water's fine."

Grant used the bottled water he kept in the refrigerator. Shanghai's water system wasn't all that reliable.

"It's damned near midnight, Maynard. Have you been sitting down there waiting for me?"

"Yeah, I have." Crest collapsed on the couch, loosened his tie, and took a long pull at the glass.

"Mai told me you did a superb job." Grant sat opposite him.

"It was good, yes. I was hoping you'd be there."

"Problems in the hinterlands, I'm afraid."

"Like what?"

"Some joker burned a few computers."

"It's getting rough, isn't it?" Crest asked.

"Well, I don't know about—"

"I was watching the committee closely, you know? There's a big division there."

"Is there?"

"Yeah. Jiang has his friends, and then there's another group. I met them all, but I'm not sure just who is on what side. But they're definitely taking sides. One group didn't spend much time talking to the other."

"That doesn't sound good," Grant said. He was afraid that his lobbying efforts might have gotten him a satellite in space, but a revolution on the ground. He hoped Jiang didn't control the votes, but he suspected that compromises would have to be made and that not all of them would go in Mai's favor.

"I have a very bad feeling that it's going to spread, Doug."

Grant agreed, but didn't want to contribute to the overall gloom. So he said nothing.

"Reason I'm here, Doug, I'd like a job."

"A job? You're shitting me, right?"

"Not in the least. The minute I walked out of that room, I knew we'd lost it."

"Can't be. I've seen some of your stuff."

"*Nada*. Nothing. We've blown a few million bucks even trying for it. This thing was decided long ago."

"You can't be sure."

"I am, though."

"Well, hell, I don't know what you'd—"

"Make me assistant to someone. Salary, ten bucks a year. I only need a title."

"Maynard, what the hell's going on?"

"With the title and a job, I can keep a visa and stay in the country."

"Why do you want to do that?"

"I want to do some exploring on my own."

"Not the tourist kind, I suppose?"

"I'm damned good at what I do, Doug. I don't take losing well. What I want to do is find out what went on behind the scenes."

"So you find out it's been rigged. What do you do with it?"

"Gets me some satisfaction that I didn't blow it on my own. Maybe I use it to convince the Consortium it's not my fault. Maybe, if I get anything hard in the way of evidence, maybe I do a documentary. Put that on the Shanghai Star network."

Crest sounded very bitter.

Grant thought it over.

"Can I get a promise out of you, Maynard?"

"Depends."

"You don't do anything illegal. Nothing that would reflect badly on MI."

"You got it. My word. I'll put it in writing, if you want."

"All right. We wait a few days to find out what the outcome is. If it goes the way you think, then you're my Marketing Director, China. Hundred thousand a year."

"Shit. That sounds like work."

"I sell computers."

"I sell 'em better. Tack on a commission."

"We'll discuss it later."

Saturday, August 27

At eleven o'clock in the morning, Grant was in his office plowing through the rough draft of the projected month-end profit-and-loss statement.

It was a loss.

Parker had offered to come in and help him, but he had told her he couldn't afford the overtime.

He was poring through the detail sheets, wondering if there wasn't something that was either in error or could be cut out, when he felt someone looking at him.

Crest was standing in the doorway, grinning. "Where's my office?"

"No lie?"

Crest came over to the desk and laid a newspaper down so Grant could see the headline. It was the English-language *China Daily.* PROGRAM CONTRACT AWARDED.

The picture accompanying the article was that of Jiang Guofeng. Trust him to use the announcement to feather his own PR bird.

"What's it say?" Grant asked.

Crest pointed to the stack of paperwork. "I can come back if you're busy."

Grant pushed the report aside. "It's not going to get any better. Sit down."

Crest turned a visitor's chair around and straddled it, resting his elbows on the back of it. "MBL gets the big one. Some Aussie outfit got a small contract to provide a natural-resources program. Kind of a Discovery Channel delivered by the mates down under. There's also a contract awarded to a Beijing company I never heard of before. They're going to do a visual *Seeking Truth.*"

Seeking Truth, formerly known as *Red Flag,* was the official journal of the Central Committee of the Communist Party.

"The Politburo has decided that they have to compete with *Gilligan's Island?*"

"I guess. I don't give them much hope for a ratings success, but then I don't suppose they've ever done any demographic studies. It's a new game when you start caring about whether or not the viewer *wants* what you're offering."

"Damn. I'm sorry about this, Maynard."

"So am I. Beyond all the Mad Avenue bullshit, I thought we could give them some quality programming. Hell, it might have taken six or seven years to develop to the point where China was getting the same thing the rest of the world is getting now. Somehow, I got this real streak of idealism going for me, Doug, and I've never been much of an idealist before."

"You going to try to change the committee's collective mind?"

"Nope. But I am going to try and find out what really happened."

"How?"

"Not a clue. I'm no investigator."

"Try talking to some of the reporters. Get in with the Western press, and they'll make introductions to the Chinese correspondents. I can introduce you to a Russian named Suretsov. He's with ITAR-Tass. Some of those people know how to dig."

"I know him. And anything I do along that line is off the payroll. I'll tell whoever runs that when I'm on personal time. You won't see any of those expenses, either."

Grant tapped his draft report. "Good damned thing. My P&L can't handle it. By the way, you *can* sell computers?"

Crest grinned at him. "I can sell anything. I need to get hold of the technical data, and then I'll build you a China-oriented campaign that'll knock your socks off."

"You call C.C. Jackson in L.A. and tell him what you need."

Crest stood up. "Okay. Right now, I've got to go borrow a computer and write a letter of resignation."

"Tell me, Maynard, what were you making at CIS?"

"Last year, six hundred thou."

"And you'll dump that for one hundred?"

"I like your outfit, Doug. Besides, with the commissions, it'll be better than six hundred."

Suretsov made his phone call to Beijing during the lunch hour, hoping to catch Makov at home. The minor functionaries of the consulate lived in a housing block two kilometers from the consulate.

A woman answered, and Suretsov spoke in Russian, as if he were someone from the consulate. "Is Arkady there, please?"

"Da."

A minute later, Makov came on the line. "Yes?"

"Do you know who this is, Pyotr?"

Arkady Makov's voice reflected his alarm. "You should not call me here!"

He whispered, so Suretsov guessed that the woman was close by.

"You do not have to say much. I am convinced of your patriotism, Arkady, and this will be a short conversation."

"Quickly!" His state of alarm was such that he did not realize Suretsov had addressed him by his true name.

"Yesterday, I hope, you should have received a photograph in the mail."

"I did! It was him!"

"The man in the park with Sytenko?"

"Yes!"

"Goodbye, Arkady."

Suretsov replaced the receiver carefully.

Well.

That was one duck in a row.

"You've been at it five days in a row," Wickersham said.

"It's only eighteen hours a day," Stone told him.

"And so enjoyable, too. I hate doing the same job twice."

Stone shut down the computer and stood up. "I still ran into some glitches when I was running the ap files."

"I know. We'll get 'em."

"Bastards."

Stone and his technicians had rebuilt two of the seven destroyed consoles, and installed two more airfreighted from California. During the installation and initial testing, however, he had discovered that a network server and an optical-storage unit had also been destroyed. The storage unit had contained most of the application programming, about twenty gigabytes of specialized software. And when Wickersham had gone in search of the backup programming, stored on optical discs, he'd found those obliterated, also.

It wasn't a major loss since Wickersham had dialled into the Chengdu installation and copied off their base programs. The customized part, for the Guangzhou installation, had had to be rewritten, though, and Wickersham's software engineers and programmers had been at it for the same amount of time Stone had been spending on the hardware.

"How are your guys doing?" Stone asked.

"I kicked 'em out. They're so fatigued, they're making the same mistakes five times. We'll let them start fresh on Monday. Hell, Mickey, we've got two weeks."

"Yeah, well, I've got a video board acting up on this unit. I'll work on it for a while more."

"Forget it. I'll buy your dinner."

"It's midafternoon."

"What'd you have for lunch?"

"Oh, lunch."

Stone hated leaving a job half done. He was a project person, and he'd work seventy hours straight to finish a chore, then take a day off. But, damn, he *was* tired.

He jotted some numbers on a sticky note and pasted it to the screen.

"Okay. As long as you're buying and we're going to the Swan."

"Christ, Mickey. That'll take three credit cards."

"You want to apply for a couple more before we go?"

Wickersham grinned. "I've got enough."

They left the building, which was on Huanshi Road in the northeastern sector of the city, and found a cab. The driver didn't race through the crowded streets—the city housed over three million people—but managed a pace better than a walk. After a few blocks, he turned south, probably to delay the trip and run up the meter.

The gardenlike campus of Old Guangdong University passed on the left. In 1926, it had been renamed Zhong Shan University in honor of Dr. Sun Yat-sen. The campus also was the site of the Guangdong Provincial Museum. Stone had been keeping a list of the museums and their addresses in his notebook, just in case he didn't run into something more beautiful.

It was ironic. He had finally landed in a city that offered a wide variety of amusements and an international cast of pretty women, and he didn't have time for either. Since arriving, he had been falling into his bed in the early morning at the White Cloud. In Chinese, it was the Bai Yun Hotel, isolated from the main city, but close to the Guangzhou Facility of the Shanghai Star Communications Network.

Guangzhou, once known as Canton, was located on a bend of the Zhu Jiang, the Pearl River, and was a major southern port, just up the coast to the west of Hong Kong. For two thousand years, it had been a center of commerce—even the Romans had visited during the Han Dynasty, which ran from 206 B.C. to A.D. 220. While the foreign China traders had been around a long time, it was the Portuguese who first got permission from the Ming Dynasty to settle Macao, seventy miles downstream. The English were prominent traders, of course, and not content to barter silver or gold for rice and tea, had utilized opium conveniently located in India. The Chinese objected to that practice, resulting in the Opium Wars.

After the second Opium War in the mid-1850s, as part of the reparations paid by China to the righteous English, England reclaimed a sandbank in the Pearl River called Sha Mian and built an enclave on it in partnership with the French. The colonial traders needed their tennis courts, sailing club, football field, and sumptuous villas, all located across bridges from the main city. Gates closed off the peasants at night.

In the early part of the 20th century, Guangzhou had a reputation equal to that of Shanghai—notorious. It was the center of revolutionary activity, Sun Yat-sen's base for the overthrow of the Qing Dynasty in 1911, and Mao Zedong's choice for the establishment of the National Peasant Movement in 1925. There was, in fact, a museum dedicated to that movement.

Now, as one of fourteen open coastal cities, Guangzhou was setting the pace for economic development. Modernization projects begun in the 1920s and 1930s had revitalized the city's infrastructure in the way of sanitation, roads, and buildings. High-rise buildings dominated the city center.

The cab cut through the eastern end of the city center, crossed a bridge onto Shamian Island, and deposited Stone and Wickersham at the White Swan Hotel, a five-star emporium featuring five Chinese, Western, and Japanese restaurants, a coffee shop, and a teahouse. There was a gymnasium, swimming pool, sauna, shopping arcade, dance floor, disco, and bars available for the bone-weary, fatigued businessman. The standard room or the three-room suites featured air-conditioning, color TV, and direct-dial phones to Hong Kong.

The two of them were in typical MI attire, jeans and sport shirts, but it didn't seem to upset any of the other guests. Most of them were dressed similarly.

"Your choice," Wickersham said.

"I think it's time for a good T-bone."

Which it was, and they had great steaks in the nearly deserted Western restaurant, then moved out to a table near the pool for drinks.

"The sun *is* over the yardarm?" Stone asked, peeking out from under the umbrella, which protected the table.

"Way over."

"I'll skip the gin and tonic, then, and go right to scotch."

It was warm, but a light breeze moving under the banyan trees took the edge off. There was a large group of Westerners around, and in, the pool. Stone's eye scanned them, seeking out those of the opposite gender who might be unattached. Overhead, they were about to lose the sun as threatening clouds moved in. Guangzhou was in a subtropical weather belt, hot and humid in the summer, with numerous thunderstorms. August and September were the prime typhoon months.

"I'm going to find something lovely," Stone said, "and then some big wind is going to come up and blow her away."

"Fortunately, I no longer worry about that."

Wickersham's wife, Linda, had elected to stay in L.A. and not transplant their two kids during their high-school years. He went to California twice a year, and she came to China three or four times a year.

"Linda coming soon?" he asked.

"She'll be here for two weeks during opening festivities on October first."

"I'm happy for you. I need to be happy for me, though. See that table over there?"

"Two guys, three gals?"

"That's the one. By the slang drifting on the breeze, they're Americans *and* computer nerds."

"But you like the population distribution?"

"It's better than equal."

"I'm going back to the hotel. Our hotel."

"Thanks for the din-din, Curt."

"You needed to get out. Don't forget to come back, though."

Wickersham drained his drink, then got up and headed for the lobby and the taxi rank. He gave Stone an understanding grin as he left.

Stone didn't waste time. Carrying his glass, he walked over to the target table.

They all looked up as he approached.

"Mickey Stone," he said, "I'm with Megatronics."

That was common bond enough. The first man rose and offered his hand. "Del Bannon. We're all with Digi-Communications."

"You've been working in Hunan?"

"Right on. But we've landed some new contracts. We're the advance party for Guangdong Province."

"Good for Tank."

"You know the boss?"

"We've met a few times."

"Pick a chair, Stone."

They were all specialists in telecommunications or computers or software, and he spent half an hour sharing anecdotes with them while he analyzed the relationships. After a while, it became apparent that the two men had real or imagined claims on two of the women, leaving the third woman twisting in the wind. Which was picking up.

She was not his type. Margaret, or Meg, Naylor was not sensual French or even California Girl. She was midwestern tomboy, with freckles lightly peppered over her cheekbones, lively hazel eyes, short-cropped brown hair. Maybe three or four years younger than Stone, but in her jeans and checkered blouse, she didn't display much voluptuousness. Definitely not as bosomy as he preferred.

She was a computer scientist out of the University of Illinois and, he judged, bright. She had a lively sense of humor.

But it just wasn't going to work out.

The rain hit in a sudden rush, and the six of them leaped up and headed for the hotel along with the rest of the crowd. In a main-floor bar, they found a big round table, and Stone bought them another round of drinks. Not surprisingly, he found himself seated next to Naylor.

"What do you do for MI, Mickey?"

"Play with the machines."

"Seriously."

"Director of Hardware Systems."

"Ahhh, one of the honchos." Her eyes caught his own, evaluated his response to her comment.

"In China, we all get our hands dirty."

"Is that what you're doing here? I heard something about sabotage?"

"Yeah, someone burned a few units. I'm trying to get everything back on-line."

"But that's not all you do."

Stone found himself telling her about his friends, their hopes for the company, the way they all worked their butts off. It was usually the other way around; Stone was a good listener, and he normally prompted women to spill their life stories.

After twenty minutes of that, she asked, "Do you like to walk?"

"Sure. I've been walking every backwater burg in China, seeing the sights."

"It's stopped raining. Let's go for a walk."

The others didn't seem to even notice their departure. Leaving the hotel, they went down to the river and walked the bank under the banyan trees. Raindrops dripped from the leaves, and the air was sweet and clean after the rain. Sampans and other watercraft plied the river, their lights bobbing lightly and splashing the water's surface with shimmery white reflections.

A block from the hotel, Stone decided he was enjoying himself.

He finally reversed the flow of information. She was from Indianapolis; her sister wanted to be a model and was in New York attempting to do so; her father was on some committee for the Indy 500; Meg had really wanted to race cars, but got scared over 180 miles per hour.

He laughed. "I really wanted to be in the movies, but got cut after my audition."

"You did?"

Watch it! Let's not get into Errol Flynn.

"But I've never been in a car above seventy. Maybe eighty."

"You've missed the greatest feeling in life."

He didn't think so.

"How long are you—"

BLAM!

He didn't know where the shot came from, but the whistle of the slug whined in his ear, and he felt the concussed air slap at him as it went by.

Stone grabbed Naylor around the waist, hugged her to him, and dove to the left, landing in the grass, rolling down a slight incline—over her twice, and into a copse of shrubbery.

"Mickey!"

"Shh. Listen!"

He felt her trembling against him. Her heart was beating double time. So was his own.

He didn't hear footsteps charging.

After a full minute, he relaxed a little.

After another minute, he relaxed a bit more.

Her head was tight against his chin, and her hair smelled good. Kind of like corn silk.

He relaxed his grip around her waist.

She struggled a bit, and he rolled away from her.

"What was it, Mickey?" she whispered.

"Someone took a potshot at us. I think he's gone."

"God! That's terrible!"

"Especially since I was told the criminals in China don't have guns."

"Don't joke!"

If he weren't so worried that the guy was out there, waiting for him to stick his head up, Stone might have thought it was a pretty good ruse to get close to a woman.

Lefant had selected one of the ballrooms of the International Hotel for his celebration party. The hors d'oeuvres were excellent, the champagne icy, the local band loud, and the two hundred guests in great good humor.

Madame Yvonne Deng was positively radiant. She felt animated in his arms as they danced to, of all things, Willie Nelson's rendition of "Stardust."

"I could take you away from all of this," he suggested.

"Could you? When? Not for a couple hours, I hope. I *am* enjoying myself."

"I was thinking more long-range, Yvonne. In two years, perhaps less, the China Division of Media Bureau will be self-sufficient, and I plan to leave the company."

"And what will you do?"

"I have a villa—a small villa, a farmhouse, really—in the hills close to Cannes. It is nice there most of the year."

Her eyes turned dreamy for a moment, then cleared. "This is a proposal!"

He smiled. "It may well be."

"We have known each other but a few days."

"As I say, there is another two years in which to become better acquainted. I mention it only as a matter of placing a tiny thought at the back of your mind."

"My home is here, Pierre. Mai needs the help I can give her."

Across his partner's bare and luscious shoulder, Lefant saw the daughter standing with Grant and the Russian correspondent—what was his name, Suretsov? Deng Mai kept glancing their way, following them as they swept around the other couples on the dance floor. It was clear from her expression that she did not approve.

Her approval or disapproval was of little consequence, now that he had the contract in hand. No. He forced himself to remember that her approval was still necessary. Her position as director allowed her to set up obstacles.

"I think Director Deng can take care of herself. She is a strong woman."

"Strong-willed is what you mean. I did my best to dissuade her from nominating her liberal choices for the executive positions, but she is determined to force the committee to become disenchanted with her."

Yvonne Deng very likely had little knowledge of the qualifications of the candidates for those positions, but Lefant had mentioned to her that Jiang's favorites were probably the best choices since it would mean less disruption.

It was nice to know that his suggestions were being passed along by Yvonne.

And gratifying to know that she was taking his side.

When the song ended, he said, "Come, let us get a glass of champagne and rest for a moment."

"But shouldn't you mix with your guests?"

"I think they are enjoying themselves as much as I am."

And indeed, they appeared to be. The members of the Information Advisory Committee, except for Pai Dehuai who had returned to Beijing on business, were chatting equably with everyone in sight. At the beginning of yesterday's presentation, Lefant had been aware of some tensions in the committee, but they appeared to have ironed themselves out by the end of the session. Shao Tsung, the national defense minister, and Jiang Guofeng were together, laughing over some joke.

Lefant captured two flutes of champagne from a passing tray, and he and his divine consort requisitioned the chairs of two people bound for the dance floor.

He felt Deng Mai's eyes on his back as they sat down, but that was all right. For the first time, he knew he had some leverage over the Shanghai Star director. He would now be a favorite with her superior.

And he had her mother well in hand.

* * *

Suretsov kept his voice low as he told Grant and Deng, "My supervisor has initiated a background investigation of Pierre Lefant."

"It may be too late," Grant said.

"We will see."

Deng looked once more to where her mother and Lefant were seated. They appeared to be enjoying themselves. The sight of them laughing and looking into one another's eyes irritated her no end. Her mother had always enjoyed life, even as a struggling politician's wife, but had never before looked so foolish in Deng Mai's eyes.

Others at the party were aware of them, also, and that irritated her further. The onlookers' all-knowing smirks appeared to be saying, "What an adorable couple. So suited to each other."

They were both in their sixties, for the love of Buddha!

She was forced to backtrack on her last thought. She had never before invoked any god, Chinese or Christian.

She brought her attention back to the conversation between Grant and Suretsov just as a waiter interrupted them.

"Mr. Grant? There is a telephone call for you."

Grant excused himself and went away with the waiter.

The Russian said, "I have not yet received a date for an interview, Director."

"Monday? In the morning?"

"I will be there. Thank you."

"What do you think of all this, Mr. Suretsov?"

The correspondent considered his response before saying, "I admit that I was a little disappointed in the selection. Having viewed the offerings of the Consortium of Information Services, Media Bureau Limited, and several of the smaller vendors, I was surprised at the outcome. MBL's programs seemed to stop short of full disclosure and lacked some sophistication, in my opinion. Of course, I am not an expert."

Deng agreed with him, but withheld her view. She thought that Lefant's sample offerings had been overly slanted to meet the committee's expectations.

"CIS's interactive component has great potential as a learning tool," Suretsov went on. "MBL's requires additional development."

"We will hope for the best."

She looked up and smiled as she saw Jiang and Shao approaching. Jiang was smiling, a rarity, and it carried into the glitter of his mobile eyes. She noted dark perspiration stains in the armpits of his tailored suit.

Shao Tsung was also smiling. They had reached some accord.

"Good evening, Minister Jiang, Minister Shao. Have you met Mr. Suretsov?"

The ministers shook hands with the Russian correspondent.

"It is a joyous occasion, is it not?" Jiang asked her.

"It is."

"And there will be further cause for celebration tomorrow," he said, turning to the reporter. "Mr. Suretsov, we will give ITAR-Tass an exclusive."

Suretsov smiled. Correspondents always reacted favorably to "exclusive."

"Tomorrow at one o'clock, the ministry will announce the name of the new president of Media Bureau Limited-China."

She held her smile, as well as her breath.

"The president will be Sung Wu, an extremely capable man and long a servant of the People's Republic of China."

Suretsov set his drink aside, produced a notebook, and wrote the name down.

Deng looked to Shao, but his expression said that he wholeheartedly endorsed the decision.

"I am happy," she said, "that so many of these decisions are behind us, and we can quickly advance to the inception of Shanghai Star."

"Exactly!" Jiang proclaimed.

The two ministers left them, and she had difficulty maintaining her composure.

It was the beginning of the end.

Her end.

Grant returned, and the dark scowl coating his face reflected her own feelings.

"What is wrong, Douglas?"

"Someone took a shot at Mickey Stone."

"What!"

"The Guangzhou police are looking into it."

"This is terrible!"

"It's starting to get serious. I sure as hell don't like my people getting shot at."

"What will you do?"

"I'm going to get serious, too."

Thursday, September 1

Stacked all around him in the small office on Changzhi Road, which was the central headquarters of the Right to Know Committee, were several hundred big-character posters exhorting the Ministry of Information to let the people learn via the Consortium of Information Services' interactive data program.

All of them useless, Zhou Ziyang now knew.

The announcement on August 27 of the advisory committee's decision had caught him by surprise. He had automatically assumed that Jiang would wait until September 1 to make his proclamation. Neither Zhou, nor as he understood it, Chiang Qing, had had a chance to make their cases with the people prior to the selection of Media Bureau Limited. He was especially astonished since, as he had learned at the presentation, MBL's interactive programming was nothing more than a toy. It allowed the viewer to engage in games, or if they understood English, German, or French, to peruse encyclopedias, atlases, and dictionaries. None were available in Chinese, a subtle form of censorship.

Then, yesterday evening, a messenger had delivered the final blow.

The final draft of a policy recommendation from the Ministry of Information to the State Council rested on the arm of the old stuffed chair in which he sat. His office did not have a desk.

There were twenty-seven pages in the document, and he had pored over each clause at least four times. For a policy which should be broad in scope, he thought, there was amazing detail.

In the arena of entertainment programming, every segment was covered, from situation comedies to drama to game shows.

Anything rated "R" was banned as pornographic unless exempted by the office of the president of Media Bureau Limited-China. Dramatic productions with violent content were to be reviewed prior to airing. The president's office would determine what types of violence were acceptable or not. The thematic slant of any program must not degrade the Communist Party in general, or the Chinese Communist Party or the PRC regime in particular.

Zhou thought that Pierre Lefant's company was going to be upset. Under the policy, most of their offerings would have to undergo extreme editing.

As to news coverage, the Xinhua News Agency, which had oversight for all domestic print and broadcast media, anyway, would continue its censorship role for news reports generated inside the country and channelled into Shanghai Star. The reportage of violence or demonstrations against the administration were to be tempered so as not to offend viewers.

The director of the All News Channel had similar responsibilities concerning international news beamed via satellite from elsewhere. The viewer was to be protected from the excesses demonstrated by some camera and correspondent teams, and the director was to ascertain the suitability of newscasts for Chinese viewers.

It was the section on protected information that dismayed Zhou the most. Not one of the points listed in his proposal had been addressed.

Almost all of the agencies and bureaus of the PRC were protected. None of the records of any ministry was available for dissemination as a matter of public interest. In most cases, the aura of national defense was decreed as the reason for such bans.

And the trade-off for these injunctions could be found in the commercial section of the document. There were almost no restrictions, other than to offensive sexual or cultural taboos, for advertising. MBL and its sponsors would be allowed to sell almost anything to any gullible buyer from age eight to eighty.

Zhou Ziyang wanted to cry.

The bright star on the horizon, that of Shanghai, was already tarnished, and it had not yet risen.

* * *

Jiang Guofeng was happy with his bartering.

He always hated to give up position, but in this case, thought it was worth it. In order to reach an accord with Shao, he had had to allow the military to have final control over both ShangStar One and ShangStar Two. Shao was suddenly concerned with the requirement to have backup, should one or the other be damaged.

He and the defense minister had an agreement in principle, and the written version would be drawn by Shao's staff and presented for signature soon.

Jiang did not believe he was giving much away. In the event of a war, the army would have commandeered the satellite anyway.

In exchange, however, he had gained something far more important—Shao's backing of Media Bureau Limited as the information provider, and Sung Wu as its domestic executive. Having seen the way the army blew, three of the undecideds had also cast their votes in favor of Jiang's recommendations. The last three would not have voted for MBL or Sung in any case.

He telephoned Pai, whom he had not spoken to all week.

"Yes, Guofeng?"

"You should have stayed for the celebration. It was quite enjoyable."

"I am certain it was. Director Deng was happy?"

Jiang laughed. "She knows her leash is much shorter now. I think she may not last the month."

"Yes, well, there are other things to worry about."

Pai sounded as if he were depressed.

"Such as?"

"That reporter? The Russian?"

"Yes."

"He is all over Shanghai and Beijing, asking questions."

"About what?"

"About the nuclear reactors."

"Have you checked on them?"

"I have," Pai said. "The International Nuclear Regulatory Agency *has* approved the designs. I flew to Chengdu and examined the reactor there personally."

Not that that proved anything, Jiang thought. His brother-in-law knew very little about energy production, nuclear or otherwise.

"And you are reassured?" he asked.

"Absolutely," Pai said, though without real conviction.

"Then we have nothing to worry us."

"That reporter—"

"Reporters also ask stupid questions, Dehuai. Forget him."

After he hung up, Jiang reminded himself that reporters also asked the right questions.

On his China Air flight to Beijing, Maynard Crest reviewed the first sketches for his brochures, mailings, and ad campaign. They had been drawn by Rock Major, one of the best creative minds in the business.

Major, along with the rest of CIS's China contingent, had been shipped back to New York. As a side deal, however, Crest had retained Major on a consultant contract, paying him out of his own pocket. If it worked out, he was sure that Grant would reimburse him. If it didn't, that's the way some things went.

To date, Megatronics, working out of its Los Angeles marketing shop, had targeted its marketing toward business users, and nothing in that portfolio was useful in a consumer campaign. Joe Blow didn't want a $9,000 computer. Well, maybe he wanted it, but he wasn't going to dig for the cash to acquire it.

Chin Li, for sure, wasn't going to come up with those kinds of bucks, or the equivalent in yuan, either.

Crest was pleased, however, with what he had learned from Calvin Jackson, MI's production manager. After their two-hour-long overseas conversation, he not only liked Calvin Coolidge Jackson, he was more impressed than ever with Doug Grant's company. And he was damned sure going to talk to Grant about stock options.

There were three levels of product for him to work with. The basic unit, the interactive controller, was being produced at a unit cost of $14.12. With freight and other overhead, they'd have to retail it at $29.95. Like C.C. Jackson, Crest thought better in terms of U.S. dollars.

Crest had asked about the television sets, but Jackson said

they'd already determined that the Japanese were going to roll up that market with high-definition monitors. MI's units were being offered without monitors, tailored to work with what the Japanese were going to put on the sales counter.

The second level unit retailed at $199 and provided rudimentary hard-disk data storage, minimal memory, and some Wickersham-designed software for word processing and data manipulation.

The top level, with more memory, 340 megabytes of storage, and outside vendor software came in at $399. Naturally, there was a wide array of add-ons available, from printers to floppy-disk drives.

In American terms, the prices were damned reasonable. For the Chinese, though, even the basic unit was going to be a strain on the budget, particularly after springing for the television monitor.

Crest had already decided that his push was going to be behind the second-level unit, designated by Crest as the People's Home Companion. He had yet to tell Grant about the name. That's where the major revenue source lay, and he would have to arrange a deal with the Chinese, maybe through the Bank of China, to establish payment-purchase plans for his consumers. He was certain the PRC wouldn't object to an interest-bearing idea.

The basic unit, to be called the People's Controller, was a throwaway. He had several campaigns in mind for it. One, he was going to approach the Japanese vendors—he already had four interviews lined up—with the proposal to sell them the unit at $15. MI would make fifty cents or so, and the retailer could include it with the television monitor as a so-called free bonus.

Secondly, for outright sales to the public, he wanted to provide a written guarantee that the purchaser could trade it in on a People's Home Companion for half of what they paid for it.

Trade-ins could be recycled for $19.95.

Damn, he thought. There's going to be a bunch of money in this. He was excited enough that he had nearly forgotten the reason he was staying in China.

After his plane landed smoothly at the Beijing airport, Crest bought a bowl of wonton soup in the terminal for lunch, then cabbed into the city. He arrived at his appointment with an English-speaking functionary in the Ministry of Commerce fifteen minutes before he was due.

He had respected punctuality in others, and he always attempted to show them the same respect. He also knew that the quality was a prerequisite in China.

When he was led into the tiny office, he offered his hand and a warm smile.

"Mr. Quan, I am most happy to meet you, and I sincerely appreciate your agreeing to see me on such short notice."

"The pleasure is mine, Mr. Crest. How can I be of help?"

Lifting his briefcase to his lap as he sat down, Crest opened it and extracted his tall stack of files.

"I am here to learn the process of registering our products for sale to the general public."

The man smiled. "It can be rigorous."

"Absolutely! It is the same everywhere. That is why I must rely so heavily on your expertise. I am a complete novice when it comes to official paperwork."

"Would I be correct," Quan asked, "in assuming that your products are connected directly with Shanghai Star?"

"Quite correct. We will sell nothing that is not associated with the network."

"Perhaps that will make it easier."

"I hope so."

Crest took out his pen and offered the man one of his brand-new business cards. "In case you need to reach me for a response to any question. I am available at any time, and my hotel phone number is listed there. And I wonder if I might have your telephone number here and at your home? In case I have a question."

He wrote the numbers on another card and placed it in his wallet. The number would help him to determine the man's home address, and if he had a wife, she would receive a bouquet of flowers. A happy wife made a happy functionary.

It would also indicate to Crest how open, or how expectant, the man was to a little grease on the palm. The official line of the government was that bribery and other forms of corruption were outlawed. Still, some lower-level bureaucrats still expected a nice gift, now and then.

The two of them spent nearly three hours introducing Crest to the process, to the myriad number of meaningless and mindless forms to be filled out, and to the expectations he might have in regard to timelines. Sandwiched in between relevant questions, Crest learned the names of other bureaucrats he should meet regarding his advertising campaign and his proposal for a Bank of China consumer-lending program. In response to Crest's query, Quan told him he was quite excited about the prospects of Shanghai Star. Under the surface, however, Quan was less than excited, Crest thought. He would learn later just what those reservations were.

He was also gratified when Quan accepted his invitation to dinner. Crest wanted, not only a satisfied bureaucrat in his corner, but one that might bubble over with interesting information.

The deputy was extremely interested in Crest's brochure sketches and Crest's descriptions of the MI products. The People's Home Companion widened his eyes.

"Are these available now, Mr. Crest?"

"The Controller should be available in quantity by the first of October. The Home Companion, I think, will be stocked in limited number by the middle of the month, and the professional model is not expected until early December."

Crest was aware that Quan's office did not contain a computer. He wondered how limited the distribution of machines was within the government, but he did not ask. He made a mental note to keep tabs on the offices he visited. A governmental market for a middle-of-the-line MI machine could generate millions of dollars.

"Would it help you determine the value of the product if you had one to test?"

Quan leaned back in his chair, and his eyes narrowed, suspicious.

Perhaps an honest man.

"I could arrange for a unit to be placed at your disposal for, say, ten days. Then I would have to take it back."

Quan smiled. "Indeed, that could be helpful."

And if he liked it, Crest would give it to him at cost, maybe a hundred bucks. It would make them both feel better.

"I enjoy doing business with a congenial man, Mr. Quan."

Harbin was a pleasant city. The European-styled architecture was dominated by pastel shades of color, a legacy of the Russians who once controlled the city. The avenues were wide and lined with trees, providing a shady, verdant overtone for the entire city. A twenty-six-mile-long embankment had been built along the Songhua River after the 1933 floods to protect the town and to provide a wonderful promenade for strolling and meeting people. One no longer met many Russians. They had come en masse, first to build the branch of the Trans-Siberian Railway, the Chinese Eastern Railway, then to flee the 1917 Russian revolution. They turned tail and returned under amnesty to Stalin's Russia when the Chinese revolution of 1946 brought the city under Chinese Communist rule.

The Songhua flowed into the Heilongjiang River, the namesake for the province, and meaning Black Dragon River. The province was a center of food production, with wheat, corn, soybeans, and beets grown on huge farming tracts in what was formerly known as the Manchurian Plain.

Tan Long took his midafternoon break from examining the department store's books by purchasing a can of Coca-Cola and walking along the river. There were many sailboats skimming the surface and dozens of young people swimming in the river, to shed the heat of the day. In the wintertime, they would be skating or ice-sailing for the Songhua froze completely from bank to bank.

Tan was feeling quite magnanimous. Just before noon, he had discovered a discrepancy in the receipts of the women's clothing department of The Number One Department Store. When he showed the twelve-thousand-yuan error to the manager, the man had become nearly frantic. He was new to the store, suffering his first visit from Tan. His visions and his dreams for months, and perhaps for years to come, would be filled with images of concrete-walled prisons and, worse, the disgrace suffered by his family when the error of his ways became public.

Tan had told him, however, that he sympathized with the man, that such things happened, and that Tan could perhaps arrange to assist him in correcting the matter. They eventually agreed that the manager would pay Tan two thousand yuan a month for six months, plus a one thousand yuan fee, and Tan would see that the accounts eventually came back into balance.

The manager was still worried, dependent on Tan, and afraid the fraud would come to light before the balance was restored. Tan himself was unworried that auditors would uncover the discrepancy since it had never been there in the first place. The store's bookkeeping was impeccable.

He was forever amazed at people. If he were innocent, the manager should have demanded an outside auditor immediately, in which case Tan's paperwork would disgorge a simple arithmetic miscalculation, and all would have been settled harmoniously. Since the man had so readily agreed to the cover-up, Tan could be assured that he had something to hide. Tan would watch him closely in the future.

When he had finished his Coca-Cola, Tan diverted his walk from the promenade, crossed the wide boulevard, and walked up a heavily trafficked side street. He was about six blocks from his hotel.

Three blocks from the river, he turned into an alley, made certain no one was watching, and produced a key from his pocket. He unlocked the small door to a single-room shed and stepped quickly inside.

He had rented the garage the day before, paying two months' rent.

Inside was a brown van, well used, with the sign of a produce market painted on each side.

On the floor beside the van was a wooden mold he had fashioned from lath and wire. He knelt next to it and tested the surface of the concrete he had poured into the mold. It was hard. Though it was only fifty millimeters thick, he had reinforced it with chicken wire while he was hand-forming the concrete.

Taking his time, Tan untwisted the ends of the wire holding the short pieces of lath in place, pulled the wire free, then pried away the short lengths of lath board and the waxed paper. What was left was a rather crude, heavily textured vase with a 200-millimeter base flaring to about 300 millimeters at the top. It looked much lighter than it probably was.

He opened the side door of the van, then squatted to lift the vase. It was heavy, but he thought he would manage it nicely.

Placing it on the floor of the van, he turned to a cardboard box already in the van. From the box, he extracted the vase filling he had prepared the night before. It was tightly wrapped in duct tape, but beneath the tape was a bundle of twelve sticks of dynamite. They shared their space with nearly four pounds of small finishing nails.

He lifted the package from the box and lowered it into the vase. The fit was nearly perfect, with 100 millimeters of space left available at the top of the vase. In that space, he inserted a small black box, then covered it all with pears, bananas, oranges, and apples.

Tan thought it looked quite enticing.

"Why aren't you home with your wife, babe?" C.C. Jackson asked.

"My wife's in China," Bricher reminded him.

"Oh, yeah. Most guys that get back to the States for a few days don't come to see me. They'd rather see someone they love."

"We all love you, C.C."

"Doug wanted you to check up on me?"

"I walked through the plant, just to make sure you weren't manufacturing erotic toys or something."

Jackson grinned. "That's a hell of a thought, Will. I could probably put a crew on overtime and make a million on the side. Where've you been?"

"I had to meet with the GE people about ShangStar Three and actually put my signature on the agreements. They're getting particular about details like that."

"Nobody trusts nobody anymore," Jackson lamented. "How long are you here?"

"A couple days. Shana wants me to look at the house, to be sure our renters are still there and haven't taken off with all the furnishings. I want to watch a few real television shows."

"After dinner, right? Janet will be unhappy as hell if I don't tow you home."

"I've been waiting for you to ask." Bricher flipped a thumb over his right shoulder, at the window overlooking the assembly floor. "Anything new? Or bad?"

"Hey, babe, my show goes on. At least for a few more days."

"Come again?"

"We didn't get the August thirty-one payment."

"Shit. I'll talk to the director when I get back. Jiang's real forgetful about things like that."

"Sure he is. Anything else you need?"

"Our new marketing man asked me to bring back some demonstration models for him."

"Crest? I think he knew what he was talking about on the phone."

"I think he's a fast learner. We'll see how he works out. How about demos?"

"I can give you the controller and the second model. Number three's still somebody's dream on a CAD program."

The engineers all worked on computer-assisted design programs (CAD).

"How many of each?"

"How much carry-on baggage you want?"

"I can get someone to haul it for me."

"Twenty-five controllers?"

"That'll do it."

Jackson turned to the computer on his credenza and called up an inventory screen. "I've got fifteen hundred of the model two in the warehouse, but they don't have any labels on them yet. Someone has yet to come up with a name, and I told Crest he might think about it. And there was some early discussion about whether to label them in Chinese or something else. No one has told me if that was resolved."

"I don't think it has been. Let me take two of them, along with a couple accessory floppy drives."

Jackson tapped the keyboard a few times, then turned back.

"We'll have 'em ready for you, babe. Hey, Panasonic's got a slick new laser printer. They came over to show it to me. It's a tiny mother and might go well with either the second or third models."

"This isn't my department," Bricher demurred.

"But you got a swell brain."

"Explore the possibilities with them, then call Mickey or Doug."

Jackson got up and walked around from behind his desk. He was a big man, and despite the spacious size of his office, dominated it.

"How's it really going over there, Will?"

"I'm a little less optimistic about the final outcome than I was a week ago. Oh, I think MI will do okay, but I think the man on the street is getting ripped off."

"I wonder about MI."

"Why?"

"You haven't heard?"

"Heard what?"

"Hell, someone took a shot at Mickey."

"Goddamn it!"

"On the street in Guangzhou, somewhere. It was close, but no cigar."

"Maybe they were just trying to scare him?"

"It worked, he told me. He was scared."

"I can't figure it, Calvin. I mean, I know the politicos are divided about the information that gets to the people. But I don't see any advantage for anyone in killing the messenger. Burning a few computers isn't going to stop anything."

"But it might delay it."

"Somebody's buying time?"

"Knock down a rocket, that'll buy time."

"A couple weeks."

"But they didn't know that," Jackson pointed out.

"Yeah, maybe."

"You know what I'd do, babe, if I was a smart terrorist?"

"What?"

"I'd pass on killing a few computers or engineers and go right to the central distribution point."

"The Shanghai building?"

"Damned right! Little plastic on the right structural members, and I'd bring that baby down. That'd buy me a couple years."

"Shit. I hope they're not as bright as you, C.C."

"Don't worry; they ain't."

Suretsov had left the office early and gone home to the small apartment the agency rented for him on Zhaojiabang Road. It was an elderly building, about five blocks from Old Town, but the rent was right.

Perhaps unknown to ITAR-Tass, Suretsov liked it just fine. With a single bedroom, a bath, a kitchen, and a living room, it was far better than any flat he had ever been assigned in Moscow. The furnishings were dated but comfortable, and he had added a bookshelf for the books he consumed voraciously.

He carried two bags of his weekly grocery-buying spree as he unlocked the door and let himself in. Taking them to the kitchen, he placed them on the small counter, then shrugged out of his jacket and tossed it on the couch in the living room. He put the perishables in the refrigerator, then poured himself a small glass of pepper vodka.

The telephone rang. It was located on the kitchen counter, and he picked it up after taking one long sip of the vodka. It burned pleasantly on the way down.

It was Fedorchuk.

"Home early?" he asked.

"My shopping day, Yuri. You know what lines are like."

"I didn't think they were as bad in Shanghai."

They were not, but Suretsov said, "Come and see."

"Maybe I will."

"You did call for a purpose? Or just to harass me?"

"Both. I will tell you, Vladimir Petrovich, you are going to owe me so many favors you can never repay them. I have had to use sources that were tenuous."

"Tenuous?"

"In terms of what people owed me. Now I owe them, and that is not good."

"I understand. Believe me, I know where my debts lie."

"Let us hope so. Anyway, first there is your Pierre Lefant. He is a millionaire, in French francs."

"That is not what I expected."

"He has an ex-wife named Margot who took his Paris home and a guaranteed alimony of twenty-five thousand francs a month, so he has some overhead costs."

"That's better."

"He is still a millionaire who owns a ten-room villa near Cannes. It is paid for."

"Perhaps his wife does not know of it."

"I think that is the case," Fedorchuk said. "It is deeded in the name of Jean Legrand. The millions also happen to be in accounts assigned to Jean Legrand."

"Your sources, though tenuous, are very adept. If the wife had known of it, she might also have a summer home."

"My thought, exactly. And my sources are capable. Following up on the Legrand name, they discovered a Marseille brokerage account in the same name. Legrand is attempting to amass another fortune of his very own in the stock market."

"We do not happen to know his investments, do we?"

"Unless he has made purchases or sales in the last couple of days, I have a copy of his exact portfolio in front of me."

Suretsov was impressed with his supervisor.

"Do you find anything of interest, Yuri?"

"Yes. He seems a conservative investor. Most of his holdings are in blue-chip stocks, both American and European. There are a few Japanese stocks. There are mutual funds and bonds. What stands out is a heavy investment, equivalent to a half-million dollars U.S., in a start-up firm called Nuclear Power Limited."

"That is exactly what I wanted to hear," Suretsov said.

"I thought it might be."

He hung up thinking that he now had two ducks in a row.

But he did not know exactly where the row was going to end.

"Those are my two ducks," Suretsov said.

Grant said, "I think you need a few more."

He also wondered why the Russian had come to him with this information. It was not something that had anything to do with him or with MI. As far as Grant was concerned, if he could find a twenty-foot pole, he should use it to push Suretsov and his investigative digging far away from him.

"Oh, I do. I am asking for your reaction."

He had met Suretsov in a bar called the Watering Hole in Hongqiao New Town at the reporter's request. The 165-acre site was halfway between the airport and downtown Shanghai and was to become kind of an industrial park of foreigners. With a trade center, exhibition hall, apartment buildings, and a wide range of recreational facilities—swimming pools, tennis courts, and gardens—the area already served a few consulates. Some of the MI people had found apartments in Hongqiao.

Grant sipped from his Chivas. "You've given me just two facts, Vladimir."

"I prefer to deal in facts."

"And from them, you want to infer some kind of conspiracy?"

"I am buying your drink, Doug, and my supervisors do not let me assign it to my expense account, such as it is."

Grant grinned. "Well, hell. Okay. A guy that looks like Lefant slips some cash to a Russian trade attaché. Lefant owns a bunch of Nuke Power. Now, because I've talked to Stone, who understands these toy reactors, I'd take a wild guess that Sytenko had access to the Topaz designs and slipped them to Lefant for a fee. Payable in installments, maybe. Lefant hands off, or handed off some time ago, the Topaz plans to Nuke Power in exchange for a hefty chunk of stock. Sytenko builds his nest egg for his American girlfriend, and Lefant hides some more assets from his ex."

"Our minds run along the same suspicious track."

"We Americans see conspiracies everywhere, but what I don't understand, Vladimir, is what the hell it has to do with me. Why are we having this meeting?"

"Before I answer that, let me ask this: Are you impressed with the advisory committee's recent selections?"

"Media Bureau?"

"And Sung Wu."

The new CEO was a pain in the ass. On Monday, construction crews had moved into the lower floors and begun finishing them for Sung Wu and his staff—whoever they might turn out to be, though many would be European transplants from MBL. Sung had shown up on the fifth floor, shuffling around at his old man's gait and poking into everything as if he owned it. Grant had to call Deng Mai down to explain that Sung Wu had nothing whatsoever to do with Megatronics or the fifth floor. She also had to explain to him that his role in the programming end of Shanghai Star was separate from the technical aspects. He did not have automatic access to the upper floors.

In a rage, Sung had called Jiang on Diantha's phone, and Jiang had to calm him down and apparently explain the facts of life to him. The man was in a blue funk now because he didn't control what he thought he controlled.

"I didn't get to see the CIS product, so I can't really compare."

"You do want to avoid taking sides, do you not?"

"All right, from what I know, the committee picked the wrong box. And Sung is not necessarily the most enlightened gentleman I've ever met."

"It strikes me," Suretsov said, "that the China of old had a Big Brother mentality. Since I come from a similar background, I am perhaps sensitive to a government that wants to control its citizens so strictly."

Grant nodded his understanding and took another drink of the scotch.

"It also strikes me that some elements in the PRC would like to utilize Shanghai Star as the high-technology version of Big Brother."

Grant had come to like the Russian, and he felt he could be a bit more open, but he wanted to be certain. "I hope we're off the record."

Suretsov smiled. "From here on, we are always off the record. Unless I warn you, of course."

"I'm disappointed as hell. With people like Director Deng in the driver's seat, this whole thing could have been the most exciting thing to happen to China in seventy years. Jiang and his friends are going to wreck the whole concept."

"Would you see Jiang as paranoid?"

"Maybe a little. Maybe I'd be paranoid if I sat around all day thinking about a billion people who didn't like me."

"Now let us go back to Mr. Pierre Lefant. If, and I am saying *if*, he is capable of bribing a Russian official for profit, could he not also be capable of *being* bribed? Again, for profit?"

"Jiang is buying him off? Giving him the contract in return for . . . what? Jiang's control of content?"

Suretsov raised an eyebrow.

"Yeah, I suppose it's possible."

"Does that not enrage you to some degree, Doug?"

"I'm not happy with it, if that's the case. But, Vladimir, my business is plastic and silicon. I don't have a damned thing to do with the program end."

"Perhaps it is because you come out of an environment where the exchange of information is almost unhindered that you do not become fighting mad. In my case, I am enamored of the opportunity to investigate wrongdoing. It is something that those in my profession, in my country, could not do for a long time."

Grant felt guilty as hell. Probably because Suretsov knew he was on sure ground. He'd have made a good life-insurance salesman.

"Let's turn this around one more time, Vladimir. What if the bribe goes the other way?"

"Lefant pays off Jiang in order to secure the contract?"

"I like that scenario better," Grant said.

"Media Bureau benefits more than Lefant. He owns only a few shares of stock in his company."

"I'll bet he's on commission," Grant said, thinking of Maynard Crest.

"All right. Let me think about that angle for a few days."

"Do that. I'm not good at this. I don't think it affects my operation."

"No? Doug, there are the incidents which *do* affect Megatronics. Sabotage. Assassination attempts."

"You're right, Vladimir. *That* does make me fighting mad."

"And if they are connected?"

Grant frowned. "In what way?"

"I do not know. However, anything out of the ordinary that happens to those associated with Shanghai Star should be of concern to you. I do not believe you should draw so fine a line between the technical and the program aspects of the enterprise. It seems to me that if Shanghai Star is unsuccessful because of its biased programming, then Megatronics will also suffer. If the world sees a disaster, the world does not question whether or not the disaster was caused by the ministers in Beijing or the electronics genius in Shanghai. They only see a disaster."

Shit. All I need at this point in my life is a logical reporter.

"You're trying to recruit me for something, right?"

Suretsov's smile displayed all of his teeth. "You are close to Deng Mai. She is close to the committee. I am hoping that you can learn something that I cannot."

Grant pursed his lips and thought it over. "You wouldn't also be thinking about the close relationship between Jiang and Pai, the energy chieftain?"

"You see? There are many avenues to explore."

"And what's the outcome?"

"From my heart, Douglas Grant, I would like to see a wrong righted. The Chinese people deserve better than they are getting."

"The appointments of MBL and Sung Wu aren't cast in concrete, are they?"

"It is a shifty world we live in," the Russian said.

"I dream about this axe hanging over my head, Vladimir. If I get too far out of line, the axe drops and I lose. My visa, at least. My company evicted, at most. Those ministers in Beijing have bigger weapons than I have."

"But you are a crafty man."

"You sure you aren't with the KGB?"

"It is the Ministry of Security and Interior Affairs now, and no, I am not."

"Let me see what I can do, but no promises."

"That is all I ask," Suretsov said, standing. "By the way, the International Atomic Energy Agency has not inspected those reactors."

"What!"

"They are scheduled, at the PRC's request, to examine them a year after they begin operation."

"Does that seem right to you?" Grant asked.

"That is because they approved the design. The agency does not anticipate problems."

"Mickey Stone does."

"I must meet your Mickey Stone. He may feel as I do."

"And that is?"

"The Topaz was designed for operation in space. They did not worry about radiation leakage."

Suretsov left money for the drinks on the table and departed. Grant got up and crossed the room to sit with three MI engineers he had spotted. He stayed an hour and had another drink with them.

It was nearly eleven o'clock at night when he went out to the parking lot and crawled into his Jimmy. He pulled out of the parking slot and followed the curving street to the entrance to the compound. Turning right, he fell in with light traffic headed for the city on Hongqiao Road. He thought about his conversation with Suretsov and found himself checking the mirror frequently.

Was that set of headlights pacing him?

Was he becoming paranoid?

He thought about pulling over to see if the lights went on by, then thought that would only prove his paranoia.

The traffic got a little thicker as he entered the city.

The lights were still with him.

The street became Yanan Road.

Instead of turning left on the street to his apartment, he turned right and drove past the headquarters of Shanghai Star.

The headlights followed him around the corner.

He turned left at the next block and drove east on Huashan Road, then took another left.

The red and yellow and blue neon lights seemed to cast sinister shadows. He couldn't help thinking about Shanghai's sordid past. A lot of people had died in this city, both before and after the Japanese occupation.

At Yanan Road, he turned west again, then right onto the street to his apartment building. There were a lot of cars behind him now, and he couldn't pick out the pair of headlights that he thought was following him.

Had they gone straight across Yanan?

All in his mind.

When he was parked in the lot behind his building, he sat in the truck for a while, looking around. The lot was well lit. Nothing seemed to be out of place.

He got out and headed for the back door, looking for the right key on his ring. Kind of like walking home on a dark night, knowing the boogeyman was behind him.

He made it.

But when he let himself into his apartment, he saw that the red light on the answering machine was blinking. The furious stutter of the light told him he had about a dozen messages.

He hit the rewind.

The first recording told him in a cracked voice, "Mr. Grant, this is Bobby Wheeler at the Harbin Facility. Look, ah," the voice choked up, "I've got three dead and six hurt bad. . . ."

Friday, September 2

The Citation was wheels-up by 1:10 in the morning, and Dusty McKelvey was still trying to soothe the air controller over the radio. It had nearly taken an act of the State Council to get an emergency clearance for the flight. Chinese air controllers preferred a week's advance notice from independent charter aircraft or, in the case of Southeast Asia Charter, which was making so many flights, at least a day.

Grant had to call Jiang, getting him out of bed, and talk him into lending his authority to the flight. The minister was reluctant to do so, but for the circumstances.

"This is not good joss," McKelvey said after he signed off with the air controller.

"What's not?" Grant was in the copilot's seat. On such short notice, McKelvey hadn't been able to track down any of the three pilots he currently had in Shanghai. That had been one of the problems. The Chinese didn't like corporate jets running around the populated eastern coast with only one pilot. They probably didn't like corporate aircraft, period.

"This shit in Harbin. The shooter going after Stone."

"Have you heard anything, Dusty?"

"Unusual? No. My guys hang out around the airports and hotel bars, but all I've heard about Shanghai Star has been on the positive side."

Grant idly watched the instruments as McKelvey levelled off at the prescribed 20,000 feet of altitude. The lights of Shanghai were far behind them, but Grant saw a sprinkling of lights along the coast as they left the continent behind and swung out over the Yellow Sea.

Harbin was over a thousand miles away, slightly east of due north, and they would be over the sea for about half the distance. Heilongjiang Province was the northeastern-most province of the People's Republic of China.

"It's going to be awhile, Doug. You might as well get some shut-eye."

"Who takes over if you get sick?"

"I'll wake you."

Grant had learned in the army to get his sleep where he could, so he loosened his seat belt, bunched his windbreaker into a pillow, and lodged his head into the headrest. In minutes, he was fast asleep.

He woke when the engines changed tone, sat up, and found that McKelvey was already lined up for his landing at Harbin.

"You snore," McKelvey said.

"Do not."

"Do, too."

"Must have been my upright position."

"Any excuse in a storm."

"What have we got?"

"On the ground? Light wind, temperature sixty-eight. It's almost five o'clock."

They were shunted off by the air controller and made to circle the airport once while another aircraft landed.

"Probably a cargo freighter," McKelvey said, adjusting the red bandanna wrapped around his forehead.

"We get delayed by cargo?"

"Happens every now and then. This part of Asia, Doug, there's some jealousy about independent aircraft. It just doesn't seem right to some of these controllers that an airplane can be privately owned and allowed to go where it wants to go. They let us know, from time to time, who's got the real power."

"Jesus." It didn't seem right to Grant, but then he recalled some of his past dealings with American midlevel bureaucrats. Everybody liked to prove they were somebody and could make a difference in their tiny parts of the world.

McKelvey put the airplane on the runway smoothly and parked in the out-of-the-way spot someone directed him to.

"I'll get the tanks topped off, Doug, then unroll my sleeping bag in the cabin. Be here when you're ready to go."

Grant unstrapped, stepped out of the cockpit, released the airstair door, and stepped down into a cool morning. Walking across the tarmac, he was met by an official who wanted to see his visa, then directed him to a gate in the chain-link fence.

In the parking lot was a Shanghai Star truck, and Bobby Wheeler crawled out from behind the wheel. Wheeler was a software engineer reporting to Wickersham, but was also in charge of the Harbin operation. Close to forty, he was tall, fair-haired, and blue-eyed. At five in the morning, with the sun breaking over the flat plains to the east, he looked haggard—hair ruffled, a stubble of whiskers coating his cheeks.

"Good morning, Doug."

"Let's go, Bobby."

They got in the utility vehicle, and Wheeler started it up, shifted to first, and gunned it out of the lot. The tires squealed as he turned onto the pavement of the highway leading to the city.

"Let me have it one more time, Bobby."

"I heard it, the explosion, from my apartment, which is three blocks away. It was nine-forty, and I tore over there. The place is a shambles."

"The people, Bobby."

"Okay, yeah. There were twelve people at work on the second floor in an open office space. The bomb went off in the first-floor reception area and ripped out the ceiling. There was some kind of shrapnel in this thing because it just shredded our guys. One American, one Australian, and one Chinese were killed. There's two Americans and four Chinese in the hospital, all in serious condition."

"The other three?"

"Scrapes and bruises. A few cuts. They were lucky as hell."

Old emotions, which Grant thought he had forgotten, were boiling within. As a platoon leader, he had felt what he thought at the time was an inordinate sense of responsibility for the men and women in his platoon; he couldn't help it. When they were attacked, he was attacked. When they hurt, he hurt. Stone's encounter with some unknown gunman had unnerved him some, but was still remote. It could have been happenstance, an accident.

This wasn't so remote. He didn't want it to be. He wanted to feel the pain. He wanted to kill someone.

"Let's go to the hospital first."

Wheeler drove into the city and to the hospital, a place that was antiquated by his American standards, but the doctors and the nurses were compassionate. One of the doctors kept apologizing for his lack of modern medical tools.

Four of the patients were under sedation, but Grant talked to one of the Americans, a kid from Tulsa, Oklahoma, and one of the Chinese, an older man who had learned his computer skills in the army. Both were heavily bandaged as a result of shrapnel wounds. The Oklahoman wasn't very lucid; he'd been injected with heavy doses of painkiller. The Chinese was more concerned with Grant's appearance in his semiprivate room than with his own injuries. It seemed unfathomable to him that the big boss would show up to shake his hand and extend his sympathy.

They stayed an hour, and Grant was thoroughly depressed by the time they got back in the truck and drove out to the Harbin Facility.

It was located on the outskirts of Harbin in a development of rectangular, unremarkable apartment buildings. In a refurbished four-story apartment structure, the Harbin Facility was a maze of offices reclaimed from bedrooms and living rooms. There were a lot of rest rooms.

It was 7:30 A.M. when Wheeler parked as close as he could get to the building. Police barricades were set up, and the street behind them was littered with police cars and fire trucks. The firemen were rolling their hoses and collecting their equipment. The cops were standing around. It could have been L.A.

After they identified themselves at the barricade, Grant and Wheeler were allowed to walk the half-block to the entrance.

The glass doors were gone.

"Were those locked?" Grant asked.

"They're supposed to be after six P.M., but I couldn't swear to it since I left at five."

Grant climbed the three stairs, stepping gingerly on shattered glass, and stepped through the portal into the reception room.

Black, sooty water stood in puddles on the carpeting. The once-white walls were scorched where they hadn't been torn apart by pieces of furniture propelled by the blast. Gaping holes into adjacent rooms revealed more carnage. Directly above where the reception desk had once stood, the ceiling had opened like a flower, almost fifteen feet across.

There was no one in the room, and Wheeler led him to the right, past the elevator stack, to the stairway. They climbed the concrete steps quickly, and on the second floor, a policeman in civilian clothes blocked his way.

"Who are you?" he asked in English.

Grant identified the two of them.

"I am Inspector Chou, Mr. Grant. Where were you last night?"

Grant didn't like the immediate quiz, but said, "In Shanghai. My plane landed at five this morning."

He asked Wheeler the same question, and was told that the manager was home with his wife. It would be checked out, Grant had no doubt.

Another security officer took Wheeler down the hallway to question him, and Chou said, "Follow me, Mr. Grant."

They went down a short hallway to the open space where twenty desks had been arranged in pairs, back to back. Six men worked at collecting evidence. In the middle of the area was the wound above the reception desk. Charred computer workstations, desks, and chairs were flung haphazardly away from the hole in the floor. Blood was spattered everywhere, now blackened into ink blots.

Grant had seen blood before, and he was just as sickened by the sight now, as he had been then.

"What was it, Inspector?"

"The bomb was a combination of dynamite and small construction nails, probably quite heavy. It was antipersonnel in nature and intended to inflict as much harm as possible. The forensic specialists believe that the charge was in a shaped container designed to exert most of its force upward."

"So, if it was placed on the reception desk, they knew beforehand that they wanted the damage to occur on this floor?"

"It would seem so," Chou said. "How often do people work here at night?"

"You'll have to check with Wheeler, but I suspect that there are at least a few here every night. We've been working hard, with the deadlines that are approaching."

"Would any one of these persons be here every night?"

"You're thinking that a particular man was targeted?"

"I try to think of every possibility."

"Again, you'd have to check with Wheeler. There will be sign-in logs around."

"Possibly at the reception desk?"

Grant saw the problem.

"The desk is gone, isn't it?"

"Yes, sir, it is."

"Our logs are kept on the computer, so there'll be a record in some database."

"Good. That is helpful."

Grant couldn't see that it would be. With the incidents in Guangzhou, this thing was much broader than revenge against one man. Shanghai Star was the target, but Grant couldn't figure out why. Jiang Guofeng and his buddies were unhappy with the Star, but their attitudes should have changed with Sung Wu in charge of what went over the airwaves.

"Do you have any ideas, Mr. Grant?"

"I wish that I did have, Inspector. I've been standing here, looking at this mess, trying to figure out why anyone thinks Shanghai Star is worth a single life."

"I am certain that there are a few."

Grant looked at the policeman, but his face remained impassive.

"Will I know where I can reach you, Mr. Grant?"

"Sure." He gave the man a business card with his office and home numbers.

"If there's a working phone, Inspector, I'm going to use it."

"Of course."

Grant turned and went back down the hall until he found an office with an unlocked door. He picked up the phone, heard a dial tone, and sat in the visitor's chair in front of the desk.

He called Deng first.

"Douglas! I heard just after midnight. Minister Jiang called me. There are three dead?"

Grant confirmed the details for her and brought her up to date.

"Look, Mai, we need around-the-clock security for all of Shanghai Star's installations. At least two cops per building. Four for yours since that's the heart of the system."

"Jiang will object to the cost."

"It'll be cheaper than paying the bills we'll keep sending him."

"I will talk to him."

He remembered those headlights following him last night, certain now that his instincts had been correct.

"And, Mai, you need some protection, too."

"Nonsense!"

"At least think about it."

"That is all I will do."

When she hung up, he depressed the reset button, then called Parker.

"Megatronics, the director's office."

"I can hear it in your voice, Diantha. You've been crying."

"Oh, Doug! I knew Dick Wells!"

"I'm sorry." He didn't know what else to say, and "sorry" was so lame.

"Is it bad?" she asked.

"Yes."

"Tell me. I've got people hanging over my desk, waiting for the details."

"There's not much to tell right now," he said, but gave her what he knew. His employees were entitled to know what was going on.

"Keep it to the facts, Diantha. Don't let rumors get started."

"I will."

"Then, let's get this out." He dictated a quick memo for all employees of MI, telling them to be cautious of where they went and who was around them. On the streets, stay with a buddy. "You might send a copy of that up to the Director's office. Mai should probably send the same kind of warning to Star personnel."

"I'll do it."

Grant replaced the phone and stood up to find Wheeler waiting in the doorway.

"You heard, Bobby?"

"Yes."

"Tell your people to stay alert. I'm not sure we'll get much help."

He had Wheeler drive him back to the airport where he found McKelvey asleep in the aisle of the passenger compartment. His opening the door and rocking the aircraft as he climbed aboard didn't disturb the pilot in any way.

Grant tapped McKelvey's bare foot with his own.

McKelvey opened one eye.

"I knew you were there."

"Come on, cowboy. Time flies."

"So do we."

McKelvey sat up, and dug into one of his boots for his socks.

"What was it like?"

"Antipersonnel bomb, they told me."

"Shitty, then."

"It was bad."

"This going to turn into a combat zone, Doug?"

"Are you looking for hostile-fire pay, Dusty?"

"Nah. I don't need the pay. But if you need a willing soldier, I'm your man. A few of my other guys, too."

Grant just looked down at him.

"Mean it, man."

"Thanks, Dusty."

McKelvey finished pulling his boots on, scrambled to his feet, and made his way into the cockpit. Grant followed him and fell into the right-hand seat.

"Shanghai bound, right?"

"No. We'll go to Guangzhou."

"Ah, shit! My plan's filed for Shanghai. They'll raise hell with us."

"That's okay. Take off on the filed plan. We'll change it en route."

"That's going to go over like grape-flavored noodles."

"It's their tough luck if they don't like grapes," Grant told him.

Deng Mai went home over her lunch hour, something she rarely did. She parked in the street, let herself in the front door, and tossed her purse on an 18th century Vile and Cobb library table now overpowering the entry. It had appeared yesterday afternoon, a gift from Pierre Lefant.

Her mother was in the kitchen, chatting with the housekeeper and eating a shrimp salad. She glowed with well-being.

"Darling! You are home!"

"Mama, where have you been?"

Deng Yvonne gave her the half-smile she thought of as secretive.

"You did not come home last night."

"You have not noticed, my young one. I am an adult. Would you like a salad?"

"I am not hungry."

The housekeeper decided to pursue another chore and left the kitchen.

"You are sleeping with him," Deng accused.

"He thinks I am fifty-three years old. Isn't that charming?"

"Did you hear what I said? Do you deny it?"

"Did you hear what I said, Mai? I am old enough to make my own choices."

"It is a terrible choice you have made, Mama."

"How would you know? Your sights are set on boorish young Americans."

"Mama!" Deng stamped her foot, and then regretted it. She rarely lost her temper, much less in such a silly way as throwing a tantrum in the kitchen.

She was in enough control to realize that accusing Lefant of being shortsighted and inept would only result in her mother's quick and vocal defense of the man. She could not raise the issues she had learned that Suretsov was pursuing, not yet anyway. She also realized that she could no longer confide in Yvonne Deng; whatever she said was likely to get back to Lefant.

"What is it you see in him, Mama?"

"What do you see in Grant?"

"Douglas and I are not consorting wildly for all to see."

"You are being discreet, then?"

The argument was not going to get her anywhere. Deng spun around and marched out of the house. She was halfway down the front walk before she realized she had to go back and get her purse.

As she could probably have forecast, her mood had not improved by the time she returned to her office. She had had little sleep last night, since being awakened by the midnight telephone call with news of the tragedy, then discovering that her mother had not come home. She had paced most of the night away, wanting to call the police, the hospitals, but knowing that Yvonne was with Lefant. Several times, she had nearly called the International Hotel to ask for Lefant's room, then refrained.

She knew that, in her mother's eyes, she was behaving badly. Certainly, the elder Deng was capable of managing her own life. She had done so quite well for many years, and Mai had not been required to monitor or direct it.

It was Lefant who made the relationship so insufferable; she would have thought nothing, or at least very little, about any other suitor her mother might attract. Part of her discomfort lay in the fact that her mother had shown no interest in anyone at all in the time since her father's death.

Further, she was on very shaky ground; she had absolutely no evidence—unless the Russian came up with something—that Lefant was anything other than what he purported to be. He just . . . *seemed* sleazy.

Miss Jiangyou had phone messages for her, but told her in some trepidation, "Minister Shao is waiting for you, Director. He insisted upon waiting in your office."

"That is quite all right," she replied to Jiangyou's evident relief.

Deng did not like the thought of the defense minister walking right through her security measures, but of course, he had the right, and the guards would not have denied him. They were probably still quaking like trees in a windstorm.

She wished only that he had called before coming.

She went into her office. Shao was seated on the sofa, and he stood up. His posture was rigid, but that was typical for him, and he bowed slightly from the waist.

She returned the bow.

"Had I known you were coming, Minister, I would have made myself available."

His gray eyes appraised her. She felt Shao had an interest—romantic or otherwise—in her, though he had never overtly revealed it. He was very conservative, and he had a large family.

"It is of no consequence," he told her. "I have been enjoying your Paris scenes."

She glanced at the pictures.

"They are gifts from my mother. They are Lautrecs, but only prints, I regret."

She took a chair opposite him, sitting sideways with her knees primly together because of the short skirt she had worn that day. Shao returned to his seat.

"How may we help you, Minister?"

"I am in Shanghai on military business, but I learned in a conversation with Minister Jiang a short while ago that you have requested full-time security at all Shanghai Star facilities."

"That is true," she said. "The incidents are quite disturbing, and I fear for the lives of Shanghai Star employees and consultants."

"Tell me of the incidents, please."

She briefed him with what she knew of each.

"I did not know of the attempted shooting of the American executive."

"I imagine that very few outside of Guangzhou are aware. The police seemed to have . . . hushed it up. At minimum, they are making very little progress."

"So, that is four incidents?"

"With the destruction of the rocket, yes. My feeling is that it has gone far beyond isolated coincidence."

"There is no such thing as a coincidence," the former general assured her.

"That is my belief."

"Minister Jiang tells me that intensive security is unwarranted."

"If I knew who was behind these attacks, I could better answer that," Deng said.

"I had an interesting discussion with Mr. Grant two weeks ago. He convinced me the army has more of a vested interest in Shanghai Star than we thought we had. This morning, after talking to Jiang, I called the Guangdong regional commander, and I learned for the first time that when the Guangzhou computers were destroyed, the army command lost data transmission. It was only for ten minutes, until some automatic procedure switched to new circuits, but still it is disturbing. Should we have lost the entire facility, defensive systems could have been in jeopardy."

Deng nodded. "In a true emergency, Minister, we could shift the outlying substations to a direct link with the satellite. There is emergency programming already installed for that eventuality, and Mr. Wickersham's team is providing army technicians with the training to use it. But, as a matter of normal operations, the military signals do pass through the major provincial facilities, which provide the routing of data and voice transmission. Those are all encrypted, naturally."

Shao smiled. "You see, Director? I do not know these things. The technology has gone well beyond my capabilities. And I am afraid to ask the general staff if they know the scope of the systems they purchased. I fear what their answer would be."

"When Shanghai Star was first proposed, full briefings were provided, but I suspect you are correct. That was three years ago. I will make it a point to arrange briefings for the general staff in the near future. It should be a full seminar, in fact."

"Invite me, please."

"Of course."

"Let us go back to your immediate problem, which I now perceive as also a national-defense concern. Minister Jiang is reluctant, for some reason, to request police security. I would like to propose that the army secure your buildings for you."

He waited expectantly, keeping his eyes on hers.

She responded cautiously. "Your offer is generous, Minister Shao. I have . . . reservations, however."

"Please state them."

After a deep breath, she said, "A visible army presence at the facilities may cause discomfort in some quarters."

"Yes, I had the same thought. Even, as you say, the same reservation. Some will think the army is attempting to exert its power over Shanghai Star. Some will think the army is aligning itself with the managing director."

"I hope my position is clear, Minister. My only objective is to make Shanghai Star perform as it is capable of performing. I would much prefer to remain neutral politically." As soon as she made the statement, she thought of Grant.

"I think that is true. However, I think it is also impossible."

She smiled, but knew that it was a grim smile.

"My position, brought to my attention by Mr. Grant, must be that there is a defense issue involved. We must protect the centers of communication at any cost."

"Could you suggest to Minister Jiang a shared responsibility? Both army and police security forces?"

Shao smiled. "Perhaps you will go a long way in politics, Director. Let me test the waters with your suggestion. If it does not gain credibility, I will be forced to recommend that the chief of staff deploy military police."

He stood up, and Deng followed his lead.

"I appreciate your discussing this with me, Minister."

"You have given me some insights," he said. "We will see if we cannot keep your empire, and mine, in separate, but whole pieces."

After he left, Deng reviewed the entire conversation. Shao had been very open and convincingly sincere in his statements.

Unfortunately, Shao Tsung was a complicated man, with very many agendas. She could not help feeling that, whatever he and Grant had discussed, Shao had learned that Shanghai Star was, first and best, a military tool.

One that he should control.

The Shanghai Bureau of ITAR-Tass had a teletype repeater connected to the Xinhua News Agency, and so he had known of the disaster in Harbin as soon as he had come into the office in the morning. It was an internal message between Harbin and Beijing, relating the bare facts, and he did not think the story would get a large play in the daily Chinese papers. Earlier, the fact that the loss of the rocket was due to sabotage had barely been mentioned. The Guangzhou events had not rated newspaper or broadcast space in Beijing.

Suretsov sat at his tiny desk and considered the implications. It was apparent to him, if to no one else, that Shanghai Star was the target of someone, probably some subversive group. He could think of no connection between the destructive incidents and Pierre Lefant. Whatever Lefant's involvement in the Nuclear Power Limited scenario, it would not serve his interests to see Shanghai Star inoperative.

So, it was a different story, but one that the Chinese agencies did not see fit to exploit. Perhaps it was time to bring some public and international attention to Director Deng's plight.

He turned to the pull-out shelf of his desk, on which rested an Apple Macintosh. Fedorchuk had been extremely reluctant to approve an outlay for a computer, but when Suretsov had located the used machine, he had finally given in. He turned it on while dialling the English information line for the number of the Guangzhou police.

It took almost twenty minutes before he located the inspector in charge of the investigation into the burning of the computers.

After he identified himself, the man seemed impressed by the telephone call, either that it was from Shanghai or from ITAR-Tass. Suretsov could not tell which.

"How may I help you, sir?"

Suretsov typed the data from the Harbin teletype copy as he talked to the inspector. "I am inquiring into the investigation of the computers destroyed at the Guangzhou Facility of Shanghai Star Communications."

"Ah! That case is closed, sir."

"How was it resolved?"

"We have arrested a man. . . ."

"His name, please."

He typed in the name of a Chinese man.

"What was the motive, Inspector?"

"He was, as they say, a disgruntled employee. He chose to take out his disenchantment with several cans of lighter fluid."

"I see. You are positive he was not paid to be a disgruntled employee?"

There was a long pause, then the policeman said, "In my profession, Mr. Suretsov, no one is ever positive."

"I understand your predicament."

He would quote the inspector, but leave the case resolution open to conjecture.

"What of the case of Mickey Stone?"

"Stone? I do not know the name."

"He is the American who was shot at last month."

"Oh, yes. Another detective is assigned to that case."

"I take it that no resolution has been achieved."

"As I understand it, a nine-millimeter shell casing was located nearby, but there have been no leads worthy of pursuit. It may have been accidental or a random shooting. Those are difficult to pin down."

It sounded to Suretsov as if the Guangzhou police were not avid investigators.

"Thank you, Inspector."

He called General Hua for a quote on the rocket loss.

He called Deng for a reaction quote, but she was out.

He called Grant, but his secretary said he was somewhere en route to Guangdong Province. He asked her to try to leave a message for him.

Suretsov wrote quickly, and he soon had the rough draft of what was shaping up as a pretty good story. He would fill it out with quotes as people called back.

He dialled the number for Minister Jiang.

In midafternoon, Wen Yito brought cups of tea into Jiang's office, and the two of them sipped the aromatic brew as they talked across his desk.

"I understand," Wen said, "that Shao Tsung spent over an hour with Deng Mai."

"That is very interesting. I wonder what they have in common?"

"There is Shao's request to you this morning to place guards at the buildings."

"Would she go behind my back to the army?"

Wen licked his upper lips with the pink point of his tongue.

Jiang did not like the development. He had barely secured the vote in the committee to place Media Bureau and Sung Wu in position, and Shao had voted with him in exchange for the emergency control of the satellites. However, perhaps now Shao assumed that Jiang owed him sufficiently to allow the defense ministry to consolidate its influence over Shanghai Star.

If at all possible, he had to keep the army neutral.

"Would Deng ask the army for security?" he rephrased his question.

"I was listening to her plea to you," Wen said. "She seemed adamant about the need for protection. And perhaps, Minister, she is correct. These affairs are becoming costly for the ministry."

Wen had not answered the question, but then again, maybe he had. Jiang knew he would be billed for the losses at Guangzhou, which were considerable. He did not have the final details relative to Harbin, but they would also be substantial considering the injuries and the loss of life. Then, too, his brief interview on the telephone with the Russian correspondent was also alarming. The man was apparently making his own inferences about the attacks on Shanghai Star people and equipment. He had done his best to contain the stories, but now, they might well appear around the world. It was not a positive image.

"I may have been too hasty in my response to Deng. If Shao becomes involved, the presence of army people will look bad for us."

"Should I arrange a telephone call to Deng?"

"No. To Shao."

The President of MBL-China had been demanding, and a trifle arrogant, with Deng Mai. The upshot, however, was that Sung and Lefant were finally allowed a guided tour of the upper floors.

When they reached the security area, badges were waiting for them, and Deng Mai met them on the other side of the steel door.

"Good afternoon, gentlemen."

Lefant smiled.

Swinging an arm wide to indicate the security precautions, Sung said, "It is ridiculous to suffer humiliation in order to survey what should be mine to examine."

"Do you know C-plus-plus, Mr. Sung?" she asked.

"C-what?"

"It is a computer language. The people on these floors understand computer languages and computer technologies. The people on your floors understand entertainment and communications programs. They are two entirely different realms. Experts in one area are not necessarily experts in the other, and difficulties can arise."

Lefant's suspicions were confirmed as Deng began their tour. She barely spoke to him, and then only when he prodded her with a question. He had overstepped his bounds with Yvonne, and now it would come back to haunt him.

He had not intended to do so, but Yvonne Deng was an enticing woman, and the evening had gone out of his control early. She also had an amazingly varied erotic repertoire, to which he had eagerly responded.

The cost was to be dear, though. Deng Mai would find ways to take it out on him; he knew it in his very soul.

Though she did not dote on him, she kept her attention focused on Sung, and the unfortunate idiot did not seem to appreciate it. Jiang would have told him, of course, that Deng had not favored his candidacy, and beyond that, it was apparent that Sung considered women outside the house superfluous.

They followed her through long passages fronting on glassed compartments containing row upon row of teal-colored plastic and metal boxes. Other compartments housed brown boxes. Lefant could have cared less, but he listened as she made explanations. "These are the transponders which convert analog signals to digitally encoded forms for transmission to the satellite . . . computers controlling antenna movements . . . console operator commands the satellite with instructions about which receivers are active and allowed to accept a signal . . . billing systems . . . these computers devoted to viewer-interactive programs. . . ."

She took an hour-and-a-half to complete the tour, possibly in the hope of wearing down Sung Wu. And in fact, he did appear somewhat frazzled by the time they returned to the sixth floor and her office. The secretary provided them with tea.

Lefant would have preferred a brandy, but he politely sipped from his tiny cup.

"Are there any specific questions to which I might respond, Mr. Sung?"

"I saw no projection rooms."

"Screening rooms? There are none. We have a master monitoring room on the tenth floor," she said. "But I believe you will have three or four production and screening rooms on your floors."

The fool still could not understand, Lefant thought. He had tried to explain a compact disc to Sung, but the man didn't have enough imagination to grasp the concept. How the images and audio signals were implanted on that little disk completely escaped him. Lefant thought Sung envisioned himself sitting in a screening room, carefully editing each program before it went over the air. He did not fathom the impossibility of censoring all of the material devoted to one channel, much less the sixteen channels that would be implemented on October 1. From the date of the contract, MBL in Europe had been hiring hundreds of interpreters and technicians and putting them to work editing the immense catalogs of program material. Two hundred people would soon be en route to Shanghai to work in this building. In the first year, there would be many reruns until the libraries were built up. Reruns, however, would not daunt an audience that had been deprived for so many decades. For Chinese audiences, they were, in fact, premieres.

Sung did not understand that he was there simply to enforce Jiang's policies. Lefant had been attempting to give the man some on-the-job training in executive leadership, leaving the details to others, but that also was proving difficult. He wanted to poke into every closet by himself.

"Our function," Deng went on, "is simply to accept your feeds. . . ."

"Feeds?"

The ass will eradicate any credibility MBL has.

"The programming provided through either your local sources or those beamed from Europe to ShangStar Two. Many of the European packages are captured by downlink and stored here for later broadcast; some will be broadcast directly to our audiences. Once your programmers have determined what goes out, when, and on which channel, the signals are sent to us and we assure that the quality is maintained, that they are fed into the correct channels, and sent to the satellite. Subscribers in the

Shanghai region receive their signals directly from us via microwave links, but in the outlying regions, the primary facilities capture the signals by way of their downlinks. They then broadcast directly to subscribers or via microwave to relay stations in small towns close to the capitals. In some of the remote areas, subscribers will receive their signals directly from the satellite with special equipment. There are many variations at work, Mr. Sung."

"You do not have programs?" Sung asked. "I understood that you had many thousands of programs."

"I think," Lefant broke in, "you may have confused the kinds of programs that are your responsibility, President Sung"—he liked to be called President—"with the computer programs of Director Deng's subordinates."

"Computer programs?"

"They are only instructions which tell the computers what to do," Deng told him.

"Let us go," Sung said, standing.

Lefant stood, looking to Deng, but she did not seem inclined to wink at him, or smile, or in any way suggest that she saw the humor in the whole thing. In fact, she seemed distracted, as if her mind were tracking on far more important issues.

Then again, Lefant saw no humor in Sung's incompetence, either.

They landed at Guangzhou at 4:15 in the afternoon. It was raining.

Little puddles of water splashed and sprayed around them as the Citation raced through them. McKelvey parked in the general aviation section, made certain the plane was well-chocked against the stiff wind and the fuel tanker ordered, then walked with Grant to the main terminal. They got Cokes and ham sandwiches to make up for the lunch they had missed.

Sitting at a tiny table next to a window overlooking the runway, Grant said, "Dusty, you've been around Asia for a long time."

"Too long."

"Why?"

McKelvey grimaced, "Oh, in a way, I kind of like it. I hung on when I went REFRAD—released from active duty—because I didn't like what was going on at home. I grew up in San Francisco. Plus, there was a bunch of money to be made here. I don't think, stateside, I'd have amassed fourteen aircraft and forty employees. If I keep getting contracts like yours, I can even retire someday."

Grant thought he could probably retire anytime; he just liked the flying.

"You like China?"

"I like Thailand best. The people are gentler. Here, they're so repressed they don't know how to act around foreigners. Sometimes, I feel like I'm sitting on a keg of dynamite. Something's going to set it off."

"But you wouldn't leave?"

"Nah. It's the kind of thing that makes life interesting."

"You're an old Asia hand. Do you understand the Chinese culture?"

"Some, but you've got to remember most of my business is down south. Until you came along, about all I had was an occasional junket to Hong Kong."

"What about the people?"

"My crews and I hang out at airports, Doug. We don't often meet the common man, but what I've noticed is that, despite the government's attempts to ignore religion, there's still a deep sense of the spiritual and the mystical present. It's a real strange mix. There's courtesy, there's downright, bare-bladed cruelty, and above all there's this desperate need to maintain face."

"Yeah, I know," Grant said. "The slightest insult can lead to war."

"Which you've got to be prepared for."

"You mentioned something like that this morning, Dusty."

"You're not going to see H-bombs, but dynamite can be devastating, too."

"I saw that. I can't for the life of me figure out why Shanghai Star has been targeted. There's a tug-of-war in the capital between the reformists and conservatives, but nothing requiring ordnance. They got what they wanted with MBL and Sung Wu."

"Skip the politicos, Doug. Shanghai Star has been hyped for

four years as the solution to the common man's knowledge deprivation. Everything in the papers has emphasized how they're going to be swamped with information. All of a sudden, that's not quite the case. You and Deng aren't going to deliver on the promise."

"Me?"

"The Green-Eyed Devil and Lotus Blossom. You're the ones associated with Shanghai Star, whether you like it or not."

"You've heard this?"

"From the travellers I meet when I'm having my lunch. Like this." McKelvey took a big bite out of his sandwich.

Damn it! It's not my fault.

Then again, maybe it was. He was so busy pedalling his bike out of the way of others, he was no longer on the right road.

Maybe it was time to run over somebody and get back on the path.

"You think the attacks against us might be coming from some populist outfit that's upset because Shanghai Star isn't turning out the way they thought it would? The way it was promised?"

"That'd be my guess, Doug. If it's not going to work right, don't let it work at all. Christ, if it was a bunch of guys from Beijing behind it, don't you think they could come up with ordnance more sophisticated than lighter fluid or dynamite and nails?"

"Shit. You're probably right."

"I am right," McKelvey said.

The pilot went to find a phone so he could check on his other flight operations, and Grant left the terminal to find a cab. The taxi got him to the Guangzhou Facility a little after six. The rain had let up, and the air smelled fresher than was normal.

The building was a newer one, recaptured by the government from the profiteers just like the one in Shanghai. It was a ten-story high-rise of bronzed glass and steel in the northeast part of the city.

Grant paid off the cab and crossed the wide sidewalk to the front doors.

They were locked, and he didn't have either a card or a code for the keypad mounted on the wall next to them. He rang the intercom button, and a Chinese woman tending the reception desk came to the door, perused his identification suspiciously, then finally let him in.

"Wickersham or Stone in the building?" he asked her.

She went back to the desk to check her terminal. "Mr. Wickersham has left, but Mr. Stone is on eight."

"Thank you."

He took the elevator up, and again had to go through a security check on the eighth floor before he was allowed to roam. As he went down the long central corridor, the lights dimmed briefly three times.

They needed those nuclear reactors soon, he thought. Leaky or not.

"Goddamn it!" came from the end of the hall, and he knew he'd located Stone.

He passed several glass-fronted computer rooms. Chinese and American technicians were at work.

At the end of the hall, he reached a small diagnostics lab and looked through the open door. With his back to the door, Stone was on a castered stool in the middle of the room, poking into the back of a Model 1001 with its rear panel removed. A pretty girl with short hair and freckles was on another stool next to him holding a multitester. He didn't know the woman.

"You want to hold it down in here? You're waking up the people in the lobby."

"Oh, shit!" the woman said, looking up at him.

Stone spun around on his stool. "I met you once, didn't I? It's been so long since I've been in Shanghai, I don't remember the name."

Grant entered and held his hand out to the woman. "I'm Doug Grant."

She rose to shake his hand. "I've seen your picture. I don't belong here."

"Meg Naylor, Doug. She's a friend of mine."

"I'm with DCT," she said. "But I'll leave."

"Don't leave on my account. Stone needs all the help he can get."

"I'm protecting her," Stone said. "Someone took a shot at her."

"I thought that was you."

"Well, I thought so, too, but then I finally remembered that I'm too likable to be shot."

Unless it's by an irate husband.

Grant tried not to reevaluate Meg Naylor.

"Really," she said. "I've got to go. I'll talk to you later, Mickey, and it was nice meeting you, Mr. Grant."

She put the tester on a counter, found a purse, and went down the hallway.

"I'm going to hire her away from Tank Cameron," Stone told him.

"You are?"

"Except she likes her job. She also doesn't like getting shot at."

"That was true?"

"We were together when it happened."

"Tell me about it."

"Tell me about Harbin, first."

Grant went through it quickly.

"Goddamn it. Dick Wells was one of my aces. This is getting out of hand."

"Mai's trying to arrange some security, and maybe that'll help. Give me your story again."

Grant listened closely as Stone went through the details. He told the story while turning off testers and a soldering iron. The details were the same as he'd heard before on the phone, only now the woman was present in it.

Grant leaned against the console, and when Stone was finished, patted the machine and said, "Now tell me about these."

It was the same story Stone had related long-distance.

"Dusty had an interesting theory, based on the simplistic destructive materials."

"Nine millimeter is not simplistic, Doug."

"Actually, it is. Dusty thinks it's some peasant group unhappy that they're not getting the full measure that Shanghai Star could provide."

"Yeah. I've heard about it. About the policy, too. Maybe he's right. Maybe the peasants are right."

"Where's Curt?"

"He went down to meet the police inspector working the arson case. Some questions about our disgruntled ex-employee."

"You don't believe that angle?"

"They keep pushing that term 'disgruntled' every time I talk to any of the cops, and it's hard to buy into. Anyone that works for us is happy as hell to have a job with future prospects, Doug. Shanghai Star isn't paying all that much, but it's a hell of a step up from what the rest of the labor force is making around here."

"You think the police are making this up?"

"I don't know what they're doing. Until I threatened to fire all the Chinese techs, they weren't going to do anything. Four days after I made the threat, they suddenly had new leads. Now, it's an arrest."

"Let's go talk to this cop of yours."

Stone grinned. "Let's. I like getting on his case."

Stone drove them in a Shanghai Star vehicle with the logo on the doors, and he seemed to know where he was going.

"You mind my saying, chief, that you look like the horse that was ridden too hard and put away wet?"

Grant rubbed his palm over the whiskers on his cheeks. "I left Shanghai without packing a bag. Didn't even think about it."

They had parked and were just mounting the front steps of the police station as Wickersham emerged from the building.

"I'll be damned! Hello, Doug."

"Hi, Curt."

"We were coming to bail you out," Stone said. "What's that inspector's name?"

"Wing."

"He still here?"

"He may have worn himself out, asking me all the same old questions."

Wickersham turned around and led them back into the station, then down a hall to the left. He stepped through a doorway, and Grant followed him.

"Inspector Wing, this is Doug Grant."

"Mr. Grant, I have heard of you."

The policeman got up from his desk and came around it to offer his hand.

Grant shook it. "I wonder if you have time for a couple questions, Inspector?"

"Surely, Mr. Grant. Please, let us all be seated."

He went across the hall and brought back another chair for Stone.

Grant took out his notebook, as if he was really interested in the answers.

"This man you've arrested, he's a computer technician?"

"A—how do you define it?—software engineer. That is what he told us."

"Programmer Three is our classification, Doug," Wickersham provided.

"Do you know why he was upset? Why he was angry with the company?"

The cop's eyes narrowed. He didn't like being on the aft end of questions.

"Only that he was angry. He has not specified the anger."

"And what did you find in his house?"

"His house? We have not looked at his house."

"Why not? We're missing computer parts, some programs. I should think you'd want to examine the house, just in case you want to bring theft charges, too."

Neither Wickersham nor Stone complained about Grant's lie.

"This, I did not know of," Wing said. "We will do this, as you suggest."

"Great. We'll go with you."

"Oh, I think that will be unnecessary, Mr. Grant."

"You'll recognize the articles?" Grant turned to Wickersham. "What is it again, Curt?"

Wickersham thought fast. "Probably on a QIC-80 format tape. It's data compressed and relates to our voice-activation module. Simple stuff, really."

"And Mickey?"

Stone had had a few seconds longer to formulate his reply. "Four VL-Buses, three Boca I/Os, a Cache Controller, and a dozen SCSI connectors. There's probably more, but I don't have the inventory with me."

"What's a Boca I/O, Inspector?" Grant knew it was an input/output device, but had no idea what it did.

"Ah . . . well, perhaps it would be helpful if we went together."

"Good! Let's go!"

Grant and his directors stood abruptly, and Wing didn't have a choice but to follow. He gathered up a couple of uniformed policemen and an address, and they all went outside and got in a police van.

It was a short ride, maybe ten blocks, to a dilapidated apartment building. The room was on the fourth floor, and the manager eagerly showed them into it after only a momentary glance at all of the police credentials.

The single-room flat was surprisingly neat. The dual purpose sofa/bed was covered with a rainbow-colored blanket, and the hot plate and tiny refrigerator on a counter in one corner were wiped clean. A few dishes were stacked beside the hot plate. In another corner was a cheap wardrobe with a few clothes hung neatly on hangers.

Against one wall was a small table with two chairs shoved under it. On the tabletop were several computer-language manuals and a Megatronics Model LT200 laptop computer. Just like the one Grant kept hidden from Diantha Parker.

"There's one of them," Stone said.

Grant knew damned well that Stone was completely unaware of a stolen laptop, but stolen it had to be. A Programmer III didn't make enough money in a year to amass the wherewithal for the top-of-the-line $4,000 model.

The inspector walked over and looked at it. "We will have to mark it as evidence."

"Exactly," Grant said. "We'll take a receipt for it."

Without invitation, Grant walked around the room, peeking behind pictures, patting down the sofa. The policeman watched him, then began doing the same.

One of the uniformed cops went through the cabinets under the counter.

Stone pointed to the floor at the base of the wardrobe.

"Look at the dust, Doug."

There was a little dust on the floor, but a straight line of dustless space about an inch wide along the base of the wardrobe.

"Let's move it, Mickey."

The two of them got on either side of the wardrobe and walked it away from the wall.

"Take a look at this, Inspector Wing," Grant said.

He bent over and picked up the cardboard box that rested on

the floor and fit under the wardrobe base. One by one, he handed Wing four pornographic magazines. By the look on Wing's face, Grant thought he wanted to examine the evidence further. So did the other two cops who moved in to look over Wing's shoulders.

While they did, Grant counted the cash.

"Five thousand, forty dollars in U.S. currency," he announced, very likely to Wing's annoyance. Without these three American witnesses, that much money would never have made it back to the police station. "That in itself is illegal, isn't it? Holding foreign cash? They only let us carry FEC." The Foreign Exchange Certificates were a bit of a hassle sometimes.

Unfortunately, they didn't find the fictional backup tape or the Boca I/Os, but Grant told Wing, "We'll go back to the station with you and file witness reports."

"It will be unnecessary, Mr. Grant."

"I'll feel better if my official report for the police matches what I tell the reporters. Curt, Mickey?"

"Absolutely."

"I always like to have the documentation agree," Stone said. "I sleep better when it does."

It only took forty minutes to fill out their reports, but another ten minutes when Grant demanded a personal copy for himself with Wing's signature on it.

Inspector Wing was not a happy man when they left at eight o'clock. Stone drove them back to the White Cloud, and Grant registered at the front desk. He bought a razor and toothbrush and other toiletries in the store off the lobby, then they all went up to Wickersham's room.

"I know you want scotch, Doug. Mickey?"

"The same."

Wickersham poured them all a drink, and they sat in chairs around the bed. Grant toed his loafers off and put his feet on the bed.

"That was damned nice work, boss," Stone said.

"I don't think the computer was stolen," Wickersham said.

"No," Grant agreed. "He probably bought it out of the ten grand he was paid."

"Inspector Wing," Stone said, "is suddenly confronted with

other motives for his accused suspect. I wonder how he'll follow up?"

"There should be enough evidentiary pressure on him to do something," Wickersham said.

"And we can add to the pressure by calling him and his bosses frequently. I know a reporter who'll also make some calls."

"What made you think of this tactic, Doug?" Wickersham asked.

"Like you, I didn't like the disgruntled-employee tag. And I wasn't certain that they had the right man, or just a patsy, and I thought that a look at his house or apartment might help determine that one way or the other."

"Then how did they pick this guy to arrest?" Wickersham asked.

Stone replied, "I know Wing wasn't going to arrest his brother, or cousin, or whatever. He had to find someone."

"And when he was forced to find someone, then I'd bet someone else made an anonymous call to give him the right creep."

"Ten thousand is a bunch of payoff money in China," Stone said. "Whoever fronted the cash has to have some resources."

"And that's the question," Grant said. "Who fronted the money?"

It was after midnight when Chiang Qing and Huzhou entered the bar on Zhongshan Road. It was a smoky place full of sailors and loud music. The wooden floor was worn and rutted and littered with paper and cigarette butts.

The few women were all "roadside chickens"—prostitutes—but Chiang did not feel intimidated in the least. Huzhou said, "The man in the next-to-last booth."

"Wait outside for me."

He backed through the doorway, and Chiang fended off one proposal as she made her way to the back of the room. The man in the booth was Chinese, but he appeared ill at ease, his gaze anxious as he watched her approach.

She slid onto the seat opposite him and did not bother with introductions.

"You understand the assignment?"

"I do."

From under her loose blouse, she removed the small flat package tucked into her waistband. After a glance over her shoulder to make certain that no one in the bar was paying undue attention to them, she passed it under the table.

"There are ten CD-ROM discs and several cassettes in there," she said.

"The money?"

"One half is there. The other half will be paid on September sixteenth."

"This is very dangerous."

"You are being paid well."

"It must be more."

"You have made an agreement," she argued. "You must honor it."

"They are very suspicious. Circumstances have changed."

"We will see. If all goes well, there may be a bonus."

"There had better be," he said, his tone growing more confident.

"And if it does not go well, or does not happen," she told him, "we pass out penalties as well as rewards."

His face blanched.

She let her eyes harden as she studied his face.

"What are you doing?"

"I am memorizing your face," she said. "I will not forget it. I expect, however, that you will not remember me."

Then she stood up and left the bar to join Huzhou on the sidewalk.

"Well?" he asked.

"He will do it."

"Finally! Finally, we do something worthwhile."

He was so simple, really. He actually believed that what was on the discs was what she had told him. Still, clandestine meetings excited her, too, and made the adrenaline levels reach new heights.

It put her in an erotic mood.

"Let us go home," she said.

"I am ready."

But not as ready as she, Chiang was certain.

Tuesday, September 6

The satcom room was in its normal state of apparent confusion. All around Bricher, his engineers and technicians yelled at one another, threw doughnuts at one another for emphasis, and generally solved problems.

He was glad to be back. His trip to the States had been a decent respite, but until ShangStar Three was in orbit, and every tiny system worked without hiccups, he wouldn't be truly happy out of this environment. Every monitor in the room was lit with displays of circuits or of messages from around the PRC. He liked talking by computer, and since the second satellite was now in place, they were finally connected to all of the facilities via computer.

China's landlines were so poorly maintained, and low-grade in the first place, that effective communications between computers had been almost nil. The lack of a decent telephonic or cable system infrastructure was one of the reasons they had opted for a wireless operation for Shanghai Star. With the insertion of ShangStar Two, their administrative linkages had improved considerably.

Bricher had a circuit-schematic up on his computer screen, using a pencil point to trace a current flow, when he became aware of someone standing next to him.

He looked up, saw the slick suit, and frowned. Then he realized which of MI's employees might wear a suit as a matter of normalcy.

"Hello, Maynard."

"Will."

At the moment, there were no extra chairs, so Bricher stood up. "Glad to have you on board. And I'm sorry CIS didn't come off on top."

"It was the will of the people," Crest answered, grinning. "This is an amazing place."

"Well, we get the job done, most of the time."

"Is there a problem?" the salesman asked, trying to take in most of the conversations going on.

"ShangStar Two's solar panel array—which collects energy for electrical uses—isn't aligned to track the sun quite right, and her communications system isn't listening to us. That is to say, she's not responding to my desire to have her ass angled up four degrees."

"That's not good, I take it? I know nothing of these technical details."

"It's not good. If she weren't twenty-six-thousand miles up, I'd walk over and kick her butt. That works with most of our stubborn equipment."

Crest smiled. "May I ask a simplistic question?"

"Sure. I need those kind."

"Why are we using satellites?"

Bricher grinned. "That's pretty basic, all right, but you'd be surprised how many people don't really know the answer. In the electromagnetic spectrum, there are any number of frequencies we can use to transmit voice and data, but many have limitations. Ultra High Frequency and Very High Frequency bands, which are commonly used, have a very localized range from the transmitter. They don't get very far over the horizon, and in a country the size of China, there's a lot of horizon. The long-range frequencies require massive transmitting arrays. The High Frequency ranges have to be controlled carefully, since the sky wave bounces off the ionosphere—'skips.' VHF and above pass through the ionosphere, though, so it tends to be less expensive and faster to transmit to a satellite for relay back to other ground stations."

"Excellent! I knew there was a reason we were doing this."

"By the way, Maynard, how are you doing?"

"My negotiations with the state-run People's Department Store are going well. I expect to have an agreement soon for them to retail our units. In fact, I now have provisional approval from the commerce ministry for our three consumer models."

"Damn, that's fast. How'd you accomplish it?"

Crest looked around conspiratorially. "You wouldn't mention it to anyone?"

"I won't even tell Doug."

"I sold a People's Home Companion to a commerce official at cost."

"What in the hell is a People's Home Companion?"

"That's the Model one-eleven home computer. I renamed it."

"And you sold it to him?"

"A gift of the machine would have been a bribe."

"At cost, you said. How much?"

"He paid me in U.S. currency that he had accumulated for many years, I think. I called it ninety-five bucks."

"Shit, Maynard. Those things cost us one-sixty-five."

"So, I made an error in arithmetic. I may make it again, if I have to."

Bricher grinned at him. "We can at least say that we sold one, I guess."

"And thousands more to come. Which brings me to the reason for my visit."

"Shoot."

"Okay. I need an impressive logo for our machines. I've got to have some made up for those you brought back with you."

"All right, a logo."

"The Shanghai Star logo is a yellow star—from the flag—superimposed over a skeletal outline of a map of China."

"Right."

"I want to use the same yellow star. It gives the MI products for China a symbolic oneness with Shanghai Star."

"I like it," Bricher said.

"But I have to make it distinctive from the Shanghai Star logo. I'll drop the map, for one thing. What I'd like is a photo, or a graphic depiction of some kind, of your satellite. I'll lay that on the yellow star."

"No sweat, Maynard."

Bricher dropped into his chair and poised his hands over his keyboard. He thought for a moment, then, leaving his schematic diagram in place, called up another menu over it. He scanned the listing and found what he wanted, then opened a file.

When it came up on the screen, it was an engineering drawing of ShangStar Two, overlaid with dimensions, lines, and arrows. He captured the image and moved it to a graphics program to erase everything but the basic silhouette of the satellite.

Crest said, "Terrific, Will! That's exactly what I wanted."

He sent it to the laser printer queue and said, "Somewhere on the back wall there is a row of printers. It'll come up on one of them."

"Thanks, Will."

"Send me a logo to paste on my desk."

"I'll do it."

Crest dodged his way around desks and engineers for the back wall, and Bricher watched him go.

Grant had told him that Crest had a hidden agenda for staying in China, but it looked as if he was going to sell computers, too. And that was what it was all about.

Deng Mai thought her life was coming unravelled, slowly but very certainly. She was losing control over so many things around her. Despite Deng's studied coldness toward her, her mother continued to see Pierre Lefant. They spoke very little in the mornings and evenings, especially as Mai was wary of saying anything that had the promise of being passed on to Lefant. Yvonne continued to cruise through her life as if she were blissfully unaware of her daughter's feelings.

Sometimes, she wished Vladimir Suretsov would hurry up and discover something completely unsavory about Lefant so that she could spring it on her mother and break up what appeared to be evolving into an extended love affair, rather than a fling. Mai might have been able to live with the fling. And then again, she dreaded bringing any pain whatsoever to Yvonne.

After Shanghai Star, Yvonne Deng was the most disruptive force in Mai's life.

But there were others. Zhou Ziyang had come to her with a lukewarm proposal to overturn the ministry's information policy, and while she told him privately that she agreed with him, she could not formally endorse the proposal. He had left her office somewhat defeated, but determined. Now she worried that he would tell others of her private support. If that got back to Jiang, it would amount to one more arrow in his quiver—a possible charge of subversion.

Minister Jiang Guofeng had ordered her to talk to Chiang Qing and attempt to reason with the woman. Jiang wanted the People's Underground to temper its criticism of the Ministry of Information. So far, Chiang had not returned her calls. The minister, however, had called several times, demanding to know of her progress with Chiang. Why Jiang was suddenly so concerned with the People's Underground, after tolerating the organization for so many years, she had no idea.

And Sung Wu was a growing problem. The man could not seem to grasp just what the extent of his authority was. He called people—security personnel, programmers, managers—on Deng's floors and gave them orders to perform tasks that were not part of their jobs. The complaints flowed into Deng, and she was forced to deal with Sung, who would not heed any woman's advice, anyway. She was certain he was feeding reports of her uncooperative attitude back to Beijing, and though the reports would be unfounded and unsupported, the prospect of having to argue her position undermined her confidence.

She worried, too, about Minister Shao Tsung. Again, she had no evidence, but she felt that he was maneuvering in the background, seeking to gain control over Shanghai Star. And if he was, she would be caught in the cross fire.

Abandoned by her mother, at least conversationally, Deng felt as if she had no one in whom to confide. She had begun to rely on Grant in a small measure for that purpose, but Grant had been out of the city for days, and she missed him.

When she was in her office, and he in his, one floor directly below her, she found her mind wandering from her work to dwell on him. More and more, she just got up and went down to be with him, fabricating any excuse for face-to-face contact. She thought her erratic behavior must be driving him crazy.

Except that she thought Grant liked her presence. Sometimes, she wished she could be as reckless as her mother, just say to hell with it, and . . .

But, no. There were images to uphold, not only for herself and Shanghai Star, but for the women who watched her every move.

Now, after her trip to Urümqi, she had no desire at all to return to her office. There would only be letters and telephone calls—all complaints—to return.

The Southeast Asia Charter pilot helped her down from the cabin and offered to carry her small carry-on for her.

"Thank you for a nice ride, but no, I can take the bag."

Crossing the apron to the general aviation terminal, she entered the building which was well populated, and went through the lobby to the front doors. She emerged onto the wide sidewalk and looked both ways along the street. Her white Pathfinder was double-parked a half-block away, and when she waved, the driver pulled out of line and drove to where she stood. He pulled into the pickup lane at the curb, stopped, and got out to take her suitcase.

"I don't know you," she said to the tall Chinese man.

"Your driver's mother became ill, and he had to take her to the hospital. Miss Jiangyou asked me to pick you up."

"Very well. Put the bag in the car, and I will be right back."

Before he could protest, she pushed through the glass doors into the terminal, shoving her way through the crowd, looking both ways until she spotted the green uniform with the gold trim. She fished her identification out of her purse.

"Officer, I am Director Deng."

He looked over the identification card, double-checking her picture.

"Yes, Director. How can I help you?"

"I would like you to question the man driving my car. I do not know him."

"I am happy to help."

The two of them walked back through the throng of people. Through the glass doors, she saw the Pathfinder waiting at the edge of the sidewalk.

As they came through the doors, the driver saw the policeman, and the Nissan's tires squeaked as he let out the clutch and shot away into the stream of traffic.

The police officer glanced after the truck. He jotted down the license number.

"That *was* your vehicle, Director?"

"It belongs to Shanghai Star."

"I am afraid you were correct to be worried."

Her life was truly coming apart. Now, she had lost her suitcase and her car.

The six men seated around Zhou's small room appeared fatigued. Though travel restrictions for Chinese citizens had been gradually eased since the early 1980s, travel within the country was still not easy. One had to obtain money for the fare, and that was usually only enough for a bus. With a bit more money, one could take the much faster train, riding in the "hard seat" class. It was so named because the hard wood of the bench seats was covered with only a thin sheet of padding under the fabric. The softer seats were more expensive and normally chosen by tourists.

These six had arrived in Shanghai from six different points in the country, and they were the regional representatives of the People's Right To Know Committee. All of them had spent all of their money on their tickets and had nothing left over for lodging or food. That would be up to Zhou, and he had borrowed blankets from his neighbors in the building. His guests would sleep on his floor tonight.

Yang, an Uzbek from Urümqi, said, "I do not see that anything we are doing is having an effect."

"I am sorry to hear that," Zhou told him, and was. "Mr. Mu?"

"In Guangdong Province, the Let Us Learn slogan has captured some attention, though it is not overwhelming. People ask me, 'Let us learn what?' Guangzhou has been the seat of many uprisings in our history, but I think not this one."

"There were attacks on the Shanghai Star facilities there," the man from Harbin said, "as there was in Harbin. Some have been moved to action."

"Is it action that helps us?" Yang asked. "Destroying the means of our salvation is not helpful."

"I think the message was clear enough," Zhou said. "Whoever is behind these attacks is saying that, if they cannot have a true and free communications network, they would prefer none."

"Does the government receive the same message you do?" Wu asked.

"I should think so, but let us go back to the campaign."

The man from Chengdu said, "I do not believe slogans are enough. We must provide more information. The people are asking from us exactly what we are asking of the government. More information."

The representative from Hohhot, the capital of Inner Mongolia, said, "Even I could not answer similar questions."

Zhou told them of what he had seen in the presentations of the Consortium of Information Services and Media Bureau Limited.

"Exactly!" Mu said. "Instead of spending laborious hours hand-making big-character posters with slogans that are less than inspiring, let us make a brochure. With that to pass out, the people would better understand what they will be getting."

"Could be getting," Yang clarified.

"Should be getting," Zhou said. "However, copying machines are not readily available. Many businesses now have them, but access for the people is limited and expensive. How do you propose we go about this?"

"Chiang has one," Yang said. "I have heard so. She sends letters to her members."

The People's Right to Know Committee was organized on the same principle of the government—national, provincial, city, and street committees. Their contact with their members was face-to-face in the street.

"I will talk to her about using it," Zhou said, "but she will want money. How do we raise it?"

"That is why we charge dues," Yang said. "What has happened to the money?"

"Expenses are always high; you know that. Then, too, we have collected pledges, not dues. Less than fifteen percent of the members have delivered on what they pledged. All of you are collectors. Have you pressed your city and street chairmen for their contributions?"

The looks on their faces gave him the answer. And put the burden on their shoulders. He did not want to dwell on the accounts of the organization.

"The people want to participate," Mu said, "but they are poor."

"We are all poor. We cannot even make copies. And if we do make copies, how can we send them to the provinces?"

"By post," Yang said, "but, yes, I understand that requires more money. It is ridiculous. We do not even have telephones to contact one another, and we are all obsessed with the notion of bringing free communication to the people."

"That is exactly why we must not waver," Zhou said. "I envision a day when all will have a telephone. Or a computer to talk to one another. Or to ask our government the questions that need to be asked."

"You have had the same vision for fifteen years," Yang said.

The fifteen years had disappeared. Now, when he needed the time, it was fleeting. He felt pressured from every side—from his colleagues as well as from Jiang. Time was running out, and he needed to make a firm statement.

"The national pilot test of the Shanghai Star system is on September fifteenth. I fear that, if we do not create a furor in the people by that time, all is lost."

"Why is this so?" Mu asked.

"The people will be so enraptured by what they see that they will not know what they have lost."

"An excellent point," Wu said. "I will use the money for my return train ticket to make telephone calls. I will demand collections and money sent to us."

"I will do the same," Yang said.

"And we will all go to talk to Chiang Qing," the man from Sichuan said. "She will help us."

Zhou was unenthused. He feared the sand of his hourglass had run its course.

Grant had been back in Shanghai for four hours, most all of them spent on the phone. He was leaning back in his chair, his feet up on his desk, with the telephone clamped against his head by his shoulder, when Crest appeared in his doorway.

Grant waved him in.

Crest had barely sat before the phone came alive. "This is Inspector Chou."

"Doug Grant. I'm calling to ask about your progress on the murder cases."

"There is little to report, Mr. Grant. The procurator has reviewed the evidence and determined that murder charges should be filed against persons unknown. The charges will include sedition and others, since a state facility was attacked."

Wonderful, Grant thought. He'd been able to figure out the charges.

"You have no leads on a suspect?"

"We have been interviewing witnesses, and potential witnesses, from the time I met you, Mr. Grant. I am not shirking my duty."

"I'm not saying you are, Inspector. I had just hoped that some bad apple had fallen out of the tree by now."

"Not since you called yesterday, Mr. Grant."

"I think it's important that we find this guy, Inspector, and set him up as an example for all of the country to see. Otherwise, we're going to have more of the same problems."

"I have inquired about you, and I understand your position, Mr. Grant. However, your daily telephone calls will not help me to do my job."

"Have you talked to Inspector Wing?"

"Wing? I do not know the name. He is from here?"

"He's from Guangzhou. He was to call you about the case down there."

"He has not."

"Then you don't know that, in that case, the perpetrator was paid off by an outside person to perform the sabotage?"

"I do not know that. I will call this Inspector Wing. Does he know who the outside person is?"

"That, I couldn't tell you," Grant said.

"I will ask. Good day, Mr. Grant."

Grant replaced the telephone thinking this daily phone call might produce at least one result, if Chou called Wing. No matter Wing's and Chou's feelings, he was still going to harass them daily.

"No progress?" Crest asked.

"None that I notice. What have you got, Maynard?"

"There're three items on my agenda. This is the first."

He slid a large sheet of paper across the desk, and Grant picked it up. There were three graphic illustrations on it, all yellow stars bordered in black. In the upper-left corner of each star was a well-defined black drawing of a satellite. Across the bottom of each star, and running off the right side of the star on yellow background, were Chinese characters. The characters for each illustration were slightly different.

"I like it, Maynard, but what is it?"

"The graphics are twice the finished size, but they are the logos for the People's Controller, the People's Home Companion, and the People's Professional Assistant."

Grant knew immediately what he was talking about. "Maynard, I think you're going to fit in just fine. This is terrific! Great names!"

"I have your go-ahead, then?"

"Sure do."

"I'll get them registered with the proper bureau and have a few made up for my demonstrators. I'll send C.C. a master so he can produce them for the assembly line."

"Be damned sure to tell him which one is the controller and which is the home companion. Calvin doesn't do very well in Chinese. I'd hate to mislabel the products."

"Done. Second item . . ."

"Hold a second. When you talk to him, check on the production and shipment of the controllers, will you? We've got to have five thousand distributed in time for the demo on the fifteenth. Panasonic is providing the monitors, and they're en route."

"I'll do that. And I should tell you that one of the Japanese companies and a European company called Computrex, which I gather is a subsidiary of MBL, is already distributing controllers."

"Damn, they're fast."

"Which is why I need you on Monday, the twelfth. All day, probably."

Grant checked his calendar. He had two meetings scheduled.

"Purpose?" he asked.

"You and I have a meeting with the purchasing people for the People's Department Stores. I've held the preliminary talks with them—with a rep named Tan, and I expect us to come away with a distribution contract. I need you to sign it."

Grant drew a line through each of his two meetings and jotted a note for Parker to reschedule them.

"Cash before play. I'm yours on Monday."

"My last item. I want your permission to begin investigating the possibilities of assembling our three units in China."

"Whoa. C.C. might come unglued on that, Maynard."

"I understand that it means American jobs, Doug. Think about it, though. Based on one of our earlier conversations, I'm targeting a twenty-percent market share. There's no way in hell that Jackson can meet that kind of demand."

"He's hoping to expand our assembly operations Stateside. Put more jobs on the market."

"I understand that. However, we can still produce the components in L.A., and that will open up some jobs. We can still manufacture completed units, say about half of the demand. Yet, if we assign half of the assembly operations to China, we accomplish several important objectives. One, we reduce labor costs and increase the profit margin. Two, we create some goodwill by establishing new jobs in China and getting some of those teenagers off the street. Three, we become part of the manufacturing infrastructure—Beijing would be loath to dismiss us and our jobs."

"Good points," Grant said, thinking about it. "What if we'd just start with the controller? It's a simple assembly, comparatively, and we could lower the retail cost even more. The initial cost of training assembly-line workers is lower, too."

Crest smiled. "You're buying into it, then?"

"Just investigate the possibilities at this point. And Maynard, this is all damned good work. Thank you."

"You'll thank me when I see my first commissions. Though, to be honest, I've really gotten into this. I think we can have a major impact on educating China."

"That's what I think, too. What else have you got?"

"That's it."

"You had a hidden agenda, remember?"

"Oh, that. I am making fast friends with minor functionaries in the Beijing government. We go to lunch, we go to dinner—

not billed to my expense account, by the way. I am slowly learning where the relationships are aligned."

"Anything pertinent yet?"

"You knew that Jiang and Pai are related? They are brothers-in-law?"

"I think I'd heard that somewhere. I knew they were close, anyway."

"Did you also know that both men are investors, through street names, in Nuclear Power Limited?"

"Damn. You're sure of that?"

"No. It's a rumor I picked up from a commerce-department clerk, and I don't know how I'd go about proving it."

"I might have a source. Let me look into it. Or you can. Get hold of Vladimir Suretsov at ITAR-Tass. I think he's got a listing of Nuclear Power shareholders."

"Thanks, Doug. I'm not sure where it would get us, but it's interesting information, don't you think?"

"What would be more interesting, is if they're both into Media Bureau Limited."

Crest smiled and stood up. "It gets more involved all the time."

He headed for the door, and when he pulled it open, Parker was standing there with Deng Mai.

Parker looked concerned. Deng was pale.

Grant came to his feet and went around his desk.

Crest said, "Are you all right, Director?"

"I will be fine, thank you."

Crest glanced at Grant, said, "Call me if you need anything, Doug," then slipped around the women and passed through the jungle.

Parker said, "She was kidnapped!"

"What!"

"I was not, Diantha. But the police think it was a failed attempt. They have been questioning me for the past hour."

"Come on in." Grant took her hand, which had a mild tremor in it.

"Water's on," Parker said. "I'll have tea in a minute."

They sat, and Deng told him of her stolen car and the possible attempt to abduct her. She was obviously shaken, but didn't want to admit it.

"I don't think it's possible," Grant said. "I'd call it probable. This is not getting any better, Mai."

"I will take more care, and you must, also."

"You were very sensible at the airport. I'm proud of you."

Parker brought in the tea, poured, and seemed inclined to stay. Grant banished her with a look, and she left.

Deng sipped the tea, and her shoulders relaxed.

"I am worried, Douglas."

"Well, I'm glad you can tell me that. I'm worried, too, but we're going to get through this."

"I never feared for my personal safety before."

Grant thought about the night he felt as if he'd been followed, but decided not to burden her with the story. It was probably all in his mind, anyway.

"Why don't you detach two guys on the security detail to follow you around?"

"I do not need bodyguards."

"Think about it, please. I'm not ready to lose you."

She turned her head so she could look directly at him, and Grant once again thought he could get lost in the depths of her eyes.

"Please." He wanted to put his arm around her, hug her, force her to listen.

He held himself back.

"I will think about it. You saw the guards on the door when you returned?"

"Yes. It was a bit of a surprise. Whose are they?"

When he had entered the building, he had been approached in the lobby by two men in civilian clothes and asked for his ID.

"I could not reach you to tell you of the accord. The information ministry and the defense ministry are sharing the cost."

"Shao and Jiang are cooperating?"

"I think they each feel safer this way. Politically."

"Maybe they'll keep our buildings in one piece."

"The people's buildings," she said, smiling.

"I'm a people."

"You're a Green-Eyed Devil."

"I'd heard that, but I don't know if it's true."

"It is. As I am the Ice Maiden."

"Nah. I think that's old hat. Lotus Blossom is the latest."

"I have always been Lotus Blossom. It was my father's doing."

"I like it. I'm sorry I never met your father."

"He was very strong on ideology. You would probably not have gotten along."

"More so than with Madame Yvonne, I think."

"Mama is having troubles. Of perception."

"I probably shouldn't get involved."

"You are like so many Americans, wishing to not get involved."

"I've blown that, I'm afraid. A couple police departments know me better than they'd like to."

"You are protective, are you not, Douglas?"

"Of my interests, yes. And if it means sticking my neck out, I guess I'll do that."

She looked down at the empty teacup. "I am losing control. Of my mother, of Sung Wu, of the information committee. I do not know what to do."

"Tell you what, Mai. You look all of them straight in the eye, and you hold your ground. I've got a few things going that might end up giving us some leverage."

She looked back at him, "Like what?"

"Let me make sure they're good, before I tell you. I don't want to give you false hopes, but I don't want you to give up, either."

"Can we start with my mother?" she asked.

"Let's start with dinner, and we'll talk about your mother."

"Hey, Jimbo, meet Meg."

James Bowie, who was standing at the edge of the dance floor scanning the crowd, revolved slowly and looked down at their table.

"Howdy, Miss Meg."

"Jimbo lets me fly his airplane," Stone explained to her.

"Hi, Jimbo," Naylor said, giving him one of those girl-next-door smiles.

"I've been looking for you," Bowie said, grabbing a chair from the next table and pulling it over. "Somebody suggested you'd be where the music is loud."

The band, hazily seen across the smoke-filled room, was well amplified. They were a five-piece Chinese combo imitating the country swing band Asleep At the Wheel, and they did a fair job. They were loudly into "Corrine, Corrina."

Stone signalled for the waitress and ordered Jimbo a beer while the pilot took a quick look at the Americans, Europeans, and Chinese prancing on the dance floor in some country line dance that had a name, but which Stone had forgotten. He and Naylor were both lightly coated with a sheen of perspiration from their own efforts at following the choreography.

Stone and Naylor had been out together a dozen times in the last couple of weeks. The duration was nearly a first for him. What was a first was that she was still the girl-next-door. She was wholesome and candid and independent and sexually remote. It was kind of a refreshing change for him.

"Do you really let him fly?" she asked Bowie.

"Only when there isn't another airplane in fifty miles."

"That's kind of what I thought."

"Hey, I haven't turned it upside down, or anything. I've got a steady hand."

"Depends on your point of view," Bowie said. "You don't want to know why I was looking for you?"

"Not if it means work. I've been working." Tomorrow, he was supposed to get the last two consoles from C.C. Jackson, and he hoped to have his center back in full operation by Friday.

Then he had to go to Harbin to check on the repairs there. He figured it would be the 21st century before he saw Shanghai again.

"Remember we took a close look at that reactor in Lhasa?"

He was suddenly more attentive. "I remember. It's on-line now, and the reports I'm getting are that we've finally got a decent electrical supply. There hasn't been a glitch due to electrical problems in ten days."

"Yeah, well I recall you made some comment about the radiation shielding? Or inadequacy thereof?"

"That it was a Topaz design. Intended for use in space."

"What's this all about?" Naylor asked.

"I mentioned to Grant that I thought it looked leaky."

"Leaky? That's a scientific term?"

"In local scientific circles, love—"

"Anyway," Bowie cut in, "I had a two-day layover in Lhasa last week, so I got a car and one of the radiation detectors from your outfit . . ."

"Why in the world do you have radiation detectors?" Naylor asked him.

"It's a combination instrument. Mainly, we check emissions from monitors."

Bowie was irked at all of the interruptions. "As I was saying? I drove out to the nuke plant, but I couldn't get very close. They had guards around the place, so I parked down on that road that runs through the valley?"

"Yeah, it was about two, three miles from the site. About five hundred feet lower, too."

"Right. I hiked in for two miles, until the terrain stopped me. I figure I was half-a-mile from the plant, a couple hundred feet below it."

"And you got a reading?"

"Thirty rems."

"Jesus! At that distance?"

"I didn't stick around. I got my sensitive balls out of there. Oops, sorry, Meg."

"I'd have taken off, too," she said. "How far is this place from Lhasa?"

"About thirty miles," Stone said.

"I thought I'd look you up because we'd talked about it, Mickey. I don't know where to go from here."

"Let me make a call," Stone said. "Don't take my girl while I'm gone."

"I'm not your girl."

That attitude was bothersome, too.

"You should watch the international newspapers in the next two days, Douglas, for the sabotage story. Then, I am running another story about you, sometime next week," Suretsov said.

"I'm old news by now, Vladimir," Grant told him.

"That is not true. My editor was impressed with the last article and demanded—demanded, I tell you—another. This one is to have more of your background, and I am calling to check the details with you."

"What's it about?"

"The tenacious manner in which you have built your company. I have talked in the United States to many with whom you have been associated. They are generally laudatory comments, by the way."

"You haven't talked to the right people, obviously." Grant laughed appreciatively.

Suretsov supposed he was not expected to like the subjects of his interviews, but he liked Grant. With the telephone tucked between his ear and his raised shoulder, he read the rough draft to Grant.

"Tex Bickell said *that?*"

"He did."

"He's never been that nice in his life. He's the toughest outside director I ever worked for. A good man."

"I detected that he had a certain . . . rough edge," Suretsov said.

"It's gotten him a couple billion dollars."

Suretsov found it difficult to think in those terms, a single man owning a billion dollars. "Now, tell me about this Silver Star you were awarded."

"You covered it in the story," Grant said.

"I only wrote that you received it. Please tell me why."

"Vladimir . . ."

"I know that you are a modest man. Overcome that for me, please."

Suretsov's fingers rattled the keyboard of his Mac as Grant related the story.

"It was early morning of the first push into Iraq. Lot of darkness, dust, and confusion. I had my platoon and a heavy-weapons detachment on two Blackhawk helicopters, and they dumped us in the middle of nowhere. As it turned out, nowhere was nearly a mile north of where we were supposed to be.

"By dawn, I'd argued enough on the radio with the company commander, and he with the operations section, that they told us to turn back. We did, and we ran smack into a pair of Iraqi infantry platoons that were retreating, probably against orders.

It was a short firefight, and I lost four wounded before they wrapped us up."

"You were taken prisoner?"

"Yeah. The Iraqis were rather jubilant over that event, and they decided to stay and fight it out. Dug into the side of a wadi and set up their heavy machine guns. Except for my wounded, they tied the rest of us—fifteen—together in a line, hands tied behind our backs, and staked us out in front of the entrenchment as a human shield."

"That is terrible!"

"That was their kind of war, Vladimir."

"What did you do?"

"About eight in the morning, it was getting damned hot sitting on the sand, and we were still in our antitoxin gear, though not the hoods, which made it even hotter. I finally got fed up, pulled the aluminum stake near me, and used it to saw on the nylon rope. We were sitting facing the entrenchment, and they didn't notice, or didn't care. Then I stood up and walked back to the wadi. It was a forty-foot walk.

"One of their officers, who spoke English, got ticked off and rushed to meet me. He was incoherent, but I demanded to see my wounded soldiers, and he decided that since I was the commander, it would be all right. They were in a depression down in the wadi."

"Were they mistreated?" Suretsov asked.

"Not too badly, but the Iraqis didn't have any medical supplies to speak of, and I was worried about them. Anyway, as it happened, this Iraqi officer was careless. He had a grip on my elbow, but he led me back past one of their machine guns. I tossed the officer on top of his gunner, grabbed the gun, turned it, and opened up down the wadi. They were lined up pretty well."

"And that was it?"

"No. As soon as my belt ran out, my guys scrambled all over them, arms tied and all. It was something of a melee for a while, but we took eleven prisoners."

"How many killed?"

"I didn't count, Vladimir."

"You did this by yourself?"

"It's rarely by oneself," Grant said. "I had a lot of well-trained men working with me. You learn to trust one another."

Suretsov finished typing his last paragraph. He would have to smooth it out when he inserted it into the draft he had already completed.

"Thank you, Douglas."

"It's not free."

"What?"

"I don't like talking about history like that, so you owe me."

"Very well. I will owe you."

"And you get to pay off right away."

"How will I do this?"

"Number one. Talk to Maynard Crest when he calls you."

"I have already spoken briefly with him. I was surprised to learn that he now works for Megatronics."

"That's right. But I think you two will have some common ground."

"All right. Number one implies number two."

"Number two. Get yourself a Geiger counter and an airline ticket to Lhasa."

Grant told him what he had learned, through Mickey Stone, from some pilot for Southeast Asia Charter.

"There is actually measurable radiation?"

"That's what I understand. I figure you're the best one to check it out."

"I hope to never be indebted to you again," Suretsov told him.

Thursday, September 8

"You are working with Madame Deng Mai."

"Well, pretty indirectly," Maynard Crest said.

"She and I went to school together," Liu Baio said.

From the dreamy look on his face, Crest assumed he wished that they still went to school together. But then, Crest wished *he* had gone to school with Deng Mai. He could understand the dream, though he couldn't fathom Liu and Deng in the same classroom. Liu appeared ten years older, and Crest supposed his life had been harder.

The two of them were talking over a Western breakfast of eggs, ham, and pancakes in the coffee shop of the Hilton Hotel. Liu was doing well with the maple syrup, having ordered an extra vat of it.

Liu was sitting across from him because Crest, after many inquiries, had learned that he was considered by many of his colleagues to be a top-notch manager, a man knowledgeable in manufacturing, and ambitious beyond the position he was in—running a plastics-fabrication plant.

It was six o'clock in the morning since Liu had insisted that he couldn't miss any of his workday, which started at eight. He was near the top of his pay scale—twenty-two—and not about to risk his income. Most Chinese workers were on a scale of one to eight, with grade eight paid about three times that of grade one. Engineers and technicians were on a sixteen-grade scale, and bureaucrats and government supervisors on a scale that ranged to twenty-six. It was easy to see where the government placed its emphasis.

"Did Mai mention me to you? I saw her at a conference a couple weeks ago."

Liu wanted an affirmative answer, of course, but Crest thought it best to be honest. "To tell you the truth, your name came up several times in conversations I had with many leaders in the manufacturing sector."

"In what regard?"

"Understand, please, that at the moment I am only exploring possibilities." Crest pulled the controller from his jacket pocket, where it had created an unsightly bulge. "Could you build these?"

Liu put down his fork and took the controller, turning it over in his hands.

"Just the case? The keyboard?"

"The whole thing. There's also an attachment that fits on the TV."

He looked at the four screws on the bottom of the case, then reached inside his jacket and came out with a small plastic case containing several tiny screwdrivers.

"May I?" he asked.

"Certainly."

Deftly, he removed the screws without dropping them on his eggs, lifted the back off, and spilled the contents into his hand. He examined the green circuit board, the contacts for the plastic keyboard, the alignment lugs.

"The electronic component would be preassembled?"

"It could be, unless you think you could build those, too."

Liu smiled. "I can assemble the whole thing. I would need to set up electronics assembly lines in the plant and train workers, but I would not anticipate problems."

"The big question, Mr. Liu, is: Would you want to do it?"

He found the faceplate and scanned the yellow logo at the top of the case. "The People's Controller—MI. Manufactured in the USA."

"Yes."

"And you are considering manufacturing them in China?" He began reassembling the unit.

"We are. I'm not certain just yet what the structure would be. Perhaps a state-owned facility, perhaps one in the free-enterprise sector. MI would be a minority investment partner, but one with the right to determine the quality standards and the administrative leadership. Would you be interested, Mr. Liu?"

"It is not my place to say, Mr. Crest. My supervisors . . ."

"Let me deal with the bureaucracy. Are you interested?"

He got that dreamy look in his eyes again, but this time Crest was sure it was for plastic keypads and silicon, rather than flesh-and-blood goddesses.

"There would be many jobs created," he said, "a great need in our country. Would this controller be the only product?"

"For now. There's a possibility that we may eventually want to introduce new models, maybe even computers."

"I am interested, Mr. Crest. I urge you, however, to use caution in who—"

"I'm not going to tell anyone of our discussion, Mr. Liu. Not yet, anyway."

Crest didn't know how anyone in their right mind could get dreamy about assembly lines. It would drive him batty.

The international editions of the *Washington Post*, the *London Times*, and a few others were available to the ministries each morning, and often, when the papers were discarded, the staffs in those offices kept pace with current events, sometimes to the discomfort of their superiors.

Jiang Guofeng read the *Post* each morning, frequently with some trepidation about what he would find. He was well aware that the world around him was filled with atrocities and rebellions. He did not enjoy reading about them, but he had an obligation, not only to the citizens of China, but to her leadership. His colleagues and superiors expected him to be aware of the trash behind the headlines.

The riot in Bosnia, for example, with four dead—one beheaded—and seven injured, need not have been presented in such gory detail, much less with a picture of the victim. The Xinhua News Agency, in its release to the PRC's media, if it released the item, would refer to a disagreement between political factions. If they mentioned the dead, they would also point out the pitfalls of multiple political parties.

Or the American sex goddess stripping off her blouse on a national television talk show in France, fortunately without a picture. The foibles and fantasies of others did nothing to promote goodwill or understanding, and such an article, even as a one-paragraph filler, had no place in a newspaper of stature.

Jiang had no objection to people learning from what they read or watched as long as there was intrinsic value present. He put the full weight of his office behind the production of documentaries heralding the history of the Communist Party or dramatic films based in Chinese culture. He firmly believed the Chinese people should be aware of their political and cultural heritages. The folklore of the American West, with its cowboys and Indians and sheriffs, did little toward true education, but he was willing to accept such tales as meaningless, escapist entertainment. If it satisfied some of the popular demand for trivia, he thought it would be harmless.

What alarmed him was the relaxation of some standards. In the 1980s, the State Council had approved the importation of Hong Kong and Japanese-made films for showing in cinema houses. These, too, were viewed as escapist fantasy by the administration, but many of the films were martial-arts movies relying on violence as their central themes. Jiang was certain the examples set had moved into the mainstream juvenile society. It was apparent in the gangs roaming the city streets and in the increase of murder and other violent crimes, especially among young offenders. He was so certain of the influence of violent films on Chinese youth that he had commissioned a study, but the research had turned out to be inconclusive, and none of the results were strong enough for him to present to the State Council.

His introspection was interrupted by a rap on his door, and Wen Yito entered. His dark eyes held a scowl.

"Yes?"

"Have you read page three yet, Minister?"

"No."

He turned the page, and his eye was immediately captured by the headline: FREE DISCOURSE UNDER ATTACK IN CHINA.

The source was the Russian ITAR-Tass News Agency—so it would be related to Suretsov's call to him, and as he scanned through the article, he noted the mention of the sabotage at Guangzhou, the attempted murder of a Megatronics Incorporated executive, and the murders at Harbin. The loss of the Long March 3 rocket and communications satellite was also detailed.

When all of the incidents were listed together, it seemed like a greater threat than when he thought of them as isolated events. He would have to complain to the national police again. And to Shao, now that the defense ministry was sharing the load. He was not happy to be cooperating with Shao, but it was better than one or the other of them vying for superiority. And Shao now seemed more involved in the information ministry's activities than ever before. Jiang assumed it was because he had, by signing the agreement, allowed the military a final say over ShangStar Two.

"Is Xinhua carrying the story?" he asked.

"I will telephone and ask. Should they be?"

"I don't think the trials of Shanghai Star are of interest to the people, do you?"

"Of course not, Minister."

Wen turned and left, and Jiang let escape a low murmur of curses. Sure as the eight hills of Kowloon and the boy Emperor Ping were truly nine dragons, the story would infiltrate the borders on outlaw television and radio waves, greatly magnified and warped. And some would blame Beijing for sabotaging its own communications network in order to keep the populace ignorant.

That was not his intent at all. Jiang fully believed in the power of Shanghai Star. He simply did not believe in the efficacy of rape, murder, and mayhem.

He knew he was not alone in that philosophy.

Chiang Qing invited Zhou and his six colleagues into her headquarters. The room was animated with her followers as they prepared campaign posters.

Zhou's friends were introduced to her, and they looked with interest at the activity taking place. The men were regional committee heads and expected to be older, but Chiang was struck by the fact that her own cadre was composed of teenagers and those in their early twenties. The disparity was suddenly obvious, and she felt as if the underground was instantly less wise than it might have been.

Zhou stepped over to a desk and read the posters:

CHANGE IS UPON US
MAKE IT COMPLETE WITH BIG BROTHER
JIANG'S EJECTION

Zhou was alarmed. "Leader Chiang, this is a direct attack."

"And so it is," she said. "Did you see the pictorials?"

She pointed to the far wall, and Zhou and his friends moved over to see the illustrations tacked there. A small-and-ragged black dragon huddled in place, clutching a television set. His nearly impotent power was represented by a minuscule flicker of flame issuing from his fangless mouth. Looming over him was a huge white dragon emitting a stream of fire—worthy of a flamethrower—from a mouth full of jagged teeth. Above the white dragon was a satellite with rays made of the characters for "freedom," "knowledge," "power," and "equality." The white dragon was labelled, "The People," and "Jiang" was worked into the spine of the black dragon.

Huzhou moved up alongside her, wanting recognition, and since she was proud of what he had done, she gave it. "Huzhou is responsible for the drawing. He has an artistic talent we have not before recognized."

Huzhou beamed and was introduced to the visitors. When he learned they were of the People's Right to Know Committee, his smile altered slightly to one of disdain. He had always thought them weak and ineffectual.

"You will bring Jiang's wrath upon you," Zhou cautioned.

"It is time. The people pay billions for Shanghai Star, and they should receive value. Minister Jiang is passé, and we will not allow him to perpetuate his bias."

The man from Guangzhou, Mu, smiled his appreciation. If Zhou was not careful, Chiang would recruit his chairmen to her own cause. His silent approval reinforced her decision to take up the battle in earnest. Minister Jiang was about to receive more than he had bargained for.

"Why are we honored with your presence, Chairman Zhou?"

"We continue our Let Us Learn campaign, but we find that we must provide more detail than the posters allow. I am hoping to persuade you to allow us the use of your copy machine."

"It is an old one and well used. It breaks down frequently."

"Still . . . ?"

"You will provide toner and paper and repairs?"

"With much gladness."

Chiang was feeling magnanimous. "You are welcome to it. It is time we cooperated more fully."

The way their faces lit up, Chiang thought she might have given them the keys to the Forbidden City.

The man named Yang said, "May your pathways forever be smooth and downhill."

"I am afraid the path is upward, but we shall reach the summit, Mr. Yang."

Eleven days after Media Bureau Limited had been awarded its programming contract, the second, third, and fourth floors of the Shanghai Star building had been painted and carpeted. Movable partitions delineated office spaces, and the furnishings were in place. MBL engineers flown in from France had installed the equipment for one production room and were working on others. Sung Wu and his executive assistant were moving into their solid-walled office today. Pierre Lefant worked out of another office with real walls next door to Sung. He had closed down one of his suites at the International Hotel.

The floors were slowly becoming populated. Lefant's staff had moved in, and another dozen had arrived from France and Germany. By the end of October, the work force would number 125, thirty of them selected from Chinese applicants. Lefant could tell already that there were going to be problems.

Twelve Chinese had been hired so far, every one of them related in some way to Sung Wu, a nepotism he seemed to take for granted as his perquisite. If they had any familiarity with information processing in any manner, he suspected it was from watching television or reading a newspaper.

Now, as much of his time was taken with arranging on-the-job training for the Chinese as it was in attempting to keep Sung Wu from tripping over his own tongue.

And next week, five of the Media Bureau Limited directors would arrive from Europe to examine the facilities and the operations. They were happy with Lefant right now—who would not be with visions of billions and billions of francs in their heads?—but as soon as they talked to Sung and interviewed the Chinese staff, they were going to be less happy.

His only argument for the board members would be the political one. He had no choice in the selections. They would understand that, but they would also be concerned about the future. If Sung and his relatives created a disaster, it would reflect on MBL worldwide. The directors would not be happy about the prospects.

He ought to talk to Sung once again, knowing the attempt would be futile.

Rising from his chair, Lefant left the office through his open door, entering the common reception area, then peeked into Sung's office. It was vacant.

He asked the pretty girl who served both as Sung's secretary and his granddaughter, "Mr. Sung?"

"He is in the screening room, Mr. Lefant."

The man spent most of his time watching movies he had never known existed. He was either enraptured by them, or irritated with their content.

"Do you know what he's watching today?"

She glanced down at a schedule on her desk. About the only work she accomplished was scheduling her grandfather's movies.

"It is *La Dolce Vita*, right now."

Lefant sighed. Sung would come back, tossing in Lefant's mailbox a thick stack of notes on how the movie would have to be altered—scenes cut, language changed. First of all, he would not have understood the director's intent, and secondly, his changes would render the story meaningless. Lefant had thought of leading each movie with the disclaimer, "Edited for Sung Wu."

It was almost impossible to believe, but his secondhand directing had ruined *Top Gun* and *The Sound of Music*. Lefant had yet to make the changes, and he was looking for ways he could avoid it.

Lefant's disgust finally rose to the surface.

"Get Minister Jiang for me."

"Immediately, Mr. Lefant."

He went back in his office, knowing it would take her awhile. She had to refer to her notes on how to use the complicated telephone system.

While he was waiting, Marc Chabeau came in.

"Sit down, Marc."

"We've got a problem—"

The telephone buzzed.

"Just a moment." He picked up the receiver.

"Mr. Lefant, this is Wen Yito. The minister is not available at the moment."

Lefant did not like Wen. There was an air of danger about the man.

"Mr. Wen, I need to schedule an appointment with the minister."

"The subject, please?"

"We need to discuss Mr. Sung's performance and . . ."

"Did you not vote for Mr. Sung? Above the other candidate?"

"Yes, but—"

"I doubt that changes will be made, Mr. Lefant."

"We still need to talk. Plus, there is all of the incompetent people Sung has hired."

"I believe the contract states that positions to be filled by nationals are to be determined by the president."

"Yes, but—"

"It strikes me that nothing would be accomplished by a meeting with the minister, and he is a very busy man. You must use the contract as your guide."

Wen hung up.

Lefant slammed the receiver down.

"It goes from bad to worse?" Chabeau asked.

"If I had known how . . ." Lefant let his statement die. "What problem? Sung's people?"

"Actually, for a change, no. We've stopped receiving transmissions from Paris."

In addition to the editing taking place in the Paris headquarters of MBL, numerous programs were being transmitted via satellite to Shanghai, captured on videotape, edited, and stored. It was going on all over the Continent and in the United States, also. MBL had contracted with a large number of production companies—some of whom had once belonged to the Consortium of Information Services, and they were preparing their products for broadcast in accordance with MBL guidelines and the Ministry of Information's policies. Some were lucky, such as game shows which only had to add closed-captions to their productions with Chinese-character or pinyin subtitles. Others had to edit more closely.

Lefant had been told that the MBL marketing people were living in advertising fantasyland. The commercial sector was begging them to take their money for ad space on all of the channels, from travel to comedy to drama. The sports channels were getting the most interest. There was a great deal of universality in basketball and soccer. And no editing other than a Chinese voice-over.

"This is a technical problem?"

"I assume so. I tried to call Will Bricher, but he is out. Do you want to speak to Director Deng?"

"No."

"No?"

"You do it. I have an appointment."

Shaking his head, Chabeau got up and left.

Lefant did not have an engagement; he picked up the phone and called Yvonne.

"Ah, Pierre! I am so happy to hear your voice."

"Are you free for a late lunch?"

"Of course. You come to my house."

"Soon," he said and hung up.

Pierre Lefant was the first to admit that Yvonne Deng had turned the tables on him. His original intention of using her as a source of information from within Shanghai Star had not evolved as planned. Instead, he had found himself hopelessly in love and taking care not to blurt out MBL secrets, which she might share with Mai.

Yvonne Deng had completely disrupted his careful life. He took long lunches, left in the middle of the afternoon, and devoted nearly every evening to her. He was having a wonderful time, and he knew it was affecting his work.

He was going to have to straighten himself out, and soon, or someone would begin to notice. He would start tomorrow.

The China Air flight landed at Gonggar Airport at 3:40 in the afternoon, and Vladimir Suretsov was met by an official from the Ministry of Energy named Asan.

He was carrying a small suitcase and a camera bag, and Asan took the suitcase from him and put it in the back of the van he was driving.

"I have confirmed your hotel reservations as well as your return flight in the morning, Mr. Suretsov."

"Thank you. Providing, of course, that I am still breathing in the morning." He was having some difficulty.

"The altitude takes its toll on visitors, yes. But you will adapt, I think."

They got in the van, and Asan started it and pulled out of the parking lot.

"We will go directly to the reactor site, then I will take you to your hotel in Lhasa."

The trip took forty minutes and passed through some of the most rugged and beautiful country Suretsov had ever seen. Huge escarpments rose on one side of the gravel road, steep slopes densely carpeted in pine on the other. The road wound along a valley floor, passed through narrow gorges, and lost some altitude. He dug a 35-millimeter Nikon out of his camera bag and shot a roll of black-and-white film through the windshield and his side window.

Suretsov was not a photographer, and though he often shot up a lot of film, not once had one of his pictures been selected for publication.

"You must enjoy your posting here, Mr. Asan."

The man smiled. "It is three years now, and yes, I do like it. We do not breathe easily here, but we also do not breathe toxic air."

Suretsov jotted the quote in his notebook, to Asan's obvious gratification. He did not know whether he would use it, but it made Asan agreeable.

They emerged from a narrow defile into a wider, though not less rugged valley. The road ahead continued to follow the bottom of the valley, but Asan slowed and pulled off onto a single-lane, gravelled track characterized by dips and rises.

Suretsov loaded a new roll of film in his camera.

This road traversed steeply up the side of a mountain, then levelled off and ended at a steel gate in a three-meter-high chain-link fence. Asan braked to a stop.

A guard came out of a small hut at the side of the gate and approached the van. He knew Asan, and the two chatted briefly in Chinese.

"He will need to examine your camera equipment," Asan told him.

"Of course."

They got out of the van, and Suretsov walked around to the front, put his foot up on the bumper, and placed the bag on his knee. He unzipped the side pockets and top. Smiling at him, the guard came up and poked into the pockets, finding film rolls and filters. In the main compartment, Suretsov had piled an assortment of camera bodies, lenses, neck straps, and a small tripod. In the jumble of paraphernalia, he hoped the small radiation-measuring device at the bottom of the bag went unnoticed.

It did.

As soon as the guard nodded his approval, Suretsov reached in the bag for another camera, with a wide-angle lens in place, snapping the switch on the Geiger counter as he did so. It would record whatever readings it took. He pulled the Canon camera out, draped it by its strap around his neck, then hung the bag over his shoulder. Carrying his Nikon, he followed Asan to the fence, and the guard unlocked a small gate and let them through.

He stopped and shot pictures of the complex with both cameras.

In his notebook, he recorded the film number and shots. He also quickly jotted down the time. His picture-taking was less a visual recording than a cover for keeping track of where he was within the compound and at what time. Later, when he reviewed the radiation record, which also notated the time, he would be able to tell where in the complex the readings were taken.

Being inside the chain-link fence made him feel vulnerable. If Mickey Stone's friend were correct, this was not the healthiest assignment he had ever given himself. He fought the inclination to speed his way through the visit and the interview.

Finishing his note, he said, "There, good. After you, Mr. Asan."

They continued walking toward the smaller of three structures inside the fence. The ground had been levelled and gravel spread over it, probably to keep down the weeds and ease the maintenance requirements. A couple trucks were parked by the fence, but that was the only indication that humans were present. It could have been deserted for all he knew.

Asan rang a bell by the single door into the windowless building which Suretsov estimated to be twenty meters by ten meters in size. A porthole opened briefly, revealing a round Chinese face, then the door was pulled open.

"Mr. Suretsov," Asan said, "this is Mr. Zhang, the manager of the plant."

They shook hands, and Zhang ushered them into a small room that appeared to be a lounge or resting area. After a short round of small talk, Zhang offered tea or coffee, and Suretsov declined. His skin felt itchy—a paranoiac, self-induced sensation, he hoped—without pouring plutonium, or uranium, or whatever down his throat.

"Mr. Zhang, please tell me, this reactor is now owned by the PRC?"

"It will be," the man explained. "After ninety days of operation, title will transfer from Nuclear Power Limited to the People's Republic. The same guarantee applies to all sites."

"And this is the first reactor to become operative?"

"It is. Guangzhou is also in operation now, and the reactor at Golmud in Qinghai Province is scheduled for start-up on Saturday."

Suretsov rapidly took notes in his private shorthand as he asked, "As manager, you report to the Ministry of Energy?"

Zhang laughed. "It is confused at the moment. Until the PRC accepts the reactor, I am paid by Nuclear Power Limited. I attended their training classes in France, and I work at the moment with their on-site consultant. All of us report to the atomic-energy bureau within the energy ministry. Mr. Asan is our liaison."

Suretsov had both of them spell their names and titles for him, then shot several frames of film of the two of them. Smiling broadly for the world.

Zhang then began the tour by showing him the bunk room and kitchen.

"We work in three-and-a-half-day shifts, and there are two teams."

"How large are the teams?"

"It is a simple reactor. There is a manager and five persons on each team."

They passed back through the lounge, then into a large, brightly lit, and high-technology room. The walls contained an array of monitor screens and digital readouts. Suretsov noted screens showing exterior shots of the building he was in, as well as the other buildings. Other screens were apparently live shots of the interior of the reactor building. Below the screens, and wrapped around the room, was a console with a dizzying number of slide switches and rotary knobs, as well as more digital indicators. Two men in castered chairs tended to the controls.

"Not surprisingly, we call this the control room," Zhang said.

Suretsov pointed to one of the monitors. "That is inside the reactor?"

"No. It is within the turbine building."

"I understand this is similar to the Russian Topaz."

Zhang gave him a funny look, then said, "Some of the design principles are similar, though the Topaz was created for a far different environment. There is really not much in common between them."

Suretsov wondered if that were true or simply the official explanation of Nuclear Power Limited.

"For such a small unit, it appears to be quite efficient."

"It is very efficient, Mr. Suretsov. When we reach our maximum output, we expect to produce two hundred and four kilowatts of electrical power."

"How is this accomplished?"

"We utilize uranium-dioxide pellets, which are approximately one centimeter in size, placed inside a four-meter-long tube called a fuel pin. The pins are then emplaced in sixteen-by-sixteen arrays known as a fuel assembly. Raising or lowering the fuel rods controls the reaction.

"The coolant in use is helium, and the moderator—to slow the fission process—is beryllium. You see, point-oh-two-five-three electron volts . . ."

Suretsov listened through a highly technical explanation of why a moderator was necessary to slow the process. He was lost after Zhang's third sentence, but figured that what was important was that the process was slowed. Rapid fission resulted in Hiroshimas, he thought.

". . . this is a pressurized water reactor, known as a PWR. It is housed in the cylindrical containment chamber you can see on monitor four."

"Oh, I thought it was in the other big building."

Zhang smiled. "That building contains the turbines and generators. The PWR in the containment structure sends superheated coolant through a closed loop that passes through a boiler. The boiler transfers the heat to steam lines leading to the turbine building where the hot steam drives the turbines connected to generators, creating electrical output."

"The reactor building, the containment vessel, then, is the critical component."

"Critical to creating energy, yes."

"And to containing any radiation?"

"Of course. It is composed of a steel lining overlaid with a one-half-meter thick coat of concrete. This shield is guaranteed to protect personnel from gamma-and-neutron radiation. Concrete has always served as the most cost-efficient shielding."

Suretsov moved closer to one of the monitors.

"This view is inside the reactor building?"

"It is. What you see is the visual check for the positioning of the fuel rods. As you can tell, they are approximately one third inserted into the core." Zhang pointed to a readout under a designation printed in pinyin. "This is fuel array four. The readout says it is thirty-four-point-four percent inserted. The camera allows us a visual confirmation."

"And in an emergency?"

"There are many safeguards. Should temperatures become too high—it will reach 330 degrees Centigrade—sensors begin to retract the fuel rods. Additionally, a manual override allows us to begin shutting down the systems by hand."

"And if you, or the sensors, are not quick enough?"

"That is why the building is designed as it is, Mr. Suretsov. If a coolant line should break, for example, releasing radioactive vapor, the containment vessel will trap it, even as we shut down the systems."

Suretsov smiled his best reassurance smile. "That is good to know. I wonder if I could take some pictures of the other buildings?"

"Certainly."

Zhang took them outside to walk around the turbine and reactor structures. Suretsov took his pictures and noted them and the time in his log. He assumed the recorder in his camera bag was keeping the same time. His skin felt even itchier as he walked around the reactor, dodging under the large pipes clad in some kind of insulation that connected the reactor with the turbine building. The high-pitched moan coming from the pipes suggested high temperatures. He would not want to be within a kilometer of the pipe if it burst, he thought.

Zhang would not let him see the inside of the turbine building.

"There is proprietary information involved. I am certain you understand."

"I do."

He thanked the man for his time and the tour, then he and Asan went back through the gate to the van.

As Asan backed and filled to turn around, he asked, "Well, Mr. Suretsov?"

"Very interesting. It will make a good article."

"The important thing, I think, is the portable nature of the reactor and the efficiency of its size to its output."

Asan was not forgetting his job as a propagandist for the ministry.

"I noted those exact points in my book."

Asan grinned, "Good. Now where? Perhaps you would like some dinner?"

"Thank you, but I think to the hotel would be best. It has been a long flight and therefore a long day."

"I understand."

He probably did not understand the urgency Suretsov felt in regard to a very long and very hot shower.

He was, however, afraid that a shower would not wash away any of these contaminants.

Grant had eaten two roast-beef sandwiches at his desk while going over schedules and budgets with Bricher and Wickersham. They had worked until seven, then Grant ran them out.

He wasn't hungry when his phone rang at 7:30 P.M. It was his direct line, so he figured it was one of the half-dozen people who knew the number.

It was Minister Shao.

So, seven people knew the number now.

"Good evening, Minister."

"Have you eaten, Mr. Grant?"

Couldn't force down another bite.

"Why, no, I haven't."

"Good. Would you join me at the Cellar in the Sky?"

"I'd be happy to. I need to run by my apartment first, though."

"There is no hurry."

He closed his laptop, with which he had been tracking numbers, and shoved it into a bottom drawer of his desk, where Parker wouldn't see it.

On the way out, he locked his office door, then Parker's. They had started locking all of the lockable spaces on the floor since Sung Wu had moved in. The man snooped everywhere. All of the personnel who had computers, but were not on the secure top floors, had protected them with passwords after discovering that someone had attempted unsuccessfully to enter some of the application programs.

In the parking lot behind the building, he found his GMC Jimmy and drove to the gated entrance. One of the guards came out—military or civilian police guards now, and Grant didn't know which this one was—and opened the gate to let him out. The parking lot had been enclosed with wire mesh fencing and the old pole barrier had given way to a chain-link gate. He felt like he was being let out of the zoo.

He drove directly to his apartment building, and since he was in a hurry, checked the street in front instead of using the back parking lot. He found a tight spot that he managed to squeak the truck into.

In his apartment, he listened to the messages on the answering machine while shedding his chinos and sport shirt. The only person he called back was Mai.

"Good evening, Madame Deng. This is Doug Grant returning Mai's call."

"One moment, Mr. Grant."

He hadn't spoken to Yvonne Deng since the night of the dinner party, but he detected a distinctly icier tone in her voice.

"Hello, Douglas."

"I got your message, Mai."

"Would you like to have a drink with me? Perhaps later?"

She was a little hesitant. Did her invitation sound too much like a date? Was her mother hanging over her?

"I'd love to, but I got a call from Shao, and I'm on my way to dinner with him."

"Shao? What does he want?"

"Something, no doubt, but I don't know what it is."

"Oh, well, maybe another time."

"How about afterward?" He didn't want to lose a chance to be alone with her, if he had a chance.

"What time?"

"Probably around eleven. You want me to pick you up?"

After a moment, she said, "I will meet you at . . . the Manhattan. Do you know where that is?"

It was one of the Western-styled, private bars that played taped country and pop music.

"In the French Concessionaire Area. Also close to where I'm meeting Shao."

"I will see you there."

Grant took a quick shower and dressed in one of his better suits. With Shao, he figured he needed a confident and classy image. With Mai, he didn't know what he needed. Her call and invitation was almost scary.

He went back down and crawled in the truck. When he found a gap in the traffic, he bolted out of his spot, then turned right at the corner, coming back to Wanhangdu Road. With traffic as thick as it was, he probably should have walked.

On Huaihua Road, he was fortunate to spot a Citroën pulling away from the curb, and he shot into the space ten feet ahead of a beat-up Mercedes. The Mercedes driver, a Chinese with a high-pitched yelp, cursed him roundly as he went by.

Grant got out of the truck, conscious of a Lada passing him slowly, swerving to avoid his wide-open door, the man in it staring at him. He was Chinese. He locked the door, went around the back of the truck, and gained the sidewalk. It took him about ten minutes to find the Ruijin Building, which was chock-full of restaurants, then to find the Cellar in the Sky on the twenty-seventh floor.

When he entered the foyer, he was greeted by a smiling maitre d' and a combo doing nice things with the Dave Brubeck Quartet's "Take Five." The restaurant specialized in 1950s-style jazz.

Shao had a table to himself, sitting facing the entrance, as was the custom for a host—and to give him first view of assassins entering the room. In the tightly packed room, Grant saw that it had been isolated to some extent, other tables moved away from it to give the defense minister a token bit of privacy.

"Minister, it's good to see you, again."

"I apologize for calling so late. I didn't know I was going to be staying over in Shanghai until just before I called." Shao indicated the chair next to him. "The music sometimes overcomes conversation."

Grant took the chair and ordered a scotch and water from the waiter.

The band slipped into a Cal Tjader number, but Grant couldn't place the title.

"It is loud, but I enjoy the music," Shao told him.

"I've been here once before. They give a nice performance."

Shao never looked as if he relaxed, even to jazz. He sat erect in his low chair, his hands on the table in front of him, one wrapped around a squat glass of an amber liquid. His posture somehow precluded Grant's slouching back in his own chair.

"I have ordered for us," Shao said. "I trust that is acceptable?"

"I'm looking forward to it."

They alternated between small talk and listening to the music—a little Josh White, there—for a half hour before the first courses arrived. The appetizer was minced pork in a dumpling, and the entree was particularly Shanghainese. Grant didn't know what it was called, but the Shanghai style of cooking featured heavier foods prepared for a longer length of time in greater amounts of soy sauce and sugar. This dish contained a wide variety of vegetables and hairy crab on a bed of noodles.

"If you do not mind the observation," Shao said, "I have noted that you use chopsticks quite well."

"I've been here three years, and I didn't master them for two-and-a-half."

"You might have starved."

"When no one was looking, I used a fork."

When their plates were cleared away, Shao ordered a fresh pot of tea and two small cups of a local white wine. It tasted like a Greek retsina.

"I have never properly thanked you for your assistance with the launch schedule," Grant said. "I wanted to do it in person."

"It turned out to be a small thing. I was happy to help."

"In terms of Shanghai Star's schedule, it was a major consideration, and I appreciate what you did for us."

Shao waved it away. "I did want to speak to you about Shanghai Star. Did you read this morning's *Washington Post?*"

"No, but Will Bricher did and told me about the article."

"It originated with ITAR-Tass. Do you know the reporter?"

"It is probably Vladimir Suretsov, who's the bureau chief in Shanghai. He has interviewed me a couple of times."

"You did not suggest his topic for him?" Shao asked with a half-smile.

"Have you ever tried to tell a reporter what to write?" Grant replied before realizing that Shao may have done just that, and succeeded quite well.

"I have tried, but with dismal results. What do you make of these attacks?"

"I've given it a considerable amount of thought, Minister, but I'm baffled."

"Come, now. I believe you know more than you would let on."

"I'm hoping the investigations in Guangzhou and Harbin come up with something solid."

"My understanding is that you have applied a great deal of pressure on Inspectors Wing and Chou," the minister said, watching Grant's eyes.

This old man has his fingers in every pie.

"I may have gotten a little overzealous," Grant admitted. "But I couldn't buy that disgruntled employee motive that Wing was peddling."

"And you quite artfully forced him into discovering that the disgruntled employee was paid by someone to accomplish his mischief."

"I'd like to know more about whoever is doing the paying."

"A tall man, thin, and Chinese."

Grant raised an eyebrow.

"Since you convinced me to pay closer attention to the communications network as a defense concern, I decided to have military investigators . . . assist Inspectors Wing and Chou. After prolonged interrogation, the suspect in Guangzhou admits he was paid by a man he had met, but one time, in Liwan Park—a tall, thin Chinese with a scar on his cheek. He does not know the name."

Grant found himself gazing toward the bandstand.

"Mr. Grant?"

"Sorry, I was thinking . . . earlier tonight, I saw a man with a very thin face."

"He was tall?"

"I don't know. He was seated in a car that went by me."

"There are a few thin Chinese in Shanghai."

"Yes, there probably are."

"What else have you considered relative to the incidents?" Shao asked.

"I certainly wasn't thinking about one man behind them all. The destruction of the rocket required some kind of sophisticated remote-control apparatus. Lighter fluid poured into computers. A nine mike-mike bullet aimed at Stone. A homemade bomb in Harbin. The methods are pretty damned diverse, Minister."

"On purpose, perhaps. To give the impression of multiple parties involved."

"That's one way to look at it."

"Who would benefit by the loss of Shanghai Star, Mr. Grant?"

"From my point of view, everyone loses." Grant took his turn staring into Shao's eyes. "What's your position, Minister?"

"On Shanghai Star? I think you—"

"Not on the network. I know it benefits the defense ministry. What about the kinds of information delivered to the people?"

Shao's eyes clouded for a moment. He smiled and said, "Minister Jiang makes some telling arguments. He sees connections between some kinds of information and some ills appearing in our society. The Premier and a few reformists in the Politburo and the State Council also have compelling arguments. They point out the . . . inadequacies in creative thinking among our people, how far behind much of the world China has fallen, and suggest that one of the culprits is the lack of knowledge about advances in science and the arts. At the moment, the two sides are about evenly divided."

"Is the battle heating up?"

"It is stagnant for the moment, now that Jiang has determined the provider. We shall have to wait until October first to see if it reheats."

"You still haven't told me your position."

"Mine must be aligned somewhat with the general staff."

"Your public opinion. I understand that. And privately?"

Shao leaned forward and rested his elbows on the table, his head closer.

"Between us?"

"Yes."

"I think Minister Jiang is full of shit."

Grant grinned.

"Societal problems, in my view, need to be solved through education and intervention. Blaming external sources only avoids the requirement to address the problems from another angle."

"You've got my vote, Minister."

"But my vote must be cast according to my vision of maintaining a balance."

"I don't expect to hear the views you just expressed on a talk show."

Shao smiled again.

"Are we beginning to trust one another, Mr. Grant?"

Grant thought that one over before saying, "Candidly, I don't think we can afford to trust each other, Minister Shao."

"Ah?"

"You have your own agenda going, and I respect that. Mine is to make Megatronics the most successful startup company in this decade. Our goals may coincide for a moment, but aren't necessarily the same. However, aside from the trust aspect, I think we can be honest with each other. I think you just were."

"Let me ask you this, then. Without it going further?"

"Stops right here."

"Not even Madame Deng."

"She won't hear anything from me."

"No pillow talk?"

"That rumor's getting out of hand, Minister. Not that I wouldn't like to see her pillow, but I've not seen her bedroom much less her bed."

Shao shrugged. "The chief of staff and I have considered the possibility that Shanghai Star should be an agency of the defense ministry."

"Uh . . ."

"Not the program side. Just the technological side since it appears vital to our interests. What do you think?"

"Well, you know the political system I was reared in. Right off the bat, I have to side with the civilians."

"Is that pragmatic?"

"I think so, yes. There's something to be said for checks and balances. I don't have to like the policies of the information ministry—which I think are too restrictive, but at least the civilians are making the decisions."

"We are only talking of the hardware component."

"It's an important component," Grant said. "If the military decides it doesn't like what's showing up on the screens, it can simply blank out channels. If you're worried about security, and

I am worried about it, I much prefer the system you came up with, sharing the load between the military and the government."

"Director Deng's recommendation. In other words, even though we don't have the information, we could control it? Or at least its distribution?"

"That's it. Whether or not that's the intent, a takeover by the military would appear dictatorial. My vote goes to Jiang on this one, Minister."

"As mine did on the decision for a vendor. Very well, I appreciate your candor."

"And I yours."

"We will have more of these discussions. I find them enlightening."

"I enjoy them, too."

Shao stood up, saying, "And we will find the tall, thin man."

"Very soon, I hope."

Grant took the elevator back to street level alone. Shao either had another appointment or a less conspicuous route for leaving the twenty-seventh floor.

The conversation loped through his mind as he walked the sidewalk, avoiding bumping into the many pedestrians. It was as Deng thought; Shao had a few motives of his own, and he probably hadn't revealed all of them to Grant. It was also interesting that he was so aware of the investigations taking place. Maybe his influence would startle some rabbits out of the underbrush.

Grant approached his truck, digging his keys out of his pocket.

He stuck the key in the lock, twisted, grabbed the handle, and pulled the door open.

"Oh, damn!"

Where's my mind? Mai's waiting at the Manhattan.

He reached in and flipped the door lock.

Then slammed the door.

For a split second, the truck was there.

Then it wasn't.

And his mind went white.

Friday, September 9

Deng Mai waited alone at a table in the Manhattan, fending off casual drunks—mostly *gweilos,* until fifteen minutes before midnight. She did not think Grant had forgotten her, but she assumed that the minister was keeping him longer than expected. She was more disappointed than she might have expected to be.

She paid for the single drink she had consumed, then left the bar and flagged a taxi. Twenty minutes later, the driver eased to the curb in front of her house.

And behind a black Lincoln parked at the curb.

The lights in the house were on.

Suspicious, Deng paid off the driver and hurried through the portal in the brick and wrought-iron fence and up the front walk. In the light from the open doorway, she saw her mother talking to someone. They stopped talking to watch her approach.

Shao?

"Director Deng, I have been looking for you."

"Yes, Minister, what is it?"

"I am afraid there has been an accident."

"Accident? What . . . who . . . Grant? Is it Grant?"

He nodded. "He has been taken to the Number 1 People's Hospital—"

"Come! Let us go!"

She did not think to ask whether Shao had intended to go to the hospital or not, but spun around and headed for his car.

Shao told her mother, "I am sorry to have awakened you, Madame Deng."

"It is all right, Minister."

Shao followed her down the walk to the car where a sergeant held the rear door open. She scrambled into the backseat, and Shao entered more sedately.

She realized she had been holding her breath. "Please excuse my agitation, Minister. I did not mean to—"

"It is quite all right, Director. I understand fully. The hospital, Sergeant."

"How is he? Do we know?"

"He was unconscious when they put him in the ambulance."

"You were there? What *happened?*"

"I would say that a bomb had been placed in his car. We were about a block away on Huaihua Road when it went off. It was a forceful explosion."

"Oh, no!"

"Yes. I called for police and an ambulance from the car phone, and we were there in seconds. I think what saved him is that he was not in the truck when it exploded. I would judge that the bomb was under the seat."

"Was he . . . I mean . . . hurt badly?"

"I could not tell. There was some blood; I think from glass. The force of the blast knocked him across the street, into the side of a passenger automobile. He was on the ground in the middle of the street when we got there and blocked off traffic. Some of the fools in cars would not even stop."

The defense minister's automobile had red and blue lights behind the grille, and the driver had turned them on. Most of the traffic gave way before them, but Deng was barely aware. She only remembered the street sign for Beisuzhou Lu as they turned onto it, the tires screaming a mild protest.

The sergeant braked to a hard stop in a no-parking zone in front of the hospital, and Shao opened the door and helped her out before the driver could come around. Together, they trotted up the steps and through the doors.

Shao had only to identify himself to the receptionist, and they were ushered down a long hallway to the trauma section. A hospital administrator, two doctors, and a nurse appeared magically.

"What is Mr. Grant's condition?" Shao asked.

The taller of the two doctors, in a blood-specked green smock, said, "He is now conscious, Minister. He is also a very lucky man."

"The injuries?"

"There is a mild concussion, two cracked ribs, a badly sprained left shoulder. There are many bruises and superficial cuts. I had to put stitches in two of them."

"Can I . . . can we see him?" Deng asked.

"For a few minutes, Director. As soon as he is moved to a room."

They waited almost half an hour, then a nurse took them down another hallway and pushed open the wide door to a room that was in semidarkness.

She stepped inside, Shao behind her.

Grant was flat on his back in the bed, the sheet pulled up over his chest. His eyes were closed. There were four adhesive strips on his forehead and left cheek. A larger bandage was taped to his bare left shoulder.

"Douglas?"

His eyes snapped open, then he grinned at her.

The grin reassured her.

"I'll be damned," he said. "The minister and the director out visiting in the middle of the night. I'm honored."

"Honored or not," Shao said, "how do you feel?"

"I have one hell of a headache, but I'd feel better if they gave me an aspirin and let me go home. Scotch might help."

"They're going to hold you overnight," she said.

"That's what the one doctor said, and I tried not to believe him. I haven't been in a hospital in a long time. I don't like it."

Deng had moved up to the side of the bed. She suddenly realized she was holding his left hand in her own. If Shao noticed, he did not say anything. He went around to the other side of the bed.

His hand felt warm and alive; that was suddenly very important to her.

"What do you remember?" the defense minister asked.

"Since I woke up on that table with a bright light in my eyes, I've been trying to recall. I know I unlocked the door and pulled it open. Then I remembered I had to see Mai, and I slammed the door. After that, it was bright-light time."

The way he closed his eyes partway, and winced from time to time as he spoke, led Deng to think he was in considerable pain. She wondered if she should call a doctor.

"The tall, thin man you saw earlier?" Shao asked.

"I thought about that, too, Minister. He knew where I'd parked."

"I told the police to begin searching for such a man. There will be thousands to choose from, however."

"I want him to myself for a few minutes. The SOB ruined a good suit."

Shao smiled. "I think a good night's sleep would be far better for you. And I have yet to drive back to Beijing tonight."

"I will stay a few minutes more," Deng told him, "and then take a taxi. Thank you for picking me up."

Shao Tsung smiled at her and left the room, closing the door behind him.

"I don't care what his agendas are," Grant said. "I like the guy."

He tried to move a little in the bed, and from the grimace on his face, she thought his shoulder bothered him the most.

"Do you need anything, a painkiller? I can get the doctor."

"I'm not real big on drugs, Mai. I turned him down the first time."

"Don't be silly. If it hurts—"

"Holding your hand helps a lot."

She blushed. "This is not seemly, I know."

"It's pretty seemly to me."

She released his hand. "I will go call Will Bricher, then come back and sit with you for a little while."

Deng went to find a telephone and gave Bricher a quick report. When she got back to the room, Grant was asleep. She stayed for an hour, anyway.

Bricher was there when he woke, sitting in a low chair drawn close to the bed.

"About time, old Hoss," he drawled.

Grant started to lift his arm, to look at his watch, and a jagged bolt of lightning in his shoulder changed his mind.

"What time is it, Will?"

"Close to nine. Way past the start of our day."

"How long you been here?"

"A couple hours. They make surprisingly good coffee in this place."

"That's what I need, coffee. And I could use a few eggs wrapped around ham."

"That's a good sign," Bricher said. "I'll see if I can flag someone down."

"I'd prefer the Dallas Cowboy Cafe."

"Hell's bells, man! You've been facing high explosives. Tell me what hurts."

Grant tried to do an inventory. His whole body seemed to throb, though the shoulder was the worst. There were a couple positions where he thought his whole being might be centered just below the knob of his shoulder bone.

"Not too bad. I've got some aches and pains. The shoulder's going to bother me for a while. The ribs seem to restrict my breathing."

"That's because they're bound, chief. How's the head?"

"Not as bad as last night. See if you can run down the guy who can sign me out." There was still some ringing in his ears, but Grant didn't mention it.

"I want to see if you can stand up on your own, first."

Bricher stood up and backed the chair away from the bed.

Grant used his right arm to throw the sheet aside and found that he was dressed in the bottom half of some hospital pajamas.

Sitting up was the worst part. He cradled his left arm against his stomach and used his right arm to lever himself upright. Black-and-blue strobes went off behind his eyes; pain lanced down his left arm; the headache came back in earnest.

He kept the momentum going, sliding his legs off the edge of the bed, finding the floor with his bare toes, settling his feet flat on the linoleum, rising from the bed.

"No sweat," he said.

"Shit, the sweat's pouring off you. I don't think we're going anywhere this morning, chief."

The medevac chopper airlifted Grant and his four wounded troopers to the closest field hospital, a beige-colored tent in a beige-colored world. As soon as he'd opened up with the Iraqi 60-millimeter machine gun, raking the wadi with murderous fire, some Iraqi soldier had gotten off a lucky shot that whanged off the side of Grant's helmet. A major dent in the helmet, a minor one in his head.

Concussion, they said, and wouldn't let him leave the tent. Antiseptic and vomit and groans. PFC Grosset, one of his own, in the bed next to him, screamed and cried when they took his leg.

Grant had to lay there, and listen, and smell, and agonize.

"I want out of this fucking hospital, Will."

"You're as dumb as some hound dogs I know."

But Bricher went and paid the bills and got the signatures. He borrowed a robe, a sling, a wheelchair, and a nurse, and got him out to a company Jimmy.

Driving away, Bricher said, "Can we skip the Dallas Cowboy Cafe?"

"Yeah, we can do that. Thanks, Will."

Bricher wasn't happy, but managed to walk him into the building, the elevator, and finally his apartment.

He felt better, just being a long way away from the hospital. The act of being upright and walking made him think he felt stronger, and in the apartment, he got a pillow and blanket from the bedroom and tossed them on the couch.

"I may watch TV for a couple days."

"Good luck, Doug. The selections are sparse," Bricher said from the kitchen.

"What are you doing?"

"I found enough here for a ham-and-cheese omelet. The eggs look like they're not more than a year old."

"You've done enough."

"Oh, you hungry, too?"

When the coffee was finished percolating, Bricher brought him a cup, along with a couple Tylenol tablets. The next trip, he came back with two plates heaped with what he called the Colonel's Famous Omelet.

The phone rang several times, and Bricher answered, assuring the callers that the boss was doing fine. Then he unplugged the phone.

They talked while they ate, outlining possible security precautions they should urge on their employees. The food was good, but Grant felt himself getting drowsy.

Bricher washed the dishes, then told him, "I'm going out and get you something for the refrigerator, then I'll go over to the office and make sure Sung Wu hasn't requisitioned all our computers."

"Be careful, Will."

"I'll watch my butt. You be asleep by the time I get back."

Grant turned on the TV with the remote, settled onto his right side on the couch to watch a local newscast, which didn't make one mention of him, and was asleep by the middle of the weather forecast.

Guangzhou, with all its sensory and sensual delights, still awaited Stone.

But Stone was busy.

At the moment, busy on the phone.

"I'm back, C.C."

"Pardon me," Coolidge said, "but I didn't know you were gone."

"I had to shoot over to Harbin for a day. This stuff you're building falls apart if I'm gone for long."

"Not *my* stuff, babe."

"It was a digital encoder."

"We sub those out, remember? Sheesh, you had me worried there. Why couldn't your techs fix it?"

"They could fix it; they just couldn't diagnose the problem, first off. With my masterful teaching, however, the next time they'll spot that glitch in a second."

"No doubt. Why you calling me?"

"Couple reasons. There was some of your stuff at Harbin that couldn't stand up to TNT. I faxed you a reorder, but there's no rush since they're desktops, and before we put the desks back, we have to put the floor back."

"Jesus Christ! Was it bad?"

"It was terrible, Calvin. We've got two guys back from the hospital, four to go."

"Two of my assembly-line teams have put a care package together for the victims and their families. It's on the way."

"Nice," Stone said. "Other reason I'm calling, I still haven't got my last two consoles. Deadline's coming up."

"Not my problem anymore, Mickey. They shipped out yesterday morning, which probably means they're sitting on a luggage carousel in Barcelona."

"Don't tell me that."

"Okay, I won't. Look, you talked to Doug?"

"I've tried a couple times, Calvin, but his phone's still disconnected. Bricher told me he pulled the plug."

"How's he doing?"

"Will says damned good, considering what happened, but he thinks Doug should have stayed in the hospital a couple more days."

"This shit keeps up, babe, I'm going to have to come over there and kick some ass for you guys."

"I'd do the kicking, C.C., if I could figure out who to kick."

Stone hung up, dropped his feet off the desk, and saw Naylor in the doorway.

"Hey, Meg. Don't you ever have to work?"

"I worked last night. I'm taking some comp time."

She came in and sat in one of the chairs. Through the glass wall behind her, Stone saw some of Wickersham's guys in heated discussion at a computer terminal. They were installing an upgrade to the billing program. Some of the programs they had installed two years ago were already obsolete; they had learned new methods as they went along. And Shanghai Star wasn't even operational, yet.

Naylor's sober and practical eyes studied him for a minute. It was getting so he liked watching her eyes. He liked a lot about her, even the freckles. He wasn't so enamored of her unwillingness to get involved romantically.

"You've got just bunches and bunches of computer experts around, right?"

"Well, I'm the expert. I've got a bunch of helpers."

"Don't have an ego problem, do you?"

"Never have."

"I thought not. Are you good at software?"

"Being modest, I'd better say no. That's Curt's department."

"Did I tell you my brother's a cop? With the Indianapolis PD?"

"That's an abrupt change of topic, but no you didn't. Is it important?"

"This guy the Chinese cops have?"

"I'm trying to follow this," Stone said. "Yeah. The disgruntled employee."

"You told me the police had him describe the payoff man to a sketch artist."

"Lousy sketch, too. Looked like Bozo the Clown with a scar."

"If MI had a decent software man around, and if MI would spring for the cost of the calls, I'd phone my brother."

"Let's put both of those ideas together, Meg. Where are we going?"

"I think I can talk Jim into lending—remember that word, Mickey, lending—you the IPD's composite-sketch program."

Stone smiled at her. "You're a doll."

"Cut that out. Yes or no?"

He shoved the phone across the desk. "It's the middle of the night there."

"That's okay. He's used to bad hours. And the department's computer center is a twenty-four-hour operation."

Stone stood. "I'm going to the next office for a phone to call Wickersham."

After he got the call, Bricher walked down the hallway and into the section of the floor housing Wickersham's software engineers. They were a less raucous bunch than his own, and they were a bit more orderly. The workstations were neatly aligned around the perimeter of the room, each divided from the one next to it by six-foot-high decorator panels. Wickersham's pseudo-office was in one corner; he had a few more decorator panels separating him from the others.

A dozen people in jeans and T-shirts were concentrating on a variety of tasks, scanning endless lines of computer instructions scrolling up their screens, running debugging programs, testing.

Six printers on a long table at the back center of the room were pouring forth endless reams of paper—documentation for new programs.

Bricher crossed the linoleum floor to Wickersham's cubicle.

The software director was on the phone.

". . . perfect, Lieutenant. Damn, I appreciate it . . . yeah, got it." Wickersham scribbled a phone number on a sticky note. "When we're done, we'll erase it . . . thanks, again."

He hung up and yelled, "Dickerson!"

A minute later, a pug-nosed young lady stuck her head in. "You called, Curt?"

He handed her the note. "That's the Indianapolis Police Department Computer Center. Get on a fifty-six-baud line and collect a program they'll give you."

"Right away."

A modem handling a 56,600-baud transmission rate was a hell of a lot faster than the 300 bytes per second that Bricher had used when he first started playing with computers.

"What's that all about, Curt?"

"Lieutenant James Naylor of the IPD is letting us borrow their composite-sketching program."

"How do we know Lieutenant Naylor?"

"Stone's girlfriend's brother."

"Stone doesn't have girlfriends."

"Well, she's awfully generous with her brother's time."

"What are we doing? You mind my asking?"

"Mickey's going to use this thing on the guy in jail in Guangzhou."

"So?"

"To find the man behind the scenes."

"We're getting in the police business?"

"The resident police don't have the latest tools. We're helping them out."

"Let's not get carried away, Curt."

"You don't want this son of a bitch caught?"

"I do. I . . ." Bricher thought about it for a minute. "Well, hell, as long as we're going to have it here . . ."

He turned to leave.

"Where you going?" Wickersham asked.

"To make a call."

Something woke Grant at a little after four.

He raised his head from the pillow on the sofa and looked around. The TV was going, showing some Chinese dance ensemble working hard. His headache had retreated to the back of his head and was a dull throb. His ears still rang. He rolled upright, holding his left arm firmly against his stomach. The pain in his shoulder hadn't gone away, but it was substantially reduced. The binding around his chest made him think he couldn't take a deep breath.

Scratch, scratch.

Key in his door.

He started to his feet as the door swung open.

"Stay put," Bricher ordered.

"You might have knocked," Grant told him.

"I was afraid I wouldn't have wakened you."

Bricher stood aside, and Wickersham entered, carrying a large, high-resolution monitor. Behind him was Diantha Parker. She was toting a laptop computer.

It looked suspiciously like his own.

He settled back on the couch. "What the hell's going on?"

Parker gave him one of her blackest looks, holding the laptop up. "Do you know where I found this?"

"Do I get three guesses?"

"In the bottom drawer of your desk."

"I don't get to guess?"

"As soon as you're well enough, I'm going to kill you."

"Ah, Diantha. . . ."

"You go around telling me you won't use a computer, and then Will tells me to grab this one. Do you know you've got some sophisticated spreadsheets on it?"

"Another guess?" Grant gave Bricher a dirty look.

"We needed a laptop quick," Bricher said.

"You want to clear the coffee table?" Wickersham asked, standing in the middle of the living room, still holding the monitor.

Bricher shoved newspapers, magazines, and a few dishes to one side, and Bricher placed the set on the table, facing Grant.

"Won't anyone tell me what's going on?"

Parker sat down next to him and put the laptop on the coffee table. Wickersham started uncoiling cables.

Bricher said, "While I putter around in the kitchen and make my famous Colonel's fried chicken, Curt and Diantha are going to teach you to draw."

"Draw?"

"You told me about some tall, thin man?"

"I don't know how tall he was."

"You just remember how thin he was. Now, we want the details."

Tan Long was in the office he used occasionally on the top floor of the Shanghai No. 1 Department Store. It was a small and cramped space, with no window to the outside world, but he was rarely in it, so it did not bother him unduly.

He was laboriously completing the report of his last journey. The required paperwork listed his accomplishments and the people with whom he had visited. Since his airline and hotel charges were taken care of via other means, he was allowed only to submit his expenses for meal reimbursement. His charges were creative in that they never reflected the actual amounts he had spent for his sustenance. Beijing would never know of the lobster, veal, and beef he consumed. Instead, they would think him a frugal person, his niggardly meals justifying his appearance.

At the knock on his door, he got up to open it.

"Mr. Crest!"

"Hello, Mr. Tan. Sorry to interrupt you, but the man downstairs said I might find you here."

"Come in, please. And please excuse the mess."

The American came into the tiny office, looked briefly around, and tried not to show his disappointment.

Tan laughed. "I realize there is not enough space in which to create a major mess, but I try hard."

"Quite all right, Mr. Tan. You wouldn't believe the disarray I leave my office in. I won't take up your time, but there's been a development you should know about."

Tan was immediately wary. The Megatronics account was worth a 20,000-yuan bonus to him.

"I trust there is nothing unsatisfactory with the document?"

"Not as far as I know. I shipped a copy off to our legal department, but no one has called me yet to raise cain. No, this concerns our meeting scheduled for Monday to sign the contracts."

"There is a problem?"

"A bit of one, yes. Mr. Grant has been involved in an accident, and at this point, I don't know if he will be able to be present for the meeting."

"I am sorry to hear about Mr. Grant. Is he seriously injured?"

"The doctors say he's going to be fine."

"Given the circumstances, I am sure my superiors would understand his absence, Mr. Crest. You could sign the documents in his place."

"Therein lies the problem," Crest said. "Only Mr. Grant is authorized to sign for the company."

Tan was immediately afraid that he might have badly miscalculated.

Tuesday, September 13

Tan had been waiting for this telephone call for three days.

Crest said, "Can we set up the contract meeting for one or two o'clock this afternoon, Mr. Tan?"

"Mr. Grant is recovered, I trust?"

"Well, I think he's a little shaky, but he insists he's ready to go bear hunting."

Since the incident had not made the newspapers, Tan was forced to improvise, "I heard a rumor . . . an explosion of some sort?"

"Yes, but they're going to get the SOB. We got hold of some sophisticated composite-sketching program, and Doug's come up with a good picture of the guy."

"He *saw* . . . the man?" Tan's voice almost squeaked.

"Oh, yeah."

"You have seen the picture?"

"Not yet. They sent it over to the police."

Tan could feel his heart thumping.

He forced himself to keep his voice level, "I will talk to my supervisor and arrange the meeting."

"I'll be out, Mr. Tan, but when you get a time, if you'd call Miss Parker?"

"Of course."

Tan hung up and sat at his desk, his stomach quivering.

Grant could *not* have seen him.

It was a picture of someone else. In the hands of the police.

Maybe the police would do nothing?

And if they did not, Tan was certain Grant would broadcast it on Shanghai Star.

On the first of October.

Or maybe on the day of the system test. Two days from now.

He felt paralyzed.

What was he to do?

Diantha Parker hovered around him like an Apache assault chopper on the hunt. She had been up to his apartment twice a day since he'd left the hospital. She cooked him meals and baked cinnamon rolls and cookies for him. Right now, she brought him a cup of coffee and a Danish and placed them on the desk.

"Diantha, for God's sakes!"

"You don't love me anymore." She got a nice pout on her face.

"Of course I do. But I'm not an invalid."

"You look peaked."

"I don't, either. I look sore, and that's not even extreme."

Not much. He was constantly aware of his shoulder. The headache was now a dull throb, down low at the back. He had two small round bandages on his right cheek and a larger one covering the stitches on his forehead. The left shoulder of his shirt was padded out with the bandage hiding those stitches. When he moved suddenly or walked for a distance, he was aware of sore muscles all over, and the wide bandage on his chest was still constrictive.

"You shouldn't have come to work this morning," she said.

"I wanted to see you. I just didn't want to be mothered to death."

"You don't take good care of yourself. Will told me about your kitchen."

"I eat with the Dallas Cowboys."

"And you hide computers."

That accusation had come up more than a few times.

"One lousy little computer. I don't want them to dominate my life. I just want it handy for a specific problem."

"You're afraid to confide in me?"

"Ahh, Diantha—"

The phone rang.

She picked it off the console before he could react.

"Mr. Grant's office . . . just a moment, please." Covering the mouthpiece, she asked, "Do you want to talk to Mickey?"

"Please."

"Eat your Danish," she ordered as she turned back to her own office.

"Hi, Mickey."

"Is there something wrong with Diantha? She sounded awfully formal."

"She found my laptop."

"Damn, I'm glad I'm not in your doghouse. How you feeling?"

"Fair. I know where all my muscles and bones are."

"Yeah. That's why I quit college football after my first day of practice."

"Before I forget it, Mickey, thank your Maggie for me."

"Meg. I did. And I will for you. That's one reason I'm calling, I took a copy of your composite down to the local cops on Monday morning. There's some army major strutting around the station now, and I gather he's from some military security unit, but he seems to have taken control. Anyway, he just called me. The prisoner says, 'Yeah, that kinda looks like the guy I met in the park.' "

"That's three of us, then," Grant said.

"Three?"

"Mai thinks it might be the same man who tried to pick her up at the airport. I don't know how good the drawing is, Mickey. I only saw him for a couple seconds, in the reflected light of headlights and streetlamps."

"He looks mean enough to me. Anything back from Harbin?"

"Not yet. I'm assuming Bobby Wheeler got a copy over to Inspector Chou."

"Here's a question: why haven't I seen it on the local TV news?"

"Good question. I haven't got the answer."

Grant had spent two hours with Wickersham, Parker, and Bricher, coming up with the face he vaguely recalled. And Wickersham had sent the photo out to every Shanghai Star facility—passed out to the security guards, as well as to the involved police units. Parker had mailed a copy to Minister Shao's office.

"Maybe I'll send a picture down to Sung Wu and see if he'll

air it on Thursday, say we're looking for the guy to answer some questions."

"From what I've heard of Sung, I'm sure he'll jump at the chance to be helpful."

"It might be a problem."

"Well, I hope something breaks soon," Stone said. "Have you talked to Suretsov? About the nukes?"

"Haven't heard from him." Grant jotted himself a note. "I'll give him a call."

"Yeah, I'd like to know what he found out, or if Jimbo is just full of hot air."

"If we're through with the peripheral crap, could I ask about computers?"

"Oh, those. Hey, we got C.C.'s shipment, plugged the honeys in, got the aps up, and it's smooth as silk. Guangzhou is ready for Thursday."

"Good man. Why don't you come back to Shanghai?"

"Believe me, Doug, I'd like to. But. Hohhot called, moaning. I'm off for there first thing in the morning."

"Shit. Nothing serious?"

"Like sabotage? No. But the network servers went down, and no one can figure out why. I don't think it's going to take long to fix."

"By Thursday?"

"Thursday at noon, guaranteed."

As he said goodbye, Grant saw Parker trying to hold off Crest at the door.

"He's not up to heavy work yet," she was telling him.

"Just for a second, Diantha. Please?"

Grant waited it out.

She looked back at him, shook her head, and said, "Two minutes."

Crest came in, grinning.

"I think, Doug, we could take those four armed guys out of the lobby and the parking lot and turn it over to Diantha. We'd be in great shape."

"I'll keep it in mind. How's our in-country manufacturing proposal?"

Crest leaned against the side of the desk. "It's in the commerce ministry, being run over by those big, slow wheels. And I've given Diantha a full report and recommendation regarding the facilities and personnel we might need. I found a guy that would make a good plant manager, I think. Then, also, I ran a copy by Calvin Jackson, and we'll need to update the report when he gets through with it. I expect he'll have a lot of changes since he knows what he's talking about and I don't."

"Damn good. How about the test day?"

"I recruited MI and Shanghai Star people at all of the facilities, and in turn, they recruited some chairmen of street-level committees in fifteen major cities. By tomorrow, we'll have five thousand antennas, People's Controllers, and Panasonic monitors placed in as many homes and community centers. We have, by the way, a major IOU with Panasonic. If they don't get their sets back, they'll expect a check."

"What the hell. We buy five thousand TV sets every day."

Crest reached in his side pocket and came out with a trifolded brochure. He handed it to Grant, who noted the now-familiar yellow-star and satellite logo.

"That's an explanation of how to use the controllers, along with a low-key sales pitch. I printed five thousand for the test population."

Grant unfolded it, but found he wasn't going to read it. The white, yellow, and black brochure had a few diagrams and photos, but was written in Chinese characters.

"You're going to have to tell me what we're low-key selling."

"I made a co-op agreement with Panasonic, and we're sharing the cost of the printing. I picked Panasonic because they're already in the People's Department Stores. What we're selling is a combo price on the monitor and the controller. I want a foothold with the controller before I start pitching the more expensive machines."

"Hell, print a million of them."

"You recall that we're in China? I was hoping for five million."

"I've got to learn to think big. Go with the five."

"Super. Then, I've talked to a couple of MBL's production people, with Lefant's permission. I want to get production started on a television campaign that coincides with the brochure. Again, Panasonic will co-op."

"What's our cost?"

"For the production time, sixty grand. For airtime, twenty thou a minute."

"Jesus. Sung Wu's getting into the harness, isn't he?"

"He's got Lefant for an advisor."

"We don't get a discount?"

"Shanghai Star will get a discount for in-house production and development, but Lefant says MI is a separate company selling a product. He's got a point, and he says it's the same rate they're charging IBM and the big boys."

"I suppose so."

"Anyway, it's cheap, Doug. Stateside, you'd be spending four times as much."

"Put the commercial together. Let's talk more about the airtime frequency."

"Got it. Last item; we're set for a three o'clock session at the People's Department Store. Tan just called me back."

"Okay. Come and get me when you're ready to go."

"You up to it?"

"Damned right."

"That's all I have, then." Crest straightened up from the desk.

Grant appreciated the man's ability to stick to his agenda.

"Anything more on your contacts?"

He frowned. "Nothing substantial. I talked to Suretsov, but that list of Nuclear Power shareholders he's got is just names, and there isn't a Chinese name on it. Some people have suggested that Jiang frequently makes side deals as a prerequisite to contracts being awarded, but there's no evidence, and all I've got is hearsay. Nothing I'd take to a DA back home."

"It's probably an expected practice," Grant said. "One of the resistances to democratization by the power bloc is the fear that the corruption will be swept away."

"I can believe that." Crest almost made it to the door before turning back. "I meant to ask if you'd gotten any feedback on your sketch."

"Mickey says that the man in custody in Guangzhou pretty much agrees with me. Mai may have seen him, also."

"That's a start. What the hell does this guy look like anyway?"

Grant pulled open his center drawer and lifted out one of the sketches, which had been printed on the laser printers. He held it up, and Crest came back to get it.

He looked it over quickly, then squinted his eyes, pulled his head back, and held it out at arm's length.

"Son of a bitch! That's Tan Long!"

"What!" Grant came out of his chair, ignoring a jolt of pain in his shoulder.

"That's the guy we're supposed to meet at three."

"You're shitting me, Maynard."

"Not when death and destruction are involved, Doug."

"Damn, I wonder which cop I call in Shanghai."

"Let's sit down and talk about this," Crest suggested.

The energy minister's secretary kept him waiting for twenty minutes, but Suretsov was accustomed to waiting for politicians. When he was finally ushered into the office, Pai Dehuai gave him a broad smile.

"Thank you for taking the time to talk with me, Minister."

"I am always more than willing to meet with members of the foreign press."

Though not happy about it. Pai did not get up from behind his desk and offer to move to the small conference table in one corner of the large office. He kept the symbol of the desk between them and indicated a small chair for Suretsov.

Suretsov took the seat and said, "I have just completed my visits to the reactors at Lhasa and Guangzhou."

"We were happy to arrange your visits."

Though not pay for them.

"You have my appreciation."

"I trust you have revised your opinion of the design?"

"I learned a great deal."

"We are quite impressed with the results we are getting from the two operational plants," Pai said.

"Did you know that one of the results is a widespread leakage of radiation?"

The smile did not leave his face, but Suretsov thought it twitched for a second.

"I am afraid I do not know what you are speaking about."

"I took radiation readings while I was at the two sites." Suretsov reached in his jacket pocket and retrieved six sheets of paper stapled together and folded. He placed it on the desk. "This is a draft copy of my article. It details my inspections, the people I interviewed, and the pattern of radiation around the reactors. I have forwarded to my superiors the tapes which recorded the radiation levels. I would like to have you read the draft, then I will call you back to get your reaction."

Pai acted as if he were afraid to pick up the report.

"According to the readings I took, the leakage appears to be heaviest at the juncture of the steam pipes entering and exiting the containment building. I am no expert, Minister, but it appears to me the shielding may be weak at that point, or that a faulty design of the containment structure allows contaminated coolant to enter the steam supply for the turbines."

"The sites are monitored daily," Pai said. "Excessive radiation would be noted immediately. I am certain your fears are groundless."

"I also lost all of the photographic film I had with me. That alone worries me."

"It could not be."

"Well, you read my article, then let me know your response."

"You have sent this elsewhere?"

"A draft copy has been forwarded to my agency in Moscow, as well as to the International Atomic Energy Agency in Vienna."

Pai did not like that at all, judging by the way his eyelids drooped.

From his other coat pocket, Suretsov extracted another sheet of paper. "This, Minister, is a roster of the major stockholders in Nuclear Power Limited. I wonder if you recognize any of the names listed?"

Pai took the sheet, scanned it briefly. "Where did you get this?"

"It was obtained by ITAR-Tass."

He barely looked at it. "I recognize no names."

"That is understandable. Many of those stocks are held in brokerage accounts. Some of the names are fictitious, I imagine. One more thing, Minister, have you met, or do you know, a man named Valeri Sytenko?"

"Sytenko? A Russian?"

"Yes."

"I have never heard of him."

"Thank you, Minister Pai. I appreciate the use of your valuable time, and I will call you this afternoon."

Suretsov felt extremely good leaving the minister's office. This was what his job was truly about.

After passing through the sixth-floor security area, Lefant met with Will Bricher in a ninth-floor room filled with computer terminals. It was less a place of bedlam than Bricher's section on the fifth floor. Only a third of the orderly rows of computer consoles were attended, most of them by Chinese operators.

The sign outside the doorway read, "Satellite Communications."

"Mr. Lefant," Bricher said.

"Good day, Mr. Bricher. I have forgotten the mission of this room."

"After the implementation phase and after ShangStar Three achieves orbit, when Megatronics Incorporated withdraws, this will be the central control room for satellite communications."

"I see. Manned entirely by national personnel?"

"For the most part. MI has a five-year consulting contract, and I suspect we'll maintain a staff of around thirty people to help with some of the tricky stuff."

"You will be here?" Lefant asked.

"Who knows? If this thing actually works, we may find jobs elsewhere. The Saudi peninsula, Africa, India—there're a lot of places could use a good TV show."

"I am sure it will work." Lefant made a mental note. If MI were to make proposals in other areas, his superiors at Media Bureau would want to know about it.

"So am I. Did we get you straightened out on your incoming signals from Europe?"

"Indeed you did. All is well in that regard. I came to see that we are in agreement on various aspects of the test."

"Mr. Sung expected that we were going to run five hundred channels."

Lefant sighed. "I know. He was not aware that the information ministry had to approve the channels for the test. One day, perhaps, he will grasp the concepts."

Bricher's grin suggested that that day would be a long, long time in coming.

"For the test day," Bricher said, "my people plan on channels two through sixteen, as approved by Jiang."

"Exactly. For six hours?"

"One o'clock through seven o'clock, Shanghai time, which is all China time. We probably should have given them some prime-time offerings."

"The information committee was reluctant to do that until they see exactly what they're getting," Lefant said.

"It figures. The advisory committee's thinking is prevalent in the regular schedule."

"Yes, it is."

The first year's schedule ran from six o'clock in the morning until eleven o'clock at night during the week. On Fridays and Saturdays, the cutoff was 2:00 A.M. The leadership apparently wanted to assure themselves that the workers got enough rest to get up and go to work on the following day.

"Have you got your feeds set?" Bricher asked.

"I did have, twenty minutes ago, ranging from sports to leisure-time activities to dramatic offerings. The All News Channel will run on Channel Two—we want Two to become a byword in the PRC. Maynard Crest got the schedule from me for a handout for the test viewers. We also want to familiarize the viewers with the distinctions between channels. If Mr. Sung has become involved, that may now be somewhat confused."

Lefant did not know why he made that particular revelation, but he thought that Sung's incompetencies were now common knowledge throughout the building.

"Want a suggestion?"

"Of what kind?"

"Why don't you ship in a few hundred really good R-rated movies with the questionable aspects Mr. Sung likes to review?"

See? Even Bricher knew that the president spent his time watching movies.

"Keep him busy?"

"Better than letting him find chores for himself, don't you think?"

Lefant could imagine wheeling a shopping cart full of video-cassettes and CD-Roms into Sung's office. The man's eyes would light with his zealous dedication toward seeking out the scenes to which his countrymen should not be exposed.

"It is a thought," Lefant agreed. "I may pursue it. But what of the test population and the equipment?"

Bricher looked at his watch. "The last report I had, an hour ago, indicated that twenty-one hundred units had been delivered and set up."

"We are certain they are receiving?"

Lefant had been anxious about the reception. Microwave-antenna towers located throughout the country accepted signals broadcast by the major facilities in the provincial capitals, and relayed the signals to the individual, eighteen-inch antennas of the consumers. Only those sets whose serial numbers were entered into the centralized computers—assuming the monthly bills were being paid—were able to receive transmissions. He agreed that the wireless broadcast was superior to laying millions of miles of cable, but he was still concerned about the reception quality.

"The provincial facilities are broadcasting a test pattern," Bricher said. "So far, our volunteer group of installers is reporting a perfect Mona Lisa."

"Mona Lisa?"

"That's what we're using as a test pattern."

"Ah. Very nice choice."

"I wouldn't worry about it, Mr. Lefant. We'll have our five thousand units in place by one o'clock tomorrow."

"How about the capital units?"

"They're in place. Every minister and important agency head is already hooked in. We took care of them, first."

"Very diplomatic," Lefant said. "Thank you."

"Anytime."

Bricher went back to whatever he was doing—instructing the Chinese, Lefant thought, and Lefant returned to the elevator.

When he got back to his office suite, he found Sung Wu waiting for him.

"Mr. Lefant, your editors will need to make changes in these last two films."

"What are they, President Sung?"

"The Sun Also Rises and *Lonesome Dove."*

"You watched *all* of *Lonesome Dove?"*

"Of course. There are unacceptable references in both works."

"But did you enjoy the stories?"

"I am not certain what Hemingway wanted to accomplish. It seems irrelevant. The other seems historically accurate."

Lefant would not have classified Sung as a scholar of American history, but decided not to mention it.

"I'll take care of it," he said, accepting the copious notes. Someday, maybe. "By the way, I expect to have a large number of offerings in the next few days. I'm afraid it will increase your workload."

"My duty is not measured by hours," Sung professed.

"Very good, sir."

Lefant went on into his office, shoved the notes in the top drawer, and jotted a quick memo for Marc Chabeau: "Find a copy of every R-rated flick you can locate in the archives. Deliver them to Sung Wu for review."

He glanced through his call slips, noting that Yvonne Deng had called four times this morning. The woman was becoming insatiable.

But then, Lefant was more than happy to answer the call.

He wondered if he could get away for a couple hours this afternoon, and was thumbing through his calendar and telephone memos when Sung's granddaughter called on the intercom, "Line four, Mr. Lefant."

She was getting the hang of it.

He punched the button and picked up the telephone.

"Lefant."

"Do you recognize my voice?"

After a few seconds, he did. The Chinese spoke a British-flavored English, quite agitated at the moment.

"Of course."

"They know!"

"What! What are you talking about? Listen, this is not a secure—"

"The Russian reporter! He has a list of shareholders in Nuclear Power. He knows about Sytenko!"

"I will call you later, on a different—"

"We must act quickly!"

Lefant hung up on the man rather than have him babble on with Sung's granddaughter possibly listening to the conversation.

Damned reporters! They got into everything, into everyplace where they were not wanted. And this one was a Russian, yet!

He did not think that the shareholder listing would be a problem. No one would connect disassociated names with anything. The problem could quite easily be Sytenko, however. Anyone who gave up his country's secrets so readily could not be considered trustworthy.

With everything else he needed to do—the system test, Yvonne—Lefant certainly did not need this distraction. He told himself there was no need for him to panic, and he hoped no one in Beijing panicked. They had to talk it out. They had to—

The intercom buzzed.

"Yes?"

"Line two, Mr. Lefant."

"I'm busy."

"Is urgent, I think."

He punched the button.

"This is Pierre Lefant."

"Where in the hell are you, Pierre?"

Ah, merde!

He had completely forgotten he was to pick up the MBL directors at the airport.

Deng Mai knew that she was driving her employees, and some of Grant's, crazy, but she could not help herself.

Miss Jiangyou did not know where to find her from one moment to the next. Deng visited every space on her floors, poked into broom closets, bothered everyone with questions. She could not seem to concentrate; every possible thing that could go wrong on September 15 fluttered across the surface of her mind, and she could not rest until she had personally examined the equipment, or the people.

The facility managers in Lhasa, Chengdu, Harbin, Hohhot, and Guangzhou assured her the electrical supplies were adequate, the computer systems fine, and the microwave transmitters working. The satellite downlinks had been tested repeatedly.

When she learned that Hohhot's data-transfer capability was impaired because of a problem in one of the network servers, her blood pressure climbed several notches. The manager tried to calm her, saying Stone was on the way, all would turn out well.

Mr. Chin, the systems manager, stopped her as she was pacing the tenth floor, stopping to peer over the shoulders of console operators.

"Director Deng."

She turned to face him. "Yes? What's wrong?"

"There is nothing wrong, Director, aside from the fact that you are making the technicians nervous. You should go back to your office, and I will call you if there is a problem. I do not expect to call you."

"You are correct, of course, Mr. Chin."

Deng did not take the elevator. She walked down the stairs so she could peek in on each floor. Everything was running smoothly. It was almost disappointing. Some kind of disruption might have taken her mind off her fears.

When she reached her office, Miss Jiangyou was waiting, disapproval barely concealed in her eyes.

"There you are, Director."

"I have not gone far," she said.

"Ministers Jiang and Shao have been calling. Mr. Grant called twice."

Deng took the message slips, shoved them into the pocket of her jacket. She did not feel like talking to any of them.

"And your mother called."

She did not want to talk to her mother, either.

"I will be back soon."

She turned and hurried from the reception area toward the security zone.

"Director! Where will you be?"

"In Mr. Grant's office," she called over her shoulder.

On the fifth floor, she found Diantha Parker at her desk, surrounded by computers and plants.

"Hello, Mai."

"Good afternoon, Diantha. What are you doing?"

Parker pointed to a laptop computer resting next to her own. "Doug and Maynard just left for a meeting, so I'm making certain the information on Doug's spreadsheets matches my own. I trust my data."

She had hoped to find Grant; she needed to talk to someone.

"I thought Douglas did not use computers."

"He lied."

Parker did not sound happy about the deception. More than likely, Parker preferred thinking that she did everything for Grant.

"He called me several times."

"He and Maynard may have identified the thin man. Someone named Tan."

"I do not know the name."

"Anyway, they're going to go confront the guy. I think they're crazy."

"This entire day is crazy," Deng said, settling onto one of the couches.

"Are you all right, Mai?"

"I am just nervous, I think. Getting through tomorrow may be a terror."

"Come on!"

Parker hopped up and beckoned her into Grant's office, shutting the door behind them. She crossed to the credenza behind Grant's desk, opened a bottom drawer, and came up with a bottle of brandy.

"Good for what ails you," Parker said.

"It is too early," Deng protested.

"I'm not going to let you drink alone," Parker said, finding two short glasses in the drawer. "After what I've gone through with Doug lately, the best thing I can do is drink his booze up."

"Diantha . . ."

"Sit down. We'll talk girl-talk and wait to see if the men find their assassin."

Huzhou kept asking her where she got the money.

Chiang Qing kept telling him it was from membership dues,

and Huzhou had such a lack of control over the Underground's finances and membership rolls, he could not safely argue with her.

He questioned her logic, too, when she gave 5,000 yuan to a street sweeper who lived in a one-room flat on Fu Xing Road in exchange for the antenna, television monitor, and controller that had been placed in his apartment by Shanghai Star.

The street sweeper preferred having the money to having the television for a couple days. He gave no thought to what he would tell the Shanghai Star person when he came to retrieve the set.

"Nonsense," she told him. "It is important that we observe this test."

While Huzhou and several others attempted to hook up the antenna outside one of the second-floor windows—they had no idea whatsoever how to align it—she read the yellow brochure that came with the set. It simply attempted to sell the television to the person using it for the test and suggested several financing possibilities. There was also a listing of the fifteen channels briefly describing what would be transmitted on each for the six-hour period of the test.

Three of the channels offered drama and comedy, but she had no interest in them. One channel would show samples of Chinese newscasts from Beijing, Shanghai, and Quangzhou. She circled Channel Four with ink. Another channel would tap into news broadcasts from Paris. She circled that one. Channel Fifteen would air demonstrations of interactive broadcasts.

Six channels scheduled sports ranging from golf to soccer to Canadian football replays. Travelogues. Zoos. Educational programs on Eleven. She circled Eleven.

Below the channels she had selected, she began to circle the programs listed for one o'clock in the afternoon. Inside each circle, she marked the time she wanted to watch, in five-minute increments.

Huzhou came back from the bedroom where the antenna was placed, turned on the set, and called directions to someone at the window. After a while, a picture appeared on the screen. The Mona Lisa.

With some more jiggling, and with Huzhou's fiddling with some controls, the picture clarified and became extremely sharp.

Chiang had never seen a Chinese television with as clear a picture.

"That is very good, Huzhou. I am amazed. You are not only an artist, but a technician, as well."

"There is no end to my talents," he said, and she could not tell if he was being facetious or not. "What are you doing?"

He circled behind her chair to look over her shoulder.

"These are the programs we will watch," she explained.

"For five minutes each? Only the first hour?"

"I do not think the test will last longer than an hour," she told him.

"I don't think he's going to be here," Crest said as they crawled out of the taxi at the People's Department Store. "I blew it when I told him we had a picture."

"Hell, Maynard, you didn't know," Grant said.

"If he *is* here, I'll hold him down and you can jump on his head."

"We'd be better off letting the cops do both of those jobs."

"Probably. We can still call them."

"I'll do some stomping first."

The pain in his shoulder and the dull throb at the back of his head reinforced Grant's determination to have a private conversation with Tan before they called in anyone with a badge.

Grant followed his marketing man through the main doors, down an aisle to a stairway, then up to the third floor.

"They've got some of their national offices here," Crest explained.

"I can't believe this Tan is the guy we're looking for."

"We'll know in a minute. If he's not present at the meeting, he's our boy."

A secretary met them and guided them down a hallway to a small conference room where four Chinese men, properly suited and distinguished, waited. Only one of them spoke English, and he made the introductions.

Tan wasn't introduced, of course, and when Crest asked about him, was told that the man had taken ill.

Grant was disappointed. He had hoped to see the man and decide whether or not he was the same one he had seen in the car on Huaipua Road.

An hour of polite talk, perusing of paperwork, and murmuring among the Chinese was required before one of the Chinese affixed his name in characters to the bottoms of several pages of the six forty-page documents. Crest, who had run a copy by the attorneys in California, read each page, nodding as he read, then passed it on. Grant accepted each sheet, signed his name with a flourish, and dated it.

While a clerk divided the pages into six neat stacks and stapled the pages of each copy together, another assistant produced small cups of mao-tai, the potent liquor preferred for toasts, and the six of them engaged in a great clinking of glasses, and broad smiles. Grant thought that the liquor might eradicate all his pains.

In the cab heading back to Shanghai Star, Grant said, "That's damned nice work, Maynard. I'm having trouble realizing how much you've accomplished, and you've been with us less than a month."

"With all of your marketing staff Stateside, and your China people working in the technical arena, Doug, I had a natural vacuum. It's easy to look good when no one else is doing the job."

"Well, I appreciate it, believe me. This was all stuff I was going to do, but I dropped the ball and let it get away from me."

"You've had other balls to juggle. What about Tan?"

"I almost produced the drawing for the Department Store execs, to see what their reactions would be."

"I don't think it would have done much good. If Tan's involved, they probably don't know about it."

"True. Maybe I'll run the Tan ID by Shao Tsung. He's one guy who seems to be able to make things happen."

Grant paid off the cab when they reached their building, and they produced their identification for the guard in the lobby, then took the elevator to the fifth floor. Entering Parker's jungle, Grant spotted his laptop on her desk.

"Uh-oh."

"Problem?" Crest asked.

"Diantha's rummaging through my spreadsheets. She's going to find all kinds of errors, no doubt."

Crest put the contracts in her in-basket. "You acknowledge errors?"

"Not to Diantha."

He pushed open the door to his office.

Parker and Deng were seated at the coffee table, a half-empty bottle of his best Napoleon brandy between them.

"You started celebrating without us," Crest said.

"What are we celebrating?" Deng asked. There was the tiniest slur in her words.

"The People's Controller," Parker said, and giggled.

Grant went around the desk and got two more glasses from his credenza drawer. He took them back to the conversational grouping and poured an inch of brandy in each, then handed one to Crest.

"Maynard landed us a nice contract with the People's Department Store."

"I saw the contract," Parker said. "Typed part of it."

"Con-grat-ulations," Deng told Crest.

Crest grinned at her, then settled into the chair next to Parker. Grant sat down beside Deng.

"Perhaps we're interrupting," he said. "Were you ladies sharing secrets?"

"We're sharing the boss's booze," Parker said.

"You should not be drink-ing," Deng said to him. "You are sick."

"After the mao-tai, this is mild." Grant sipped from his glass.

"Mai's afraid Shanghai Star's going to fall apart at the last minute," Parker said. "Told her it wasn't so."

"Good for you, Diantha."

"What's the worry?" Crest asked.

"I had a dream," Deng said.

"A dream?" Grant asked.

"Diantha . . . knows dreams are real."

"Her spirits talked to her," Parker clarified.

"My father," Deng further clarified.

"What'd he say?" Crest asked.

"Terrible . . . things will . . . happen."

Grant didn't know about dreams but thought that, if he didn't get some dinner in her soon, terrible things might indeed come to pass.

Jiang Guofeng and his assistant, Wen Yito, were talking in his office after their workday when his friend Pai arrived unannounced.

The energy minister appeared flustered. His tie was partially undone, his collar open, his hair ruffled as if he had been running his hands through it. He refused a seat and paced in front of the window, his hand clutching a mangled set of papers.

"Your day has been long, Dehuai?"

"My day has been horrible." Pai looked pointedly at Wen.

Wen looked back at him, his gaze steady and unintimidated.

"You may speak without reserve," Jiang said. "Yito is aware of all things."

"It is that Russian correspondent. Suretsov?"

"The one who questioned you at the media demonstration? He called me once on the telephone."

"The very one! Look at this!"

Pai shoved the papers at him, and Jiang spent a few minutes scanning them.

The article was not a good one. Jiang felt the onset of disaster, but managed to stave it off. Nothing positive ever came out of panic.

"Is it true?"

"How should I know? I have sent inspectors."

"Have you spoken to Lefant?"

"The arrogant snake hung up on me!"

"Please relax, Dehuai. We will get to the bottom of this."

"Suretsov is digging where he is not welcome. And he has a list."

"A list?" Jiang asked. "What kind of list?"

"Of the Nuclear Power shareholders."

"That is of little concern. Our holdings are in French names. There are no connections to be made."

"But that stupid oaf Sytenko may provide all of the necessary connections."

"Sytenko? What does he have to do with it?"

"Suretsov knows about him."

That was indeed a problem.

But not an insurmountable one.

Jiang inclined his head to one side, thinking, then glanced at Wen.

Wen smiled.

Thursday, September 15

Tan Long could not imagine where he had gone wrong. He had only to look at his surroundings to know that he had gone wrong, however.

The stinking one-room flat in which he sat was located on the fifth floor of a dilapidated, hundred-year-old building in an alley off Jinling Road in the Old Town. Ostensibly, it was rented by a fifth cousin of Tan's, but the cousin knew nothing of it. The flat had been empty for nine months, a bolt-hole on which he was now happy to have paid the rental. It was also a sanctuary he had thought he would never use.

Dumped in one corner next to the bare mattress resting on the floor were all of the belongings to which he could now lay claim. One duffel bag and two large backpacks contained all of his money, nearly 100,000 yuan and the equivalent of 5,000 dollars U.S. in six different currencies—francs, marks, lira, piaster among them. Upon leaving his office on Tuesday, he had closed out his meager bank accounts. The rest of the money came from three caches around the city and from his apartment.

Also in the bags were a couple changes of clothing, some gemstones he had collected over the years, a 9-millimeter Glock semiautomatic pistol, an AK-47 7.62-millimeter assault rifle, and five fragmentation grenades. There were five full magazines of ammunition for each weapon. His entire worldly belongings.

He could never return to his apartment, with its fine furnishings. His Lada automobile was also taboo, left parked on the side street near his building.

Tan sat on the mattress, a small transistor radio softly chirping next to him. It was tuned to a Chinese news station, but he had heard nothing about himself on it.

Yesterday afternoon, however, when he had gone out to purchase groceries, he had stopped in a small appliance store to buy the radio, and he had been startled to hear his name announced as the store owner made change. Glancing across the room toward several television sets, he had been more startled to see his picture displayed.

It was not a drawing, but a snapshot taken several years before, and one last seen in his own bedroom. The police had been to his apartment.

He had quickly engaged the store owner in a conversation regarding battery life and bought extra sets in order to divert the man's attention from the newscast.

Tan listened intently and was surprised it was not the police—the Ministry of Public Security—searching for him, but the army. For questioning, the announcer said.

He did not understand that, and he had spent the night listening to the radio news, but there had been nothing to enlighten him.

Munching a soda cracker for his breakfast, Tan considered his position. The situation was dire, though not impossible. The police—or the army, if that was the case—would have found nothing incriminating in his apartment or his automobile. All of that was jammed into the bags on the floor beside him. Perhaps they were truthful in only wishing to question him.

Yet, if anyone could identify him, like Grant, then he could not allow himself to be detained. He could not go anywhere near his apartment; his block committee would have been informed, and everyone who knew him would now be alerted. If they had checked with his supervisors at the People's Department Store, they would know he was not visiting stores in other cities. His excuse of sickness would now be suspect. His only recourse was to run, but that posed many problems.

Tan was so accustomed to going anywhere within the country, at practically any time, that he was now totally deflated by his inability to move.

His freedom of movement—with his airline pass—was how he had gotten into this mess, of course. It had started simply enough, doing favors for people, carrying small packages from one city to another. Then, because of the risk, he had started demanding fees, which were readily paid. Then, as he became accustomed to the extra income, he took greater risks for higher fees, performing small acts of revenge for people who moved in shadowy circles. Most often, he did not know their names, but there were several who provided referrals for him at the cost of a small commission. His sideline activity had mushroomed. Truthfully, he had revelled in his increasing expertise. He took pride in his masterful planning and smooth execution. On one side of his mind, of course.

Tan Long did not consider himself a violent man. He and his six siblings certainly had not been raised that way. In his everyday persona, he was actually quite meek. He preferred to think of the contracted activities as performed by a different self, a schizophrenic personality with whom he was only mildly acquainted. He borrowed that personality as necessary to enhance his monetary holdings.

The fact that he was sitting in this hiding room with assault weapons at his side was disconcerting. It was as if his two sides were being forced to blend.

Tan thought it was fate that guided him, but he also suspected that he should have thwarted fate and abandoned his clandestine business many months before.

Now, it was too late, and he must leave Shanghai and China forever. It was not something he looked forward to. He had never been outside the borders of the PRC before, and he was not certain what he would find.

Shanghai was a port, with many avenues of escape to the sea, but since he was Shanghainese, it could be assumed that the authorities had clamped a tight surveillance on the waterfront. He had already destroyed his airline pass, so not to be tempted by the ease with which he had used it in the past.

Guangzhou or Kowloon.

Either city would allow escape to the sea. Passage could be purchased on tramp steamers or junks. Reaching either port was the difficulty. The train and bus stations in Shanghai were as out-of-bounds to him as the port or the airport.

He needed transportation—an old truck or a motor scooter

would be ideal. Private citizens touring the country in automobiles were too conspicuous.

Tan uncrossed his legs, shut off the radio, and stood up. He left the flat, locking the door—and his worldly goods—behind him, then descended the five flights to street level. There was no telephone in the building, and he had to walk the length of the alley to Jinling Road, survey the pedestrians for anyone unnecessarily interested in him, then dart across the street to a pharmacy. Inside the front door was a telephone that the enterprising proprietor allowed the public to use for a fee.

He placed change on the counter, then called the memorized number.

The telephone rang several times before it was answered. "Yes?"

"You must do some things for me."

"Who is this?"

"You know."

After a long moment, the voice said, "You fool! You have been seen!"

"I need a truck. Or a motor scooter."

"It is out of the question. I have neither."

"You owe me. I will take the truck or the scooter in lieu of my final payment."

"Final payment! You have yet to accomplish the task for which you contracted. I see no obligation here."

Tan knew he had failed. The results were inescapable, and the pride of his alter ego had suffered extensively.

"If they take me, they take your name, also."

There was no response to that.

"I will still take care of my bargain, but I need the—"

"I know where I might obtain a truck. But you must deliver on your commitment first."

The dial tone sounded in Tan's ear.

Will Bricher had four phones going, and his assistant was on two more lines. He would drop one phone, grab another, issue an order, then go to the next phone.

He had noted a distinct difference in his telephones. The line to Chengdu, which was now operating on DCT systems, had a much higher degree of clarity. He would mention the fact to Tank Cameron the next time he saw him.

On the Urümqi line, he had Wickersham. Wheeler was his contact in Harbin. The Chinese facility manager was on the Hohhot phone. Stone, back in Guangzhou since nine o'clock this morning, was handling the communications there. At the next desk, through his assistant, he had contact with the satellite-systems manager upstairs and the facility supervisor in Lhasa.

A white phone resting faceup on the desktop issued a garbled murmur. Bricher tucked it against his ear and said, "You got a problem there, Mickey?"

"Hell, no. What I've got is a bunch of people packing the monitoring center to watch TV. I do have a question. Why aren't we doing this on the data link?"

Bricher looked across the room to where six consoles were in operation. Their operators were in direct communication with all of the ground facilities—the major provincial stations and the relay stations—via satellite data links. At another row of consoles, four technicians were ready to intervene if the Chinese satcom controllers on the tenth floor ran into problems they couldn't handle.

"We *are* on the data link, Mickey. I still want a voice backup for the first hour."

"Just in case?"

"Just in case."

"You've become a pessimist, Will."

"I'm an optimist who's aware of bombs and bullets."

"I was closer to the bullet."

"Better you than me. Hold on." Grabbed another phone. "What's up, Wheeler?"

"I just had an antenna-alignment computer go down."

"What! How in hell—"

"Power surge. We're switching to the backup now."

"Snap it up. We're at the starting gate."

Bricher looked up at the clock on the wall.

The digital readout stated: 12:54.

Six minutes until Shanghai Star reached out to the people.

Bricher wanted the first contact to be flawless.

The headquarters room of the People's Underground in Old Town was jammed. Chiang estimated that nearly sixty people had finagled their ways into seats on the floor. Less than a third of them were members of the underground, but the rest had learned somehow that a Shanghai Star system test-television was available.

She should have charged them admission, she thought.

Huzhou had located a large box, placed it on a desk, and mounted the television on top of that, getting it high off the floor. Everyone had a clear view.

Chiang and Huzhou sat in chairs near the front, less than five feet from the set, having to look upward at it. Huzhou held the controller tenderly. The people behind babbled pleasantly. There was an air of excitement. This was a momentous event.

Chiang hoped it was as momentous as she expected it to be. It was not likely to be what Jiang Guofeng had hoped for.

She looked at the schedule she held and told Huzhou, "We want Channel Six to start with. After five minutes, go to Channel Eleven."

"The visitors will complain."

"It is my television. I paid for it."

Zhou Ziyang, not having a television set nor being part of the test program, had asked a neighbor across the compound if he might watch with him. The neighbor, already besieged by relatives and friends, had reluctantly agreed. There were twenty people in the small living room, chatting comfortably, excited, chiding the neighbor about his good fortune in being selected for the test.

The neighbor, surveying his living room, did not act as if he were fortunate.

Zhou suspected that this scene was being enacted all across the country. Those who had been selected for the test and provided with the equipment would have gathered their kin and neighbors around the television. If there were 5,000 units in operation, Zhou thought that there were probably over 100,000 viewers.

It was a festive occasion, though Zhou could not bring himself to partake in it. He thought of it only as a victory for Jiang Guofeng, and a slap in his own face.

Deng Mai had invited the principals close to her to view the test from the Shanghai Star master monitoring center. Miss Jiangyou was flattered to be among them, Deng knew, and she watched her secretary with affection as the young lady moved among the guests, passing out cookies.

Chairs had been brought to the center and set up behind the consoles facing the monitor wall. It was crowded, but no one complained. A group from Media Bureau was in the front row: Lefant, his assistant Chabeau, some MBL directors from Paris, and several of Sung Wu's aides. Sung Wu himself had preferred to view the test from his own office. In his place, Lefant had invited Yvonne Deng, who looked radiant, though she often cast soulful glances in the direction of her daughter and Grant.

In the second row were Shanghai Star managers, engineers, and supervisors. Mr. Chin, the facility manager, had a seat reserved, but he was in and out.

In the last row, she was seated next to Grant and Crest. Diantha Parker and several engineers and administrators from Megatronics completed the row.

Grant looked at his watch. "You're about to go on, Mai."

She felt herself blush. Every time Grant looked at her, she recalled getting drunk in his office and his forcing her to eat, then taking her home. The most favorable aspect of that night was that her mother was not home when Grant delivered her to the door. Yvonne Deng would have thought the worst. Deng had never been drunk before, and the memory embarrassed her. Conversely, she recalled that she and Diantha Parker had had a delightful conversation, talking of homes and family and events and taking her mind away from her troubles. It was confusing.

At precisely one o'clock, fifteen of the monitors on the wall lost the test pattern and displayed the yellow-star and map-outline logo of Shanghai Star. A rolling drumbeat, increasing in crescendo, accompanied the logo.

The drums abruptly ended, then the logo faded away to be replaced by Deng Mai's face. Every channel was carrying the same introduction, taped previously.

Her voice did not sound like her own, she thought. On the screen, she was speaking *putonghua,* and the speech was duplicated in English subtitles.

"Comrades and countrymen, I welcome you to the Shanghai Star Communications Network, an agency of the Ministry of Information. My name is Deng Mai, and I am director of the network.

"We at Shanghai Star are proud of what has been accomplished in the last four years, since your Politburo introduced the concept." She went on to describe the technical triumphs, the satellite communications, and the dedication of Chinese workers to achieving the goal. At Grant's insistence, she had avoided praising the efforts of the foreign consultants and contractors, and kept the focus on the Chinese.

On the screen, she stepped to the left side as a photograph of Energy Minister Pai Dehuai zoomed into focus on the right.

"I would like to introduce you to the gentlemen responsible for bringing to you this tremendous breakthrough in technology for our nation. First, the members of the Information Advisory Committee. This is Minister Pai Dehuai, a member of the . . ."

As a photo of each of the committee members appeared on the screen, Deng introduced them, finally ending with Jiang Guofeng. She then took a leisurely pace with others of importance—the Politburo members, the Premier, the Party Chairman. No one of import was omitted.

The committee had not been aware of this introduction, and she hoped that it pleased them. She could imagine their smiles as they sat in Jiang's conference room.

"We hope that you become quickly accustomed to Shanghai Star and all that it has to offer. We bring you, not only television, but the world."

Her image faded away.

Those in the control center applauded, and that only embarrassed her further.

Grant leaned over toward her and said, "That was nicely done, Mai. You're going to be a star."

"But I do not want to be a star, Douglas."

Stone was in the main monitor room of the Guangzhou facility, along with a dozen people who didn't have a current assignment. In addition, he had invited Meg Naylor to watch with him, and she had brought along four DCT people. Her boss, Tank Cameron, was there.

It was a circus, everyone having a good time. Someone arrived with a couple cases of Budweiser, and Stone, not wanting to offend anyone, had accepted a can.

Every few minutes, Bricher said, "You still there?"

"Still here, Will."

The control room had an advantage. One wall was composed of forty monitors, and fifteen of them were lit with Director Deng's introduction. As the individual channels took on separate programming, they would be able to shift their attention from one channel to another. As Deng slowly faded away, the fifteen differing channel logos came up, ranging from Channel Two, the All News Channel, to Channel Sixteen, the Global Sciences venue.

Stone sipped his beer, leaned forward to shift volume controls and cut off the audio for all the channels except Two. Listening to fifteen at once was impossible.

He said to Naylor, "Here we go."

And then an amazing thing happened.

The members of the Information Advisory Committee were seated around one side of the large table in Jiang's conference room. He sat at the head of the table, with Pai Dehuai next to him. At the far end was Shao Tsung.

The alignment along the table seemed to follow ideological lines, with Jiang's supporters closest to him and the reformists nearer Shao's end.

Some of them had appeared ill at ease, a bit anxious about what they were to see. The introduction by Deng Mai had softened them, though, and Jiang had to give the woman some credit. She knew how to flatter.

He was certainly impressed. It never hurt to have his picture displayed next to those of the Premier and the Party Chairman. Never had his likeness been displayed to so many people at once. Jiang considered other possibilities for Shanghai Star.

He spoke to Wen Yito, who was standing behind him. "We will first want to watch the world news."

"Of course, Minister."

Wen pressed some buttons on the controller, and the picture on the screen at the side of the room changed from Channel Four to Channel Two.

On the screen, the Chinese narrator behind an elaborate and curved desk, with a large numeral "2" on the front, began to speak in Chinese.

"Good afternoon, comrades. . . ."

"Put the English on the screen, Yito."

Wen selected more buttons to push and English subtitles appeared.

Jiang glanced at the committee members, then back to the narrator.

And discovered that the narrator was no longer there.

The Channel Six introduction to the movie *Gone With the Wind* became erratic for a moment.

Chiang Qing leaned forward in her seat, peering upward at the flickering images on the screen.

They stabilized.

Clarified.

Evolved into a picture of a Caucasian man. Naked. With a large, erect penis. Walking slowly toward a nude woman with a wide mouth and wonder in her eyes.

The audience behind her gasped.

Chiang exclaimed, "Wonderful!"

Zhou's neighbor host had selected a game show for his first trial of the Shanghai Star network. It was advertised as a clone of the American program *Wheel of Fortune*, produced in Australia.

After a spluttery start, with flashes of light and color, a large wheel with colorful spokes appeared. Zhou's first impression that something was amiss came with the announcer's voice. He was not speaking Chinese or English, but a language with which Zhou was not familiar.

Down in the right corner of the screen was a small logo that suggested the program originated in Italy.

The camera angle changed to show the contestants.

All women. And all naked.

The young girls in the living room giggled nervously.

The young boys did not.

"What the hell!" Grant yelled.

With fifteen screens to choose from, Deng Mai could not tell which horrified her the most. The Channel Two News was showing years-old, very graphic footage of brutality in Bosnia—severed limbs, rapes, executions. The Channel Eleven movie channel displayed a trio of women engaged in sex acts. Even the comedy channel carried an animated erotic show. One of the sports channels was running a revealing female volley-ball game.

One of the news channels featured a black man calling for revolution, with scenes from the Los Angeles riots in the background.

The sensory array nearly overwhelmed her. She felt the heat rush to her face. Her vision dimmed, as if she were about to faint.

"Stop this!" Pierre Lefant screamed.

Deng felt as if her world had come to an end.

Mickey Stone was not often baffled or surprised.

The scenes gushing from the monitor wall stunned him.

It was fully three minutes, as his eyes darted from one screen to the next, before he realized all was not right.

The phone was still caught between his shoulder and the side of his head, and he said, "Will!"

"Kill the transmission," Bricher said.

On the console, he found the master transmission switch, and flipped it.

"Killed," he told the phone.

The monitors stayed alive, still repeating the signals captured from the satellite, but the Guangzhou Facility's transmissions to the relay stations had ceased.

The digital readout on the panel said so.

Then the incoming signal was interrupted and the monitors went black.

"Jesus Christ!" Naylor said.

Stone told her, "We are in a world of hurt."

The committee sat in silence for five minutes after the screen went blank.

Jiang could not believe the enormity of the fiasco. It was far, far worse than he had anticipated. As soon as the Bosnian footage had appeared, Wen had flipped through the channels only to discover scene after scene of disgusting visual impact.

When no one appeared willing to speak, and when Wen finally shut the television off after the transmissions ceased, he finally said, "I want everyone associated with Shanghai Star placed under arrest."

Pai added his signature. "I agree."

"I will call the Ministry of Public Safety and have them come to arrest us," Shao Tsung said.

"Wait a minute!" Pai yelped.

"Are we not associated?" the defense minister asked him. "Can you say that we are not responsible?"

"Deng is responsible," Jiang said. "Even this three or four minutes of broadcast is devastating for the people."

Shao leaned forward to place his arms on the table. "Do you say Director Deng is responsible for the loss of the Long March Three? She killed the people at Harbin?"

"Of course not! But this . . . this excrement that appeared on our screen . . ."

The Minister of Commerce interjected, "Shanghai Star did not provide the excrement, Guofeng. The programs originated with Media Bureau, the provider for whom you lobbied us so well."

Jiang did not like the tone. This could turn back on him.

"She—" he began.

"Sabotage," Shao said. "Just as in the other incidents."

"What is worse," Pai Dehuai said, "is that every one of our pictures was displayed prior to the broadcasts. All of us are linked to this . . . to this massacre."

"I would not call it a massacre," Shao said.

"Deng is responsible for that, for placing us in jeopardy," Jiang insisted, attempting to find some damning connection for her.

"There will be reporters swarming through the building," Shan Li, the labor minister, said. "We must make a strong statement."

"And a unified one," Peng Zedong of Materials added.

"Let the reporters wait," Shao said. "Whatever we come up with must also satisfy all critics in the State Council. As well as the Premier."

"Will you make a suggestion?" Shan asked.

"If you wish. Arrests are out of the question. An overreaction on our part will only fan the flames that will be building in the State Council, and in the country. Foreign correspondents have gathered here for this test. We do not seek world condemnation, I think. I would recommend, Minister Jiang, that as our spokesman, you approach the reporters with the notion that we assume this is yet another case of sabotage against Shanghai Star. The Russian correspondent has detailed the other cases internationally. In fact, it is lamentable that we did not carry his story in the domestic media. It would have given us foundation for this position."

Jiang did not like it. "Someone must pay for creating this humiliation."

"Then, look to your own choices, Guofeng," Shao told him. "Arrest Sung Wu and Pierre Lefant. Be prepared for an exclamation of protest from the French."

By the time Grant got through the security section, commandeered the first elevator, and descended to the fourth floor,

Bricher was exiting another elevator on four. A troop of engineers and techs was behind him.

"Which way?" Grant asked him.

"Follow me."

The two of them led a pack of angry men and women as they raced down a hallway, slid around a corner, and came up against a locked glass door. The white lettering on the door read: PRODUCTION CENTER ONE—MEDIA BUREAU LIMITED.

On the other side of the door, a dozen men and women were milling about the room in apparent confusion.

Grant yanked on the door handle. It didn't budge.

"Open the goddamned door!" he yelled.

People looked at him, but didn't move.

He banged his fist on the glass.

Finally, someone reacted and trotted toward the door, then pushed the panic bar to open it.

Grant shoved him aside and barged past him.

"Who's in charge here?"

A diminutive Chinese man stepped forward. "Mr. Grant, you should not—"

"You?"

"Well, yes, I—"

"Get everyone on this shift into another room and count heads. I want to know who's missing."

"What! No one is—"

"Now, damn it!"

The man glared at him, but started ushering his people out of the center.

Grant turned to his satcom director. "Will?"

Bricher surveyed the group outside the door and started pointing at them, picking five men and two women. "Inside. I want every external circuit traced. The rest of you guys can either stand guard here, or go back upstairs."

Grant hadn't been in this room before. It had been constructed by MBL engineers and was long and narrow, with a console extending the full length of the right wall. The console had a dizzying array of controls and small monitors, and above it was a glass partition, which looked into a parallel room. That room was accessed by doors on either end of the console and contained floor-to-ceiling banks of video players, laser-disc players, and CD-ROM drives. From the console, a platoon of production engineers could select live feeds coming via satellite from Europe or North America, local feeds from within China, or any of the media drives in the next room, then direct them into the correct channels for broadcast via Shanghai Star.

"It's got to be here, doesn't it?" Grant asked Bricher.

"That's right. Okay, guys, let's—"

"Hold it!"

Grant turned to find Lefant and Chabeau elbowing their way through the crowd outside the center. The two of them fought a path to the partially open door, pulled it open, and came to a stop in front of him. Grant wasn't going to step aside.

"What do you want, Pierre?"

"This is MBL property. You have no right to be here."

The shock Lefant must have undergone as soon as his carefully prepared programs failed to materialize had transformed into anger. His eyes blazed, and he tried to stare Grant down.

Grant wasn't a happy soul, either. "You think I give a shit, Pierre? I'm not going to stand around and have you bury your problems. Will, go take your look."

"If we have to tear the place apart?"

"Then tear it apart."

"You cannot do that!" Lefant insisted. "I won't have it!"

"Not your choice," Grant said.

Bricher and his team headed for the glass door on the right end of the console. Pulling it open, they swarmed into the media room.

Chabeau tried to step around Grant, but Grant threw his left arm up and pressed his hand against the smaller man's chest.

"Get out of my way, Mr. Grant."

The kid thought he was tougher than he looked.

"There's a door right behind you, Chabeau. You can either open it and walk through, or I'll run your head through the damned glass."

Chabeau paled a trifle, but he was going to brazen it out. He grabbed Grant's wrist and tried to pull it away.

"Go get Mr. Sung, Marc," Lefant told him.

Grant thought the young Frenchman was relieved at the diversion. Under his breath, he said, "Fuck you, Grant," then spun around on his heel.

Lefant started to say something, but was interrupted by a shrill scream.

Everyone in the hallway rotated toward the front of the building.

"AIEE!" some woman yelled again.

The crowd surged toward the source of panic, and Lefant ran with them.

Grant pulled the door closed and made certain it was locked.

He walked through to the other room and found Bricher and his engineers standing in front of the wall of video drives. Bricher had found a schedule and was calling it off. "Tape deck one-twelve, *Gone With the Wind,* Part I."

A woman punched an eject button on the correspondingly numbered deck, pulled the tape out, and said, *"Gone With the Wind,* Part I."

"One-twenty-one."

"Gone with the Wind, Part Two," another engineer called back.

They went through eight before Bricher said, "Correct programs, correct decks, Doug. Unless they're mislabelled. We'll have to check that."

"If not, there's got to be another source, then."

"All right, everybody! Pop every deck in the place."

The satcom engineers swarmed along the banks of decks, hitting eject buttons. Within a couple minutes, one woman said, "How about *Debbie Does Dallas*? We looking for that?"

"That's one of them," Bricher said.

Grant followed him over to where the woman stood.

"There'll be fifteen program sources," Grant said.

"I already had it counted, Doug."

They found the contraband media loaded in fifteen CD-ROM and cassette decks along the floor at the left end of the room.

"Let's pull it apart," Bricher ordered.

Grant heard a banging and looked to the corridor door where Lefant was slamming the flat of his palm against the thick glass.

Ignoring him, he watched as latches were released and banks of playback decks were swung outward, allowing the engineers to see the maze of wiring behind them.

Lefant continued hammering on the door.

"This is going to be simple," Bricher told him.

"You think so? Looks like spaghetti to me."

"Yup."

In five minutes, a man wearing the name badge "Cotter" came over.

"Minor rewiring job, Will."

"I thought as much."

"The production guy hits the button for deck one hundred, and he gets the proper green light, but what happens is that deck forty-two activates also, and forty-two is wired to send the actual signal when a timed solenoid flips a switch. Deck one hundred isn't sending anything, then."

"Inside job, then," Grant said.

"Yup."

"Document the wiring, will you? And confiscate all the contraband? Then we'll keep the place hostage until the cops or somebody important gets here."

"We'll do it carefully. There may be fingerprints on some of those tapes or CDs, though I doubt it," Bricher said.

Grant went back to the control room and opened the door for Lefant.

"We've got it figured out, Pierre."

"Sung's dead," Lefant said.

Minister Jiang Guofeng said, "Dehuai, this may have backfired."

"It will be all right. You will see. I am much more worried about the other."

The two of them were in Pai's office, where the energy minister kept a bottle of vodka. They were drinking it straight, without ice.

"You handled the press conference well," Pai said, "though Shao and Peng were infuriated at your additions."

"I felt the statement had to be much stronger than we were simply investigating an act of sabotage."

In fact, the damnable correspondents had nearly overwhelmed him with a broadside of questions, and feeling the sting of their barbs, Jiang went beyond the statement agreed to by the committee to announce he was suspending the contract of Media Bureau Limited until further notice, and that he was ordering an investigation into the personnel and procedures of both Shanghai Star and Media Bureau Limited.

The press conference was fifteen minutes behind him, and Jiang was just beginning to feel his adrenaline level lower. He had wondered at the time if he should not have more information from Shanghai before meeting the reporters, but telephone calls to Shanghai Star confirmed only that confusion reigned there. Then the Premier had called to demand that Jiang make an announcement immediately, to draw the television and print media away from him.

"The correspondents make life difficult," he told Pai.

"Absolutely! The damned Russian continues to tread where he is not welcome."

"What did you tell him? About the reactors?"

"That his data must be in error, that ministry inspectors found no evidence of high-radiation levels. I believe he now mistrusts his own investigation. It comes down to it being his word against the word of the government."

"And what of the shareholder list?"

"I did not respond, other than to say I knew none of the names."

Jiang mused for a moment, then asked, "Do you have documentation of these inspections?"

"Of course. They have been completed by my own handpicked inspectors."

"Was there radiation leakage, Dehuai?"

Pai waved a hand lazily. "Minimal, Guofeng. What is important here? A negligible amount of leakage, or the power to operate your Shanghai Star?"

Jiang almost asked about the levels of radiation, then decided he did not want to know. But he wavered. He did not want to be known as a man who poisoned the atmosphere of his country. His holdings in Nuclear Power Limited were minimal at the moment—about $500,000—and were a gift from the company for his assistance in contract negotiations. However, when the contract was completed and all ten reactors were operating, his shares promised to be worth ten times the current value. It was simply a nest egg.

But radiation *poisoning?*

"The government must always present a united front, Guofeng, or the counterrevolutionaries will take it from us."

"This is true."

He sipped his vodka as Pai responded to his intercom.

"We were not to be disturbed," Pai told his secretary. "What? How urgent?"

Jiang waited.

"It is Director Deng for you, Guofeng."

"I do not want to talk to her."

"You should."

Shaking his head in resignation, Jiang stood and crossed the room to the desk, taking the receiver from his friend. "Minister Jiang."

"I am glad I found you, Minister."

"It is you who should be talking to the reporters, Director Deng."

"I thought it best to refer them to the ministry. I have a report for you."

"Report, then."

"Mr. Grant and his assistants located the source of the illicit material . . ."

Grant, again. Always Grant involved.

". . . and found that the Media Bureau production center had been sabotaged."

As I declared to the committee.

"There was no penetration of the Shanghai Star system," she went on.

Ah! Immediately after I tell the world I suspect the Shanghai Star processes. Madame Deng, you must be removed from my life.

"There are a number of suspects, and the military police are interviewing them."

"The army? How is the army involved?" Jiang demanded.

"I am sure I do not know. They arrived quickly and took over the investigation from Mr. Grant."

Shao. He is getting back at me for the press conference.

"We are rescheduling the test for tomorrow at one o'clock," Deng said.

"You will do no such thing."

"But, Minister, it is important for both Shanghai Star and the ministry to demonstrate a quick recovery."

"Not until I discuss it with the committee."

Jiang hung up before she could protest any further, and told Pai of the conversation.

"But who would do this?" Pai asked. "You told me—"

Jiang did not want that debate and was relieved when the phone buzzed again.

He was less relieved when Pai said, "Yes, Director," and handed over the phone.

"What is it, now?"

"I was unable to tell you, Minister, that Mr. Sung succumbed to a heart attack."

"Now, you have told me," Jiang said and dropped the telephone in its recess.

"What was that?"

"Sung is dead. It was a heart attack."

"I can understand that. I nearly had one, myself."

"We will have to find a suitable replacement."

"Perhaps someone less elderly," Pai suggested.

Jiang went back to his chair and his glass of vodka.

And the intercom buzzed again.

"If she is calling back once more, tell her I have left."

Pai responded to the intercom, complained about the interruptions, then picked up the phone.

When he replaced it, he was smiling.

"What?"

"Finally, there is good news!"

"Are you going to tell me?"

"The Russian trade attaché was killed in an automobile accident."

"I know," Jiang said.

It was close to midnight when Tan Long found his answer.

As was his custom when preparing for a contracted operation, he had spent hours on the planning. The time devoted to anticipating every contingency—and an alternate plan of action for each—had always served him well. He could recall no mission he had undertaken which had gone according to the first plan. Yet, each had reached a fruitful conclusion because he was prepared for the unexpected.

His contract, for which he had already received 30,000 yuan—his best contract ever—called for the elimination or severe disability of the American Douglas Grant and the Shanghai Star director Deng Mai. He did not question *why* the contractor wanted this to occur; his only concern was *how* it was to happen.

Already, he had failed twice, though the contractor would not know of his aborted attempt to abduct Deng Mai at the airport. For this last time, he had decided he could be less stealthy. After all, he was not going to stay in Shanghai.

With that factor apparent to him, Tan had opted to worry less about noise and confusion. He would simply open fire with the AK-47 on the two of them as they exited the building on Changning Road. In the turmoil that ensued, he would abandon the rifle and slip away to meet his contractor and obtain his truck. If necessary, he could also eliminate the contractor. In fact, he probably should do so.

And during the day, as he assembled his sets of contingency plans—a taxi might not be available, a guard might get in the way, Grant might be armed—a realization slowly dawned on him.

He let it dwell, linger, swell in his mind throughout the evening, until it flowered.

It was so simple, he was amazed he had not thought of it before.

He did not need the contractor.

Everything he required for the completion of his contract, and his escape from Shanghai, was right in front of him.

Tan Long smiled for the first time in days.

Friday, September 16

Deng Mai slept fitfully and was wide awake at four o'clock in the morning. She slid out of her bed, pulled on a robe, and went down to the kitchen to make coffee. She had been spending so much time in Grant's office, with Diantha Parker's coffee, that she was coming to prefer it over tea.

She was hovering over the coffeemaker when she heard her mother's footsteps coming down the stairs.

"I thought I heard a little mouse."

"Do you want coffee, Mama?"

"Please. You could not sleep, either?"

She poured two cups, and they sat at the table, opposite each other. Yvonne Deng's eyes were slightly reddened with fatigue. The tiny wrinkles at the corners of her eyes and mouth were apparent without her makeup. Deng thought, this morning, Yvonne's face was a reflection of her own.

She also thought that too many weeks had passed since the two of them had spent time in the mornings, just talking.

"Yesterday was the worst day in my life."

"It was not. There have been bad days before, and there will be bad days in the future. They will be outweighed by your good days."

"Mama, Jiang is determined to evict. At five o'clock, we were inundated by investigators. They are all over, digging into files, interviewing everyone."

"And what will they find?"

"Nothing." But she knew that they could discover whatever they wanted to discover, if it met Jiang's needs.

"See? You worry unnecessarily. Think of poor Pierre. His contract is under suspension; he is undergoing the most intense scrutiny."

Deng did not want to think of poor Pierre. What about poor Mai?

"You cannot be worried about Lefant?"

"Of course I am. If Media Bureau loses this contract, he will lose his livelihood. He will have to go to his farmhouse and subsist on his pension."

Whatever Lefant did, Deng did not think it would be on a minuscule pension.

Yvonne tasted her coffee, wiggled her nose in mild distaste, and asked, "Have you considered at all who might be behind these attacks? This sabotage?"

"It is not my job, Mama. The police, the ministry—"

"So you do nothing? What if it is the ministry itself?"

"Mama! That is ridiculous."

"Is it? Who is it who would most like to discredit you?"

"This episode has brought discredit on the entire ministry, as well as the information committee. Jiang would not do that."

"I have frequently noted," Yvonne said, "that politicians may be cunning, but not necessarily bright."

Deng suspected that Jiang fell into that category, but she still did not believe he was a man who would condone murder. "We have our differences, Mama, but not differences that would generate such retaliation."

"And the thin man who is a suspect? Why has he not been apprehended?"

"The police—"

"May not be looking for him with any diligence," Yvonne finished for her. "Why do you suppose it was the army who showed up at your door yesterday?"

"Minister Shao—"

"Is quite a charming man. I liked him the minute he—"

"Mama! May I finish a sentence?"

Yvonne smiled and sipped from her cup.

"Minister Shao, I believe, maintains the balance on the committee. If Jiang is trying to control either the committee or the media, Shao would act to neutralize him. I suspect Shao sent the army to investigate so as to have his own control over evidence. The man is devious."

"But favorably impressed with you, Mai. He may have romantic inclinations."

Deng did not see that, in the least. Well, maybe. Shao, however, was too intelligent to carry out the quest. "There, you are quite wrong."

"How many ministers of national defense take the time to seek out young ladies late at night and squire them to hospitals?"

It was time, Mai thought, to change the subject.

"What if Lefant is a suspect? He works closely with Jiang, and if Jiang ordered this . . . this sabotage, as you suggested, Lefant would be the one to carry it out."

"I doubt that, Mai."

"If so, he will be deported."

"Then, I may go to his farmhouse in the south of France with him."

"Mama, you cannot!"

"Do I tell you that you cannot socialize with Douglas Grant?"

"I do *not* socialize with him."

"What were you doing the night he was blown up?"

Mai clamped her lips tightly together.

"And who rushed off in panic to the hospital to see if he was alive or dead?"

"I work closely with him, Mama. . . ."

"Yes. I see that."

Deng decided her mother was becoming impossible to reason with.

Let her run off with Lefant.

Mai no longer cared.

Diantha Parker pushed the office door open.

"Minister Shao is here to see you, Mr. Grant."

Some people impressed Parker with the need to call him mister.

"I'll see him right away, Diantha."

The defense minister was dressed in an immaculately tailored gray-and-silver pin-striped suit. In his jeans, Grant felt underdressed as he went to shake hands.

"Good morning, Minister."

"How are you, Mr. Grant?"

"I may survive, but yesterday was nerve-wracking."

"It was, was it not? I wanted to talk to you about it."

Grant ushered him to a seat. "How about coffee or tea?"

"Thank you, no."

He wondered why he was seeing Shao so frequently of late. Even during the military applications phase of the project, centered around ShangStar One, he had never met the defense minister. He, Bricher, Stone, and Wickersham had liaised with minor bureaucrats and the generals responsible for technology and communications.

"I wanted to thank you," Shao said, "for your quick response yesterday in securing the production room and sequestering the staff."

"I was a little ticked off at the time. I probably offended a lot of people."

"They will get over it."

"You didn't happen to pin down the perpetrator?"

Shao offered a grim smile. "Yes. Major Cho, in charge of the investigation, has a suspect. He is a young man, a programmer, employed by Media Bureau. He is quite frightened, and he tells us that it was only a practical joke."

"A practical joke for which someone paid him?"

"Ten thousand kuai. An expensive joke, I think."

"The paymaster wouldn't be a tall, thin man, by any chance?"

Another grim smile. "Unfortunately, no. This man, who first made contact with him, was short, with long hair and spectacles. The delivery of the media and the money was made by a woman, middle-aged and otherwise unidentified. The suspect, despite strong threats, remembers nothing else. It was dark during both contacts."

"It is always dark," Grant said.

"Yes, it is."

"May I ask, Minister, why the military is conducting this investigation?"

After a short time of reflection, Shao said, "Like you, I wanted a quick response. Occasionally, the police bureaucracy is slow to react . . . and infrequently, important evidence becomes . . . mislaid."

Diantha Parker's research indicated that the Minister of Public Safety was a moderate man, working diligently at instituting the State Council's reforms in favor of the accused in the justice system, but that he had some tenuous ties to Jiang.

Grant considered his next question for some time before uttering it, "Shall we talk about what we think?"

"Precisely why I stopped by, Mr. Grant." He looked around the room. "I assume we are in privacy."

"As a matter of fact, I had one of the techs sweep the office late yesterday afternoon. Maybe I'm becoming paranoid."

"There are no listening devices?"

"I don't believe there ever has been a bug in here."

"I know you take pains," Shao said, "to remain politically neutral. Except in the instance of the launch date, of course. I presume you are also a man who thinks."

"From time to time, I give it a try."

"Would you tell me what you do not tell to others?"

Grant leaned back in his chair and laced his fingers over his stomach. The movement gave him a little twinge in his left shoulder. It was getting better, but he had to be careful of sudden moves in the wrong directions.

He studied his visitor. Shao hadn't gotten where he was by being a compassionate man. He might empathize with others, even care deeply about some issues, but his emotions would never get in the way of hard decisions when they were required. He'd once been a general, and Grant had always been leery of generals.

Yet, Grant felt there was some kind of sympathetic link between the two of them. He thought that both of them understood that either would do whatever was necessary to protect his interests. If, however, their diverse objectives might be reached by common means, then sharing could be helpful.

"Even at the risk of offending you or your national interest?" he asked.

"I have been offended many times in this life. I have found that it is not fatal."

"All right. So what you and I are both interested in is who might be behind the attacks on Shanghai Star."

"Correct."

"My prime suspect is Jiang Guofeng."

Shao's face didn't register much surprise. "That is interesting. Why?"

"I have absolutely no evidence, Minister. This is only a theory, but I have felt that he wanted more time to solidify his position, to eliminate the director; the incidents that might have delayed initial operations would have played right into that scenario. I think he fought hard to delay the launch of ShangStar Two."

"And the events of yesterday?"

"When the opening couldn't be delayed, the next step was to discredit the network. It would give him a rationale for terminating Deng Mai."

"Fortunately for Deng, Mr. Grant, you acted quickly to pinpoint the source of the problem. If it had been left unresolved, or if the evidence had evaporated, Jiang might well have been successful in removing her." Shao drummed his fingers on his kneecap. "Let me agree with your theory in part. Just the theory, mind you; not necessarily the facts, which are not clear. I cannot, in my own mind, think that Jiang would destroy rockets or cause people to be murdered. He might be capable of creating a diversion to cast suspicion on the principals. If he was behind it, his scheme has turned out badly for him. You have seen today's news?"

"Local TV, this morning. I thought they were nice, given the circumstances."

"As they must be. However, there were veiled innuendos regarding the ineptness of the advisory committee. Many will read behind the words to see that the ministry is in trouble. In the political realm, Jiang and the committee are under high stress, and that includes myself. If Jiang is an instigator, he miscalculated. A few badly slanted news stories, or outright lies, would have been enough for him to question the competence of either Deng or Sung, and perhaps lead to their removal. Sung may have been a sacrificial lamb, intended to go down with Deng."

"Not Lefant?" Grant asked.

"Based on the lobbying effort that took place in the committee, it is my assumption that Jiang and Lefant had arrived at a prior accommodation. I think the Frenchman is safe. Or was until your intervention."

"What you're saying, Minister, is that if Jiang had been more subtle, he might have succeeded in ousting Mai, but since this was so . . . outrageous, the criticism is broader based."

"And it has caught him, and me, in its clutches. The ministry and the committee are, after all, the responsible bodies."

"We may never know what really happened," Grant said.

"It is possible. Major Cho can be quite persuasive, however."

"If you don't think Jiang is involved with the early incidents, who then?"

Shao crossed his right leg over his left knee. "Oh, there are many possibilities. There are fringe radical groups, gangs, whatever. I have a personal concern about the People's Underground."

"That's Chiang Qing's group?"

"Correct."

"It seems to me that she's in favor of Shanghai Star."

"In favor of what it could be, yes. But she is difficult to decipher. She may have decided that, since the network was not going to fulfill her fantasies, the PRC would be better off without it."

Grant recalled a similar conclusion drawn in a conversation with Mickey Stone.

"You have met her?" Grant asked.

"No, but I have read many reports about her. In the past, she has been a minor irritant for the government. In the last few weeks, her attacks against the information ministry have accelerated. That is also true of the People's Right to Know Committee."

"I'd bet you've had both groups under surveillance."

"Of course. And on the days in question, both Chiang and Zhou have been accounted for."

"But they have large organizations?"

" 'Large' is a relative term. They are sizeable, yes, and even if we knew every member, we would be unable to watch them all. The reason I prioritize them highly on my list of suspects is that, though they scream for free information, they have been disappointed to some extent."

"You don't think Shanghai Star is all it could be, Minister?"

"No, but I have to live with compromise."

"Don't we all?" Grant grinned.

Shao returned it. "There is, perhaps, a slim window of opportunity here."

"Which is?"

"You might mention to Director Deng that, should she quickly make a recommendation for her candidate for the Media Bureau presidency—Ming Xueliang, I believe it was, in replacement of Sung Wu—it might be favorably viewed. The committee is in some disarray at the moment."

"I'll do that, Minister."

"Is there anything else we might beneficially discuss, Mr. Grant?"

Time to get everything off my chest?

"Do you know a Russian correspondent by the name of Vladimir Suretsov?"

"No . . . but I may have seen him somewhere before, perhaps a party. I've seen the name somewhere recently. One moment." Shao closed his eyes while he tried to recall something. "Yes. I saw the name on a memo circulated yesterday afternoon. He is to be ordered out of the country as persona non grata."

That surprised Grant. Or maybe it didn't.

"Do you know who originated the memo?"

"Pai, I think. Yes, it was Pai Dehuai."

"That's interesting as hell, Minister. This is completely unrelated to my problems, but I learned from Suretsov, and also from one of my executives, about a problem with the nuclear reactors."

Shao sat up, completely attentive.

Grant told him the story.

"And this Suretsov thinks that Jiang and Pai might be secret investors?"

"That information turned up as a rumor picked up by my marketing man. Suretsov was going to confront Pai with what he knew."

"I see. You come up with interesting information, Mr. Grant.

I wish that our intelligence services were as effective. How did you learn of the confrontation?"

"Suretsov told me."

"He has written articles about you for the international press, has he not?"

"Yes, though I haven't read them. He also thinks Lefant paid off a Russian attaché named Valeri Sytenko for the designs of the reactor."

"Sytenko!"

"Yes. Something wrong?"

"Sytenko was killed in Beijing yesterday. A traffic accident."

"Damn. That's a happy coincidence."

Shao stood up. "And perhaps not. Lefant was involved?"

Grant rose, also. "Vladimir had some eyewitness who identified Lefant as a man giving Sytenko some cash. I don't think Suretsov deserves to be kicked out."

"I will see what I can do. And I will look closely at this accident of Sytenko."

"I wish you well, Minister."

"I wish me well, too, Mr. Grant. I did not plan to become a policeman."

Maynard Crest leaned on his hands on the front of Grant's desk.

"I'm going to miss Diantha," he said. And everyone else, Crest thought.

"You're what!"

"I've come to tender my resignation, boss."

"For Christ's sake, Maynard! You haven't been here three weeks. I need you."

"That's nice to hear, Doug, but I came to China for the Consortium. I think I've got a chance to get back in the driver's seat after Lefant's debacle."

"Have you talked to someone at CIS?"

"Yeah. They said to give it a shot."

"Well, shit! I don't want to hold you back, but damn it, you've done some good things for us. I was planning on more. How about a consulting contract?"

"For after-hours stuff? Sure, we can work that out."

"Great!" Grant offered his hand across the desk, and Crest shook it warmly.

"You've got wonderful people, Doug, but I feel some loyalty to my old outfit."

"I understand. What about your other mission?"

"I had a long talk a couple days ago with Suretsov."

"His name's been coming up today. What'd you talk about?"

"Lefant. I think I've found a way to get back at that asshole."

"How? Wait. I don't think I want to know."

"Probably just as well. Jiang, I don't know about."

Until Sunday, when he met with the information ministry minion in Beijing.

Then, he might have a little surprise for Jiang Guofeng, Minister.

At the Guangzhou Facility of Shanghai Star, it was mostly get in line and wait.

The equipment hummed. It had been checked, double-checked, and triple-checked so many times, Stone was certain it would snap to attention if he looked harshly at it.

The MI experts spent their time with their Chinese counterparts in training sessions. There was nothing to do until they got the go-ahead for another test.

For the first time, Mickey Stone had a real chunk of free time. He could have gone back to Shanghai to make his daily calls to all of the facilities. Instead, he hung around with Curt Wickersham, who had come back from Urümqi, in the morning and wandered around the city in the afternoon, waiting for Meg Naylor to get off work.

The morale among the troops wasn't the greatest. After the fiasco, half the Chinese personnel worried that they would be fired for some undiscovered connection to the sabotage. The MI people, Stone included, worried that the Premier or some bloc of politicians in the State Council would cancel their contract.

Stone had ducked out of work right after lunch, reluctantly taking a beeper with him, and headed into the city to get his mind off both the contract and Naylor.

Naylor mystified him, and he hadn't yet figured out how to deal with her.

He spent an hour touring the Peasant Movement Institute, located in a 16th-century temple of Confucius. He liked the glazed ceramic animals trimming the roof, but had difficulty imagining Mao Zedong and Zhou Enlai using the place to train peasants and students in Communist doctrine. He *could* imagine the students heading out into the provinces to spread the word, like Mormon missionaries. In the restored student dormitories, he looked over the towels, mugs, and toothbrushes and decided that some restorations didn't have to go so far.

He wandered next door to the Exhibition Hall of the Revolution, built four hundred years after the temple, and spent nearly two hours looking at the photographs and documents sacred to the Party. Mao and Zhou were prominent in the photos, of course, and there was even a model of the boat used for the first meeting of the Party in Shanghai in 1921. He wondered why someone in the United States hadn't saved Washington's boat after the Delaware River got itself crossed.

Most of the documentation was Chinese to him, being composed in Chinese characters, but he dutifully studied his history until his beeper sounded off.

It took awhile to find a telephone and call the unfamiliar number.

"Mickey, where are you?"

"Consorting with Mao, Meg. Where are you?"

"We shut down early, and a bunch of us came down to the White Swan."

Stone looked at his watch. "I'll be there in twenty minutes."

"Why don't I meet you back at your place?"

"My hotel?" he asked hopefully.

"No, silly. Shanghai Star. I had a thought. Can you get on the Internet?"

The MI people were utilizing data channels regularly now, but the fact that they could access the Internet wasn't widely known, and Stone said, "Probably."

"Super! I'd like to send some e-mail."

"See you there."

He cabbed back to the building and waited in the lobby so he could guarantee her reliability to the guards on the door.

When she arrived, all bubbly enthusiasm and freckles, he signed her in.

Naylor was wearing Reeboks, jeans, and a blue-checked blouse. She looked ready to climb a tree. Stone couldn't figure out why he was wasting his time. He could be in Shanghai, chasing something besides cyberspace.

He found them a vacant office with a computer, turned on the lights, and offered her the seat behind the machine. He pushed someone's picture of home and family aside and sat on the corner of the desk.

"All yours, madame."

She turned on the computer and turned to rest her elbows on the desktop, looking so earnestly at him. She always gave him the impression of being so open and candid, it sometimes scared him.

"The Chinese don't know about this, huh?"

"Well, they do, and they don't. We told them they would have the eventual capability to link up their scientific institutes, universities, hospitals, and the like on a computer network, and we've set aside forty channels to carry the traffic. There's an additional forty channels reserved to add to that if necessary, though I think we can develop a civilian or public usage for some of those."

"What's it called?"

"What else? ChinaNet."

"And Shanghai Star is the backbone?"

"We think of it as a spine."

In the United States, the earliest big network had been developed by the Defense Department, connecting it with its scientific and industrial contractors. That had evolved into the Internet, adding universities and research concerns and supported by the National Science Foundation in the beginning, then transferring to private proprietorship for its underwriting. That was the "backbone" of the system, and a variety of commercial enterprises—Prodigy, CompuServe, America Online, Delphi, and even the very basic Free-Nets—allowed individuals entry into the system, an "on ramp" to the super highway.

In the Shanghai Star system, though part of it utilized fiber-optic cable, most of the user contact would be through microwave transmission. Many people didn't realize, when they dialled a long-distance call, that much of their conversation with Aunt Peg in Minneapolis spanned the continent from one microwave-relay tower to another. The difference in the PRC was that the small and inexpensive fiberglass antenna dishes, like their telephone companies' big brothers, carried two-way traffic. That allowed the interactivity between the viewer with a People's Controller and a program like CIS's encyclopedia.

"And you haven't told the information ministry?" Naylor asked.

"Well . . . I think they know, deep in their little hearts, that the capability is there. They know we're going to hook up the scientific circle. It's just that no one's come right out and said, 'Hey, as part of the bargain-basement price, you're also getting ChinaNet.' "

Or, later, the Internet. Jiang and his buddies would come unglued.

The computer screen had come to life, producing a Windows graphics screen. Naylor turned back to it and double-clicked her way into the communications program.

"How do I get there from here?"

Stone gave her a telephone number. "That gets you into the Shanghai Star system. Don't pass it around, please."

"Of course not."

With a couple more commands, he got her into Channel 461, one of the dedicated channels.

The screen was black now, with a single query in white letters: ACCOUNT NUMBER?

"We're pretty primitive at this point, on this end of the system," Stone told her. "No fancy GUI."

GUI was the acronym for graphical user interface, where icons and pictures and clicks by hand-guided mice allowed novices to navigate computers with relative ease.

"Do I get to use your account?"

Stone gave her the number, and once she had access, she keyed in her address: "copguytwo@aol.com."

"Who's copguytwo?" Stone asked.

"My brother Jim."

"Ah."

He slid off the desk, intent on finding himself some coffee while she corresponded with family.

"Don't go away," she commanded.

He sat back down on the desk.

With deft fingers, Naylor tapped away at the keys for a moment, then asked, "Michael Stone your real name?"

"What? Of course."

"Social Security number?"

He gave it to her.

She keyed it in.

"Statistics?"

"What the hell are you doing, Meg?"

"Statistics?"

"Five ten, brown, brown, thirty-two."

She wrapped up her letter, then posted it via e-mail.

"What's going on, Meg?"

She turned to face him, and again, he was struck by the sincere, earnest expression on her face.

"I'm running a police background check on you."

"What!" He came off the desk.

"My brother's very protective. He doesn't want me falling in love with someone he doesn't know about."

Stone, who was never at a loss for words when it came to women, didn't know what to say.

"It's happening, you know?"

He nodded.

"Is that all right with you, Mickey?"

"When does your brother check on his e-mail?"

"I am to leave the country by Monday at noon," Suretsov told Grant.

He had come to the Shanghai Star building in search of Grant and happened to run into him in the lobby, as Grant was returning from some meeting.

There were a few dozen people passing through the lobby, and

Grant waved him to the side. They stood next to the public telephone near the front doors.

"They give you any reason, Vladimir?"

"I am simply declared persona non grata."

"But you have a good idea?"

"Certainly. I showed my article to Minister Pai."

"And your article said?"

"Around the nuclear reactor at Lhasa, there is an apparent radiation level of approximately sixty roentgens per hour. At the juncture of transfer pipes with the containment structure, it rises to nearly ninety. At Chengdu, the readings were slightly lower."

"Not good," Grant said.

Suretsov shook his head in resignation. "Yuri Fedorchuk, who is my editor, wanted me to take more readings next week, to see if the levels increased. I will not be able to do that because I will not be in the country. I was hoping to convince you to get them for me."

"Is your article going to be published?"

"I have the firsthand, eyewitness account with recorded evidence, and I have Pai's denial. It will be published."

"What else are you doing?"

"Fedorchuk sent a copy of the article to the Atomic Energy agency in Vienna."

"Maybe they'll come out and investigate?"

"I hope so, but I think Pai will invoke the agreement with them. They can investigate a year from now." Suretsov sighed. "A year from now will be too late."

"Why?"

"I know nothing of reactors, Doug, but Fedorchuk has conversed with experts who suggest that it's possible the reactors are losing coolant. Not only is the atmosphere being poisoned, but the loss of coolant could lead to a meltdown."

"Ah, damn! How soon?"

"His experts have asked for copies of the design from Vienna. They will examine it."

"Those things should be shut down until they know."

"It is not likely to happen," Suretsov said. He could not believe how wrapped up in this he had become. He was supposed to investigate and write the stories, like Clark Kent. Superman was to save the world, or, at least, China. "Could you arrange for someone to take additional readings, Doug?"

"If you're not here, yes. But don't pack your bags just yet, Vladimir."

Suretsov raised an eyebrow.

"I heard about your deportation this morning. Shao is going to bat for you."

"The defense minister? Why?"

"I asked him to."

Grant continually surprised him. Suretsov did not know whether to feel relieved, or anxious.

He might actually have to go back to the reactor sites himself.

"The Consortium is reforming itself," Crest told him. "And they asked me to give you a call."

"I understood that you worked for Grant now," Lefant said, moving the telephone to his left hand so that he could jot notes if necessary.

"Oh, that was until this morning."

"And why are you calling?"

"I wanted to talk about your leasehold improvements and the equipment you've installed on floors two, three, and four."

"What of them?"

"The CIS will buy them from you, should your license be revoked."

"We have nothing to discuss, Mr. Crest."

Lefant slammed the phone down.

The gall of the man!

He punched the private number for the Information Ministry.

Wen Yito answered.

"I want to talk to Minister Jiang."

"The Minister is not avail—"

"Now!"

Wen was silenced for a moment. "I will see if I can interrupt his meeting."

Lefant doubted there was a meeting, but he had to wait five minutes before Jiang came to the telephone. Outside his office door, which he was not allowed to close, he could hear the men from the information ministry and the army's security section rifling through file drawers and cabinets. Earlier, there had been a confrontation of some kind when Ministry of Public Safety officers had shown up and been denied access by the army officer, Major Cho. He could imagine that tensions were running high in Beijing.

"Yes, Mr. Lefant?" Jiang's tone suggested he was not aware of any tension.

"You and I have an agreement, Mr. Jiang. I want these people out of my offices. I want this suspension lifted."

"What you want and what is possible are two entirely different things."

"There is nothing to be found here. You know that. It is an exercise in futility."

"You must be patient. There are protocols to be followed, Mr. Lefant."

"Protocol be damned! I am tired of being persecuted. You made promises—"

"Mr. Lefant, did you know that Mr. Sytenko died?"

Jiang hung up.

But the threat was left hanging in the air.

At 4:36 P.M., Tan Long approached the gate to the parking lot in back of the Shanghai Star building. He walked the sidewalk in a thin crowd of pedestrians. Dressed in denims and a sweatshirt advertising a Chinese rock band, he had his backpack in place and his duffel bag hanging from a strap over his left shoulder. He could have been one of thousands of transients. He wore a dark felt hat, shapeless with use, and its floppy brim helped to hide the scar on his cheek.

Nearing the gate, he slowed his pace, and one of the two guards on the other side of the chain-link fence immediately noticed. Both guards had assault weapons slung across their chests.

Tan smiled at him, swerving toward the gate.

"This is a funny place for security police. A parking lot?"

"If you do not have a car or a pass, you need not worry. Continue to wherever you are going."

Tan withdrew his hand from his pocket and held the fragmentation grenade in front of him, against his stomach where it would not be seen by those passing behind.

Both of the guards immediately noted the absence of the safety pin.

"Wha—"

"You will open the gate. Do it now. Do not touch your guns."

Reluctantly, the man opened the gate.

Deng Mai came down from the sixth floor, and Grant met her at the elevator, then got on with her. A steady stream of MI and Shanghai Star people packed the elevators, en route to their homes at the end of the workday.

Because of the crowd in the car, they didn't speak until reaching the lobby.

"The investigators still on your floors?" he asked.

"There are at least a dozen. It is, I think, overkill."

They walked side by side across the lobby to sign out at the reception desk, then took the wide corridor to the back of the building. Grant pushed open the door and let her precede him into the parking lot.

"You do not have to do this, Douglas."

"I told you on the phone that I'm driving you home every night until they find this Tan guy. I'm just carrying through on my conviction, Mai."

She smiled.

"What's so funny?"

"With all of the bandages, you do not look like a knight in shining armor."

He grinned. "The manufacturer recalled my armor."

Grant dug his keys out of his pocket as they approached the Jimmy. It was one of six vehicles parked at the back of the lot, up against the wall of a neighboring building. He moved up the right side of the truck and stuck the key into the lock.

Then looked up.

Assault rifle.

AK-47 Kalashnikov. 7.62 mike-mike. Big holes.

Held at waist level by a tall thin Chinese.

Tan. Or, at least, he was the man Grant had seen the night of the bombed truck.

He had stepped out from hiding behind the front of the truck.

"Douglas!" Mai yelped.

"You will be silent," Tan said. "Get in the truck, Mr. Grant, from this side. Slide over behind the wheel."

"Listen, Tan—"

Tan moved the muzzle of the rifle to the right, training it on Deng.

"Be quiet!"

Grant shut up, but swung his head around, looking for the guards, though he had little hope of finding them. Not if Tan was right here.

"Look in the other car," Tan said.

He glanced into the window of the Pathfinder next to him, saw nothing, looked into the rear-door window.

Two bodies.

The closest one had its throat slit. The sun was still high enough in the west to illuminate the dull-red coating on the dead soldier's shirt.

Grant heard Mai gasp when she followed his example and looked.

"Do you understand my determination? Get in the car." Tan kept the rifle aimed at Deng.

Grant pulled the door open, slid into the car, then across to the bucket seat behind the wheel.

"Madame Deng, you are next. In the passenger seat."

"Douglas?"

"Do as he says, Mai."

She slid along the side of the truck and climbed into the seat next to him.

Tan slammed the door shut, went back to the front of the truck and retrieved two bags, then tried the rear door, only to find it locked.

"Unlock this!" he called.

If Grant had had the engine running, he might have tried to bolt, but decided that would have been stupid, GMCs weren't quicker than AK-47s. He hit the electric switch on the armrest to unlock the doors.

Tan threw his duffel bag and backpack into the back, then got inside to sit behind Deng. Grant heard him unzipping something, tried to see what was happening in the rearview mirror, but didn't have the right angle. Tan rummaged around.

"Mr. Grant, you will look back here."

Grant turned in his seat as he was told. As he watched, the man took a thin loop of wire, reached forward, settled it over Mai's head, cautioned her when she began to struggle, then snugged it up around her throat. With the other end of the wire, he took a couple wraps around the muzzle of the Kalashnakov, which was pressed into the seat back. Aimed directly at the level of Mai's heart. Then he dropped a jacket over the rifle. A casual glance from outside would reveal nothing.

He also had a pistol—looked like a Glock automatic—stuck between his left thigh and the seat cushion.

And beside him on the seat, three fragmentation grenades. Once he was certain Grant had seen all of the armament, Tan spread a sweatshirt over the grenades and up against his leg, covering the Glock.

"Do you understand, Mr. Grant?"

"I understand."

"Turn around and start the truck. The gate is unlocked, and you will only need to push it open with the bumper."

"Where are we going?"

"Do as I say."

Grant turned back, taking a quick glance at Deng. Her face was very pale, and her lips trembled. He reached over and squeezed her forearm, trying to reassure her.

"Grant!"

Fumbling with the keys, he found the ignition key, and started the engine. He backed out in a wide swing, looking for someone, anyone, coming from the building.

No one. They were all using the front door.

Shifting to low, he eased up to the gate, honked once to warn pedestrians, then shoved the gate with the truck. It swung wide to the left, and he pulled across the sidewalk and into the street. He had to stop for traffic until a '61 Chevy let him into the traffic lane.

"Turn right," Tan ordered.

Grant spun the wheel and drove onto Huashan Road.

"You will do nothing to attract attention, Mr. Grant."

"Right."

They made two more right turns, and when they reached Yanan Road, Tan ordered him to turn west, headed out of the city toward the airport.

"If you want a way out of town, Tan, I can get one of our airplanes."

The killer seemed to be considering that option. One that probably hadn't occurred to him.

"I'll ride along as your hostage. We let Madame Deng go."

Grant's first priority was to get Mai out of harm's way. The second was to get Tan in the airplane with himself and Dusty McKelvey. He had a sudden faith in McKelvey's violence potential.

"You will drive where I tell you to drive," Tan Long said.

Sunday, September 18

At six o'clock in the morning, which he figured was a decent time, Bricher called Grant at his apartment.

Still no answer.

He'd tried calling until midnight last night. Grant hadn't told him he had anything planned for Saturday. He usually worked part of his weekends, but with the convalescence time Grant needed, Bricher thought he might have decided to get away for a few hours.

He was sitting at the kitchen table, trying to be quiet, though he had put the coffee on. It perked away cheerfully. This apartment wasn't really big enough for two adults and two teenage boys, and Bricher sometimes thought longingly of the big, rambling farmhouse in which he'd grown up. Then, he thought about Chinese families of eight or ten living in the same space he was in now and felt guilty about his extravagance.

"You're supposed to sleep in on Sundays, then be bright-eyed for church," Shana said as she came into the kitchen.

She was wearing a loose robe, which didn't hide some lusty curves.

"Forgot about church," he said.

There wasn't a Baptist missionary within miles, and they had been going to the nondenominational services conducted at Hongqaio New Town since arriving.

The coffee wasn't through perking, but she whipped the carafe out of the machine and poured two mugs quickly.

"Here."

"Thanks, love."

"Are you still trying to find Doug?"

"Yeah. This isn't like him."

"Did you call Deng Mai?"

"I've been afraid to."

"Why?"

"If she's not home, maybe they're off somewhere together."

Shana raised both eyebrows. "You're kidding?"

"Anything's possible. I'll try her house." Bricher got up and went to the living room to find his address book. He came back and sipped coffee while he looked up her home number.

The telephone rang once. Didn't even get through the first ring.

"Mai?"

"Ah, no. This is Will Bricher," he said, trying desperately to remember the elder Deng's first name or title. "I'm with Megatronics Incorporated."

"Yes. Mai has mentioned your name."

"Is she home by any chance, Madame Deng?" he asked, hoping he was right on the title.

"Perhaps your Mr. Grant would know where she is. I certainly do not."

"Well, that's why I was calling. I'm trying to locate Mr. Grant."

"Oh! I knew it! They have run away together!"

The connection was abruptly severed.

Bricher sat there, feeling somewhat lost.

"That was quick," Shana said.

"I don't know what's going on. Mai's mother thinks they've run off."

"Eloped? That's exciting!"

Shana always liked a good romance. She had stacks of the paperback variety sitting around the apartment. Patricia Werner's *Treasured* was leaning against the toaster.

Bricher thumbed through his address book. He didn't want to call Jiang, though he had the number. Grant had said that the defense minister had become rather cordial in recent days, but he didn't have that number, and he didn't think he had the time to chase one down through Beijing on a Sunday.

Hua.

Bricher had both the headquarters and officer's quarters numbers. He got the long-distance operator—residence telephones didn't have direct-dial long distance—on the line and gave her both numbers, then hung up.

He and Shana were on their second cups of coffee when the phone rang and he picked it up.

"Mr. Bricher, this is General Hua."

"I'm sorry to bother you so early in the morning, General. I was going to bother Minister Shao, but I don't have his number."

"Is there a problem?"

"I can't find Doug Grant." He thought for a moment, then added, "And I think Director Deng may have also gone missing."

"They are together?"

"I don't know. But neither of them would take off voluntarily without leaving a message somewhere."

Hua didn't hesitate, but said, "I will try to reach the minister, then one of us will get back to you."

He hung up and said, "Shit."

Shana said, "It's Sunday, Will."

"They could have been gone for thirty hours or more. And I've been sitting on my butt."

On Friday night, they had driven for twelve hours, stopping once for gasoline. Shortly past dawn, they parked the truck behind a pig shed on the farm of a man Tan apparently knew. They sweltered in the closed truck throughout the day, and Tan allowed them out only to relieve themselves. He fed them crackers, dried beef, and sips of water from a canteen. When they were seated in the unmoving car, Tan wired their hands behind them, using a thin, plastic-coated wire like that used in floral shops, slid the wire beneath the cushion, and then tied it to the frame of the seat.

On Saturday night, they drove for another eleven hours.

But they did not get very far, Deng thought. The PRC discouraged automobile traffic between cities as a matter of national defense. Tourists were expected to travel by air, rail, or waterway. The security concern was not the only obstacle. China's roads were in dreadful disrepair, and what there was of them were clogged by horse- and donkey-drawn carts carrying farm products to market. The carts made passage slow until well after midnight and from before dawn. To manage an average speed of forty kilometers per hour was an admirable feat. She estimated they had travelled about 1,000 kilometers. They had passed through Changsha in the early morning, and she suspected they were now near the Hunan Province town of Hengyang. That would put them about 400 kilometers from Guangzhou, directly to the south, a little further to Hong Kong.

They had been stopped twice by provincial police, suspicious of a vehicle travelling at night, but Grant's and Deng's papers and identification, along with a story of emergencies at a microwave-relay station, had erased the suspicion. Mai's pleasant explanation in Chinese had soothed the policemen.

And now the truck was parked, of all places, next to the small building housing the base equipment for a microwave-relay station. The logos on the truck doors matched the logo on the chain-link fence surrounding the antenna farm. It was a perfectly natural camouflage.

The gate had been locked, but Tan had blown the padlock apart with one shot from his pistol. He had repeated the feat on the lock of the steel door to the building, having to shoot that lock twice.

The inside of the windowless building was jammed with electronic equipment. In a small space near the door was a workbench with a stool in front of it. Tan sat on the stool and toyed with his guns.

Grant was seated on the bench; his arms wired at the elbows and wrists behind him, then hooked to a bent nail in the wall. Deng was seated on a collapsed cardboard box on the concrete floor, her bound hands snugged up against a wall stud behind her.

She was hungry, almost salivating, as she watched Tan crunch soda crackers, but she would not admit it to him.

She was fatigued, feeling the weight of it on her shoulders, yet she could not sleep and had not closed her eyes since Tan first pointed his gun at them.

She was also terrified.

Tan had not allowed them to speak to each other for the entire journey. And he spoke very little, had revealed nothing of his plans for them, or for himself. Instinctively, however, Mai knew they were doomed. They were alive only because they were useful to Tan as hostages, for easing the suspicions of policemen. As soon as Tan Long saw his way to freedom, they would be shot.

She knew that.

It caused her to review her life and wonder if she had any regrets.

When she looked at Grant, she knew she had one regret.

Grant had been stoic for the whole ordeal. He did as he was told. Several times, when she thought of attempting an escape, he seemed to sense her mind and cautioned her with a look or a gesture. He had touched her lightly on the forearm twice when he was driving, only to be warned by Tan. She had opted to follow his example; she would not give Tan the pleasure of knowing her fright.

If he could sense her thoughts, then she, too, had a mental perception of Grant's mood. She thought there was a great deal of repressed fury just below the surface, ready to spring forth like a jack-in-the-box. And yet, he remained calm. Seated unceremoniously on the workbench, his shoulders were still high and back, his head held erect. There was a pride there that he was not going to release.

And without warning, he winked at her.

Mickey Stone was lying in bed wide awake at 8:15 A.M., staring at the ceiling. Beside him in the queen-sized bed was . . . empty space. But he had been thinking about that space filled with Meg Naylor.

He wished to hell Lieutenant Jim Naylor would get on the ball and complete his background check. Stone had never before wanted a police examination so much.

The hell of it was, he found himself thinking about her all of the time, now.

Dumb, huh? Like some love-struck puppy.

He'd never been in love before, didn't know what it was.

But if he was in love, it was sure as hell going to screw up the schedule he'd outlined for his life.

Bye-bye memoirs.

He didn't really expect to have that memorial to his professional prowess oohed and ahhed over by tourists in the year 4000. But those personal memoirs had been in the back of his mind for a long time. Here he was, thirty-two years old, and not a quarter of the way through a list like Errol had compiled.

And then again, he didn't feel particularly saddened by the failure. . . .

The phone beside the bed rang, and he let it go three rings, hoping whoever it was would give up.

Then thought it could be Meg, calling from her lonely bed.

He rolled over, grabbed the phone, and pulled it to his ear.

"Mornin', whoever."

"Mickey, we've got us a situation."

"Will? What kind of situation?" Stone sat up and threw his legs over the side of the bed.

"Doug and Deng Mai are missing."

"Goddamn it! When?"

"I don't know. Shao Tsung sent some people over here—the Shanghai Star building—this morning and found the two parking-lot guards with their throats cut. It could have been as early as Friday evening; had to have been, in fact. The two guards were on that shift."

"How in hell did that happen?"

"The parking lot doesn't get protection on Saturdays and Sundays. There was no shift to relieve them. They weren't missed."

"And no sign of Doug?"

"None. Nor of Mai. Her secretary last saw her at five-forty on Friday. She didn't go home Friday or Saturday night, and her mother thought the worst."

"The worst?"

"That she'd eloped with Doug. I don't know what that's all about. I only talked to her briefly, but Shao talked to her this morning. Shao's on his way now by plane."

"What's been done?"

"According to Shao, he's alerted the police and the army. There's an all points bulletin, or whatever they call it here, out for them."

"Do we know anything else?"

"Just that we're missing a white Jimmy. Shanghai Star logos on the doors. Number sixteen on the tailgate."

"Damn! What do we do?"

"Sit tight, I guess," Bricher said. "Shao's got more troops than we do."

As soon as Bricher hung up, Stone called the general aviation office at the airport, had to wait a couple minutes for an English-speaking clerk, then asked if anyone from Southeast Asia Charter was hanging around.

A couple minutes later, he heard, "McKelvey."

"Dusty, Mickey Stone. There's a chance Grant and Deng have been kidnapped."

"Shit, you don't mean it?"

Stone told him what he'd learned from Bricher.

"If it's this guy Tan they've been looking for," McKelvey said, "why wouldn't he just kill them?"

"He's got to know there's a manhunt on for him. Who better to pick than Grant and Deng for hostages?"

"You think he's on the run?"

"I haven't had time to digest this, Dusty, but that's my gut reaction. Unless they find the truck somewhere."

"That truck will stick out like a hitchhiker's thumb. You don't see many new trucks—utility vehicles, anyway—on Chinese highways."

"That's what I was thinking."

"You want us to go looking?"

"What have you got available?"

"Let's see . . . there's a Lear and a Citation here . . . another Lear in Shanghai . . . another one in—"

"Don't pull the rest of them in. Look, Dusty, if you were on the lam out of Shanghai, where would you go?"

"Assuming I couldn't hop a ship in Shanghai?"

"I understand they've got a big cork in that port."

"I'd head south. Hong Kong."

"Me too. Or here. Could you make some low flights over the obvious routes?"

"What's the time frame?"

"Deng was last seen a little before six on Friday. I don't know about Doug, but they were probably together."

"That's a long damned time, Mickey. And this is one hell of a big country."

"I don't want to sit around twiddling my thumbs."

"I don't, either. Let me see what I can put together and I'll call you back."

Stone decided to skip shaving and went right to the closet for clean jeans and a shirt. He hated waiting for phone calls.

Crest's contact didn't show up at ten o'clock like he had promised.

Crest had been loitering beside one of the five gracefully arched bridges spanning a stream near the Meridian Gate of the Forbidden City for twenty minutes. He walked back and forth with his hands shoved in his pockets, and thought of himself as caught within a box in a box in a box. The Purple Forbidden City—purple related to the North Star and indicating the emperor's palaces as the cosmic center of the universe—with its moat and thirty-five-foot-high walls was within the walls of the Imperial City, which was within the walls of Beijing.

After having been levelled to the ground when the Ming drove the Mongols from China, Beijing was rebuilt in 1407, and twenty-four emperors of the last dynasties, the Ming and Qing, ruled from the Dragon Throne of the Forbidden City for five centuries, until the last dynasty was overturned in 1911. A ruler rarely left the city and its hoards of treasure, priests, ministers, princes, concubines, and eunuchs; and no one was allowed to enter without permission. Six thousand cooks catered to the daily needs of the inhabitants.

Within the 250 acres of the city, palaces had sprung up over the centuries, protected by the massive walls with four towers at each corner—huge pavilions topping each tower—and the towers over each of the four gates. Crest had made the tour once, struck by the notion that the lavish living of the emperors contradicted many of the names of the fifty-odd structures: Gate of Heavenly Purity, Hall of Supreme Harmony, Palace of Earthly Tranquility, Palace of Abstinence. He could understand that, after five hundred years, a few of the peasants grovelling in poverty got ticked off at the authorities living in elegance and opulence.

Much of the treasure gathered from all corners of the empire had disappeared—sold off by ousted officials, lost to fire, and looted by the Japanese during the Sino-Japanese War. After a period of neglect, the city had been undergoing renovation as a museum, and new collections of jade, paintings, bronzes, and porcelain were on display. The gardens were lavish and peaceful.

Crest knew some mavens of Wall Street and of Madison Avenue who would have liked to buy the place as a summer home.

Lu appeared at 10:40 A.M., with a wife and three youngsters in tow. Crest couldn't believe he'd brought the whole family along, but they were good cover. He wondered how the man supported three kids. With the official policy of one child per family, extra kids didn't receive free schooling and medical support from the state.

Or perhaps that was why Lu was interested in Crest's paying proposition.

After looking around him, Lu sent the family across the central bridge toward the Hall of Supreme Harmony and wandered toward where Crest stood at the bridge.

"Mr. Crest, it is a pleasure to see you again."

"And you, Mr. Lu."

The man appeared to be only slightly nervous. He wanted to be polite, but he wanted to get this over with quickly.

"What did you find?" Crest asked.

"As you requested, and when I had the opportunity, I perused the minister's private file drawer. It was locked and posed something of a problem, but I was able to overcome the obstacle."

That was a hint that the job was worth more money.

But Crest had been planning a bonus, anyway. He glanced about, then withdrew the envelope from his jacket pocket and handed it over.

Lu's brow wrinkled in question.

"Thirty thousand kuai."

"I had hoped for U.S. dollars."

"They are illegal within the country, Mr. Lu. I have FEC, if you prefer."

Foreign exchange certificates were used by visitors to the country rather than renminbi—the "people's currency," which was measured in yuan.

"This will have to do," the clerk said.

He handed Crest a small slip of paper.

"That's it?"

"I do not have access to a copy machine, Mr. Crest. In the whole file, that was all that struck me as odd, since the names were in English. Good day, sir."

Lu went on over the bridge, leaving Crest with a 30,000-yuan scrap of envelope, on the back of which was written: "Phillipe Margolin, Enrique Marquez."

After a moment's thought, Crest decided the two names might be worth the value. He went back toward Tiananmen Square and looked for a taxi.

Thirty minutes later, he was back in his hotel and had Suretsov on the phone. He had located him at the ITAR-Tass office.

"Vladimir, it's Maynard. What are you doing in the office?"

"Packing. Just in case Doug is overly optimistic."

"If he talked to Shao for you, I think you're clear. You'll get a little note of apology."

"I wish that they would hurry it up, then. Have you talked to Doug?"

"Not for a couple days. Why?"

"I have been trying to call him, but no one is answering his office or apartment telephones. Not even an answering machine. Where are you?"

"Beijing."

"Your contact?"

"I didn't get much out of him, Vladimir. Two names that were stuck in our target's files."

"They are?"

"French and maybe Spanish. Phillipe Margolin and Enrique Marquez."

"Hold one minute, please."

Crest heard papers rustling in the background.

"Yes. I have them."

"On the shareholder list?"

"Their holdings are equivalent to that of Jean Legrand. It would be a half-million American dollars. Each."

"I was pretty sure they'd be there."

"This is wonderful, Maynard. We can publish—"

"No, we can't. All I've got is the names."

"Not the stock certificates?"

"Those will be held in the brokerage account."

"A paper? A letter?"

"Just the names."

"Bloody hell! We have nothing, then."

"Well, we have an idea that our two ministers are using those names, one or the other." Crest wasn't going to mention Jiang's or Pai's names on the phone. "I think they were in the file just so our man wouldn't forget what his name was in France."

"I will ask my supervisor if he can trace these names to any other enterprise."

"That might be helpful."

"And what," Suretsov asked, "did you do with the Jean Legrand name?"

Crest almost laughed aloud. "On Friday, I called Madame Margot Lefant in Paris. She was very interested in the name."

"I thought that you might do that, Maynard."

"Do you approve?"

"I am a journalist. I neither approve nor disapprove."

"I don't hear you crying."

"I do not cry when I smile," Suretsov said.

Zhou Ziyang had been expecting a call for two days.

Mu had called him from Guangzhou. Yang had called him from Urümqi. Both had been excited by the fiasco of the Shanghai Star system test, and the potential for making changes in the policies of the information ministry. Their workers were out in force, passing out the brochures that had been printed on Chiang's copy machine. Small demonstrations were erupting everywhere.

It might have made Zhou happy.

But he still had not received the telephone call he expected.

So he got his bicycle and rode it down to the Old Town and climbed the stairs to the headquarters room of the People's Underground.

Chiang, the young man called Huzhou, and a half-dozen others were present.

"Chairman Zhou," she said, "would you like tea?"

"I would."

She gestured to one of her subordinates, then invited him to sit in a chair drawn up to the desk. Everyone was sitting around the same desk.

"Did you enjoy the example of Shanghai Star programming?" she asked him.

"It was abominable."

"Precisely what Minister Jiang feared, I think. I found it enlightening. There were sex acts that many of the people have only imagined before." Chiang laughed with her delight.

"It does not serve our purpose, Leader Chiang."

She was not listening to him. She went on, "It always amazes me that the leadership in Beijing is so intent on keeping pornography from the people. Sexuality as a sinful pastime is a Western concept, propagated by Christians and psychoanalysts. It does not have a place in the Orient. I think Beijing is afraid of having the people enjoy themselves."

Zhou repeated himself, "Still, it does not serve our purpose. We should be striving to enlighten, to educate."

"Oh, I believe many were educated. Have you seen our dragon posters?"

"Yes. There are squads of policemen on the streets, tearing them down."

"Minister Jiang is not happy with me. I expect to hear from him soon."

"It is getting out of hand," Zhou said. "There is a demonstration scheduled for tomorrow in Fu Xing Park. I have heard many speak of it."

"It is time," Huzhou said.

"There could be casualties. The police will not allow it."

Huzhou grinned.

Chiang turned on him, her face a mask of anger. "You arranged it, Huzhou!"

"Of course. If you will not act, then I must."

"You fool! I have already acted," she said.

At 4:00 P.M., Jiang Guofeng's airplane landed at the airport and parked in the general aviation section. He descended to the ramp on the airstairs wheeled into place, then followed the policeman, who met him, to the terminal.

Once inside, the policeman pointed toward the closed door of an office. "In there, Minister."

Jiang strode across the floor and opened the door.

The office was utilized by customs officials and contained only a table and four chairs. Chiang Qing was slouched in one of the chairs, a police officer standing behind her. He had not seen her in person in four years, and he thought she looked somehow jaded, past her prime.

Jiang gestured, and the policeman left, closing the door behind him.

"Good afternoon, honored cousin," she said. "You have gained weight since I saw you last."

Jiang shook his head in . . . what? Despair? Frustration? He sat in the chair opposite her.

"Qing, you have jeopardized us all."

"It is you who paid me to discredit Deng, if you will remember."

"It is I who have kept you in money and out of prison for ten years," Jiang said. "We had an agreement. You should have honored it."

She sat up in her chair and her eyes blazed. "So that you can go on living your pampered life? So that I can tiptoe about, shouting useless slogans, just so you can prove to your brothers in the inner circle that you are in control of the radicals? Cousin, the time has come for that shit to end."

"It is you who chose your life, Qing."

"It is you who twisted it, Guofeng."

"Only when you came to me for funds. Who was begging?"

"Fuck you!"

"You are completely out of control."

"You are losing control." She sat back, laughing. "Were your friends shocked by their new television?"

"You were to have simply replaced two news videos," he said, his anger rising.

"I thought everyone should have some fun, not just the outdated old men on the information committee. Did you, or did you not, have fun?"

"And now this demonstration tomorrow."

"That is not my doing," she insisted.

"The police say the Underground is organizing it."

"Not at my order."

"Then, it is you that have lost control, is it not?"

"I still determine my fate," she said, deadly serious now. "You would not want Shanghai Star to know of our arrangement, would you?"

"They cannot know, if you are dead," he told his cousin.

Grant had slept for a few hours in the afternoon, lodging his head back against one of the studs of the wall behind him. His hands felt numb from the wire wrapped around his wrists. His upper arms ached from the position in which his elbows were tied. His left shoulder was no longer a shoulder, but a dull throb. He longed to unwrap the bandages from his chest so he could take a deep breath.

He was still tired, but more tired of the inactivity and the satisfying images he conjured of the things he would do to Tan as soon as he got the chance.

The man was too careful. He had not yet made any mistakes that Grant could take advantage of. There had been a few times when Grant might have made a move on him, but with Mai present, Grant would not take unacceptable risks. He had considered turning the truck over in a ditch, for one, but not with Mai shackled to the passenger seat with a wire around her throat.

Tan was sound asleep, leaning back against a power-supply cabinet as if he had not read the "Danger—High Voltage" sign in both English and Chinese. The Glock was in his lap, and the assault rifle rested on the floor next to his right leg.

Grant looked at Mai. Her head was nodding forward, jerking back, her eyes half-closed. She was in that netherworld of half-sleep, and he wished she would sleep, if just to conserve her energy.

Just looking at her brought his rage into full bloom. Tan was going to pay dearly for the humiliation.

"Hey, Tan!" he yelled.

Mai jerked awake.

Tan came off the floor quickly, dropping into a crouch, trying to find the safety on the rifle.

"Getting nervous, are you?"

"Be quiet, Grant."

"What? No mister? Are you losing your courteous side, too?"

"What do you want?"

"It's getting dark. Time you made your preparations."

Tan went to the door, shoved it open a few inches and peered outside. Dusk was falling rapidly. He slipped outside and closed the door. After a while, Grant heard the clanking of a bucket and guessed that Tan was draining the gas tank of the emergency generator next to the shed. He'd funnel a few gallons into the truck.

"How are you doing, Mai?"

"Douglas, what will we do?"

"We'll be patient. Something's going to turn up. He's not that bright, and he's going to make a mistake."

"Do not try to cheer me up."

"Got to. I don't want you sulking when you take me to dinner in Guangzhou."

She frowned. "Do you think that is where we're going?"

"That's where we're going. I don't know if Tan is going to make it."

She tried to smile, but didn't succeed very well.

Her suit hadn't weathered the journey. She no longer had the jacket on, and her white blouse was smeared with dirt. In her position on the floor, the skirt was hiked over her knees.

Which looked damned good, he thought.

And while he was trying to get his mind off her legs, Tan came back.

As in the previous night's ritual, he untied Deng first, then gave her five minutes to eat some dried meat and crackers, then sip from a half-gallon container of water. Then he shoved her roughly through the door.

"Tan!"

The killer looked back.

"You treat her like a lady or you're going to die much slower." Grant let some of his anger and frustration translate into the conviction of his voice.

Tan blinked at him, didn't say a word, then followed her out.

He would tie her in place in the truck, then put the wire around her neck.

When he came back, he showed more caution in dealing with Grant, and Grant regretted his outburst.

"I should just kill you now," he said.

"You probably should," Grant agreed. "If you don't, and if you have plenty of that wire, I'm going to take a couple wraps around your scrawny neck and pull slowly. You'll know some pain before your head comes off."

Tan studied him for a minute, then took the Glock from his belt, released the safety, and held the muzzle against the side of Grant's head. It took Tan longer, working with just his left hand, to get the wire undone.

When it finally released, Grant swung his arms forward, to get the circulation going. Needles of pain shot along both arms. His left shoulder screamed its relief.

Tan backed away from him. "Eat."

Still working his shoulders and arms, Grant slid off the bench, then squatted to pick chunks of meat from the wrapper on the floor. He chewed slowly, trying to get the tasteless gunk to go down. He grabbed the jug of water and upended it, chugging as much as he could.

"Hey! Not so much!"

Grant lowered the jug. "You should have planned ahead. You want me to fall asleep and drive off the road?"

"I will drive."

"And get picked up right away. You know there's an alert out for that truck by now?"

"We will take the back roads."

"Every road in the damned country is a back road."

"Be quiet!"

The automatic was aimed directly at Grant's midsection. He didn't want to take a bullet in the stomach by pushing the man too far, so he shut up.

When he was finished with what passed for his meal, Tan had him back up against the wall while he repacked his duffel bag. Then they went out to the truck.

"Get behind the wheel," Tan ordered.

Grant went around the back of the truck, opened the door, and slid in. Mai looked at him, and her eyes were wide and fearful.

He knew why.

This was the last leg of the trip. He guessed that Guangzhou was less than 300 miles away, 350, maybe.

He'd have to do something long before dawn.

Unfortunately, nothing had yet occurred to him.

Mai groaned when Tan tied the wire to the AK-47's barrel. He knew that whenever he hit a pothole, the weight of the weapon jerked the wire and caused her pain.

He was going to enjoy killing this son of a bitch.

Suretsov was in his flat when the message arrived, brought by a soldier in uniform. He thanked the man, then tore at the seal and ripped the envelope open.

Reprieve.

His visa was restored and he was offered apologies for an unfortunate error in paperwork processing.

When he realized he was standing in the open doorway, he went back inside.

Thank whatever lords there might be for men like Douglas Grant and Shao Tsung. He would find an appropriate way to thank them, knowing that, with Shao, he could not be obvious. The debt was incurred, would not be spoken of, would not be forgotten, and would someday be repaid.

And still, he was thankful. To have been ejected from the PRC for simply doing his job was an ignominious way to complete his tour.

He called the operator and placed a call to Fedorchuk, then sat down to wait for it to be completed.

It turned out to be quicker than anticipated. The phone rang in two minutes.

It took another minute to relate developments to Fedorchuk.

"At any rate, Yuri, I am not returning to Moscow."

"I hope not. I have work for you."

Fedorchuk did not exude his normal lighthearted good humor.

"You have learned something from the Margolin and Marquez names?"

"No, not as yet. I have talked to a representative of the International Atomic Energy Agency in Vienna. They have been in contact with Beijing—"

"With whom in Beijing?"

"They did not say. The man told me that they have been denied an examination visit to the reactor sites at Lhasa and Chengdu. It was explained to them that the reporter's data had been falsified and was intended only to create a spectacular story. The energy ministry's own investigators discovered no unsafe radiation levels."

"Yuri, that is a lie."

"It may well be. In fact, Vladimir, I am certain that it is. I could not obtain a statement from the Agency for publication, and my calls to the Premier and to Minister Pai have not been returned. We are at a standstill with this article."

"You must go forward—"

"We are still considering it, but, Vladimir, there is more disturbing news. The Russian experts who read your article, examined the tapes, and studied the possible designs that could be derived from the Topaz, are worried."

"Worried? About what?"

"They think there is a coolant loss taking place. Especially in the Lhasa reactor."

"Leading to a meltdown of the core?"

"Yes."

"How soon?"

"They would not be specific. The professor in charge told me, 'A day, a week, who knows?' "

"This is disastrous, Yuri."

"It could well be. And I am not certain where to turn. You told me that Grant had interceded for you with Shao in regard to your deportation?"

"He did."

"Perhaps you could discuss it with Grant and he could talk to the minister?"

"That is not possible. I learned two hours ago that Grant is missing."

"What? And you have not written it up?"

"I have telephone calls out, trying to get information, Yuri. Deng Mai is missing, too."

"Vladimir, you have many tasks to complete. Get started on them."

"She is in Hong Kong," Yvonne Deng said. "They have married against my wishes."

"Mai told you she was marrying him?" Lefant asked, relaxing the telephone pressed to his ear. He had been talking to her for nearly an hour, and his hotel room had darkened as the sun went down. He found it difficult to become concerned about Yvonne's fantastic worries. He had problems of his own.

"No."

"I do not think you have raised a daughter who would take such a drastic step without consulting you, Yvonne."

"I did not think so."

"Then wait until you hear from Minister Shao before you upset yourself with conjecture."

Lefant thought the prospects more readily favored the abduction of Grant and Deng by some unknown person. By late evening, the rumors surrounding the duo's disappearance had been flying around the Shanghai Star building, the Dallas Cowboy Cafe, the International Hotel, and the settlement at Hongqaio New Town. China suddenly seemed a more dangerous place to him, especially after the Russian was killed and Jiang made the subtle threat toward him.

He would not voice his supposition to Yvonne, of course. He was seriously considering a retreat to France. He would prefer to take Yvonne with him, but while Mai was missing, he could not raise the question.

"Perhaps you could come to my room, and we will wait together," he offered.

"No. I must be near the telephone. In case they call."

"I hesitate to mention, Yvonne, that the telephone is busy."

"Oh. Yes. I must get off."

"I will call you later, to see if there is news."

"Thank you, Pierre. I appreciate your concern."

He got up, turned on the lamp next to the sofa, and went into the kitchenette for a fresh pack of cigarettes and a glass of brandy. Lighting a Gauloisse, he took a long drag, then went back to the living room and the sofa.

He sat in the semidarkness and looked out on the lights of downtown Shanghai. Though he did not like the city, he had sometimes thought the view to be romantic. Now, it just seemed sinister.

His entire weekend had been spent in his rooms at the hotel. Chabeau had called several times, the first time in regard to the apparent kidnapping of Grant and Deng. Lefant could establish no way in which the abduction should affect him.

But there were other intrigues afoot, he thought. Jiang's revelation that the Russian was dead—certainly executed—had sounded a jarring note. He did not know why Sytenko had become a threat, but the death was an omen not to be ignored.

Lefant was not a murderer; he could dredge up no image of himself in that capacity. He was simply a businessman, and no one ever denied a businessman his right to make a profit. He merely assisted others in completing transactions.

And yet, if his name were connected to other names, he might well be looked upon as an accomplice, an accessory, something . . .

He had found himself looking over his shoulder on his way back to the International on Friday.

And he had secluded himself for the weekend. He dreaded returning to work tomorrow. The investigators would still be there. And while there was, he was certain, nothing for them to find, Jiang's committee might well use the sabotage as an excuse to remove him and MBL from Shanghai. He almost looked forward to that consequence. He was ready to return to France.

In fact, he had mentally composed a letter of resignation several times. He would take what profits he had and move to the beaches of the Mediterranean.

Except for Yvonne. He yearned for her. He had composed a picture of their future together. But perhaps she could come later. . . .

The telephone ring startled him.

Reaching forward, he lifted it from the cocktail table.

"Lefant."

"Pierre, this is Jacques. I have been trying to get through to you for half an hour."

He glanced at his watch: 8:15 P.M.

"It is one in the morning there, Jacques. Why are you calling?"

"Because I am your attorney, and because I am at a party that started on Saturday night."

"I do not see the connection."

"It's about Margot."

"Margot? She is there?"

"No. But the city prosecutor is. I am informed that Margot is bringing a civil action against you on Monday morning. And the prosecutor is to file criminal charges."

"What! This cannot be!"

"Pierre, did you, or did you not, hide assets, including a house and stock holdings, during the divorce litigation?"

How would she . . . ?

"Of course not!" he lied loudly.

"Under the name Jean Legrand?"

"Ridiculous!"

"Well, until I get to the bottom of this, you had better stay away from Paris. Stay right where you are."

When he hung up, Lefant's heart was beating double time.

Monday, September 19

At two in the morning, Grant's office was full of people. Will Bricher had command, by virtue of his seat in Grant's desk chair. On the sofa and in chairs imported from other rooms were most of MI's senior staff. Wickersham had come in the previous evening from Lhasa, and he was nervous and restless enough that he was personally making the second pot of coffee.

Maynard Crest and Diantha Parker were in the visitor's chairs drawn up close to the desk. Bricher was aware of Parker's red-rimmed eyes. She'd been crying.

Miss Jiangyou from Deng's office was also present, and she appeared to be in about the same condition as Parker.

The group had begun to gather about ten o'clock last night when a report came in that Shanghai Star's vehicle number sixteen had been stopped, then released, by police in Zhejiang Province late on Friday night. The policeman had noted three people in the truck that Grant was driving. He hadn't thought there was any problem, and the paperwork had been treated routinely. But then the military issued a request for information about the truck, and some clerk had discovered the stop report.

Since then, there hadn't been anything new, and the group engaged in desultory conversation while occasionally stealing a glance at the telephone in front of Bricher.

At 2:12 in the morning, the primary line buzzed, startling everyone. Conversation died.

Parker leaped from her chair, but Bricher grabbed the phone first and punched the button with the blinking light.

"Bricher."

"Mr. Bricher, this is Minister Shao."

He hit the speaker button, so the others in the room could hear the conversation. "Yes, Minister. Is there anything new?"

"The truck was detained by Hunan Province police early on Sunday morning—before dawn. All was in order and it was allowed to proceed."

Bricher tried to recall the map. "They're not making much progress, Minister. I suppose Tan's keeping them off the road during the day."

"That is the consensus of the police and military leaders. We are of the opinion that Tan hid the truck during the day on Sunday, somewhere south of Zhuzhou. They probably got under way again around dusk last night, five to six hours ago."

"That would put them in Guangdong Province now," Bricher said.

"Exactly."

"What are you doing?"

"We have alerted air-force helicopter patrols in the region, but they have been told not to approach too closely, in fear of lives. At his request, General Hua has been placed in command of the surveillance aircraft."

"Thank you, Minister."

"Spotters with radios are being placed on the roads leading into Guangzhou, as well as to the east, on roads to Kowloon. If the truck is identified, they will only make reports. We should be able to track it soon."

"Thank you, sir. I appreciate your letting me know."

Bricher depressed the disconnect bar, released it, and punched the button he'd programmed for Stone's hotel room.

Parker looked desolate, and Bricher gave her a hopeful smile.

Stone didn't answer his phone. Bricher dialled the desk and was told Stone had gone to the airport, leaving the number for him. He punched it in, reached the general aviation terminal, and asked for Stone.

"Hey, Will. What've you got?"

Bricher brought him up to date.

"All right. Good. We've got a chance, then."

"Damned right. McKelvey have any planes near Shanghai?"

"I can check with him, but it'll have to be by radio. He's airborne."

"Tell him to send something to me, Mickey. I'm leaving for the airport now."

"Got it, Will."

Bricher stood up. "Curt, you're in charge here. Stick by the phone."

"Will do," Wickersham said.

"I'm going with you," Parker told him.

"I'm going, too," Crest said, pushing out of his chair.

He wouldn't deny Parker, but he said, "Maynard, you don't even work for us."

"Au contraire. I'm a consultant."

"Okay, come on."

They were down in the lobby, headed for the back door, when a man coming in the front door—arguing with one of the guards—yelled at Crest.

"Maynard!"

Bricher stopped and looked back.

Crest said, "Vladimir, what are you doing here?"

The Russian trotted up to them. "The Xinhua News Agency wire said that there was a national search for Grant."

"Yeah, we're going to go looking."

"May I go with you?"

Crest looked to Bricher.

He shrugged. It was turning into a real carnival.

It took them half an hour to get to the airport, and then they had to wait an hour before Jimbo Bowie arrived in a Citation.

Most of the lights were illuminated on the floors occupied by the Ministry of National Defense. Jiang passed through the security checkpoints on the identification card clipped to his breast pocket and was admitted to the minister's suite of offices.

He found a large group assembled in one of the conference rooms. Military and public-safety officers were gathered at the table, and a maze of telephone wires crisscrossed the floor, attached to a battery of telephones on the table. If the telephones were not buzzing, they were gripped in the hands of generals and bureaucrats.

Jiang wondered why Shao had taken such an interest in this event, as to assume control over it. If there was some connection between the defense minister and Deng or Grant that Jiang had overlooked, it could pose problems in the future.

Shao was pacing the floor near the windows, and when he saw Jiang, he changed course to meet him.

"Are you also working nights, Guofeng?"

"I just returned from Shanghai, Tsung. The situation there is quite tense. People are already beginning to gather at the park, and it is not supposed to start until one o'clock this afternoon."

"The demonstration?"

"Yes."

"Let them have it," Shao suggested.

"They do not have a permit. To let it proceed would establish a precedent that we do not want to have set."

Shao acknowledged that truth with a curt nod. "Yes. I agree."

"The police in Shanghai worry that they will not be able to maintain control. They are estimating that as many as thirty thousand will gather."

"This is instigated by the People's Underground?"

"I have talked to Chiang Qing. She swears not, that it is some faction using the Underground's reputation."

Shao studied him for a long moment. Did the man have knowledge regarding Chiang Qing and Jiang? The head of the defense establishment was privy to so many sources of intelligence, it was always difficult to decipher just what he did know.

"Do you want to defuse the event, Guofeng?"

"Of course."

"Call Mr. Bricher at Shanghai Star and tell him to conduct the system test tomorrow . . . that is to say, today."

"Today?"

"Have him place extra television sets around Fu Xing Park. The crowds will gravitate to the televisions."

Jiang was truly concerned that the demonstration would escalate into violence. It would rattle their currently positive public-relations image internationally.

"When?" he asked.

"The demonstration is scheduled for one o'clock. Have them start at noon."

"I don't know if they can be prepared that soon," Jiang said.

"Test them."

"Very well. But what contingencies should we—"

"I will alert the area commander and have him prepare mobile vans as well as troops. As soon as we have a command function in place, we will fly to Shanghai."

Shao returned to his pacing.

Jiang spoke to a sergeant and told him to call Shanghai Star. As he waited for the call to be placed, he wondered where Pai Dehuai was. His brother-in-law had been incommunicado ever since Shao and a few influential State Council members had engineered the countermanding of the Russian correspondent's deportation order.

When the sergeant held up the phone for him, he took it.

"Mr. Bricher?"

"No, Minister. I am Curt Wickersham, the software director. Mr. Bricher is flying to Guangzhou."

"Very well. Mr. Wickersham, I want the system test to be conducted today, beginning at twelve o'clock."

"Today, sir?"

"Can it be done?"

There was only a moment's pause. "Of course, Minister. I will have to locate Mr. Lefant, and we will prepare the programming."

Jiang was about to tell him of the requirement for television sets to be located near the park when a general at the other end of the table called to Shao, "Minister! They have found the truck!"

With two corpses in it, Jiang hoped.

Shao appeared unruffled at the news. "The occupants?"

"There is one body," the general told him.

Tan Long was pleased with his analytical ability.

It had always been exceptional, as he had proven time and again in his reports of the operations of the department stores, or in his evaluation of the conditions surrounding a contractual mission.

It was the frequency of the aircraft that had alerted him. Long before dawn, he had become aware that helicopters and airplanes were flying very low and following the roads. He had seen their lights from time to time and ordered Grant to turn off the headlights and drive by the thin illumination of the parking lights.

He had been certain they were looking for the truck. They may have also learned of the two times the truck had been stopped by police. Normally, he supposed, those kinds of reports were not filed in a central location. If Beijing had discovered the police reports, it indicated that a national alert may have been issued. It also suggested that the police were tracking him to the south, toward Guangzhou. The airplane searches confirmed that, as far as Tan was concerned.

So, when he saw the headlights of a truck approaching them on the narrow road, he said, "Slow down, Grant, and turn across the road."

"That's idiotic—"

Tan fired the Glock once. The bullet zipped by Deng's head and starred the windshield. The concussion filled the compartment and made his ears ring.

Deng screamed.

Grant glanced first at Deng, then immediately slowed, turned to block the road, and stopped.

"Get out and flag down the driver."

Grant got out, and the approaching truck—a twenty-year-old Volvo with a flatbed stacked high with crates—eased to a stop next to them. The driver climbed down from the cab to see what the problem was.

Tan rolled down his window, shifted the automatic to his right hand, and shot the driver twice. His face registered shock as he collapsed in the truck's headlights.

It took less than five minutes to transfer to the other truck, after he ordered Grant to place the body of the driver in the back of the GMC and drive the vehicle into the ditch at the side of the road.

Again, he told Grant to drive, and he placed Deng in between them on the single seat, the muzzle of the AK-47 pushed up under her chin.

At the next intersection of provincial roads, Grant turned west as he was told. If the police wanted to search to the south, that was fine with Tan.

Within forty minutes, they were approaching the small village of Qingyuan. Tan spotted a copse of trees at the edge of the village.

"Drive the truck into those trees."

Grant apparently wanted no more of gunfire; he complied readily, easing off the road and threading the hood of the truck between several large trees. The back end stuck out in the clearing, but there was no help for that.

During the long drive, Tan had assessed the characters of his hostages. Deng was frightened, but not totally acquiescent. She was worried. Grant had exploded verbally several times, but Tan thought he was like most Americans—all mouth. He was certainly afraid of the guns, and he was solicitous of Deng Mai's safety. Tan had discovered he could control Grant with any gesture that threatened Deng.

He got out of the truck first, then motioned Deng outside. She slid from the center of the seat, stepped down on the running board, then to the ground. He double-checked the wire binding her wrists in front of her. Then he told Grant to get out on this side, unwound more of his floral wire, and wrapped it around Grant's wrists ten times. He tested it and thought it snug enough. The circulation in his wrists might suffer, but Tan was not worried about it.

Grabbing his backpack and his duffel bag, he motioned with the AK-47, and the trio started toward the village, circling it to the south. With dawn just breaking in the east, some villagers were already up and beginning their day.

They followed a trail through the woods that was probably centuries old, and ten minutes later, arrived at the edge of the river. It was a tributary of the Hongshui Xi and joined with that stream some fifty kilometers west of Guangzhou. The Hongshui then flowed southward down the peninsula to reach the sea at the Portuguese port of Macau. If he could reach the border town of Gongbei, Tan felt he would encounter no difficulty in crossing into Macau.

The river edge and the docks in the village were jammed with watercraft. The aroma of cooking fires drifted on the breeze coming downriver.

Tan turned his hostages northward, and they walked the packed earth along the river until he found an unoccupied sampan with a small diesel motor.

Prodding Deng in the back, he forced her over the prow. Grant followed without urging. Tan released the line tying the boat to a tree stump, then shoved it from the bank as he clambered aboard.

The overhead sun shield was made of aged canvas, and he told Deng and Grant to sit on the thwart beneath it. He was careful as he stepped between them to the aft end of the boat and dropped his baggage in the bottom. The boat drifted from the shore and started downstream as he tied a length of wire from their wrists to heavy eyebolts attached to the gunwale, apparently used to secure cargo.

Waiting until the sampan had drifted a hundred meters downstream, Tan searched for a starter, but found none. He had to wrap a rope around a crankshaft extension and pull it seven times before the motor started. It was unmuffled and loud. He found the throttle cable and worked it until the engine idled more quietly.

Then he headed the bow downstream.

In a few more hours, he estimated, he could kill his prisoners, ensuring his final payment on that contract, and then launch himself into the freedom of the outside world.

The outside world still worried him a little.

He was supposed to be looking at the ground, but every once in a while, Suretsov glanced up and looked around at the nearby airspace. He was somewhat fearful that there would be a midair collision with himself as the focal point.

Besides the Cessna he was on with Bricher, Crest, and Parker, there was another white business jet making circles to the north of Guangzhou, and at least eight airforce aircraft. They ranged from fighters to helicopters to transports. He didn't recognize their specific silhouettes.

Suretsov had never been on a corporate jet before, and he thought that the cabin of this one was much smaller than he might have anticipated. It was also less luxurious than he would have guessed, and he supposed that was because Southeast Asia Charter's aircraft served many roles. He could see marks on the cabin sides that were probably the result of careless loading when the seats were removed and the airplane was used as a cargo plane.

He was not certain why he was here. For most of the night, he had been trying to telephone Mickey Stone when he finally learned of the news release.

And so here he was, feeling a little giddy whenever the pilot tipped the plane to the left or right as he made his circles.

He also knew where Stone was.

The cabin's overhead speakers broadcast the conversations between the two aircraft chartered by Megatronics. Occasionally, he heard someone named Dusty talking to someone named Jimbo. Stone talked to Bricher, whom Suretsov had only known by name and title.

"Hey, Jimbo?"

"Yeah, Dusty?"

"What's your fuel state?"

"Another twenty minutes, I'm going to have to put down and top 'em off," Jimbo said. From what Suretsov heard of the conversations, it had taken him awhile to figure out that Jimbo was the pilot of this craft.

He had also learned, in a conversation between Bricher and Wickersham, that the Shanghai Star system test had been suddenly scheduled for later in the day. Bricher had given Wickersham some instructions, then told him that he would oversee it from Guangzhou.

The four of them in the passenger cabin had been shifting from one side of the airplane to the other to peer through the small windows as it followed some kind of search grid set up by Dusty. He had not been much help, he thought. Everything on the ground appeared normal to him. Normal traffic, normal people cultivating fields, walking the roadside toward one village or another.

Earlier, they had flown over the spot where the Shanghai Star truck had been found. It was surrounded by five police vehicles, all of them with their blue lights flashing. Men were searching through the weed-choked ditch and the surrounding fields looking for evidence, Suretsov assumed.

He looked forward in the cabin and saw that Bricher was holding a microphone as he leaned against the cabin wall looking through the window. Suretsov stood up and made his way forward along the narrow aisle, crouching because of the low ceiling. He sat in the chair opposite Bricher.

"Mr. Bricher?"

The man turned to look at him.

"Is it possible to talk to Mickey Stone on that microphone?"

"Yes. They're on a frequency separate from the airport and the army. Why?"

"Well, sir, I was looking for Mr. Stone when I came to the building this morning. I thought he would be the one to talk to, since Mr. Grant . . ."

"Talk about what?"

"A nuclear-reactor meltdown."

Bricher's eyes enlarged. "Now, what?"

"May I talk to Stone?"

Bricher handed him the microphone.

Bricher showed him the button. "Press that when you talk."

He pressed the stud. "May I speak to Mickey Stone, please?"

A minute went by, then the overhead speakers filled with Stone's voice.

"Is that you, Vladimir?"

"It is."

"I thought they were kicking you out of the country."

"There have been second thoughts. There may be third thoughts. I have learned from Russian scientists that the Lhasa reactor may be in danger of meltdown."

The radio squawked as Stone overrode him. "Meltdown! How?"

"They think the radiation emission is a result of coolant loss."

"Son of a bitch!" Jimbo said, leaning back to call through the cockpit doorway. On his own microphone, he said, "I told you, Mickey!"

"Shit!" Bricher said. "What the hell's going on here?"

Suretsov tried to tell him the story briefly. It was difficult to do.

"What has Pai said?" Stone asked over the radio.

He pulled the microphone close to his lips. "He will no longer talk to me. His statement for the record denies any malfunctions with the reactors."

"Damn it!" Stone said. "You there, Will?"

Suretsov handed the microphone to Bricher.

"I'm here."

"What are we going to do about this?"

"I don't see as it's our problem, Mickey. We've got another task at the moment."

After a pause, Stone said, "Yeah, you're right."

Which left Suretsov at a loss. He had been hoping to find an ally in Stone.

He was about to try again when the speaker erupted.

"Jimbo!"

"Yeah, Dusty?"

"I'm at your . . . radial two-five-zero. Over a village named . . . let me check the chart . . . Qingyuan. There's a truck stuck back in the trees."

"Funny truck?"

"I didn't think much of it, except that it looks like a bunch of people are looting the boxes off the back of it. Grabbing and running."

"You think that's Doug's new transport?"

"Not anymore. We've got a river here."

"And a boat?"

"There's a million boats."

"Fuck," Jimbo said.

"I'm going to take a low ride down the river. You coming?"

"I need JP-4, buddy."

"Go get it."

As McKelvey levelled out over the river, Stone leaned his head against the porthole. There weren't a million boats, but it was a damned close guess, he thought.

The Lear was maybe two hundred feet above the surface, dragging its heels as much as possible. As they whipped overhead, the occupants of sampans, barges, and small freighters craned their necks to look up at them.

The shores of the river were thick with growth, but frequently, he glimpsed paths winding along either side of the stream.

Above the roar of the engines, he called to the cockpit, "How in hell are we supposed to recognize it, Dusty?"

McKelvey yelled back, "One! It's going downstream. Two! It's probably going faster than anything else. Three! It's got three people on board."

Stone wasn't sure that last guide was going to help. Most of the sampans had a small sun shelter amidships. He shifted his focus farther to the south, trying to see beneath the canvas on the boats before the plane shot over them.

He didn't think he was going to have much luck. The boats were crowded with either freight or passengers, and it was difficult to count heads.

In the back of his mind, he stored the message he'd gotten from Suretsov. Damned reactors! Jesus! It seemed like everything was coming to a head at once.

But Will Bricher was right. They had another job at the moment.

Dick Krebs, one of the techs who had come along to help in the search, asked him, "Where's this river go?"

"I think it eventually ends up at Macau."

Five minutes later, the river joined another coming out of the west. McKelvey banked a hard left at the confluence and followed the stream to the southeast.

"What's the river, Dusty?"

"Hongshui."

Stone almost said, "Gesundheit," but decided the moment wasn't right for levity.

He was thinking, though, that the closer Tan got to a border, the less need he had of Grant and Deng.

McKelvey must have been thinking the same thing. He called, "About ninety miles to the frontier, Mickey."

"Let's find 'em, for Christ's sake!"

"They may already be there," McKelvey said.

"Yeah."

The sampan was making about twenty miles an hour, Grant thought, moving faster than other boats and sampans headed in their same direction. Tan had been slowly picking up speed in the last hour, apparently with the smell of freedom and victory in his nostrils. Whenever Grant looked back at him at the tiller, five feet behind Grant, the man's face appeared to be a shade more lively.

Despite the fact that Tan must be tired, he didn't give much appearance of it. He had donned an old jacket that had been left in the boat to assume the identity of a river dweller. This river rat, however, had his Kalashnikov resting on the seat beside him, covered with a scrap of canvas; the Glock stuck in his waistband under the open front of the coat; and two grenades under a rag on top of his duffel bag, which was placed close to his feet. On the starboard side of the boat was a shallow wooden box with a few rusty tools in it. Several times, Grant had eyed an old pair of pliers, with something akin to deep yearning. He hoped Tan hadn't noted his interest.

Probably not. Tan kept a wary eye on Grant and Deng, but he also had to watch the marine traffic, as well.

There was a lot of shipping on the river, most of it small boats. A few larger boats towed barges loaded with wheat or rice. Once, they passed a tour ship headed upstream, sixty people gathered at the rails, faces shining in the sun. A hydrofoil gave them a wide berth as it overtook them and then sped out of sight ahead. The river was wide and the water appeared murky, dark with the pollution of centuries.

The old diesel engine droned on with an ear-numbing racket that precluded any conversation, even if Tan had allowed them to talk.

He wasn't exactly certain where they were, but judging from a vague memory of the area's map, he didn't think they had far to go before they reached Macau.

Grant didn't want to reach Macau. He'd been there before,

and didn't think much of it. More important, he thought, Tan would find hostages a burden in the Portuguese colony.

He assumed that a search for them was in progress. Any number of times, he'd seen low-flying aircraft working the region to the east. There were a few choppers, a couple of C-130s, some fighters—probably Shenyang F-12s—at below-normal altitudes. The problem was, they were in the wrong area, apparently searching on the assumption that Tan was headed for Guangzhou. The location of the abandoned Jimmy would have given them that clue.

He glanced over at Mai. She sat slumped on the thwart, her bound hands in her lap, a length of the wire securing them to an eyebolt near her seat. There was no back to the bench, and she rested sideways against the gunwale.

She was staring at him. The area under her eyes was smudged with old makeup and fatigue. Her hair was in disarray, windblown, and he found it appealing. What was left of her tailored suit would make a good stack of rags. Keeping his face forward, away from Tan's view, he gave her a smile.

Mai shook her head negatively. He hoped it wasn't in defeat, but she refused to smile. He wanted to hold her in his arms, to reassure her. He wiggled his thumb, aiming it upward. Then she gave him a half-smile.

Grant had the notion that, when he got out of this, he was going to be a hell of a lot less neutral, politically and socially. He had some things that needed to be said to Jiang, and to Mai.

That he was going to get them out of this predicament, he had no doubt. He had been working on it.

He'd been watching Tan for almost three days now, studying his moves, his demeanor. Grant thought the Chinese assassin was a great deal less confident in himself than he attempted to project. The man exerted his control over them with his weapons, but Grant read him as being more personally selfish than intrinsically evil. He was scared and trying to overcome it with bravado. He wasn't sure enough of himself to engage in any dialogue, afraid that Grant would talk him out of his grand plan, perhaps. Every verbal opening Grant had tried had been met with the demand for silence. He would never have gotten Tan to admit to the Harbin killings, but even without evidence, Grant was damned certain that Tan was responsible for them.

He wasn't making any mistakes on that score. Tan would kill if necessary. Grant could call up a clear image of the parking-lot guards, their throats slit. The poor damned farmer who'd been driving the Volvo truck was shot down without apparent remorse on the part of Tan. It was so matter-of-fact, it was chilling.

All of that only underscored the fact that Tan needed Grant and Deng as his hostages, at least until he reached the border.

Not gonna happen, asshole.

Grant had been setting him up, psychologically. He'd given him some lip from time to time, but had otherwise remained docile, doing what he was told, exhibiting his fear of a bullet. Grant knew guns, and he was rightfully afraid of them, especially in the hands of a man who seemed uneasy with them.

Grant had also been at work, mechanically. Flopped against the side of the boat, as if he were near the end of his emotional well-being, and to hide his activity from the man in the stern, he had been working on the wire. The thin, plastic-coated wire was nearly insurmountable when it was wrapped around his wrists ten or eleven times. Rotating his wrists in opposite directions, he had attempted to flex one or more of the strands enough to break it, but he hadn't succeeded. The four strands leading from his wrists to the eyebolt, about eight inches long, were a different story.

Nearly an hour before, awkwardly forcing his hands into a position near the tethering wires, using his thumbs to work one strand at a time back and forth—trying to keep his elbows from moving and giving him away, he had eventually snapped all four of the wires. Then he hid the fact by repositioning the wires in the eyebolt.

He couldn't separate his hands, and they felt numb because the wire had cut off some of the circulation, but he was free to leap around the boat.

Knowing that would draw fire from the AK-47. Judging by the way the man handled it, he didn't think Tan was very good with the assault weapon, but at close quarters, it wouldn't matter.

His major concern was Mai. If he started something that resulted in the sampan going bottom up, she'd be pulled under with it. He didn't want her breathing polluted water.

What he needed was a good diversion. He'd been watching for it, for anything, since the moment his tether was broken. If that hydrofoil had passed closer, rocking the sampan, he might have had a chance then.

That was history. He kept watching downriver, looking for a ship or another hydrofoil, and trying to think of a way he could use either if it appeared.

He heard his diversion before he saw it.

The increasing crescendo of turbofans.

Grant spun his head around to look beyond Tan, up the river.

He immediately picked out the distinctive head-on silhouette of a Learjet.

It was low, not more than three hundred feet off the river, and coming at them directly down the center of the river.

Three, four miles away.

Coming fast.

Tan had turned back to look at it, too.

Deng called to him above the roar of the diesel, "It is Dusty!"

Unfortunately, with Grant and Deng hidden under the canopy, Dusty McKelvey or anyone else on board wouldn't see this sampan as distinctive from hundreds of others on the river.

Grant stood up, turned, and stepped over the thwart.

"Hey, Tan! I've got to pee!"

Tan spun around, pulling the automatic pistol from his belt.

Stone had moved up to kneel on the deck between the pilot's seats, straining, with a pair of binoculars McKelvey had produced, to examine the boats plying the waterway. There were so damned many of them, and most of them appeared to have been built by the same boatbuilder, who had only one design in his head.

The antiquity of the design seemed in direct counterpoint to the sleek business jet he was aboard. The other counterpoint was the difference in speed. Even if they found the damned boat, he didn't know what an unarmed airplane travelling at two hundred miles an hour could do about it.

"Keep looking, Mickey," McKelvey said.

"I *am* looking, damn it!"

His eyes felt like they were crossing, trying to pick out the detail of tiny people on tiny boats. He kept scanning, moving the binoculars from side to side, peering a couple miles ahead. Most of the southbound boats were on the right side of the river, but some ignored that right-of-way. Occasionally, he lowered the binoculars and looked with his naked eye to make certain he wasn't missing a boat or two on the east side of the river, which didn't appear in the field of the binoculars.

The Cessna Citation Jimbo Bowie was flying had gone on to land at the airport, and McKelvey's copilot had switched the radio frequency to that used by the air-force planes. Those pilots were speaking Chinese, however, and the background chatter only disrupted Stone's concentration.

He trained the binoculars on a small cruiser, counted heads on the stern deck. Five. Moved on to another boat, a Chinese junk. Too big.

On to another.

A sampan.

Someone at the tiller, another standing in front of him. Couldn't make out the details.

"Slow down, Dusty."

"Ain't going to go slower, Mick."

"Shit! That's it! Put her on the deck."

"Goddamn it! Tell me where!"

Stone leaned over the throttle pedestal and pointed through the windscreen.

Tan Long's attention was divided between Grant's demand to urinate and the oncoming airplane.

He held the pistol on Grant's stomach. "How did you . . . ?"

Grant held his hands up so that Tan could see they were still wired together.

"Damn it! I've gotta unzip," he called over the diesel roar.

Tan's head whipped back toward the plane.

Grant was gratified to see that it was coming down. The pilot—whoever it was—had deployed the flaps to increase his lift and slow his speed. It looked as if it were on a landing approach to the river, with Grant at the head of the runway.

Less than a hundred feet off the water.

A mile away?

The perspective made it look as if the Lear barely cleared the masts of a southbound junk.

Then, it was really on the deck, bare feet separating it from the surface of the river.

Coming directly at them.

Tan looked back at him, waved the pistol menacingly.

"Sit down!"

Grant was outside the canopy, and he went to his knees right where he was.

The roar of the turbofans intensified.

Tan looked back again, then shoved the tiller hard to the right.

The sampan lurched over to the right as it turned left.

The plane tracked them.

It looked to Grant as if the nose of the Learjet was going to take the canopy off.

"What the hell are you doing!" Grant yelled, pulling the man's attention back to him.

In front of Tan, Grant bent over, as if terrified of the coming collision.

Tan's face paled. He looked back over the stern again.

Half-mile away?

No more time. With his toes lodged against the side of the sampan, Grant shoved forward and up, with all of the strength in his legs, thrusting his hands out in front of him.

His chest hit the tiller.

His clenched fists caught Tan's wrist as they chopped down.

Tan yelped, but the pistol flew from his numbed hand, clattering on the deck, and spilling into the open pit of the engine compartment.

In a panic, Tan swung hard with his right hand, catching Grant on the side of the head before he could get his feet under him. He went sideways and tumbled to the deck as Tan fell to his side, fighting to get the assault rifle freed from its covering chunk of canvas.

The sampan had taken on a starboard heel in the tight turn,

but as Tan released the tiller and it centered itself, now started to regain its equilibrium.

Grant rotated on his right hip, lashing out with his left leg. The flat of his shoe sole caught Tan in the knee, and he felt something snap.

Tan screamed.

And Grant found himself staring at the duffel bag in front of him. Quickly, he grabbed one of the grenades, fumbling with his bound hands, pulled it to his face, and yanked the pin with his teeth.

He held it high for Tan to see.

With intense pain constricting his face, Tan finally freed the rifle, aimed it at Grant, and . . .

The Learjet shot overhead so close that the shrill scream of the jet engines threatened to burst eardrums. The turbulence of its passing rocked the small boat violently.

In his fright, Tan almost slipped from his seat as he ducked his head. The muzzle of the assault rifle jerked upward, and a burst of three rounds made a feeble sound in the aftermath of the Learjet.

Grant got his right knee under him, leaned forward, grabbed Tan's waistband, and tumbled the grenade into his pants.

"Aiee!"

The man dropped the rifle, scrambling to grab himself; to find the grenade, ripping his pants apart.

Grant got his forearms under Tan's legs, and heaved upward.

Tan went over the back of the boat, splashing into the wake, disappearing for a moment below the surface.

Three seconds later, there was a dull thump.

And a small geyser.

Monday, September 19

"That wasn't very elegant," Grant told her as he kicked the gearshift to neutral and awkwardly reduced the throttle setting with the loose cable. "It wasn't nearly as graceful and heroic as I had planned."

"You were magnificent, Douglas."

He bent over to retrieve the rusty pliers from the toolbox, then moved back to her, stepped over the thwart, and knelt on the deck in front of her.

She held up her hands, the wire freed from its anchor.

He smiled at her, pleased. "Damn. I wish I'd known that. I was worried about you going down with the boat."

She had worried about it, too. Deng did not think she would swim well with her hands tied together.

Grant slipped the pliers between her wrists, pinching her skin, then snipped the first wire. Quickly, he unwound the wire.

The stinging, needlelike sensation in her hands was so welcome she almost cried. The boat was still rocking from side to side, slowing in the middle of the river, but she felt such a sense of relief that nothing bothered her.

She smiled up at him.

"I'm glad to see that smile. I was afraid you'd forgotten how."

"I followed your lead, Douglas. I thought we were supposed to appear beaten."

"That's right. We were."

"Give me those."

She took the pliers from him and tried to work them in between his hands as he spread his palms apart. It was a tight fit, but she got them in place, pressed the handles together, and watched as two wires parted. Then she unwound the rest of it.

He flexed his hands.

"I was worried about us," she confessed.

"Nonsense. I don't take well to captivity."

"You are being optimistic."

"I always try to be."

Almost unbidden, her arms rose and went around his neck.

"Thank you for being optimistic."

His hands pressed against her waist, balancing him as the sampan rocked in the wake of another boat. His eyes were locked on hers, and she saw something new and ageless in them. She had seen it before, had never acknowledged it.

He leaned toward her, and their lips met.

She felt suddenly feverish, pressed forward, tasted the salt on his face, absorbed the soft firmness of his lips. Her heartbeat increased.

When they parted, Grant said, "That makes it all worth it, Mai."

"Douglas . . ."

She was suddenly aware of people chattering, and she looked back to see several boats gathered around them. Several men asked her what had happened.

The sound of an approaching helicopter added to the din of the inquiries.

"What do I tell them, Douglas?"

"Everything's all right."

Grant rose from his knees, grimacing a bit. His activity must have aggravated his cracked ribs and bad shoulder. He stepped to the back as she told the drivers of the small fleet accumulating that there was nothing to concern them.

They were suspicious of the *gweilo,* however, and stared at him with open hostility. She told the man in the closest sampan, "He is known as the Green-Eyed Devil. He follows the Mandate of Heaven."

That did not appease the man, but by then, Grant had dug around in Tan's duffel bag and backpack. He came up with bundles wrapped in paper and slowly unwrapped one. She saw that the packaging was a sheet used for a big-character poster. It held several bundles of yuan notes. Grant grinned to himself and started tossing the rubber-banded bundles of currency to the other boats. He opened another package and tossed those bundles, too.

The occupants of the other boats yelped with glee, scrambling over their decks to retrieve the money. Some of the packages contained American currency, and Grant dumped that back into the duffel bag.

"We'll let the cops have the U.S. currency and the ordnance," he said. "They like to have evidence to play with."

She thought he enjoyed throwing the money around. These people would certainly remember the Green-Eyed Devil.

Grant took a look at a couple of the big-character posters, folded them, and stuck them in his pocket. When he was out of Chinese notes, he waved at the other boats, then engaged the gear and advanced the throttle. The boat moved slowly away from the potential, and now rewarded, Samaritans.

Deng got up, her back stiff from sitting on the hard-plank bench for so long, and moved back to sit beside Grant.

"They will pray for your return tonight," she told him.

"I'm just hoping they'll buy TV sets, Mai."

She laughed, relieved that she could. "Where do we go now, Douglas?"

"Straight to shore, I think."

He pointed upward, and she saw the Learjet circling them, and an army helicopter approaching. Dusty McKelvey must have called for the helicopter.

She waved at the jet, and it waggled its wings, then streaked to the northeast.

The helicopter divined their purpose and circled back toward the shore to land.

"Before we get bogged down in investigations, I'd better tell you I'm in love."

She took his left hand in hers and rubbed the wrist, trying to restore the circulation, staring down at the creases left by the wires on his wrist.

"I am in love, too, Douglas."

"With me, I hope."

"Mama will shoot me."

"She can't be nastier than Tan Long."

"Yes, she can be."

The helicopter settled to the tarmac behind the terminal, and as soon as the rotors began to slow, a swarm of people rushed forward to meet the passengers.

Vladimir Suretsov trailed along with them. He had his recorder out and his notebook ready. No matter what else was going on, a story was a story.

A military officer stepped down from the passenger compartment first, then turned back to help Deng Mai to the ground. Grant followed, but wasn't given any assistance by the officer.

Bricher and Stone were the second to greet them. Though he had talked to Stone on the phone, Suretsov had not met the man until Dusty McKelvey landed. Suretsov had gone around, getting everyone's name, along with the correct spellings.

Diantha Parker raced ahead of everyone, grabbed Deng and gave her a big hug, then transferred her attention to Grant, hesitated, then threw her arms around him.

"God, I'm happy to see you both. You look marvelous!" Parker was crying.

"I think, Diantha," Deng said, "you have been drinking again."

"And I think, Mai, we'll steal some more of the boss's booze."

"That is a welcome thought, Diantha."

"God, Diantha," Grant told her, "who's running the empire?"

"To hell with the empire," she said.

Bricher said, "You don't know how glad I am to see you, Doug." He threw his arm around Grant's shoulders and gave him a big hug.

Grant said, "Ow."

Bricher said, "Oops. Sorry."

Stone told Deng, "You're a sight for my eyes, sore or not, Director. And Doug, I thought I warned you about hanging out with department-store buyers."

Deng said, "Hello, Mickey. I cannot be a sight. I have been in these clothes far too long."

"We'll throw those out and get you new ones," Stone said.

She was indeed a damsel in distress, Suretsov thought. Her skirt was torn in several places, and her blouse had been ripped at the side seam, revealing the bra beneath it. There was a patina of dirt and grease smeared over her clothing and her skin. And with all of that, Suretsov was reminded of Gina Lollobrigida in any of her movies; no matter the dire situation, her beauty shone through. All of the men around him, he was certain, were intensely aware of the luscious, if grimy, curves.

Grant's appearance was no better. His jeans were torn at the knee, and his sport shirt had lost several buttons. He looked ragged and tired. The stubble on his face had trapped dirt.

Bricher and Crest led Deng to one of the utility vehicles, which had been driven right onto the apron, and helped her into the backseat.

Suretsov followed Stone and Grant to another truck and crawled into the back with them.

Somebody got into the front and started the engine. Two more people crammed themselves into the front passenger seat. The atmosphere was one of lively banter. Suretsov understood a little of what Grant's employees thought of him.

Grant eyed the recorder.

"Jesus, Vladimir! Already?"

"It is my job, Doug."

"I haven't even briefed the cops yet."

"All the better. That will make it really exclusive." Suretsov grinned.

"I've got one question, first," Stone said. "By the time we circled back to the boat, Tan was gone. Where did he go?"

"Over the side," Grant said.

"So, are they out there on the river, looking for him?"

"He shouldn't be hard to find. He'll be in a lot of pieces."

"What?"

"He had a frag grenade in his pants when he went over."

"Shit!" Stone said.

Suretsov tried to grasp the image, then decided he didn't want it.

While the driver fought his way through the traffic, following the other Shanghai Star vehicles, Grant told them about the ordeal he and Deng had endured. "To me, at least, Tan seemed to be a lost, lonely, and misguided man. I don't think he was cut out for the role he was playing."

"Tell me again, Doug, how you killed him."

Grant looked at Suretsov for a long minute. "I wanted him alive, Vladimir. I wanted to know who was paying him."

"But—"

"Let's just say he was juggling a grenade, lost his balance, and fell overboard."

Stone watched them both, waiting for Suretsov's reaction.

"That is what you will tell the police?"

"That's it."

"That is how I will write it, then."

Grant turned to Stone. "Mickey, where the hell is the hotel?"

"We aren't going to the hotel, Doug." Stone looked at his watch. "Will tells me we're going on the air in an hour and fifteen minutes."

"But what about the reactor?" Suretsov said.

"What reactor?" Grant asked him.

When they reached the Guangzhou Facility, Stone found a secretary, gave her a thick wad of yuan, and sent her out to get a change of clothing for Grant and Deng.

Mai headed for a rest room, and Grant found one labelled *nance* in pinyin.

He emptied his pockets into one basin: wallet, keys, change, penknife, money clip with a few notes, the posters he'd found wrapping the currency. He stripped off his clothes and dumped them in the trash barrel, and took a standing sponge bath. Stone helped him unwrap the bandage around his chest.

"You want me to find a replacement, Doug?"

"I'll skip it, Mickey. It feels good to breathe. Suppose anyone's got a razor?"

Stone went out and came back with a rechargeable electric razor. While he ran the razor over his face, Stone caught him up on the news, finishing with Bricher's interpretation of the sudden decision to move ahead with the system test. "There's some big demonstration planned by the People's Underground for one o'-clock. Will thinks that Jiang is trying to divert attention from it."

"I hope he's successful," Grant said, bending over the sink to wash his hair with soap. "This month has been bad enough without capping it off with a riot."

Crest pushed open the door and stuck his head in. "Doug, there's some inspector out here who wants to talk to you."

"Tell him that, until we're on the air, I'm tied up. Probably a couple hours. In fact, Maynard, give him a seat where he can watch whatever happens. If we have another disaster, he can arrest us all."

By the time he'd rough-dried his hair with paper towels, the secretary was back with shorts, jeans, and a blue shirt with a button-down collar. He dressed quickly, retrieving his wallet, keys, and change from the adjacent washbasin. He stuck the folded posters in his hip pocket, then bent over to pull his running shoes on and tie them. The shoes were filthy. Bending over didn't help his chest much, either, but he felt as if he was through with the bandages. The shoulder was probably a few days behind in its recuperation.

He and Stone stepped back in the hall to find Deng emerging from the women's room, the one marked *nuce.* Her face was scrubbed clean, she had combed out her hair, and she was wearing new denims and a pale-yellow blouse. They fit her like they were supposed to fit.

"You were able to wash your hair," she accused.

"You look marvelous."

"I do not. My purse is in the truck, wherever the truck is."

"Your whole laboratory's gone, then," Stone said. "However, I don't see as how you need it."

"Thank you, Mickey, but we need to find Will."

"In the monitoring center, I suspect."

"Or we could just skip the whole damned thing, and catch a plane for Bali," Grant suggested.

She smiled, but he didn't think she took the suggestion seriously.

They took an elevator up two floors and found Bricher at a console in the monitor center surrounded by Chinese and American engineers, and telephones. Mai went right to a console and called Shanghai.

"Mickey," Bricher said, "you want to track down Lefant and find out how he's coming along?"

"Will do." Stone headed for another phone.

Grant heard Mai talking to her mother. He assumed she was relating her return to safety, and not her new relationship with Grant. He saw Suretsov and Crest in one corner of the room, and he knew what their topic was likely to be. Well, he'd see if he could do anything about it.

He backed out of the center, crossed the hall, and looked into an office. It took him a second to recall the name of the young woman. She was a software specialist.

"Georgia, can I borrow your office for a few minutes?"

She looked up. "Oh, sure, Doug. I'm happy you're back, by the way."

"Not half as happy as I am."

"I bet." She hopped out of her chair, all energy and zest that Grant didn't think he'd ever match again, and left him alone.

He sat in the cushioned chair, feeling as if he could go right to sleep in it, and dialled the number for the defense ministry in Beijing. He asked for Shao.

"Minister Shao has flown to Shanghai, Mr. Grant."

"Do you have a telephone number?"

While he dialled the new number, Grant checked the clock on the wall: 11:40 A.M. Twenty minutes until Deng once again appeared on five thousand television sets.

It took awhile. The man who answered the phone had to find an English-speaker, then the next man had to transfer the call to some special number.

"Mr. Grant, I am pleased at the outcome of this episode. I have a sketchy report from a helicopter pilot, but one day soon, you and I will have to sit down together so you can tell me what really occurred."

"That may be a short conversation, Minister."

"I believe not. I recall your telling me that you did not relish captivity."

"This one took longer. Look, Minister, is it pretty tense over there?"

"One can feel the tension in the air. Our estimate is that over thirty thousand people have gathered in the park, and more are arriving."

"And the army?" Grant asked, fearful of another Tiananmen Square.

"I have alerted the brigade here, but not yet ordered any action."

"Tanks and the whole enchilada?"

"Enchilada?"

"It's a Spanish word. An American idiom."

"Yes, the whole enchilada. I do not like this, Mr. Grant, but the Premier and many of the ministers are fearful of allowing this to proceed much further."

"Why are you waiting then?"

"Your Mr. Wickersham has placed nearly thirty television sets around the park. We are waiting to see if the broadcast will possibly defuse the situation."

"What about your local Shanghai television stations? Are they covering this?"

"Ah . . . no."

"Why don't you get them out there with a couple cameras? We'll put these people on the screen and let them look at themselves."

"It is not a good idea," Shao said. "Knowing they have the publicity may excite them to extremes."

"Or show them that you're not afraid of criticism. Of letting the nation judge your tolerance."

Shao sighed. "I will order the cameras out, but I will have to talk to others."

"I understand. Now, the reason I'm calling. Do you remember our discussion about the nuclear plants?"

"I do."

"Suretsov's information has been reviewed by Russian scientists, who think the reactors, particularly the one at Lhasa, are in imminent danger of going into meltdown."

"This is true?"

"I don't know crap about it, Minister. I don't think, however, that Suretsov is a man I'd ever distrust. I wouldn't want to take the chance that he's wrong."

"He has shown his information to Minister Pai?"

"Pai won't talk to him. Pai claims everything is hunky-dory, yet he won't allow the Atomic Energy people in Vienna to examine the plants."

Grant heard another long exhalation of air. "This may be ticklish, Mr. Grant. There is a large bloc of people who are very proud of those reactors. Pai has substantial support for the program, and he will have the backing of many. I do not see intervention taking place quickly. And in any event, with the crisis in Fu Xing Park, I will not raise the issue until we have some stability."

"Minister—"

"That is all I can do. We will have dinner next week."

Shao hung up.

"Shit."

Grant got up and went back across the hall. He watched the feverish activity. The way Bricher handled telephones would drive Grant nuts in about five minutes.

Nine minutes to go.

Crossing the room to Stone, he tapped him on the shoulder.

Stone looked back at him.

"Still have Lefant on the line?"

"Yup."

"Let me talk to him." Grant took the phone. "Pierre, this is Doug."

"Stone told me of your escape. I am glad to hear of it."

"Thanks. You know what's going on in the park, right?"

"I do. The reports from observers are not good. The mob is unruly and hostile. They are not waiting until their announced time of one o'clock to begin."

"You're getting reports?"

"Curt Wickersham has a number of people out there, taking care of the television sets. They have portable radios."

"Okay, good. Look, I think Shao's going to allow one of the TV stations to cover this thing. I need to have you ready to accept a local feed and put it on Channel Two."

"I can do that."

"And tell Curt to have his people at Fu Xing Park tune those sets to Channel Two. We'll let them see themselves as stars."

"Is this a good idea, Doug?"

"You're in good company. Shao has the same reservations."

Grant was a bit surprised at Lefant's immediate acquiescence. The man sounded somewhat defeated. He handed the phone back to Stone and said, "Mickey, get Suretsov and meet me across the hall."

Maynard Crest followed along, and the four of them assembled in an office, which was too small for four big men.

Grant related his conversation with Shao.

Suretsov did not look happy.

"Vladimir, how much faith are you putting in the report of your scientists?"

"Russia has good scientists," Suretsov said, defensive.

Grant could acknowledge that to some extent, but he wasn't looking for a debate on how much technology from foreign research and development had been acquired by the KGB for the Soviet Union.

"Convince me," he said.

"According to Fedorchuk, four of these men wrote a treatise on problems at Chernobyl *before* the accident occurred there. The report was buried."

"Shit, that's good enough for me," Stone said.

"What do you think, Maynard?" Grant asked.

The salesman said, "I only know enough to be worried. But until I goose Lefant out of his chair, I'm at your service, Doug."

"Well, Shao isn't going to do anything right away. What do you want to do, Vladimir?"

"I do not know what action to take, Doug. I know they must be shut down."

"I can turn the suckers off," Stone said, "if I can get to the controls."

Grant picked up the phone, called the general aviation section, and had McKelvey paged.

"Dusty, want some combat pay?"

"Fuckin'-A!"

"Get the Citation ready."

Grant had to dig out his wallet and find his list of numbers before dialling the next one. It took only two minutes to run down his man.

"General Hua, this is Doug Grant."

"Yes, Mr. Grant. Besides congratulating you on your recent actions, what can I do for you?"

"What do you think of radiation poisoning?"

"I do not like to think of it."

Grant told his story briefly, including Shao's reservations, then added, "General, I'm going to read a list to you. I'd like to have you think about it quickly, then turn your back on me."

After a moment, Hua said, "What is the list?"

Grant enumerated the items he'd been thinking about.

Hua hung up on him.

Fu Xing Park, created in 1909 and not far from the city center, was an appropriate site, Chiang thought. The First National Congress of the Communist Party of China had been held nearby, and it was only fitting that a counterrevolutionary movement should be initiated in the same location as a symbol of the revolution.

This assembly was not of her creation, of course, but since it was here and now, she felt as if she should involve herself in it. Jiang Guofeng had effectively disowned her, anyway. With the cessation of his "dues," paid so that she would maintain a moderate stance, she was going to have to generate an income in some fashion. This could be the start of a much greater role for her.

The noise created by the swelling crowds had alarmed the animals in the small zoo. Over the dull roar of the mob, could be heard the squeals and brays and honks of restless and frightened creatures. That, too, was apt, she thought. Let the whole world scream its indignation, and cry out for freedom.

She even caressed a momentary thought of invading the zoo and freeing the inmates, but knew it would be fruitless. A large contingent of policemen had surrounded the zoo.

The park was lushly overgrown with huge shade trees and foliage, a favorite spot for a cool walk in the heat of day. The normal strollers had, however, been chased away by Huzhou's fanatics.

She did not know where they had come from. The majority were young. There were students of secondary- and collegiate-age groups. There were obvious gang members. In smaller knots, she noted older persons—thirties, even fifties—and she supposed they were sincerely supportive of the cause. For the most part, though, she interpreted the rowdy youngsters as simply looking for an excuse to demonstrate a rebellious urge, while hidden in the anonymity of a monstrous mob.

Chiang could not count them.

The park was overflowing with humanity. They spilled into the streets, went shoulder to shoulder through the flower and shrubbery beds. Somewhere near the center of the park, a public-address system was attempting to capture attention, but was not succeeding well. The rebel call of youth was strident and cacophonous. Alcohol in many forms was changing hands steadily. So were drugs, she noted. This was viewed by most as a party.

The police were in evidence, but understated. They had blocked off the streets around the park to traffic, as the young people took them away from the automobiles. They were in riot gear—clear plastic shields, batons, rifles slung over shoulders, gas masks hanging around their necks, but were making no demands as yet. She saw no evidence of army units.

She had to fight her way across the street, and upon entering the park, met an almost solid mass of sweating flesh. She pulled unknown shoulders, shoved elbows, slipped past, ducked under arms, wrestling her way toward the infrequent blare of the PA system. Someone grabbed her breast, and she turned and slugged the bastard with her fist. His eyes were so dazed already from some near overdose of narcotics that her attack meant nothing to him.

It took her fifteen minutes to battle her way to a makeshift stand erected on the grass. Across the front of it blazed *her* banner: THE PEOPLE'S UNDERGROUND.

Her banner.

Huzhou paced on the small deck, shouting into a handheld microphone.

Her assistants attended him, passing out handbills, raising fists in salute to his oratory.

Her assistants.

". . . THE DETERMINATION OF THE PEOPLE WILL BE HEARD," he yelled into the microphone, and the amplifiers magnified it into booming phrases, which erupted from the five speakers and pounded the eardrums, heating the blood, accelerating pulses. "NO LONGER CAN WE ALLOW THE GREEDY MINORITY IN BEIJING TO MANAGE OUR LIVES! BIG BROTHER WILL NOT . . . CANNOT! . . . HIDE THE WORLD FROM US!"

Chiang knew she had lost.

Everything was gone. The organization was now Huzhou's. It was likely to be penniless, without the hidden resources provided by Jiang, but still, it was no longer hers.

Jiang had cast her aside, and now Huzhou did the same. She did not know how she would live.

"Set us free!" intoned Huzhou.

"SET US FREE!" the nearby crowd responded.

"Again! Set us free!"

"SET US FREE!"

"Give us the world!"

"GIVE US THE WORLD!"

By the time she made her way back to the street and across it, the chant was rolling through the park, screamed by thousands of voices.

She walked away with shoulders slumped, her head down. When she found a side street, she turned into it and kept walking. She did not know where she was going. Vaguely in the direction of Old Town.

Behind her, the chant grew louder and stronger. Loose windows rattled in their frames as she passed them.

Two blocks away, she turned a corner.

And there they were.

Tanks and armored personnel carriers.

Dozens of them lined up in the center of the street. Soldiers in helmets, carrying assault weapons, stood in ranks alongside them.

She hurried on, homeless for the moment, but not at the center of the coming bloodbath.

Once again, Will Bricher was on the telephone to every Shanghai Star facility in the country. He had Curt Wickersham in Shanghai managing the central console.

He was talking to Wheeler in Harbin when he heard Wickersham's exclamation from another phone: "What! Goddamn it!"

"Hold on," he told Wheeler and switched phones. "What's going on, Curt?"

"One of my teams trying to set up a TV at the park was just overrun."

"Anyone hurt?"

"No. But they trashed the TV."

"Well, hell, just send another one out. We can't worry about it now."

Bricher looked at the clock on the wall: 11:59.

"What's it look like, Curt?"

"Everything on-line. I've got so many green lights, I'm turning pale."

"Good." He dropped that phone and grabbed another. "Mr. Lefant?"

"I am here."

"Run 'em."

He heard Lefant giving an order to someone, then: "Mr. Bricher, all channels are broadcasting."

"Thanks." Monitors on the wall in front of him flickered to life.

"Will!" Georgia yelled. "Grab line nine."

"Can't."

"It's the defense minister."

"Don't go away, Wheeler," he said into the phone, then punched nine on the console. "Will Bricher, Minister Shao."

"I could not reach Mr. Grant."

Bricher looked around the room, suddenly aware that some familiar faces were missing. Stone was supposed to be here, for one. The correct monitors on the wall were all showing Deng Mai's welcoming speech. He wondered how many people were watching. On such short notice, they hadn't been able to notify all of their test population of the broadcast.

"It's a little hectic, Minister. I don't know where he's gone."

"I am, Mr. Bricher, at my last ditch. Will you see that the local television broadcasts are aired?"

"Happy to, Minister. Bye."

He grabbed Lefant's phone. "You still there?"

"I am here."

"Interrupt Channel Two with the local Shanghai feed."

"Very well."

Two minutes into the broadcast, with no porno flicks showing up on any of the monitors, Bricher figured the Shanghai Star network was running smoothly.

Something else might well blow up, somewhere else, but he'd finally accomplished his job.

Jiang Guofeng, along with Minister Shao, Minister of Materials Peng Zedong, and several other members of the Information Advisory Committee, were sitting in a military-command van parked next to a police-command truck on Zhaojiabang Road, three blocks from Fu Xing Park.

The Premier was on an open line to a general seated at one of the telephone consoles. Jiang supposed that the Premier had a roomful of close advisors present, as well as his television set.

One of the monitors in the van was connected to a microwave antenna provided by Shanghai Star and displayed the live coverage on Channel Two. The news reporter had abruptly supplanted the last half of the introduction by Deng Mai which, as far as Jiang was concerned, was not a loss.

The reporter was impressed with his newfound fame. Talking over the pictures, he kept reminding his audience that this was a ". . . newscast of historical importance, being broadcast simultaneously to all parts of the People's Republic over the new Shanghai Star network."

Those in the van, including several generals and police commanders, were less interested in the dialogue than in the images captured by the television camera, which was obviously located on a rooftop across Chongqing Road from the park. The thickly forested area prevented the camera's eye from seeing all that was taking place, but as it roved, it halted on clearings, on the street, on young people climbing into the trees.

The whole gathering was disgusting, Jiang thought. These young people could better serve their country by engaging in productive work. And when the camera caught five-second snapshots of citizens who were obviously thirty, forty, or fifty years old, he felt momentary disquiet. No one in the van was directing the aiming of the camera, so they had to rely on the discretion of the cameraman.

They sat on the stools and leaned forward to watch, and to hear.

Above it all, heard over the television audio, as well as directly from the street through the open door of the van, was the chanting of nearly forty thousand people. The chant would die away, the young man on the rostrum near the center of the park would bark for a while, then the chant would resume.

No one knew who the young man was. Jiang was mildly relieved that his cousin was not present.

One of the police commanders was called to the doorway of the van, and when he came back, he said, "One of our undercover operatives has just learned that the leader is apparently a man named Huzhou. Does anyone know the name?"

No one did.

The camera panned to the intersection of Chongqing and Fu Xing roads. A pickup truck was parked there, with a television set in the back. They could not see the picture, but it was obviously the same view they were seeing. Gradually, a few of the rally-goers gravitated toward it and began watching. The crowd around the truck grew steadily.

"How many of those are there?" Peng asked.

"I do not know," Shao told him. "Wickersham was going to try to get around thirty, perhaps more."

"For this mob, we would need a thousand sets," Peng said.

The camera eye suddenly jumped to the north. A fistfight had broken out among twenty or thirty youths.

"That is it!" Jiang said. "We must act, before this spreads. Send the troops."

"Not just yet," Shao said. "A few bloody noses will not hurt us."

The rioters were mostly drunk. Their wild swings failed to inflict damage. The fighting died away, leaving five or six teenagers sitting stupidly in the gutter.

Shao went off to take the telephone line to the Premier from the general. Jiang watched him as he attempted to persuade the Premier from ordering the soldiers in.

Shao was becoming entirely too soft.

The view on the screen went black for an instant, then rebounded with another image from a different point of view. Another camera had been set up. It took Jiang a few seconds to orient himself, realizing that the camera view was now from the south, still across from the park and on another roof.

A new narrator took over. "We have just gotten into position. Below us, on the street, about five hundred people are trying to get a look at a television set placed on the sidewalk. Hello, everyone! Can you see yourselves?"

The camera tracked across the street, then zoomed in on the center of the park.

"There!" Jiang called. "That is the traitor!"

The man marching back and forth across his stage was young, wearing a black jacket, with long hair caught under a leather thong. He waved his microphone around, spoke heatedly into it.

Turned, came back toward the camera, unaware of it.

"Oh, no!" Peng yelped.

"What is it, Zedong?" Jiang asked.

"My son!"

Pierre Lefant stayed in the master production room, pacing up and down behind the men and women manning the consoles. Frequently, he checked his watch, as if he could not trust the clock on the wall.

Having viewed many demonstrations in the streets of Paris, Lefant was not alarmed by the current situation in Fu Xing Park. He knew, of course, that it could turn ugly at any moment. What was most interesting was that it was being shown at all on Channel Two.

His agreement with Jiang ordained that MBL would never air any footage that was in the least way detrimental to the administration, to the Party, or of a political nature. And here, on the first day, was a live broadcast of political dissension.

He did not know what was taking place among the politicos, but if this newscast was any indicator, he estimated that Jiang was losing, if not control, at least his edge of power. And with its loss, the agreement would also deteriorate. The Russian correspondent could be partially to blame. His snooping about for names might have unnerved Jiang and his brother-in-law.

He could no longer worry about Jiang and Pai. They had, after all, accepted their payments—their shares of Nuclear Power Limited—cheerfully. Lefant had lived up to his part of the bargain. He understood that Jiang was trying to control the extent of the damage. The death of Sytenko was an example of that, and he assumed that Jiang had ordered Wen Yito to take care of it. The scenario that was frightening, of course, was that, if Jiang thought that Lefant could undermine his standing, he might well send Wen to visit Lefant.

And Lefant had his own problems. He had checked with Jacques again this morning, and the attorney confirmed that the Paris prosecutor was seeking an indictment against him for fraud. Margot had filed suit to claim half of his Cannes house, and any other assets he might have hidden. Plus damages. Damages to what? Her frivolous reputation?

He had known it was serious when he called his broker to sell off his holdings, especially the Nuclear Power Limited stock, and discovered that his accounts in the name of Jean Legrand had been frozen.

"Is there anything wrong, Mr. Lefant?"

"What? Oh, no, mademoiselle. Continue what you are doing."

Lefant found that he was motionless in the middle of the room, staring over a young woman's shoulder at her monitor. A chef was preparing a chicken for some fabulous recipe on the culinary-arts program.

He turned and headed for the door, stopping to tell Chabeau, "Marc, I am going to rest for a couple of hours. You are in charge."

"Of course."

As the glass door closed behind him, he wondered if Chabeau knew how a couple of hours could stretch into weeks and months and years.

In his office, he unlocked the security box in the bottom drawer of his desk and withdrew his collection of Foreign Exchange Certificates. Rifling through them, he estimated they would exchange at the current rates for nearly 20,000 francs. He shoved them into his jacket pocket, next to his passport. There was also an eight-millimeter videocassette in the lockbox, and he transferred it to his jacket pocket.

He almost left without telephoning, then decided he would have to make at least a short call.

"Pierre!" Yvonne Deng said. "Have you seen the television?"

"Too many of them, my dear."

"I mean, the riot!"

"It is not yet a riot, Yvonne."

"But it is dangerous."

"These things happen all the time. It will resolve itself. You will see."

"I hope you are right."

"Of course I am. Yvonne, I am calling to tell you I must leave Shanghai for a few days."

"A few days! But, Pierre, we were planning dinner tonight. We must celebrate Mai's escape!"

"It is a problem with my ex-wife. I am certain it will prove fruitless, but I must attend to it."

"What day will you return? I will look forward to it with yearning!"

"A week? I do not yet know."

"But you will call me?"

"Certainly."

If they had telephones in Kenya, or wherever it was that his airplane tickets would take him.

Certainly not France.

Lefant left his office, headed for the elevators.

He paused in the reception room, thinking. In Kenya, he would not need insurance. And some people needed deserved retribution for the shabby way they had treated him.

Withdrawing the videocassette from his pocket, he handed it to Sung Wu's granddaughter. "Take this up to Director Deng's office."

"She is not there, Mr. Lefant."

"Then give it to Miss Jiangyou."

Guangzhou to Xichang in Sichuan Province was a 750-mile hop. Dusty McKelvey risked the engines of his Citation at top revolutions and better than 400-miles per hour to put them down on the rocket center's airstrip two hours after leaving Quangzhou. It was 2:40 in the afternoon.

The Citation had a full passenger load of eight. In addition to Stone, Grant, Suretsov, and Crest, McKelvey had recruited four of his pilots. He and Jimbo Bowie were in the flight compartment.

Stone had had some time to consider the kinds of adventure he got himself into. This was something Errol Flynn might have done, he thought.

Flynn probably wouldn't have called his girlfriend before embarking on the adventure, however.

"Meg, I've got to run out of town for a bit."

"You're avoiding discussing the report, right?"

"What report?"

"The one my brother just faxed to me."

"Ah! Did I pass?"

"Do you realize you've had four speeding tickets in five years?"

"I vaguely remember paying them. I'm a good driver, Meg, just a fast one."

"You told me you didn't like fast cars."

"Not the Indy kind. What else did you learn about me?"

"Nothing. The lieutenant approves."

"That's a relief."

"Hurry back. We've got things to do."

The flight to Xichang went swiftly, what with Stone's fantasies about Naylor's "things to do."

When McKelvey backed off on the power, Stone peered through his window and found that the airstrip was deserted. Searching the skies, he didn't see one airplane. He heard McKelvey calling for air control, but no one responded to him.

The pilot leaned back and called through the open door, "What now, Doug?"

"Go ahead and land, Dusty. I think they don't want to acknowledge we're here."

Together, McKelvey and Bowie deployed the flaps and landing gear, and brought the plane in smoothly. As soon as they were down, slowing rapidly, Grant crawled out of his seat and went to crouch in the doorway to the flight deck.

"Right there," Grant said. "See it?"

"I see it," Bowie said.

Stone didn't see it.

Near the end of the runway, McKelvey spun the plane around in a 180-degree turn and stopped at the left edge of the runway.

Grant undogged the door and pushed it open.

"Come on, Mickey."

Stone scrambled out of his seat to follow Grant down the airstair.

It was hot in Xichang. The dry air hit him in the face like he remembered deplaning in Phoenix, Arizona.

Sitting in the weeds at the edge of the runway were two duffel bags. Grant grabbed one, and Stone hefted the other. It just about pulled him off-balance, a hell of a lot heavier than he had expected.

The two of them ran back to the plane and clambered up the steps. Stone heaved his bag into the aisle and turned back to pull the door up.

"Hit it, Dusty!" Grant called.

McKelvey ran the throttles up, and the Cessna accelerated down the strip.

Stone sat sideways in his seat and unzipped the duffel bag.

Reaching inside, he pulled out one towel-wrapped object.

"What the hell's this, Doug?"

Grant had the other bag open, retrieving something that looked suspiciously, to a novice such as Stone, like a grenade.

"What you've got, Mickey, is a Kalashnikov AK-74 assault rifle. What I've got is a stun grenade."

"Jesus," Stone said. "It must be nice to have friends in high places."

"In military high places, yes. Just remember, we were never here."

Grant looked pointedly at Suretsov, who was in the seat behind Stone.

"I have been asleep for the last three hours," the Russian said.

Nuclear reactors don't explode. The superheated steam they generate expands and blows the container apart—if the container isn't strong enough. Then the fissile material takes about 30,000 years to cool off.

But they don't blow up.

Grant kept reminding himself of that.

As they cleaned and assembled the weapons in the cabin, which had become pretty tiny for eight big men, Suretsov told them, "There are more deaths attributed to mining uranium than to accidents in nuclear plants. The pollutants from coal-fired generating plants kill more people than do nuclear reactors. But these reactors . . ."

"I don't care about the process so much," Crest said, "as the results. If they're losing coolant, then that allows the core to heat up?"

"Correct," Suretsov said.

"But the steam is supposed to be contained in the reactor vessel in the event of an accident?"

"Again, correct."

"If it's built right," Stone said. "I only saw the Lhasa plant, and it didn't look right to me. I can't say it any better than that—it didn't look right."

Suretsov and Crest had both refused a weapon, Suretsov because he said he was a noncombatant and Crest because he thought he'd shoot his foot off. But Suretsov was armed with a 35-millimeter camera and Crest was carrying a video camera. Grant wanted a photographic record of this foray.

"So the steam escapes vents to reduce the buildup of pressure," Crest went on, "and it's radioactive steam. That's what happened at Chernobyl and Three Mile Island."

Suretsov nodded.

"Well, I'm glad I came along, but I don't know what the hell we're doing."

"Mickey's going to shut it down," Grant said.

"Just like that? No one's going to object?"

"That's why we're carrying firepower," one of the pilots said.

"We don't want to use it, however," Grant cautioned. "We just want to command enough respect to get in there."

He began feeding 5.45-millimeter rounds from a box on the floor into one of his magazines.

"When I visited the Lhasa site," Suretsov said, "there was but one guard on the gate. We should not encounter heavy resistance."

"Good," Grant said. "My first and only order is, nobody shoots anyone. Crank 'em off skyward if you have to, but let's avoid killing anyone."

"And if they shoot at us?" a pilot in a backseat asked.

"If you know what you're doing, shoot to scare."

"I know what I'm doing."

Looking back at the grizzled veteran, Grant believed him.

"Hey, pilot!" Grant called. "Where are we?"

"At least an hour out, Doug. It's a six-hundred-and-eighty-mile jaunt."

Grant loaded another magazine and decided two would be enough.

McKelvey's people looked like they knew what they were doing. They were all combat vets of one kind or another. He'd issued them each an AK-74 and four stun grenades. Stone was still fumbling with his weapon. With luck, he'd never find the safety. And he was just as happy that Crest and Suretsov had elected to go unarmed.

He checked the safety of his own weapon, though it was not loaded, then propped it against the fuselage wall. He turned and settled himself in his seat, prepared to wait out the next hour without worrying about it too much.

"Doug!" McKelvey called. "Phone for you."

The set was mounted on the bulkhead in front of him, and Grant lifted it from the hook.

"Grant."

"This is Shao Tsung, Mr. Grant. I had a great deal of trouble locating you."

"Sorry about that, Minister."

"Where are you?"

Grant figured lying wouldn't help his cause. "En route to Lhasa. I want to see that reactor for myself."

"I would not bother."

"Oh?"

"The Lhasa reactor just went into runaway meltdown."

"Goddamn."

"Yes. The personnel have been evacuated, but they managed to withdraw the fuel rods from the core before they ran."

"The containment vessel?"

"Burst. The entire vicinity is irradiated."

Grant felt sick. He didn't know what the environmental conditions were like at the moment, but if there was any wind at all, the radiation could spread over thousands of square miles before it settled.

"Winds?" he asked Shao.

"Out of the south, but moderate. The city should be protected, at least for the time being. The experts"—his tone suggested they were less than expert—"feel that the danger zone will encompass an area of thirty kilometers by eighty kilometers."

"But they haven't been there to check?"

"No. They are guessing."

"People are going to die, Minister."

"Yes, that is true. Over many months, I fear. I have ordered army and air-force units into the region to assist in evacuation and containment."

A little after the fact.

"And the other sites? You're shutting them down?"

"I have no control, Mr. Grant. Minister Pai insists this is an isolated incident. He will not close the Chengdu site or stop the construction elsewhere. Qinghai is scheduled to activate this week."

"Minister, you're going to have repetitions of Lhasa all over the country."

"Mr. Grant, this radio frequency is not secure. Let me say that balances are delicate."

Balances in the State Council, Grant understood.

"And that taking a strong position could initiate a schism."

Grant could picture ministers and deputies taking potshots at each other from either side of the assembly hall. With real pots. Or real shot.

"What I have is a nuclear reactor melting down and, at the moment, a mob on the edge of eruption. I feel I have no control over either, without creating a much larger explosion."

"I read you, Minister."

"*I* have a lack of control."

The emphasis suggested something to Grant.

"Have you talked to General Hua?"

"As a matter of fact, I have."

Hua had to protect himself, and Grant didn't fault him for it. But Shao knew Grant's little team was armed to the teeth. Strictly against Chinese law, of course.

"You know what I'd do?" Grant asked.

"What is that?"

"I'd get a TV crew out to the Lhasa site and put that on Channel Two. It's a real-world crisis that's a hell of a lot more important than screaming one's head off in a park on Monday afternoon."

"It is, as they say, hard news?"

"Those people in the park want access to hard news, Minister. Give it to them."

"I will. Good luck, Mr. Grant, and good day."

"Good day, Minister."

The conversations in the passenger compartment had died away as they tried to listen to Grant's half of the conversation. McKelvey and Bowie both had their heads stuck in the doorway to the flight deck.

Grant turned sideways in his seat.

"Lhasa melted down."

"Shit!" Stone said.

"I intensely dislike being an oracle," Suretsov told them. "How bad is it?"

"Shao doesn't really know yet, I don't think. He didn't mention any direct deaths, but they're estimating a contaminated area about thirty by eighty kilometers."

"That's gone for a couple thousand years," Stone said. "About a minute in time for the Chinese."

"They closing the other plants?" Crest asked.

"No. I had to read between the lines, but I suspect that Pai and his camp are taking a hard stance on this. Shao's afraid that if he interferes, he's going to create a governmental crisis. Shao's an honorable man, I think; he doesn't want to bring the government down."

"Shit," Stone said. "What's more important here, the government or a few-thousand lives?"

"Anarchy would not help anything," Suretsov said. "That much, I know. I also know that there is a great deal of corruption involved."

"But Shao has no evidence of that," Grant said. "Do you?"

"Nothing concrete, no," Suretsov admitted.

"So, what now, boss?" McKelvey asked.

Grant hoped that what he'd heard underlying his conversation with the defense minister was a tacit approval from Shao.

"Turn it around, Dusty. We're going to Chengdu."

The command van had become a hostile zone, Jiang thought.

Shao sat near the telephone to Beijing like some imperious dictator. After the announcement of the disaster in Lhasa, issued first to governmental leaders by Pai Dehuai's office, Shao's discussions with those in Beijing had been heated. Someone, possibly the Premier, had temporarily stifled the argument.

From what Jiang could hear, Shao had argued for the immediate termination of the portable nuclear plants, but he had been overruled.

Jiang was himself stunned, though he tried his best not to display his feelings. Could Pai have actually covered up deficiencies, put the countryside at risk? It was unthinkable, but it was possible. Jiang and Pai had been so eager to accept Lefant's proposal. What was simpler than accepting a half-million-dollar U.S. block of well-hidden stock in return for something so simple as a media contract and a power contract? Who would be hurt? Who would be the wiser?

By morning, if not already, Jiang's stock would be worthless. He did not even feel the loss, never having partaken of the power that that wealth might have given him. It was just as well; he would never go near the stock.

Now, however, the consequences were becoming manifest. Pai would dig in his heels, admit to nothing, and try to salvage the reactors in the attempt to salvage his stock value. In Beijing, Pai and his supporters would be debating the issue. Jiang assumed the Premier, wanting to save face, was taking their side. If they lost, the Premier would lose everything—his titles, his positions, his prestige.

And in the command van on Zhoujiabang Road, the tensions were also at apogee. Jiang and Peng were isolated at one end of the van. The commerce minister had moved to Shao's side, and while the generals and colonels and captains manning the consoles and radios divided them, it was clear where their loyalties must lie.

Peng Zedong would be of no assistance in a debate. Since the discovery that his son was one of the orchestrators of the park demonstration, the man had been totally disconsolate. To have a son humiliate his father in such a way was a near death experience. Jiang expected that Peng would submit his resignation within hours.

Which left him alone. He would, when the time came, have to exert his authority in unequivocal terms.

The time was close at hand, he thought. It was now 3:20 in the afternoon, and the hooligans had had center stage for over three hours. And on television, no less!

The police and the military had by now established intelligence posts surrounding the park, and the information flowed into the van steadily, in addition to the images televised by the news teams. The military men with their headsets kept providing oral descriptions of small outbreaks of violence, a smashed window, an overturned car.

Shao resisted the suggestions to dispel the crowd with armed force. He was waiting for something, but what? This could go on for hours, and the longer it went without retaliation, the more harm was done in those households that were viewing it live. They would begin to assume that the government could be tested on any policy.

The young man at the center of it all—Huzhou or Peng?—was not running down. He was enjoying his notoriety, and the television screen often showed his face.

On the perimeter of the crowd, many had turned to the television sets, enamored of their own bits of national prominence. The national anchors for Channel Two News had been located and galvanized into action, and now they occasionally broke in with commentary and analysis. It pained Jiang to hear them laud the government's patience.

"Wait for a moment," one of the anchormen said, "the message in the park seems to be changing."

The camera zoomed in on Huzhou, who was screaming,

"TELL THE WORLD! TELL THE CITY! LET US REACH OUT TO ALL OF SHANGHAI!"

The fool was urging them to run through the streets.

Jiang stood up. "Shao! This has to stop now! They will terrorize the city."

Shao held up a hand for silence. He was talking on the telephone to someone.

"Do it now," he said.

Suddenly, the announcer on Channel Two said, "We are going to interrupt this broadcast for an announcement of a national tragedy. In Lhasa this afternoon . . ."

"No!" Jiang shouted.

"Please be quiet, Minister Jiang," Shao said.

He slumped back on his stool. He was minister of nothing if he could not determine what the fools in the media reported.

The television screen switched to a mountain view, and the camera—seemingly from a long distance away—panned slowly until it settled on the three odd buildings of the nuclear reactor at Lhasa. The backdrop of the mountain seemed serene and peaceful. But there was a white mist hanging in the air, a small plume of white rising from the container building.

". . . no fatalities reported as yet, but the medical facilities in the city are reporting a tremendous infusion of persons concerned that they may have suffered radiation poisoning. As we speak, several units of the army, including emergency medical teams, are boarding aircraft for transport to Lhasa. . . ."

"Minister Shao," one of the generals reported, "our observers are reporting the story is infiltrating the mob. The fringes have gone quiet. The chanting is dying away."

"That is not all that is dying," Shao said.

The Citation passed over Chengdu at 3:45.

"The airport's closed," McKelvey reported.

"They say why?" Grant asked him.

"By order of the Ministry of Energy."

"Pai's trying to keep his plants going," Stone said.

"I'm beginning to feel like a man without a country," Grant

said. "Maybe they won't let us land anywhere. Where's the plant?"

"Forty-five kilometers to the southeast," Suretsov said.

"Let's take a look, Dusty," Grant said. "What's it look like, Vladimir?"

"The structures are the same as those at Lhasa, but it is set in the middle of a flat field, surrounded by a three-meter-high chain-link fence with razor wire at the top. There is a guardhouse at the gate."

"What's the road situation, Vlad?" McKelvey asked from the cockpit.

"There is a paved highway a half-kilometer from the gate."

"That's probably going to be good enough for me, Doug."

"You sure?"

"We may have to take a couple passes, to scare off any motorists."

Minutes later, they were circling over the site. Grant surveyed it through his porthole and confirmed Suretsov's description.

"There's a small difference, however, guys. The defenses look as if they've been beefed up."

Looking down, he saw the rectangle of the fenced area. It was surrounded by fields of stubble. The wheat had been harvested sometime ago. The ground looked soft and green, the result of a rain shower earlier in the day.

Less pastoral was the presence of three trucks parked just outside the gate of the nuclear plant. He could count at least twelve guards patrolling inside the fence. There would be another one or two in the guardhouse.

"Do you suppose those are army or police?" Stone asked.

"I would think they belong to the energy ministry," Suretsov said. "They have their own security detail."

From the highway up the narrow track to the gate of the plant, there wasn't a single bit of cover. Not a rock, not a tree, not a sign to hide behind.

"A frontal assault is only going to get us dead," Grant said.

"So will a rear assault," Stone added. "The suckers cut the wheat too early."

"So, we'll bomb 'em," McKelvey said.

"What?"

"Let me make one more circle, to let that truck get farther down the road, then I'm going slow to near-stall as I come back over. Stone, you push open the door a couple inches, and Doug, you drop a handful of grenades when I tell you to."

Grant wasn't too sure of the tactics, but there didn't seem to be a better option. He started collecting grenades from everyone.

"I need a string, shoestring, anything," he said.

Crest went to his knees in the aisle, grabbed one of the towels that had been wrapped around an assault rifle, and began tearing it into strips.

"Good, Maynard."

Grant knelt down beside him and placed all of the grenades in another towel. There were twelve in all. The two of them tied strips to each of the pull-rings on the grenades.

"Let's not make any slips here," Crest said.

"These would only stun you for about fifteen minutes, Maynard. Not too lethal as ordnance goes."

"I'm not in the mood to be stunned, Doug."

"You've got a point."

"Hurry it up back there," McKelvey called. "I'm about to go low-level."

Crest tied all twelve of the strips together on one end. Grant gathered up the four corners of the towel, making a bag for the grenades, then took the end of the pull-cords in his other hand. He stood up and moved next to Stone at the door.

"Anytime, Dusty."

The airplane slowed drastically. The tail went down and Grant shifted his feet to maintain his balance. Through the portholes, he could see how low they were. A fence flashed by in an instant.

"The door now, Mickey!"

Stone turned the handle, then shoved against the pressure of the slipstream.

The door suddenly jerked free, and Stone jammed his shoulder against the fuselage wall to keep it from flying wide open, probably tearing away from the airplane.

The wind-scream stifled any conversation.

With his left hand, Grant held the bag of grenades close to the narrow opening. They were heavy as hell.

"Hurry up, damn it!" Stone yelled over the wind.

A second.

Another.

"Now!" McKelvey yelled.

Grant released the bag, making certain it dropped outside the airplane, and a second later felt the jerk of the cords in his right hand as the grenade pins were pulled.

Then he released the cords and helped Stone pull the door closed.

The Citation accelerated, throwing them back into the seat behind Grant. Stone landed on top of Grant.

"I didn't know you cared." Stone grinned at him.

"Think about Margie."

"It's Meg. And I have been."

Stone worked his way off Grant just as the plane went into a tight left bank, McKelvey keeping the power on to maintain his lift.

"Stow all stewardesses," Bowie yelled back at them.

A few seconds later, the Cessna levelled off, and the gear thunked down.

The rumble of wheels rolling on asphalt followed, and Grant pulled himself out of his seat to cross the aisle and retrieve his weapon. Pulling a magazine from his hip pocket, he slapped it in place.

"Load and lock," he called out.

The four pilots responded with simultaneous clicks as their magazines chocked into place. Stone took awhile to figure his out. Crest held up the video camera.

"Hey, Dusty," Stone asked, "did we hit them with the grenades?"

"How in hell would I know? I don't have eyes in the back of my head."

"Great. Now you tell us."

Grant remembered times like this. The humor, even strained humor, always seemed to come out before men went into combat. It hid some unease, some misgivings, some doubts.

He had misgivings, himself. He was responsible for these seven men. He didn't want to lose any of them.

"I'm going to roll for another two hundred yards, then jam on the brakes," McKelvey said. "We'll be right in front of the road. Jimbo, you hold the fort and keep the engines turning."

"Shit, Dusty!"

"I write the paychecks, remember? I'm in on this thing."

Eight men. Eight damned good men.

Suretsov was down by a window, straining to see the compound. "I see a few men down. The grenades had some effect."

"Good," Grant said. "Keep your heads down. No unnecessary heroics, please."

He heard a couple pings.

"There's a couple of 'em shooting at us," Bowie said.

Grant put his back against the cockpit bulkhead, and when McKelvey finally hit the brakes, managed to stay on his feet. As soon as the plane was stopped, he slapped the door lever and pushed the door open.

Looked out. Saw a road.

A long way down the road to the gate.

Leaped from the plane and sprinted to the left of the road.

Heard a rifle shot.

Zigzagged.

Another shot.

A small fountain of dirt erupted a few yards to his left.

He went flat on his belly, bringing the Kalashnikov to his shoulder as he hit the ground.

No targets.

He couldn't see one man standing within the compound.

Crest landed on the ground next to him.

A few more shots from the plant. The rattle of a long burst. Coming from the guard shack.

"Don't shoot to kill," Grant yelled.

The men from the plane were spreading out around him, also taking advantage of earth, since nothing else presented itself in the way of cover.

"That camera work?"

"Just a sec, Doug. Yeah. Tape running."

"Good."

Grant sighted the Kalashnikov on the side-rail fuel tank of a truck parked near the gate, then squeezed off a burst of three.

Another burst.

The tank holed, and gas began to flow.

Nothing else.

He aimed for another truck, and this time, he got a reaction.

The tank may have been partially empty, full of fumes, because it blew with a thunderous boom, and was followed by a swoosh of flames. In seconds, the truck was engulfed, the canvas covering its bed burning bright.

The first truck also ignited, then exploded in yellow-orange flame.

The guards in the compound—four of them—began running. The rest were probably incapacitated by the grenades. One man leaped from the doorway of the guardhouse, scooting like a wounded bull elk for the safety of the control building.

Then they were up and running, covering the distance to the fence rapidly.

The gate was off limits, within the sphere of the burning trucks, but one of the pilots reached the fence and began working on it with heavy wire cutters.

McKelvey heaved a grenade toward the running guards, but it fell short.

Grant was the first one through when the pilot held a flap of the fence aside for him. Stone was right behind him, then McKelvey.

He looked back to see Suretsov taking pictures.

As the men came through the rip in the fence, they spread out to form a shallow arc advancing on the control center.

There was confusion at the center. The men inside, aware of the attack, weren't about to open the door for anyone. They had locked the guards out.

The guards took one look at Grant and his posse, and began dumping their weapons in a pile, raising their hands.

"The energy people aren't trained as well as the army," Stone said.

"I hope to hell not," Grant told him. "Dusty, you want to grab a couple guys and round up all the guards?"

"Done, Doug."

As he approached the control building, Grant motioned the prisoners aside with the muzzle of his weapon. They were happy to oblige.

He walked right up to the door, aimed the rifle at the lock, and fired two bursts of three into it.

The lock disintegrated.

He reached out and pushed the door open.

Seven men waited inside for them. As soon as they saw Grant and Stone enter, they moved as a group to the side of the room.

Grant all but ignored them, he was so thankful at the lack of resistance.

"What do we do now, Mickey?"

"It may take awhile to figure out. Get Vladimir and Maynard in here to record our visit."

Suretsov and Crest came inside and began shooting pictures, keeping the faces of any of the raiders out of the shots.

Stone walked around, studying the instrumentation and controls. After what seemed a long time to Grant, he found a wide handle connecting several levers, and began to pull it toward himself.

One of the scientists issued a yelping reprimand in Chinese.

Stone pushed the handle the other way, slowly.

Grant moved up beside him.

"You sure you've done this before?"

"First time for everything. See those digital readouts?"

Grant followed his pointing finger to a couple of displays that were beginning to show diminishing numbers.

"That tells you something?"

"Primary and backup readouts. The plant was operating at seventy-eight percent output. It's headed for zero right now. I don't know how to shut down the steam turbines, but if they don't stop on their own, they'll probably come apart, or something."

"How do we keep it there? At zero?"

"We pull a few boards out of the computer."

"Or put some bullets in it?"

"That'll do it, too."

Grant and Stone stepped back, and Grant emptied the rest of his magazine into the base of the console.

"Doug, you'll never make a computer man."

"Why?"

"That wasn't the computer."

Grant showed Stone how to release his safety, and Stone went over to a cabinet at the side of the room and shot it thirty times.

The din and gunsmoke filled the room. Grant's ears rang when he stepped outside again.

"Shall we go home?" Grant asked.

"Let's," Stone said.

Saturday, October 1

Chiang Qing was awake early, before 5:30. She lay with her eyes open, staring at the ceiling for a while, then prodded Huzhou.

He grunted.

"Get up. We want to watch the news."

"You should not expect miracles, Qing. Nothing has changed."

But it had. After Huzhou's grand demonstration had fizzled so badly, and so quickly, overshadowed by the disaster in the west, he had returned to the headquarters completely despondent. No one listened to him, he complained.

They had listened for a while, she consoled.

He had been convinced the government had purposely created the reactor problem in order to deflate the power that was building in Fu Xing Park. In the days since, as the death toll mounted in the Xizang Autonomous Region—now ninety-seven, with over seven hundred identified as suffering from various levels of radiation poisoning—Huzhou had given up that conviction. Still, he was depressed, and not even her offer to share the leadership of the organization—though quickly accepted—had lightened his spirits.

He wanted action, but none was forthcoming.

The two of them dressed quickly and went to the room where seven members had already gathered. The girl from Hefei had made tea, and she poured cups for them.

Huzhou sat on the floor, leaning back against a desk, and turned on the television with the remote controller.

"Soon," he said, "someone is going to realize that we have not paid a subscription, then we will have our television cut off."

"We cannot afford a subscription," she told him.

"We will have to find work."

She did not respond to that. Her work was inciting the government to change; she would simply have to concentrate on rebuilding membership.

At precisely 6:00, the Channel Two logo blossomed on the screen. A few minutes' worth of credits scrolled upward over the logo, then the logo dissolved to reveal the anchorman speaking in *putonghua*.

"Good morning to all our viewers on this first day of our regular programming."

He gave them all a reassuring smile, then went on. "You will notice behind me, to my left, a large thermometer. Please keep watching it in the days and weeks ahead. The thermometer represents the number of our subscribers, and I am proud to say that, with the start of our year, the Shanghai Star Communications Network already has one hundred and sixty-four thousand subscribers. The numbers should escalate quickly, given the reports we have heard throughout the country of shortages of equipment and waiting lists for installations.

"Now, the primary story of the day, as reported by the Shanghai Bureau of ITAR-Tass. The Ministry of Energy yesterday confirmed that Pai Dehuai has resigned as minister, citing personal reasons. The resignation follows ten days of intense investigation into allegations surrounding the portable nuclear reactors supplied by Nuclear Power Limited. The examinations have been conducted jointly between the energy ministry and the International Atomic Energy Agency, and the report acknowledges deficiencies in the design of the reactors. No one at Nuclear Power Limited would respond to inquiries, and there are reports in France that the company is seeking bankruptcy protection.

"The report of the commission also mentions the actions, without commendation or condemnation, of a small group of people who forcefully terminated the operations of the Chengdu reactor. The group is still unidentified, but the commission expressed its belief that, had they not acted, the Chengdu reactor might also have experienced difficulty within seventy-two hours.

"Somewhat related to the reports from the Ministry of Energy, the office of the Premier has announced that October fifth will be a national day of mourning for the victims of the Lhasa meltdown.

"In other news from Beijing . . ."

"The Premier is still in office because Pai has stepped down," Chiang observed.

"Mr. Pai may commiserate with my father," Huzhou said. "They can revel in their memories of the glorious days of the revolution."

Chiang did not respond.

No matter what Huzhou said, she thought the current events a miracle.

Deng returned to her office at 9:20, after it was apparent that Will Bricher and Mr. Chin had everything well in control. Miss Jiangyou was waiting for her and looking very contrite.

"What is it?"

She held out a small cassette.

"What is this?"

"I am so sorry, Director Deng. It was delivered here from Mr. Lefant on the nineteenth. There was so much going on that . . ."

"Do not worry about it. I am sure it is inconsequential."

She took the cassette, went into her office, tossed the cassette on the television console, and went to sit at her desk. The console was a gift from Grant. It had three screens and several video playback decks. With the remote control on her desk, she could instantly monitor any of the broadcasts taking place.

She picked up the phone and called her mother.

"Have you been watching, Mama?"

"What? Oh, no. I thought perhaps Pierre might call today."

Yvonne Deng thought Pierre Lefant would call every day. Vladimir Suretsov had told Mai of the criminal and civil actions lodged against Lefant in France, but Mai was not going to mention them to her mother. She did not think that anyone would ever again hear of Pierre Lefant.

And she hoped that Yvonne would soon get over the man.

Deng Mai was getting on with her own.

"Mama, I called to say that I will not be home for dinner."

"You will be with Mr. Grant?"

"Minister Shao has invited us to be his guests."

"And afterward?"

"I do not know yet."

"Very well."

Yvonne Deng had stopped chastising her about Grant, ever since the first night she had stayed with Grant in his apartment. Her skin still flushed, and she still felt dizzy whenever she recalled their first night together. The twenty-first of September. She would remember it like an important anniversary.

And for her, it was.

"Are you daydreaming?" Grant asked as he came in.

"Close the door, please."

He closed the door.

"About you, yes," she told him when she thought they were in privacy. She got up and went to meet him, wrapping her arms around his waist. He felt so strong.

"We're going to have to get ourselves kidnapped more often."

"That will not be necessary. Why are you here?"

"I have a meeting this afternoon, and I wanted you to verify something for me."

"Of course, but wait! There is a message from Lefant."

"Lefant? What kind of message?"

"I do not know, Douglas." She told him about the tape.

He gave her a quick kiss and said, "Let's see what's on it."

"You are more curious than romantic," she accused.

"I'm both."

He let go of her and moved to the television sets. After examining the cassette, which had no label, he bent over, popped open a small deck, and inserted the tape. Deng went to the desk for the remote control and turned on one of the screens.

The image on the screen was of a hotel room. For a while, nothing happened, then Lefant appeared, coming onto the screen from the left.

"Pretty dark," Grant said. "Not enough lighting, and I'd bet the camera's hidden somewhere in the room."

"But why?"

"We'll soon see, no doubt."

Nothing happened, however, until Grant took the remote from

her and engaged the fast-forward. When the knock on the door came, quite loud, Grant slowed the machine and turned down the volume.

Lefant went to the door and opened it.

"I apologize for our tardiness, Mr. Lefant," Jiang Guofeng said as he and Pai Dehuai entered the room.

The rest of it was about what she expected. When it was over, Grant started the rewind.

"What does this mean, Douglas?"

"For one, I'd guess that Lefant was feeling a bit of remorse."

"Should I give this to Shao tonight?"

As he mulled it over, he went to the console, opened a cabinet door, and found a blank VHS tape. She watched while he started two of the decks, copying the smaller format tape to the larger format at high speed.

"No," he finally said.

"No? But this is evidence of Jiang's complicity."

"So, what would happen? He'd retire, just like Pai, and that would be it. You don't think the Premier wants any public trials, now that they're likely to be carried on Shanghai Star?"

"No. You are correct."

"It's a tough world, Mai. You've got to be tough, too, if you want to get ahead."

"Douglas, Suretsov believes that Wen Yito may have killed the Russian attaché."

"It's possible. Probably not provable. Not from what we have here, anyway."

"But—"

"Just think about it. Now, what I came for. Do you recognize this, and where it might have come from?"

He unfolded a big-character poster and showed it to her. She translated it for him, and told him the source.

"That's what I thought. Thanks."

The tapes were done copying, and he took them out of the decks and placed them on the desk in front of her.

"Douglas, what—"

"It's your call, Mai. I'll see you tonight."

He bent across the glass top of the desk to give her a kiss, then turned and left, leaving the door open.

It took her a moment to relish the sensory pleasure of his kiss, then she looked down at the tapes.

Shanghai Star was beginning to bring the real world to the people of the PRC.

It was a real world.

And she was part of it.

"Miss Jiangyou!"

Her secretary responded at once, coming to the door. "Yes, Director?"

"Take these tapes. The small one is to go in the vault. Call for a courier and have him deliver the other to Minister Jiang in Beijing. It is to be done as soon as possible."

"Of course, Director."

Most of the rest of her day went very well. There were cards and flowers from well-wishers, congratulating her on the successful implementation of the network. There were no black orchids. Minister Shao sent a small painting by Lautrec. This one was not a print, but the real thing, and she was impressed, not only with his thoughtfulness, but his memory.

There were dozens of telephone calls in the same vein.

There were a number of miscues, miscalculations, and outright dead air transmitted over the network as Media Bureau employees made mistakes, and though they were rectified quickly, the complaints flooded in. She dealt with each of them.

At 4:20, Jiang Guofeng called.

His voice seemed constricted. She did not think he was at all himself.

"Madame Deng, it appears that the network is meeting all of your expectations."

"And yours, Minister?"

"Ah . . . of course."

"I believe you received a tape cassette this afternoon. Have you viewed the *copy?*" She wanted to emphasize that it was a copy.

If he had not been certain who had sent it, now he was.

He took some time before saying, "Yes. I have viewed it."

She surprised herself with how much steel she could put into her voice. "Now, we will forget it. I think you have some recommendations from me on your desk. You have had them for a week."

"Yes, yes, I do."

"Let me review them, Minister. One is the suggestion that Ming Xueliang be named president of the programming group. The second is that the Consortium of Information Services be designated to replace Media Bureau Limited. The third is that the ministry reconsider its information policy, perhaps devising a simpler document that reflects many of the concerns raised by Zhou Ziyang and the People's Right to Know Committee."

"I have them right here before me," Jiang said, still in that slightly choked voice.

"I would like to have the first two confirmed by Monday afternoon and the last by the end of the month."

"Director . . . uh . . . yes. I do not see that as a problem."

"Thank you, Minister."

After she hung up, she thought that Grant was correct. It might not be justice, but it certainly assisted in accomplishing tasks.

Grant parked his Jimmy, the third one he'd been issued in two months, on Changzhi Road at five o'clock.

So, he was going to be a little late.

It was 5:06 by the time he located the tiny office, knocked on the door, and was admitted.

"Mr. Grant, I am honored that you have chosen to visit me."

Zhou Ziyang bowed and backed his way into the office. Grant followed for only two paces.

He unfolded the poster and held it up for Zhou to see.

"That one of yours?"

"Indeed, it is."

He unfolded another.

"And this one?"

"Yes, sir."

Zhou appeared proud of his work.

"I found these, Mr. Zhou, wrapped around a large amount of Chinese currency in the possession of one Mr. Tan Long, who is now deceased." He started refolding the posters. "The posters, naturally, will have your fingerprints on them, and when the police get done with the currency, I'm certain they will find your fingerprints on it, also. The charges will involve murder. You mentioned honor a moment ago, Mr. Zhou. Enjoy it while you still have it."

Zhou's face collapsed. He looked so stricken, Grant thought he might be having a heart attack. He didn't give a damn.

Grant turned and left the office. He went back and got in the Jimmy and sat there for a moment. Now, of course, he wished he hadn't been so free with the money, tossing it around to all the boat people.

It was one reason he'd never make a good cop. He didn't have any respect for evidence.

Starting the truck, he drove back to his apartment, where he took a long time having a drink and a shower. He was dressed in his second-best suit—he still had to replace the first—and was on the twenty-seventh floor of the Ruijin Building by seven o'-clock. He waited in the foyer of the Cellar in the Sky and listened to someone credibly re-creating Josh White until Shao Tsung arrived with Mai.

Once they were seated at the minister's table, Shao said, "I fear I am going to be impatient, Mr. Grant. I feel the need to ask a question before our meal is served."

"Be careful, Minister. That's a very American trait."

Shao sighed. "I know. You visited Zhou Ziyang today?"

"I did. And yes, I recall that you keep him under surveillance."

Mai gave Grant a quizzical glance.

"Did you know that Zhou hanged himself about an hour after you left?"

Mai gasped.

"I hoped that he might," Grant said.

"Do you know why?"

"Mr. Zhou wasn't ready for our brave new world, Minister. Like some others, he thought it was getting away from him."

"But Douglas, he tried so hard to make change beneficial to all."

"And he also saw that he wasn't succeeding, Mai. He wanted desperately to slow things down. He needed to protect his self-respect at any cost."

"You will tell me the story, Mr. Grant?"

"Let us have our dinner, and then I will tell it. I warn you, though, that it's a long one, and it doesn't have much evidentiary support."

Shao nodded and waved for a waiter.

And Mai reached under the table for his hand.

THE AUTHOR

William Lovejoy is the bestselling author of mystery, suspense, and thriller novels, including *Red Rain, China Dome,* and the cyber thriller *Back\Slash.*

A Vietnam veteran, he has served as a college assistant professor of English and director of planning, as a state college president, a college system chief fiscal officer, and a management consultant. Currently, he is the research and planning officer for the Wyoming Community College Commission and is at work on his next novel.

SINS AND SCANDALS!
GO BEHIND THE SCENES WITH PINNACLE

JULIA: THE UNTOLD STORY OF AMERICA'S
PRETTY WOMAN (898, $4.99
by Aileen Joyce
She lit up the screen in STEEL MAGNOLIAS and PRETTY WOMAN She's been paired with scores of stunning leading men. And now, here' an explosive unauthorized biography of Julia Roberts that tells all. Rea about Julia's recent surprise marriage to Lyle Lovitt—Her controversia two-year disappearance—Her big comeback that has Tinseltown talking— and much, much more!

SEAN CONNERY: FROM 007 TO
HOLLYWOOD ICON (742, $4.50
by Andrew Rule
After nearly thirty years—and countless films—Sean Connery is still on of the most irresistible and bankable stars in Hollywood. Now, for the firs time, go behind the scenes to meet the man behind the suave 007 myth From his beginnings in a Scotland slum to international stardom, take a intimate look at this most fascinating and exciting superstar.

HOWARD STERN: BIG MOUTH (796, $4.99
by Jeff Menell
Brilliant, stupid, sexist, racist, obscene, hilarious—and just plain gross Howard Stern is the man you love to hate. Now you can find out the rea story behind morning radio's number one bad boy!

THE "I HATE BRENDA" BOOK (797, $4.50
By Michael Carr & Darby
From the editors of the official "I HATE BRENDA" newsletter come everything you ever wanted to know about Shannen Doherty. Here's th dirt on a young woman who seems to be careening through the head galaxy of Hollywood, a burning asteroid spinning "out of control!"

THE RICHEST GIRL IN THE WORLD (792, $4.99
by Stephanie Mansfield
At the age of thirteen, Doris Duke inherited a $100 million tobacco fortune By the time she was thirty, Doris Duke had lavished millions on her lover and husbands. An eccentric who thumbed her nose at society, Duke's circl of friends included Jackie Onassis, Macolm Forbes, Truman Capote, Andy Warhol and Imelda Marcos. But all the money in the world couldn't buy the love that she searched for!

Available wherever paperbacks are sold, or order direct from the Publisher. Send cover price plus 50¢ per copy for mailing and handling to Penguin USA, P.O. Box 999, c/o Dept. 17109 Bergenfield, NJ 07621. Residents of New York and Tennessee must include sales tax. DO NOT SEND CASH.